996

P9-CJU-704

Discarded by
Santa Maria Library

FIC M
Hautman, Pete, 1952-
The mortal nuts : a novel /
c1996.

mended 11/13/15 nw

96   97   98   01

ILL MAR 01

ILL JUL 10

GAYLORD MG

ALSO BY PETE HAUTMAN

Short Money

Drawing Dead

Pete Hautman

THE MORTAL NUTS

A NOVEL

SIMON & SCHUSTER

SIMON & SCHUSTER
Rockefeller Center
1230 Avenue of the Americas
New York, NY 10020

This book is a work of fiction. Names, characters,
places, and incidents either are products of the
author's imagination or are used fictitiously. Any
resemblance to actual events or locales or persons,
living or dead, is entirely coincidental.

Copyright © 1996 by Peter Hautman
All rights reserved,
including the right of reproduction
in whole or in part in any form.

SIMON & SCHUSTER and colophon
are registered trademarks of Simon & Schuster Inc.

Designed by Kathryn Parise

Manufactured in the United States of America

10   9   8   7   6   5   4   3   2   1

LIBRARY OF CONGRESS CATALOGING-IN-PUBLICATION DATA

Hautman, Pete
The mortal nuts: a novel/Pete Hautman
p.   cm.
1. Agricultural exhibitions—Minnesota—Fiction.   I.Title.
PS3558.A766M6   1996   813'.54—dc20
95–53356   CIP

ISBN 0-684-81000-X

ACKNOWLEDGMENTS

Becky Bohan, Marilyn Bos, Charlie Buckman-Ellis, Andy Hinderlie, Mary Logue, Tom Rucker, George Sorenson and Deborah Woodworth—I thank you for all your help and support over the past six years, and for saying nice things when I read those first tentative chapters more than six years ago. I thank Mike Hildebrand for his linguistic support, and I thank Bill Stesin, "still one of my ten best friends," for telling the tales that made this book possible.

For Tuck

Chapter

"SHE DON'T SEEM SO BAD, Ax. Get 'er tuned up, maybe a new set of shocks."

"I got a hundred eighty thousand on it. They start to go at a hundred eighty thousand." Axel Speeter gripped the wheel hard, trying to suppress the shimmy that had developed thirty thousand miles before. It was a good truck, but getting old, the way things do. He looked at the speedometer. Fifty miles per, about as fast as he dared go, cars passing him on both sides, people in a hurry.

Sam O'Gara rolled down the passenger window and expelled a wad of Copenhagen. "Hell, Ax, they start to go at a hundred eighty *miles.* That don't mean you got to buy yourself a new truck every Monday morning."

"I had this one ten years. I don't want to have to worry about my truck busting down during the fair."

"You worry too much, Ax. Plus, you don't never listen to me."

Axel Speeter shrugged. He worried just the right amount, he figured, because when it came to the Minnesota State Fair, he couldn't afford to take chances. And he always listened to Sam. They'd been friends going on fifty years. But that didn't mean he always trusted what he heard. He rested his right hand on the Folgers can on the seat beside him.

Sam said, "What you got in that can?"

Axel ignored the question. "Look, I want to buy a new truck," he said. He drifted into the right lane, pulled off the freeway onto Highway 61. "You going to help me or not?"

"I say I wouldn't help? Hell, I'm riding shotgun, ain't I?" Sam was looking at the coffee can. "You're still a goddamn peasant, ain't cha, Ax?"

"What's that supposed to mean?"

"I don't know anybody's told you, but they got these things called banks now, guaranteed by the government of the United States of America."

Axel clamped his jaw.

Sam muttered, "Goddamn peasant. Prob'ly got it all buried in your backyard."

"I don't have a backyard, Sam. I live in a motel."

"Well, there you go."

Axel thought, There he went where? Sam was always saying stuff that meant nothing and acting like it proved whatever crackpot point he was trying to make.

Axel said, "Goddamn right I do."

Sam looked at him. "Goddamn right you do what?"

They drove for a few blocks, neither man talking.

"I just want to make sure I don't get stuck with a lemon," Axel said.

"You know what they say about lemons."

West End Ford came into view on the right, a block ahead. Axel turned on his signal and started to slow down. "What do they say about lemons?" he asked.

"I don't remember," Sam said. "Something about lemonade."

———

King Nelson leaned a hip against the immaculate hood of a new Bronco and watched the two old men through the showroom window. The big one was kicking the tires—literally kicking the left front tire of the white '94 F-150. A lot of the old farts did that, kicked the tires. What did they think, that there might not be air in them? That the wheel would fall off? King didn't know what they thought.

King remembered the big one from the day before. The old man had crept into the lot in a beat-up '78, got out, and walked straight to the row of "certified preowned" pickups.

At first, King had thought the old man wasn't serious, just a lonely old dude who had stopped in to waste his time, but after a few minutes the guy . . . what was his name? King scanned his memory. Some part of a car. Dash? Hub? Axle! . . . Axel had zeroed in on the white '94 F-150, a more modern version of the rust-speckled, creaking wreck he'd driven into the lot.

An inch or two taller than King's six one, Axel had veiny, chiseled, deeply tanned forearms and wide, sloped shoulders. He must've been a monster when he was younger, King thought. Axel's eyes were yellow at the corners, with green irises and pupils of slightly different sizes. The top of his head shone smooth pinkish brown, sprinkled with a few dark freckles, framed by two swaths of thick white wavy hair over each ear, which met in a curly little ducktail above the collar of his white short-sleeved shirt. He seemed like a nice enough guy, but kind of slow on the uptake. Yesterday King had thought he'd had the sale wrapped, but then the guy—Axel—had backed off, saying he'd have to have his mechanic check it over.

And here he was, back as promised, with his mechanic—a scrawny old dude in greasy coveralls and a quilted, visorless welder's cap—under the truck now, looking at god-knows-what, while Axel walked around kicking the other three tires and examining nearly invisible chips and dings on the truck body.

King decided to stay inside for a while, let the mechanic finish looking things over. They'd be in a more decisive mood after the sun worked on them for a while.

———

"Carmen's going to like it," Axel said.

Sam said, "Say what?"

"I said Carmen's going to like it. She hated that old truck of mine."

Sam wriggled out from under the truck. "Carmen the nudie fountain dancer? Thought you shipped her off someplace."

"I did. She's in Omaha." Axel did not like being reminded of Carmen's naked fountain dance. He wished he'd never told Sam about it. "She's going to medical school," he said.

"You're shittin' me. Carmen wants to be a doctor?"

"Actually, she's studying to be a medical technician. You don't need college for that. It's sort of like being a nurse."

Sam scratched his grizzled jaw. "Huh. She didn't never strike me as the nursey type."

"She's a good kid. Just got in with a bad crowd." Bad company and drugs, that was what had inspired Carmen to strip her clothes off, middle of the day, and dance nude across Loring Park. She'd been arrested, on that particular occasion, while cooling off in the Berger Fountain.

"I'm flying her back to work the fair," Axel said. "She's doing much better now, Sam."

Sam shook his head.

Axel said, "What?"

"I didn't say nothing."

"Good."

"I tell you one thing, though. I wouldn't want her changing *my* bedpan."

———

King waited until the two of them were standing, looking at the price sticker, arguing, then he left the cool showroom and strode confidently across the hot tarmac. The two men stopped talking and watched his approach. He was ten feet away, still bringing his smile up to full power, getting ready to offer his hand, when the mechanic, all squints and wrinkles and dirty fingernails, jabbed a forefinger at the side of the truck.

"What about these here stripes? He ain't paying extra for no dee-cals."

King stopped and opened his mouth, not sure what to say.

"I like the stripes, Sam," Axel said.

"That don't mean you got to pay for the fuckers."

"Why not? You don't think I can afford stripes on my truck?"

"Only a damn fool pays for looks."

King said, "There's no charge for the stripes."

Both men glared at him as though he had cut in on a private conversation.

"The stripes were there when we took it in on trade," King explained, wishing he'd kept his mouth shut.

Sam crossed his arms and spat, missing King's tasseled loafer by four inches. King took that as a bad omen but not a sale-killer. He started to tell them a few things about the truck, give them the canned sales pitch, directing his best lines at the big one, Axel. Axel listened, rocking back and forth on his heels, pushing out his lips now and then and licking them with a pale tongue. King tried to draw him out a little, asking him how he would use the truck, asking what he did for a living, asking how he liked the weather lately, asking what he thought about those Minnesota Twins.

"What about these here square headlights?" Sam interrupted.

King explained that the new halogen headlamps were brighter, lasted longer, and were more attractive than the old round ones.

Axel said, "I don't like 'em."

King ignored the unanswerable objection. He asked Axel how heavy a payload he would be carrying. Guys liked that word. Payload.

Axel shrugged. "Lots of tortillas," he said.

King said, "Tortillas?"

"That's right," Axel said. "Lots of tortillas. I'm gonna need a topper too."

Sam had climbed into the driver's seat. "Jesus, Ax, you get a load a this radio? I bet you gotta go to school or something to run the fucker."

As Axel looked at the radio, King told him about its automatic search function and ten available station presets, five AM and five FM.

Sam said, "FM? He don't need FM."

"I like the FM," Axel said.

"Since when did you listen to anything except 'CCO?" Sam asked.

"Carmen's going to like it," Axel said. "She hated my radio."

Sam said, "So who the hell you buying this for?"

King smiled weakly, almost wishing this Mutt and Jeff team would just up and go down the street to the Chevy dealer, buy a truck off of those assholes.

"Speedometer says twenty-five nine," Sam said. "How far'd you spin 'er back?"

"Excuse me?" As far as King knew, they hadn't spun an odometer in three years, not since the state attorney general had taken a personal interest in a truck his son was buying.

"I said, 'How far you spin it back?' It's a simple damn question."

"Those are original miles," said King.

"What the hell's that mean, 'original miles'?"

"I mean the odometer is accurate."

"I don't doubt that. What I want to know is, how far'd you spin 'er back?"

"What about this air bag?" Axel asked, reading the embossed letters on the steering wheel. "I don't want the air bag."

King was confused, but happy to be talking about something other than the mileage. "You don't want the air bag?"

Axel said, "How do I know the son-of-a-bitch won't just go off?"

"Go off?"

"I'm driving down the highway and the son-of-a-bitch just goes off."

"That won't happen," said King.

Sam had his head down under the dash. "My best guess is, the way these pedals are worn, she's got better'n fifty thou on 'er."

Axel said, "For cryin' out loud, Sam, the man says the mileage is what the mileage says it is."

"You don't want to know what I think, why'd you bring me?"

Axel grunted. "Good question."

King could feel himself starting to lose it. It was hot as hell out there. The sun felt like an iron on the yoke of his peach-colored shirt, which was turning dark around the armpits. It wasn't healthy, this work, walking from an air-conditioned showroom out into the heat, back and forth. That was why so many car salesmen had heart attacks. The two old men, who didn't seem to mind the heat, were both examining the steering wheel again.

Axel said, "What do you think, Sam?"

Sam shook his head. "Air bag ain't a bad thing to have, Ax. You run into something, you might like it."

"Yeah, and it might blow up right in my face, never know what hit me."

Sam muttered something, scratching his beard.

"What's that?" Axel asked.

"Nothing," Sam said. "Wouldn't make no difference what I said."

"Fine. So what do you think? Think you can monkey-wrench it?"

"Shit, Ax, I could monkey-wrench a gorilla."

Axel turned back to King. "You mind we take it for a spin?"

King took a deep breath, dredged up a smile, pasted it on his face, and handed Axel the keys. Ignoring his own best instincts in favor of company policy, he said, "I'll have to ride along, of course."

Sam snatched the keys and hopped into the cab. "C'mon, then. Let's have us a look at what this fucker can do."

A few minutes later, King felt his facial tic start up again. It had been months since it had bothered him, but Sam had coaxed it out. The old bastard must have kept a whole army of guardian angels busy to have lived so long. His idea of a test drive was taking it up to seventy-five on a residential street, then locking up the brakes, leaving about five dollars' worth of rubber on the tarmac.

"Brakes seem good," he commented. And that was only one of Sam's several "diagnostic tests." When they finally bounced over the curb back into the lot, missing the driveway by six feet, King had to excuse himself, go to the rest room, and sit down on the toilet for three minutes of deep-breathing exercises. It hadn't helped. His cheek was twitching every four seconds.

His only consolation was a feeling of gratitude at having survived. Axel seemed to have been equally shaken up by Sam's driving. When he rejoined the pair outside, they were heatedly arguing the truck's price. He might as well have been invisible, for all the attention they paid him.

"Wouldn't go a dime over twelve," Sam was saying.

The sticker price on the F-150 was $14,975—not a bad price, King thought, unless you considered the test drive the vehicle had just endured. That and the fact that Sam was probably right about the odometer reading. They didn't spin odometers at the dealership anymore. They mostly bought the vehicles pre-spun.

Axel shook his head. "Too low. There's no way they'd even consider that," he said.

True, King thought, happy to have Axel arguing his case.

"How about fourteen even?" King said to Sam.

Sam growled, ignoring him. "Goddamn it, Ax, even with the topper she ain't worth more'n thirteen."

"Sam, you told me it was solid."

King decided he'd do best by keeping his mouth shut. He found himself staring at the tattoo high on Axel's right wrist. A faded blue blotch. He couldn't tell what it was intended to represent.

"It's solid, but I sure as hell wouldn't go fourteen."

"You think it's worth thirteen?"

"They throw in a topper, maybe."

King Nelson's head was swinging back and forth, trying to follow the negotiation.

Axel said, "With the topper I'd definitely go thirteen five."

Sam crossed his arms. "Pay what you want for the fucker. See if I give a damn. You don't never listen to me anyways. You know I'm always right."

Axel shrugged. There was right, and there was right. He rolled his wide shoulders, then turned a yellow grin on King. "I'll pay you thirteen five, including the topper. And I'll need to pick it up tomorrow."

King closed his eyes and inhaled slowly through his nose, the way his doctor had recommended. It didn't help. His cheek was jumping like a bug on a griddle.

"Why don't we step inside," he said. "Get out of this sun, see what we can work out."

The figure they arrived at, nearly half an hour later, was $13,590. King knew he was going to get reamed by the boss on this one—the truck should have gone for at least fourteen. The difference would come straight out of his commission. He'd have to invent some story. Tell the boss he was matching an offer from one of the other Ford dealers. Or it was for his girlfriend's father. Something like that. Or maybe he'd just quit, get back into telemarketing vinyl siding. At least in that business he hadn't had to actually look at his customers. He focused on the sales contract, transcribing numbers and filling in the blanks, doing what he had to do to get the pair on their way. Axel had excused himself. King assumed he'd gone out to his truck to get his checkbook, but when he returned he was carrying a Folgers coffee can, the two-pound size.

———

"So you happy now?" Sam asked, firing up a Pall Mall.

Axel nodded. "I think we got a good deal," he said.

"Coulda got better."

"Maybe, maybe not. I think we did good." Axel pulled out onto Highway 61, brought the old truck slowly up to forty-five. He was looking forward to driving the new one. The salesman had promised to have it ready, complete with topper, first thing in the morning.

"You're a goddamn peasant, Ax. I ever tell you that?"

"Not in twenty minutes, at least."

"You really gonna bring that Carmen gal back for the fair?"

"Sure. She's worked for me five years now. The fair is my life. I've got to have good help. Besides, she hasn't seen Sophie since Christmas."

"Thought those two didn't get along."

"They'll do okay. You know how it is, mothers and daughters. Like I said, Carmen's changed, she's matured. She'll get along with her mom just fine. She's not this wild kid anymore."

Sam rolled his eyes and expelled a cloud of brown smoke, filling the cab. "I ain't sayin' nothing."

Chapter

2

JAMES DEAN FOUND HER up on the balcony, sitting at one of the tiny, bolted-down tables, staring through the railing at the undulating mosh pit below, hundreds of bodies bouncing and writhing to the music. It was only ten-thirty, but the band—four guitars, an electric banjo, and a drummer—had the pit rocking to a punk salsa version of "Proud Mary." Dean stopped a few yards away, watching Carmen watch the dancers, watching her keep the beat by tapping a red polished nail on the stem of her margarita goblet. Her other hand, hanging over the railing, held a forgotten cigarette, nearly half of it turned to ash. Carmen's face looked slack and stupid, from which Dean inferred that she had been waiting for him for some time. At least three margaritas, he guessed. He smiled, running a hand over the top of his shaven head, enjoying the way the fresh stubble massaged his palm.

Carmen, by contrast, had lots of hair. Long and thick, waves that were not quite curls, black under the club lights but auburn in the sun. Dean had once told her she looked like a shampoo commercial.

"I look like a *commercial*?" she'd said, rolling her chocolate eyes. Tonight she had on a sleeveless top, some kind of thin, shiny black fabric with a lace inset above her breasts. Dean wondered whether she was wearing a bra. Sometimes she did, and sometimes she didn't. One sticky, humid afternoon he had actually seen her, at an outdoor concert, remove her bra without taking off her shirt.

Dean had never had much luck with women. Perhaps it was because he was a little strange-looking, or perhaps it was because all women were fucking gold-digging bitches. But Carmen Roman was different. Carmen liked him straight out. And tonight Dean was at his best. Two thin rings pierced his left eyebrow, hanging down so that he could see the lights glinting from the polished gold. He had on his new riding jacket, the plastic antitheft strip still anchored to the left sleeve, his thin, muscular torso naked beneath the black leather. He stepped up to the table and sat down across from her.

Carmen did not look at him. "People are animals," she said, speaking as though they had been sitting together for hours.

Dean pushed his head forward. "People are what?"

Carmen laughed as if she had been told a joke. She dragged the frosted goblet toward her mouth and leaned over it, pressing her breasts against the edge of the table, a few strands of her dark hair settling atop the crushed ice. She pursed her full lips around the thin plastic straw, wrinkled her brow, and sucked.

The mangled edition of "Proud Mary" thumped to an end; the band immediately launched into something that may once have been "Summertime Blues." Dean hunched his shoulders against the sound. He asked her again, "People are what?"

Carmen looked up from her drink, the straw still in her mouth.

"Animals," she said, letting the straw fall back into the drink. "Axel says people are animals." Carmen always found James Dean a bit startling to behold. In her head, when she thought about him and he wasn't around, she saw a black leather jacket, a shaven head, a couple of rings in his brow, and a sort of blank, ordinary face. But each time she actually *saw* him, it surprised her. Dean's head was small and well-shaped, but he had somehow got the wrong set of features. His oversize root-beer-colored eyes were the first thing that hit her, then his skin tone, a yellowish sand color. And then—she always had the same thought—where did his nose go? It was there, of course, but you had to look for it. It was almost like a baby's nose. If people were animals, she thought, James Dean would be a bald monkey. Or a hairless Pekingese.

He was blinking those doggy eyes at her right now, like he needed a treat. Carmen pushed her hair back over her shoulder. She said, "Axel's got this thing about animals. I ever tell you he's got a tattoo of a kangaroo on his arm?" She tipped her head to the side and watched blue smoke curling from the end of her cigarette. The ash had fallen off at some point, probably onto one of the moshers below. Carmen closed one eye and moved the cigarette back and forth, making zees. "He eats ketchup on everything. You ever see a guy put ketchup on a taco? Christ, I can't believe I'm going back to do the fair."

"So don't go."

"I need the money." She took a final drag on her cigarette, stabbed it into the ashtray.

"How much do you make?"

"A couple of thousand, maybe." Her mouth opened in a silent, smoky laugh. "Maybe more."

"He's paying for your school and stuff, right?"

Carmen frowned. "I'm not doing so good at school. I don't think I want to be a med tech." She reached a forefinger into her wrinkled pack of Marlboros and placed the last bent cigarette between her lips. She fumbled with her disposable lighter, turned it right side up, lit her cigarette. "Axel's gonna have a cow. Christ. What's he expect from me? It's not like he's so perfect. He's the one that lives in a Motel 6."

"Was that true, what you were telling me about him? The other night?"

"What's that?"

"About him keeping all his money in coffee cans. At the Motel 6."

Carmen drew back, squinting at him. "I told you that?"

"You said he keeps it in Folgers cans. You were pretty wasted."

Carmen regarded him for a moment, watched his nose come in and out of focus. "I think I'm a little wasted now," she said. "Speaking of which, did you bring it?"

Dean reached into his jacket and produced an amber prescription bottle. Carmen's features twitched into life. She took the bottle, held it to her ear, and shook it.

"How many?" she asked.

"About forty," Dean said. He hadn't counted, he'd just grabbed the bottle and taken off. Mickey would be pissed, but he'd just have to deal with it. Life is so ironic, he thought. He could walk down the block anytime and come back with weed, crack, dust, you name it, but try to find a few Valium, one of the most commonly prescribed drugs in the country, and he ends up having to steal it from his own sister.

Carmen said, "Thanks, Dean. You know, it's really hard to score here in Omaha."

"You just have to know the right people," Dean said.

Chapter

3

SOPHIE ROMAN WATCHED Axel Speeter order the chicken-fried steak again, after all she had told him, never mind the cholesterol, the saturated fat, the calories. Axel folded the menu and pushed it away. The waitress, a blue-eyed blond girl with an outstate smile, asked him what dressing he wanted on his salad.

"Honey," he said, grinning, "I don't need no rabbit food. You just bring me that steak and a Co-Cola."

The waitress returned his smile and wrote carefully on her pad. She looked at Sophie, who was glaring at Axel. Sophie closed her menu and handed it to the waitress. "I'll have the spinach salad. And a glass of white zinfandel."

The waitress marked her pad, beamed again at Axel, and started toward the kitchen.

Axel swiveled his head to watch her walk away, then turned back, to find Sophie giving him her pinched, bloodless look.

"You are so crude," she hissed. "This is a nice place. You don't call people 'Honey' and call their salad 'rabbit food.' You don't have to go around acting all the time like a dirty old man."

Startled, Axel pushed back into the padded red vinyl. What was going on here? First Sam calling him a peasant, then Sophie telling him he was a dirty old man.

"Don't you know how to act?" Sophie continued. "Don't you care what people think about you?"

"Sophie . . ." Axel looked puzzled. "What are you talking about? That little girl likes me just fine. Besides, I am what I am."

"Calling their salad 'rabbit food.' Looking at her that way. Like you got no class. Like some dirty old man. And you should eat your salad anyway, what with your heart and all."

"Look, I got to be a dirty old man eating food I like. Tonight I like chicken-fried steak." Axel grinned.

Sophie tried to hold on to her frown. God, what a picture he made, she thought. He was wearing his usual uniform: white short-sleeved shirt, black trousers, and black suspenders. His green eyes glittered in his big red face. She tried to keep her face rigid, but Axel wouldn't stop smiling. He knew he could get her with that smile. Sophie's cheeks loosened; she gave a short laugh and looked away.

The waitress delivered their drinks and a bottle of Hunt's ketchup. Axel winked at her. The waitress smiled back.

Sophie said, "What did you just do?"

"Not a thing."

"You winked at her, didn't you? Goddamn it, Axel, that's really low-class."

Axel shrugged and sipped his Coke, avoiding Sophie's eyes. Sometimes she reminded him of her daughter, Carmen, even resembled her a little if you looked past the bleached hair, the layers of makeup, and the harsh lines framing her mouth. It wasn't something he cared to dwell upon.

"Have you talked to Carmen?" Sophie asked, as if plucking the thought from his mind.

"She's flying in tomorrow. I booked a room for her."

"You'd think she'd want to stay with her mother." Sophie lifted her wineglass by the stem, keeping her little finger well away from the others, and took a long swallow. "It would save money. Pay me the money instead of the Motel 6." She drank again from her wineglass, beginning with a delicate sip, then tipped the glass all the way, draining it.

Axel said, "Well, you know Carmen—she needs her space. It was hard enough getting her to stay at the Motel 6. She wanted me to put her up at the Holiday Inn."

Sophie shook her head, twisting the stem of the now empty wineglass between her fingers. At least Carmen had some taste; she'd taught her that much. She flagged down a passing waitress, a harried-looking woman carrying four loaded plates on her arms. "Excuse me—do you think I could get another glass of wine?"

"I'll get your waitress."

"Do you think you could just get me another glass of wine please?"

How was she supposed to keep track of who was her waitress? She had enough problems keeping track of her daughter. The waitress paused, about to say something, then shrugged and walked off to deliver her orders. Looking across the dining room in the other direction, Axel waved his hand, then pointed down at Sophie's wineglass. Fifteen seconds later, the young blond waitress appeared with a glass of wine, set it quickly at Sophie's elbow, and smiled at Axel. Sophie glared at her as she walked away.

"They'd never make it at the Taco Shop," she said.

"Who?"

"These waitresses. They have an attitude problem."

"They have a tough job."

"Why do you think Carmen won't stay with me?"

"Says your trailer's too small."

"It's a mobile home, and it's not so small."

"She's going to be spending twelve days working with you at the fair."

"Working *for* me," Sophie said. It was an important distinction. This year, Axel had made Sophie the manager of Axel's Taco Shop. This year she would be in charge.

"That's right," Axel said. "But you still have to spend twelve days working with her."

Sophie frowned and sipped at her wine. Axel had a point. Twelve days at the fair was like twelve months in the real world. The fair produced a sensory overload that stretched time to the breaking point. Twelve days serving tacos with Carmen would be more than enough.

"She's coming in tomorrow?"

"I'm picking her up tomorrow. In my new truck."

"You got a new truck?"

"I'm picking it up tomorrow."

Sophie nodded. Since Axel seemed to be in a spending mood, buying a new truck and all, this might be as good a time as any to talk condiments. She plucked a sugar packet from the bowl on the table and waggled it under his nose. "You know these little sugar and salt things?"

"Yeah?"

"Do you think you could buy them from me instead of Restaurant Supply?"

Axel's eyes narrowed. "Why?"

"I mean, if I had a bunch of condiments, would you buy them from me?"

Axel sighed. He wasn't sure what this was about, but somehow he knew it was going to cost him money.

———

Sophie wanted to go straight home after dinner, and that was okay with Axel. She'd been sniping at him all night. He knew it was out of nervousness. Making her the manager, maybe that had been a mistake. It had seemed like a good idea a few months ago, but now, with Carmen coming back, maybe it wasn't so good after all. He wasn't sure how Carmen would take to working under Sophie.

He dropped Sophie off at her mobile home in Landfall and got a perfunctory kiss on the cheek by way of thanks. Axel waited for her to let herself in and turn the light on, then guided the truck out of Landfall.

At 11:45 P.M., the state fairgrounds were dark and mostly silent. Axel drove in on Dan Patch Avenue, rolled the empty streets. Lights showed in a few of the buildings, and he heard the occasional buzz of a power saw, the pounding of a hammer. Axel turned off his headlights and let his truck chug along at an idle, feeling his way around the familiar grounds. He could almost hear the crowd, smell the smells. He drove up Cooper Street to Machinery Hill, circled the silos and pole barns and tractors, then zigzagged down toward the midway. The big rides were already in place, but most of the setup would take place in a frenzied but orderly burst of activity tomorrow, the day before the fair opened. Some fairgoers, mostly the kids, thought of the midway as the heart of the fair, but Axel knew better. The midway was nothing more than a bright pimple on the west end of the fairgrounds, a lure for young people. The true heart of the fair was the livestock. Axel drove past the Swine Barn, the Cattle Barn, and the Horse Barn, each of which covered an entire block. He drove up Judson Avenue, between the Poultry Building and the Coliseum, a building shaped like a gargantuan concrete Quonset hut. These were the edifices around which the fair had erupted. Without the animals, the Minnesota State Fair would be an out-of-control street party, a beast without a soul. For half an hour, Axel slowly idled his truck around the fairgrounds, sometimes seeing what was there, sometimes seeing bits and pieces of the past thirty years. Axel ran food concessions at dozens of county fairs and special events, but none of them even came close to the Minnesota State Fair, the cornerstone of his business and of his life.

Finally, he stopped his truck on Underwood Street, at the base of the mall. White picnic tables and benches were scattered at random angles over the grassy, football-field-size expanse. Axel let his eyes rest on a small white building. Even in the dark he could read the freshly painted sign: AXEL'S TACO SHOP. A smooth, peaceful feeling settled in his gut. Everything would be okay. He and Carmen and Sophie and the rest of the help would settle into a rhythm. His new product, the Bueno Burrito, would be a huge hit.

This would be a great fair. For the moment, he was as sure of that as he was that the gates would open, that the crowds would come, that people had to eat.

Chapter

4

"HOW COME YOU WANT ME TO GO?" Dean said. He was lying naked atop the rumpled bedding, watching her step into her panties, white ones printed with little pink bows, feeding his eyes on her smooth thighs, her crisp tan lines, and those incredible tits, each two-tone hemisphere bearing a dark, inviting nipple. Her body could not be better, he thought. At age twenty-one, she had achieved perfection.

"I don't want you to go. But I got to go, and you don't live here." Carmen wriggled into a pair of jeans, then sat down on the edge of the bed. Dean sat up and wrapped himself around her, grabbing one breast in each hand.

Carmen broke free and stood up. "My head hurts, James Dean."

"Call me just Dean, okay?" He liked his name, James Dean, the only thing his mother had given him that he liked, but it bugged him when people called him by it. It was like they were calling him James Dean but they were meaning somebody else.

Carmen said, "Okay. My head hurts, Just Dean. Look, I got all this stuff to do. I got to go to the laundry, and then I got to go to the institute, 'cause I'm gonna be gone for two weeks. I might be able to get them to let me do Anatomy over again or something, you know? I'll tell them I've been sick, or my mom died or something. Was I drinking margaritas last night?"

"You said you hated it, going to school."

"I do hate it. But Axel will be really pissed if I flunk out." Carmen pulled a pink-and-white Reebok onto one foot, tied it. "I hate the fair too, but I've got to work it. I'm not like you. I've got responsibilities."

"To who? A guy lives in a motel and keeps his money in coffee cans?"

"Axel's done a lot for me."

"What? He sends you to school and you hate it. He pays you a lousy two thousand bucks to work your butt off for two weeks. What's that? I thought you said this guy was rich. If he's so rich, how come he doesn't pay you more? For that matter, how come you don't just grab one of those coffee cans?"

Carmen stared at her feet. Dean was not that smart of a guy, but sometimes he took the words right out of her head. She'd been thinking a lot about Axel's coffee cans lately.

"You scared of him?"

"Axel?" She thought for a moment. "He's an old man." She put on the other Reebok, stood up, found her cigarettes on the floor, lit one.

"So maybe I oughta go with you."

Carmen did a double take, expelling an involuntary smoke ring. "You wouldn't like it." The idea of Dean coming to Minnesota struck her as bizarre. Dean was a separate thing, an Omaha thing. He had nothing to do with Axel, nothing to do with the state fair.

Dean said, "We could borrow a couple of coffee cans and head down to Puerto Penasco."

"Head where?"

"Puerto Penasco. It's in Mexico, down on the California gulf. I met a guy once lived down there. He said there were a lot of cool people down there, Americans, and you could get a villa with a cook and everything for a couple hundred bucks a month. If you have money, you can get anything down there."

"Anything? Like what?" she asked.

"Anything. And they don't have any AIDS. It hasn't gotten down there yet."

That sounded a little fishy to Carmen, who after all had not slept through *all* her classes. But the concept of being a rich gringo in Mexico did have appeal. The only problem was, first, Axel would not easily let go of his money, and, second, she would be with Dean. She liked him okay for this and that, but she didn't see him as a full-time gig.

"Look, I gotta get going, okay?" She pulled an orange Bugs Bunny T-shirt over her head; somehow got it past the cigarette in her mouth and over her ample breasts.

"So you saying you want me to leave?"

Carmen sighed. "Look. I got to go out. I got to go get some aspirin or something. My head hurts. I got to go to school, okay? I got to go to the laundry. You can stay here if you want. I don't give a shit. Okay?"

Dean sat up, swung his legs over the edge of the bed, saw himself in the mirror. He liked his body. It was thin, and not very tall, but he loved the way his muscles moved under his skin. Dean stood, watching his abs ripple. He picked up his jeans. "That's okay. I got to go anyways. I got things to do too."

Carmen scratched under her T-shirt as she watched him dress. "You shave your head every day?"

"Depends." He zipped his jeans. "Some days I just like to let it grow."

She let her shoulders drop, relaxing now, regarding him with the same regret and relief she might bestow upon an empty bottle. "You want to know something? If you let your hair grow out? You still wouldn't look like James Dean."

———

Forty-five minutes before her flight was due to leave from Gate 34 at the Omaha airport, Carmen tasted her Rob Roy and smiled at the nurse in the mirror. She liked what she saw. She sipped the Rob Roy again. Strange, but not bad. It had seemed like the sort of thing a nurse might order. Maybe next time she'd try a White Russian. There were so many drinks to try.

Carmen liked the feel of the white uniform. She twisted to her left, then to her right, breasts pressing hard against the stiff fabric.

She'd bought it used, from a uniform company, just for fun. Originally she'd thought of wearing it when she graduated, sort of a gift for Axel, but since graduation now looked about as likely as winning the lottery, she decided to show it off for her homecoming. What the hell—she'd bought the thing; she might as well try it out.

To her surprise, she found that she liked being in it. She liked the idea of being a nurse, white poly-cotton wrapping her like armor, smoking cigarettes and drinking a Rob Roy in an airport cocktail lounge on a Tuesday afternoon, getting a double take from every suit that stopped off for a beer. She liked that it messed with their heads, like a prizefight or a powerful new car, making their juices flow. Must be a hormonal thing, she thought. A biological process. Axel would love it. He had this thing about medical paraphernalia. Nurses and pills turned him on. But he hated doctors and machines. Carmen took a hit off her Marlboro, watching her reflection, seeing the smoke frame her face, filter through her hair. Carmen liked her hair unbound, never putting it up or tying it back no matter how impractical or uncomfortable it became. She was constantly pushing it over her shoulder, brushing it off her forehead. Sophie had once warned her that wearing her hair long and loose would make guys act crazy around her.

"A girl does with her hair like she wants for her body," Sophie had told her. "You quit messing with your hair like that and they won't be bothering you all the time."

The problem with Sophie's suggestion was that Carmen sort of liked the way men bothered her. She liked the sense of control, and of danger. Even old Axel couldn't keep his eyes off her—seventy-three years old, probably hadn't got it up in decades.

The hair was nice. Carmen wrapped a thick strand around her index finger, let it fall free. The strand remained curled for a moment, then slowly unwound. Good hair. But it wasn't the hair men looked at. It was the boobs. Axel probably wouldn't notice if she shaved her head like James Dean. God, what a strange guy *he* was. A good guy to know, always bringing her stuff, but weird-looking and sort of spooky. All he ever wanted to do was go back to her place and fuck. He seemed to think he was her boyfriend or something.

She had met Dean only a couple of months before, through his sister, Mickey, another student at Eastern Nebraska Institute of Medical Specialties. One night Carmen and Mickey and a couple of the other students had gone across the street to Bailey's Pub, and Dean had joined them. Carmen remembered her first impression: What a geek! Since then, Dean had popped up with increasing frequency, and she'd gotten used to his appearance. She thought it was interesting that he'd been to prison. Thirty months on a drug rap, he'd told her. They'd gone out dancing a few times. Dean had a peculiar style, bouncing around like a barefooted kid on a hot sidewalk. It was embarrassing. His performance in the bedroom was similar—frantic and arrhythmic. The guy didn't even have a car.

Thinking about Dean recalled the image of the blue Valium tablets in her carry-on bag. The thought sent a smooth wave rolling down her spine. A definite plus, where Dean was concerned. The Valiums would get her through the ordeal to come. The memory of the smell of the Taco Shop assaulted her: twelve days of hot grease, taco sauce, Sophie, and Axel Speeter. She shivered and dug in her purse, looking for a Tic Tac or something. It seemed unreal, almost impossible to believe that she was going back to do another season at the Minnesota State Fair. For a lousy six bucks an hour, plus whatever fell out of the till. A cash business like that, what did he expect?

There was one Tic Tac way down in the corner, covered with lint. Carmen dipped it in her drink and wiped it off with a little square napkin from the bar. She inspected the mint, popped it in her mouth, and looked up. The bartender, older and balder even than Axel, watched her. The Tic Tac was wintergreen, her favorite. She finished the Rob Roy and ordered a gin and tonic. How did Sophie stand it, having dinner with Axel every Sunday all year long? For that matter, how did Axel stand being around Sophie all that time? Carmen recalled the red mole on Axel's left eyelid, its three white hairs, and the smell of Mennen Skin Bracer. One thing about Axel, he smelled okay in spite of being seventy-three, which was in Carmen's view the next thing to having died already.

The second drink pushed Axel and Sophie to a small stage at the back of her mind. Another drink, and they would become like characters in a movie. Then, if she got really loaded, it would be like they were characters in a movie she had heard about but never seen. Her shoulder muscles relaxed, and she smiled. Carmen was good at imagining, making movies in her head. She drank some more gin and imagined herself driving, a red Corvette with the top down and the stereo turned way, way up. Where was she going? Puerto Penasco? That sounded good. Who sat in the passenger seat? James Dean. No, change that. She looked again. It was still James Dean, but not the bald one. It was the dead one, the rebel without a cause, one sneakered foot propped on the dash, squinting at the horizon. She imagined coffee cans in the trunk, filled with fat, rubber-banded rolls of money. Hundred-dollar bills. That would be the way to live. She tried to recall whose picture was on the hundred. The face that swam into view looked a lot like Axel Speeter.

Chapter

5

"**It looks like a junkyard, Sam.** I can't believe they let you do this."

"None of their business what I do, my own damn property."

"This is a nice part of town. Don't your neighbors complain?"

"Sure they do. I get letters and shit from the city telling me to get rid of 'em. I send 'em to my kid's lawyer, he takes care of it."

They were looking at Sam O'Gara's backyard in the company of eleven vehicles in various degrees of disintegration. There were two Volkswagen Beetles, a '67 Camaro, three Chevys from the early sixties, an unidentifiable car with fire-blistered paint and all its windows blown out, the front half of a hood-scooped early seventies Dodge Charger, and three trucks: a badly rusted red flatbed and a green step van, with Axel's 1978 Ford F-150 pickup truck, the newest addition to Sam's auto graveyard, trucked between them. Sam's mongrel hounds, Chester and Festus, had tired of growling and snarling at Axel and were busy christening the new truck by pissing on its tires.

"Looks to me like it'd take more than one lawyer," Axel said.

"Yeah, well, this fella, he's a good one. Tells 'em I'm an artist. These ain't cars, they're sculptures. He gives 'em a bunch of First Amendment shit, scares hell out of them. It won't be no problem, you leaving your truck here. It's got this aesthetic appeal, kinda like that Venus of Milo."

"It's still a good truck. Never know when I might need a backup."

"That's the way I figure it. You was right to hang on to her. You can't have too many vehicles."

"I don't know about that," Axel said. "You might just have done it, Sam."

"Yeah, well, one more sure as shit ain't gonna make no difference. How you like your new one?"

"It's okay. Real smooth. No rattles or anything, except ever since you disconnected the air bag there's a sort of clicking in the steering wheel every time I turn a corner."

Sam shrugged and looked away. "That ain't nothing."

"And I still haven't figured out how to work the radio." Axel looked at his watch. "I've got to get going. Got to pick Carmen up. Thanks again, Sam. We ought to get a game up someday. You and me and Tommy."

Sam said, "Yeah, we got to do that, Ax. Sometime we got to do that. Been too fucking long, the three of us."

———

On the way across town to the airport, Axel amused himself by trying to figure out just how long it *had* been since he'd sat down at a card table with Sam O'Gara and Tommy Fabian. It didn't seem that long ago, but the last specific game he could remember was the one in Deadwood, South Dakota. That had been in '63, he believed. Axel was sure they'd played cards on and off for a few years after that, but Deadwood was the last game he remembered clearly.

They'd been at a hotel called the Franklin, playing draw poker, he remembered. Never his best game, but one he could win at if he played his cards tight. Sam was sitting on the biggest stack that night, maybe seven or eight thousand, a lot of money back in those days. Axel wasn't far behind, having just raked in a nice pot on the strength of a pair of kings. Even Tommy, who'd been hitting the sauce a little too hard, was a few hundred dollars to the good.

The other four players—a rancher named Bum, who claimed to own his own spread out near Belle Fourche, a pair of cowboys who worked for him, and a businessman who'd driven out from Rapid City—were steadily losing. The rancher and his boys had pumped about three dimes each into the game, with the businessman down only a few hundred. The way Axel recollected it, he'd had a feeling about those cowboys from the start, though he hadn't said anything to Sam or Tommy at the time.

As usual, Sam and Tommy and Axel had been exercising their three-way partner routine, signaling the strength of their hands to one another to squeeze out the maximum number of raises when one of them caught a good hand. It wasn't exactly cheating, in Axel's view, but that didn't mean it was fair, either. In any case, Tommy quickly became too drunk to signal properly, so Axel had simply been playing his own cards, playing conservative and winning.

Tommy, who could irritate a squeal out of a dead pig, insisted on calling the rancher "Bud." The rancher kept on correcting him, getting more prickly every time he had to explain his name was Bum, not Bud. Each time, Tommy would say something like, "You mean like a ho-bo?"

It had started out, Axel supposed, as a strategy to throw the rancher's game on tilt, and it had worked. But he was wishing Tommy would ease up. Bum was almost out of money anyways, so it didn't make sense to keep on needling. But that was Tommy.

At four feet eleven inches, Tommy was by far the smallest man at the table, an accident of birth that he used to justify a nasty streak all out of proportion to his size. Axel had met him back in '44, when they were both in the merchant marine, sailing supplies out of Brisbane, Australia, to support the Allied efforts in the Solomons. They had matching kangaroos tattooed on their wrists, souvenirs of a four-day weekend in Sydney. Axel couldn't remember their significance, but a lot of the guys had them. He didn't think about it much anymore. It was a long time ago.

Tommy Fabian had grown up working fairs and carnivals in the Midwest, and he had the carny's contempt for a sucker. He figured he could say just about anything, and if some sucker got upset, fuck 'em, he'd just move on to the next town.

That night in Deadwood, with most of a bottle of bourbon in him, Tommy's mean streak was glowing. By two that morning, the game was showing signs of winding down. The businessman had long since descended into a melancholic haze, without the heart to call any sort of bet at all, and the three shitkickers were on tilt, throwing what little money they had remaining after every lousy hand they got dealt. At one point Tommy was dealt trip aces before the draw. He bet, was raised by Bum, and reraised. Everybody but Bum folded. Bum called Tommy's raise, then drew two cards. Obviously, Tommy figured, the rancher was drawing to three of a kind. Which made his own three aces a very strong hand indeed. Once again, he bet heavily, was raised, reraised, and was finally called by the rancher, who, it turned out, had been drawing two cards to fill a six-high straight. It wasn't the biggest pot of the night, but Bum was delighted to have some cash flowing his way for once. Tommy, on the other hand, had been mortified by such a display of fool's luck. He would have won the money back in time, but Tommy, being Tommy, couldn't let a bad beat go without making some kind of crack.

"Guy draws two to a straight. What the fuck kinda poker's that? I was sittin' on the nuts. No way you should've called my trips."

Bum said, "I won, didn't I?"

"Well, it was a dumb play anyways. What I get, playing cards with a guy named *Bud*."

Bum, dragging the pot toward him, looked at Tommy and said slowly, "My name is *Bum*."

"You mean like a wi-no?" Tommy exclaimed, widening his eyes.

"As in 'bum steer,' which I got a feeling is what we're getting in this here game."

If ever there was a time to shut up and act nice, this is it, Axel thought. Naturally, Tommy did no such thing. He was too loaded to exercise anything resembling common sense, but not quite loaded enough to pass out like a civilized drunk.

"Only problem we got in this here game is you boys don't know what the fuck you're doing, *Bud*," Tommy said.

Axel didn't remember exactly how Bum had replied. As best he recalled, they'd played a few more hands, but the air over the table had gone thick and foul, and the game broke up shortly thereafter. He remembered walking out to his car with Tommy and Sam—he had been driving a '56 Lincoln back then—the clean winter wind cutting through their jackets. Bum and his two cowboys had followed them out of the hotel, walking down the narrow, snow-dusted sidewalk about fifty feet behind them, laughing and making jokes about how broke they'd gotten. Their forced cheeriness seemed strident and out of place. When they were a block from the hotel, another block to go before they reached their car, Axel remembered saying to Sam, "Keep on walking. We get to the car, hop in fast."

He realized now that this had been his mistake. The farther from the hotel they got, the bolder and more confident the cowboys became. What he should have done, he should have forced a confrontation right outside the lobby, before the cowboys were ready, while they were still maybe undecided. Odds were, they'd have backed down. It was always best to be the instigator. You couldn't just wait for shit to happen to you, or sure as shit, shit would happen to you.

One of the cowboys yelled, "Hey, we don't even got twenty bucks left to get our willies dipped. How 'bout you boys buy us each a lady, just for good feelings' sake, hey?"

Tommy, who was apparently even drunker than Axel had given him credit for, stopped and turned back toward the trio, unzipped his Wranglers, and unleashed a stream of urine. A cloud of steam rose from the frozen concrete.

"You can dip 'em right here, suckers!" he crowed.

At that moment, Axel abandoned any hope that they were going to make it out of Deadwood intact. The cowboys dropped their pretense of cheeriness and picked up their pace. Tommy let out a cackling howl, waved his cock at them, then took off running. He made it about twenty feet before tripping and skidding on his belly down the icy sidewalk.

Axel planted his feet and, trying to look as large and menacing as possible, waited for the cowboys to come to him. Sometimes it worked. But not that night. The two younger cowboys didn't even slow down. The first one ran straight into him, landing a glancing blow to his jaw. Axel hooked an arm around him, throwing him against a light pole, but the other one leapt onto his shoulders, slamming his fists into Axel's temples. Axel started spinning, trying to throw the cowboy. He caught a flash of Tommy being lifted by Bum, feetfirst, his tiny fists flailing without effect at the rancher's prominent abdomen. He saw Sam trying to get into the Lincoln, discovering that the car was locked. Then something hit Axel on the side of his knee, sending him sprawling. He heard something pop. His face hit the sidewalk.

The next thing he remembered was Sam breathing whiskey fumes in his face, asking him if he was all right. Axel's knee felt decidedly wrong. He tried to straighten his leg. It moved a few inches, then something caught. Tommy sat on the sidewalk in a daze, exploring a bloody mustache with his tongue.

"How come you look so fucking good?" Axel asked Sam.

"Me? Hell, once you bit the dirt, Ax, I just handed 'em the dough," Sam said. "What the fuck you expect?"

The cowboys were gone, along with most of their money. Sam still had his original poke, a few hundred dollars he'd tucked in his underwear, and Tommy had a hundred-dollar-bill in his left boot. Axel didn't have a dime.

Sam said, "You got to learn to protect your poke, Ax. You might just as well give it away. And you—" He turned his attention to Tommy. "You got to learn when to keep your yap shut. You hadn't been riding that Bum fella, this never woulda happened."

Tommy said, "Hey, you're the ones just let 'em take us. Didn't even fight back. Where the hell were you while they was shaking me upside down? Besides, you shouldn't've let me drink so damn much. I mean, don't you boys know nothing?"

Axel stood up, ignoring the spikes of pain from his knee. He limped over to Tommy and put his hands on his shoulders.

Tommy said, "What?"

Axel still felt bad about putting Tommy in the trunk, but it was a lot kinder than what Sam had suggested. They'd let him out an hour later in Rapid City, had a few drinks, and by the next night they were driving through Wyoming—Axel stretched out on the back seat with his knee wrapped in Ace bandages—looking for another game. They'd kept their partnership going for a few more months, but after the Deadwood incident Axel knew he'd lost his edge. He just didn't have the heart for it anymore. Then Tommy got into the minidonut business at the Minnesota fair, and Sam took off for Alaska to try and win a fortune off the oil jockeys—an ill-fated adventure that had lasted less than a year. Axel spent a few years in the hotel business, and a few more selling land in the Dakotas, before letting Tommy talk him into getting himself a joint at the Minnesota State Fair. He'd bought the taco concession in '69.

Now they were all a lot older, all living in the Twin Cities, still friends. They talked about getting together for a little three-man, just for old times' sake, but it never happened. They were all busy doing other things.

———

As the Boeing 727 settled into its final approach, Carmen thought again about the Valiums in her bag. She dug out the vial and shook out three of them, then reconsidered and put one back. She'd had four miniature Smirnoffs during the flight. She didn't want to pass out in the terminal. She swallowed the two pills dry, closed her eyes, and imagined that she was landing someplace else. Puerto Penasco.

After the plane landed she stayed in her seat and let the other passengers file past her. There was no hurry at all. Axel would wait. Once the aisle cleared, she gathered her bag and made her way carefully toward the front of the airplane. The cabin, empty now, seemed tiny and toylike. She thought she could feel her hair brushing the ceiling, and she liked it. The stewardesses waiting at the front had shrunk to four-foot-high Barbie dolls. Carmen grinned at them, mirroring their mouth-only smiles.

"Bye now," they said, their mouths moving in tandem.

Carmen laughed.

———

Axel was wearing a pair of red suspenders. The tufts of white hair around his ears were trimmed back, as were his nose hairs. He reeked of Mennen Skin Bracer. His dentures gleamed in the fluorescent light. Carmen, still wearing her stewardess grin, stepped into his arms, pushed herself up onto her toes, gave him a quick kiss, then stepped back and forced her eyes to focus.

She was always surprised by his size. The Axel in her memory was a medium-size old man. The Axel of the present stood three inches over six feet. She could see way up into his nostrils. And she always forgot his freckles. He had freckles like a little kid; when he grinned he sometimes looked like a balding, wrinkled, green-eyed, oversize eight-year-old.

"Well, here I am," she said, staring up at the mole on his eyelid.

Axel frowned. "You smell like liquor."

Carmen shrugged and set her bag on the floor between them. "I get tense. I hate airplanes, you know? Besides, don't I deserve a drink to celebrate my first year of school?"

"You're too young to drink hard liquor."

"I'm twenty-one now, Axel."

"Too young," he repeated stubbornly. If he had his way, the legal age for drinking would be forty-five.

Carmen changed the subject. "So how are *you* doing? How's your blood pressure?"

"All over hell. Goddamn doctor has me eating stuff you couldn't give away in Ethiopia. A guy can't live on leaves and roots, you know?" He looked at her uniform, pointed a big, speckled hand at her chest. "They let you wear that now?"

"I wore it for you. How's my mom? How's the Taco Shop? How are the chips this year? Are they rancid again? I don't want to be serving no rancid nachos this year. Come on." She moved off down the concourse. "I got a suitcase at the baggage claim."

Axel watched her move away in the white dress—wrinkled and slightly damp now from the long flight, sticking a little to the back of her thighs. He could tell by her walk, as if the floor was covered with foam rubber, that she'd had more than a couple of drinks. He picked up her bag and followed.

"That goddamn Helmut tried to give me that same shit all over again," he said. "Rancho Rauncho or whatever it is all over again, and you know they smelled the same as last year? I think he must make them in his basement, probably changes his oil about once a year. Teach me to buy Mexican from a Norwegian. I told him a guy ought to make chips a guy would want to eat. Told him to cornhole his corn chips. I'm buying from the Garcias this year."

Carmen laughed. "Good for you. Did you really say that to him? Was Sophie there? You telling Helmut to shove his corn chips. I bet she about shit."

"Where do you learn to talk like that?"

"From you," she said over her shoulder.

Axel muttered to himself as he followed Carmen toward the baggage claim, his eyes moving from her white shoes to her white cotton dress and back again. He hated it when she teased him. But he liked the uniform a lot. She looked good in it. He liked the idea of her flying in to help him. And this year he would make sure his nachos were the best. Twenty-five years in the business, he had learned you do not cut corners on product quality. People come back a year later and tell you you got shitty chips, you better have an answer for them.

It took forever for Carmen's bags to arrive. Axel tried to ask her about school, but Carmen's bubbly energy seemed to have deserted her. She replied in monosyllables, yawning repeatedly. After a few minutes, she sat down on a bench and stared at the baggage carousel, her eyelids almost closed.

On the way out to the parking lot, Axel carrying both her suitcase and her overnight bag, she stumbled twice, nearly falling.

"Are you okay?" he asked.

Carmen smiled dreamily and nodded. "Just a little tired," she explained. She didn't seem to notice that Axel had a new truck. She got in it the same way she would have climbed in his old one, didn't look around it or ask him anything, just planted her ass on the seat and waited for him to drive. He was disappointed. He had hoped to impress her with his new wheels, hoped to show her he wasn't such an old fogy after all. Wow her with the AM/FM radio and the sport wheels and the lariat stripes.

He had to laugh at himself. What difference did it make what she thought? She was just a kid. He wished she wouldn't drink so much. A girl shouldn't grow up so fast. He pulled out onto the freeway and brought the new F-150 up to fifty miles per hour. He wanted to turn on the radio, show her how you could turn a knob and make the sound go from one speaker to another, something he'd figured out on the way over, but when he turned his head to say something she was slumped against the door, her mouth open, snoring. She looked young, her face smooth and childlike. He remembered the day she had come to work for him—a bright-eyed, elfin high schooler overflowing with girl energy. That was five years earlier, but he remembered it like yesterday.

It had been a few days before the fair. He'd been scrambling to get the restaurant ready, trying to get a crew lined up, interviewing the kids sent over by the State Fair Employment Office. He always asked them to send him all the Mexican girls, because it gave his taco stand that authentic south-of-the-border look. The employment people always gave him a bunch of shit about equal opportunity. Most years he ended up with a stand full of tall, blond, blue-eyed boys and girls.

The day he met Carmen he had been down under the counter, scraping up some congealed grease from the previous year, when he heard a voice say, "Hey, anybody named Axel in there?"

He stood up, to discover a dark-haired girl chewing gum and smoking a cigarette, shoving her burgeoning breasts up against the edge of the counter. "You Axel?" she asked.

Axel watched her blow a bubble.

"That's right. Who are you?"

The bubble popped, leaving a tiny cloud of cigarette smoke floating in front of her face. She grinned and said, "My name's Carmen. I think you're supposed to give me a job or something. How much money will I make?"

It had taken him all of five seconds to fall for her. She wasn't Mexican, but he hired her anyway.

Two days later, when he caught her pocketing a five-dollar bill, he did not love her less, though he watched her more carefully. And now? He had to be honest with himself. She wasn't a girl anymore. She was a full-blown woman, practically bursting out of her nurse's uniform, reeking of alcohol and cigarettes, snoring. Still, a wave of tenderness passed over him. She was someone he could nurture and protect, someone with whom he could share his seven decades of wisdom and experience. Like a daughter. Although it was hard not to stare at her tits sometimes.

He wished she could be trusted. He was waiting for her to change, for her grasping, childlike impulsiveness to mellow into responsibility. Maybe someday she would appreciate all he had done for her, maybe take care of him when he got old. That felt good. He liked thinking of her as a nurse, pressing a cool hand to his forehead.

The blast of a horn sent Axel back into his lane. Some kid in a Chevy, asshole kid driving too fast, swerved around him. Axel gripped the wheel and focused on his driving, his heart hammering. He wasn't used to this new truck. All the dials were in the wrong places. The steering wheel felt stiff, and you had to put on the seat belt or it would beep and flash at you. And the engine: he'd taken one look at it and closed the hood—you had to have a goddamn computer to change the spark plugs. At least Sam had taken care of the air bag situation. He drove, listening to Carmen's snores, happy not to have to worry about the thing blowing up in his face.

Chapter

6

MICKEY DEAN, dressed in her Go Big Red gym shorts and tank top, sat curled up on the upholstered rocker, reading a book, holding it between her bony knees. She didn't look up when her little brother clomped into the apartment, dragging the toes of his big black boots as he crossed the room. Her cat, Isabella, tensed up, a ridge of fur rising on her back. James shrugged out of his jacket, let it fall to the floor, and walked past Mickey into the kitchenette. She saw fingernail scratches on his back. She thought she knew whose. The cat fled into Mickey's bedroom.

Mickey heard the sound of a pop top.

"That better not be the last one," she shouted.

James shuffled back into the living room, holding a Pepsi.

"If that's the last one, you better go out and buy some more." Mickey glared at him, her oversize red-plastic-rimmed eyeglasses pushed up on top of her brittle blond hair. She was a big girl, nearly six feet tall, hard and lean, elbows and knees and shoulders sticking out everywhere, weak blue eyes, small mouth, and a beak like a roadrunner. She and her brother Jimmy looked as unlike as any two people on the planet. Even their skin color. Hers was pale, while James's skin had a dusky, almost khaki tint. Different fathers. Possibly different mothers as well—the Dean family history was somewhat muddled. Sandra Dean, their mother, looked like a seriously obese Barbra Streisand.

All Mickey knew for sure was that she'd grown up with James in the same miserable Council Bluffs rambler, watching Sandra drink herself unconscious daily. Mickey hadn't been back, hadn't seen her mom in six years, not since she took off on her seventeenth birthday and got herself a job printing T-shirts, a job she still held. A year after Mickey left home, her brother James had dropped out of school and quickly established himself in the Omaha–Council Bluffs drug trade, selling weed and acid and a few other items to former classmates. He'd lasted about five weeks before landing in the youth rehab center at Geneva, Nebraska, for six months. When he got out, Mickey found him a job with the T-shirt company, working in the warehouse. That had lasted a few months, until the warehouse manager found James asleep, again, on a stack of red 50/50 XXL raglan-sleeve sweats. James had disappeared from her life for more than a year after that. The next time she heard from him he was in jail, about to be sentenced for trying to sell three ounces of North Platte Green to an Omaha narcotics officer. That time, he was nineteen years old, and they'd sent him to the state penitentiary in Lincoln. Mickey had approved of the sentence. Maybe that would be what it took to open his eyes.

For the past ten weeks, since James had been released from Lincoln, he'd been staying with her. Sleeping on her couch. Eating her food. Being mean to her cat. Leaving the toilet seat up.

He had definitely changed. For one thing, he was shaving his head nearly every day now, leaving little hairs all over her bathroom. He had those gold rings in his eyebrow. Something else had changed too. James had never been a particularly caring or empathic young man, but after thirty months in Lincoln he didn't seem to give a shit about anything. He especially did not give a shit about his big sister, who happened to be supporting him.

Mickey said, "You're a parasite, James, you know that?"

He dropped onto the cat-shredded couch, put his boots up on the coffee table.

"You look for a job today?" she asked, staring at his boots.

"Sure. I looked all day long."

"You can't stay here forever, you know. I said you could stay for a few weeks, just till you got a job."

James Dean shrugged. "What you reading?" he asked. He tipped back the Pepsi and let a quarter ounce of cola slip into his mouth, held it there, enjoying the sensation of bubbles on his tongue.

Mickey held up the book, one of her poetry books, a big fat brown one. He leaned toward her and read the title: *The Complete Prose and Poetry of John Donne.*

"Read me something," he said. Mickey liked to think she was the smart one. It calmed her down when she could show off her education, act like she knew everything.

"Are you going to go look for work tomorrow?"

"Absolutely. C'mon, Mick. Read me something. Maybe it'll make me a better person."

Mickey frowned, trying to stay mad. Dean turned his mouth into a smile, giving her his cute big-eyed little brother look. It got her every time. She flipped through the book, looking for something. She cleared her throat and lowered her chin, just like when they were little kids and she would read to him.

"Any man's death diminishes me," she read, *"because I am involved in mankind."*

Dean interrupted. "What's that supposed to mean?" He liked to ask her what poems and things meant, see what kind of bullshit she could come up with.

"That means that we are all brothers. And sisters."

"I met a lot of guys in Lincoln weren't my brothers," Dean said.

"You just don't get it."

"Sure I do. Let me see that." He grabbed the book. "Show me where you were."

Mickey pointed at a highlighted paragraph. Dean furrowed his brow and read. "The guy can't spell for shit," he said. "'No man is an Iland.' No *s*. That's not how you spell it."

"You are so ignorant. That's the original spelling, the way they used to write."

"What he's saying," Dean said, reading further, "is that you are a part of me."

Mickey hesitated, then nodded uncertainly.

He was getting it now. "So I can do whatever I want with you. Like you are a hair on my head."

She shook her head. "No, no, no," she said. "You're missing the point, as usual."

Dean said, "Oh, I got the point, all right. The man's saying what I knew all along. You are just a part of me. I pull the string, you jerk." He faked a punch at Mickey's face; she jerked her head back.

"See? You're a part of me."

Mickey stood up. "You're worse than ignorant. You're ignorant and stupid on top of it." She snatched the book and went into the bathroom. Dean heard the toilet seat bang down.

Dean stared at the closed door, the word *stupid* stuck in his ears. He was not stupid. He was right. What the guy John Donne was saying was something Dean had only recently come to suspect: that the world and all things in it were simply extensions of himself. He thought about Carmen. Was she part of him too? He thought about her laughing, drunk and loose, letting him smother himself in her soft flesh. How many nights in Lincoln had he lain in bed dreaming of exactly that? He'd been thinking about her a lot lately. Maybe Mickey was right. Maybe it was time to move on. When Carmen returned from Minnesota, he could just move in with her.

He heard the toilet flush, then the distinctive click of the medicine cabinet opening.

Uh-oh, he thought.

Five seconds later, the bathroom door slammed open, hitting the wall, and his sister stomped out. "You shit!" She hurled the book at him. Dean ducked; the book hit the wall above him and dropped onto his lap. "You little worm!" Dean felt the fear in his belly, his body remembering all the times she'd beat him up when they were kids. Mickey would hold her long arms out to the sides, hands forming rigid claws, being the monster, and he'd have to run and hide, because if she caught him—she always caught him—she'd punch him repeatedly, over and over, in the exact same spot on his shoulder, until he started bawling and begging.

She was really mad; no telling what she'd try to do.

"You shit, you better give them back to me."

Dean said, "Take it easy, Mick. C'mon now—"

"You sold them, didn't you?" She towered over him, her shins against the low coffee table.

"I didn't sell them." He grasped the book, holding it up to have something between them. "I gave them to Carmen."

"Carmen *Roman?*" From the way Mickey's face bloomed red, Dean knew he'd made a mistake. "That *bitch?*" Mickey did not like Carmen. Carmen had that effect on most women, Dean had noticed.

"You can get more. Just call your doctor, tell him your purse was stolen or something." He knew he shouldn't be afraid. He'd faced worse in Lincoln.

Mickey lifted one long leg and stepped over the table. Her hands came down on his bare shoulders, nails digging deep. She moved her face in on him. Dean's body went rigid, every muscle quivering.

"Get out," she said.

Dean slammed the book against the side of her head. Mickey's hands came up off his shoulders; her body straightened above him, wavered, then went backward over the coffee table. Her feet flew up, her head hit the hardwood floor. Dean winced at the sharp sound, the book still clenched in his hand. For a few seconds, she did not move. He stared at the bottoms of her Nikes—purple, white, and gray—propped up on the table. He heard a sudden intake of breath, the feet came off the table, Mickey tipped her head forward and looked up at him, her face frozen in an expression so odd that Dean almost laughed. For a moment, very brief, he thought everything would be okay. Mickey rolled to her side, got onto her hands and knees, and climbed to her feet. Without looking back, she tottered into her bedroom. The door closed. Was she all right? Dean didn't want to follow her into her room. He sat quietly on the sofa, surprised to discover that he really didn't care whether she was all right or not. It was her own damn fault. He'd only been defending himself. He looked at the book in his hand and smiled. The title stood out crisp and clear against the buff-colored cover. He could see the fibers in the paper. He explored the room with his eyes. Everything he looked at came back in hard focus, as if his vision had suddenly improved. He liked the sensation that went with that. He tried to define it but could only come up with the word *big*. He felt big inside his skin. He could feel the air pressing against his taut integument, holding him in. Opening the book, he read a few lines at random. The archaic language struck him as profound, though puzzling. *"Oh doe not die, for I shall hate / All women so, when thou art gone / That thee I shall not celebrate / When I remember, thou wast one."*

What the hell was that supposed to mean? Waste one what? One doe? Dean closed the book and set it on the coffee table. The old-fashioned spelling was really throwing him.

He decided he'd better check on Mickey. He knocked on her door. No response. He pushed the door open and looked in. She was on her back on the bed.

"Mick?" he called out. She didn't twitch. He entered the room and took a closer look. Her eyes were both blackened. How had that happened? He could hear her breathing through her mouth. Dean backed out of the room and closed the door. Let her sleep. She could sleep all day long, for all he cared.

Chapter

7

SOPHIE ROMAN PRESSED the Play button on her pink Emerson boom box, eased a heaping teaspoonful of International Coffees orange cappuccino into her cup, watched the pale powder sink into the hot water, stirred. The sweet sound of Luciano Pavarotti's voice poured from the speakers and echoed from the paneled walls. She lifted the coffee cup, closed her eyes, and inhaled the exotic aroma of Italy. Had she ever visited Italy, she was sure, the sweet, spicy brew would have returned her to that little café in Milan—just as promised in the commercials. This would be her last morning to herself before the fair started. She wanted to make it special.

Sitting at her fold-out kitchen table, the sun warming her taupe-colored velour robe, Sophie celebrated the deal she had made with Axel. It would, she believed, go down in Sophie history as a marketing triumph. Axel had agreed to buy her collection of condiments sight unseen, for their full wholesale price. The whole lot. Sophie knew from his weary acquiescence to her demand that he had not fully appreciated the scope of her program. For the past year she had loaded her purse at every meal out, stuffing it with sugar packets and ketchup pillows, like money in the bank. Axel would probably have his next heart attack right there in her kitchen.

She had separated her booty into eleven Folgers cans, now lined up neatly on the kitchen counter of her mobile home. Domino sugar packets overflowed one can. Sweet'n Low nearly filled another. The other Folgers cans contained, in order of decreasing volume, Heinz ketchup packets, salt packets, Equal, black pepper, Taco Bell hot sauce, Burger King salt, and coffee creamer. The last two cans were filled with miscellaneous condiments such as artificial horseradish, pickle relish, and barbecue sauce. Sophie reversed the Pavarotti tape in her pink boom box, lit a Virginia Slim, and congratulated herself on her foresight, industry, and bargaining skills.

The quantities were written in eyebrow pencil on the side of each coffee can. There were 443 sugar packets. She had actually counted only 419, but her count may have been off, and besides, Axel would never take the time to recount. Sophie wasn't sure of the exact wholesale value of her hoard, but it had to be a nice chunk of cash. She thought two, maybe even three hundred dollars for everything would not be unreasonable. She turned up the volume on the boom box, sipped her cappuccino, and gazed out the window toward Tanners Lake. A strip of water showed between Laurie Armstrong's sagging pale-gray Artcraft and the Redfields' double-wide.

With the extra money she could buy a yellow metal awning for her home. She knew exactly what she wanted. She'd seen the metal awnings on other homes. They were popular at Pine Creek Village, an upscale mobile home park down in Eagan, where they got three sixty a month for a single lot. That was a lot of money. Sophie would put her money toward an awning any day. With a nice awning across the front of her home, she could have the classiest-looking home in Landfall. Not that that would take much, given the motley collection of "manufactured homes" that surrounded her, not one of which had ever been profiled in *House Beautiful*.

A tiny, incorporated village of 685 souls, Landfall clung like a barnacle to the eastern margin of Saint Paul, bordered by Tanners Lake on the north and west, I-94 roaring by on the south, and 694 squeezing against it from the east. At one time, Landfall had been a thriving community, with its own grocery store, beauty parlor, liquor store, and community center. Now the fiberglass-and-aluminum homes were disintegrating from age and neglect. The only surviving business was the Village Spirits Shop.

Sophie thought about something else then, something she'd been saving in the back of her mind. The bonus. Axel had promised her a bonus this year. If they had a good year, he'd promised to take care of her, give her a share of the profits. But he hadn't said how much. "Let's just wait and see how we do," he'd told her. Numbers flickered behind the curtain in her mind. She let herself peek. Was that a thousand? Two? Five? She could buy a new car, put a payment down on one of those Saturns, replace her aging Plymouth. Wait. She squeezed her eyes shut. She could see it. A real house. One you could walk through without the dishes rattling. A house with a basement. A place to go when the tornadoes came.

She couldn't think about it. It was too exciting, and too unreal. Instead, she looked at the watch Axel had bought for her at a fair in Iowa. That was a real, solid object. Like the condiments, it was in her possession. A classy gold ladies' watch with the cubic zirconiums that you couldn't tell from real diamonds. A house was one thing, but looking good was important too. She reached across the table and ejected the Pavarotti tape. That was enough opera for one day. It was time for Phil Donahue, then Jenny Jones. She always looked good. Then Oprah. She looked good too.

———

Dean woke up on the sofa with the TV still going, Phil Donahue talking to three black couples. He was in his sister's apartment. It continued to surprise him, almost every morning, to discover that he wasn't in his cell at Lincoln. Mickey's door was still closed. She hadn't come out all yesterday afternoon or evening. When he'd checked on her around midnight, she hadn't moved. He yawned and sat up. The black couples were arguing, but he couldn't figure out what about. Donahue also seemed at a loss. Dean never could figure out black people, even before his thirty months in Lincoln, where he'd actually had to share a cell with one of them, and where, first day in, he'd been accused of *being* one on account of his curly hair and dusky skin. His first night there, his cellmate, a guy named Chip, whose skin was the color of a chocolate-chip cookie including the chips—some sort of skin condition—had asked him what way he was going. At first, Dean thought it was a come-on, an invitation to bend over and hug his pillow, but Chip had quickly made it clear that he was talking politics, not sex. "You got two ways to go here, a kid like you," Chip had explained. "You hang with the brothers, or you hang with them Air-yan mothafuckas."

"I don't hang with nobody," Dean had told him.

Chip had said, "Then you fucking bait."

"Anyways, I'm white."

Chip raised an eyebrow. "An' I'm the fucking man on the moon."

"Fuck you."

Chip had laughed. "Ain't no two ways about it—your mama went and got herself some dark meat, boy."

Dean almost jumped the guy right then and there. He had held himself back only because Chip had been hitting the iron pile for years and looked like a polka-dot Mike Tyson and would probably have killed him. Also, it might have been true. Dean didn't know his father, and his mother had never been very selective about her dates. This wasn't the first time Dean had been called a nigger, but it was the first time he'd been called a nigger by a nigger.

Chip turned out to be a nice guy. Eighteen years into a thirty-year bid, he'd learned to get along with just about everybody. He said he didn't care what way Dean decided to go. "You seem like a good kid," he'd said. "I'm just sayin', is all. You got some choices to make, boy. You go with the powers, or you wind up in Punk City. Ain't no two ways 'bout it."

The two powers, according to Chip, were the Black Muslims and the Aryan Circle. There were other affiliations as well, but those were the only ones likely to accept him. "Punk City," also known as Protective Custody, was where all the snitches and baby-fuckers and weaklings ended up. That wasn't an option, so far as Dean was concerned. He decided to go with the Circle, since they scared him only half as bad as the Muslims.

Chip recommended that Dean shave his head.

"You lose the hair, you can pass for white bread all day long, boy."

So Dean had shaved off his kinky, ginger-colored mat and done his best to fit into the Aryan Circle, most of whom, it turned out, were not bad guys, and just as scared as him.

An advertisement for bathroom cleanser, a talking brush, jerked him back to the present. He found the remote between the sofa cushions and turned off the television.

Ten weeks out of Lincoln, and so far nothing had turned up for him. He supposed he could get back into dealing, buying and selling ounces and grams. It was easy money, but chancy, likely to land his ass back in jail. That was the thing about dealing. The mathematics was for shit. Ninety-nine times out of a hundred you did the deal and that was that. The problem was, to make a decent living at it, you had to make a lot of deals, which meant you had to have a lot of customers. Sooner or later, someone was bound to fuck you over. No, to make money in the dope business you had to move the big weight, three or four deals a year and no more. The problem with that was the same as in any other business—it required an initial investment, a reputation, and connections, none of which he had. He knew plenty of people in the business, sure, but all of them were small time and most of them were in jail. Lousy way to make a living anyway, hanging out with people who were all the time fucked up and broke. He'd learned his lesson. Aside from scoring for Carmen, he'd been more or less behaving himself—hanging out, killing time, keeping his eyes open, waiting for the right situation to present itself.

The phone rang. Dean tensed up. Mickey would not sleep through a ringing phone. He watched her door. At twelve rings the caller gave up. Dean opened the bedroom door and looked in. Mickey looked the same as before, only paler. He walked to the bedside. Her eyes were open slightly. He reached down and touched her face. She was cool. He felt her neck but could detect no pulse.

A wisp of sadness came and went, leaving nothing behind. He looked at his right hand, curled it into a fist. He was stronger than he had thought. Well, shit happened. Now he had to deal with it. Obviously, he couldn't call the cops. He'd be back in Lincoln, accident or no. He packed his few articles of clothing in Mickey's gym bag, then added the John Donne book and the three hundred dollars she had stashed in her drawer. He found another forty-odd dollars in her purse, along with the keys to her Maverick.

It was another hot day in Omaha. Not even noon yet, and the seats of the Maverick scorched him right through his jeans. He drove to Ames Avenue, turned left, no destination in mind yet, letting the flow of traffic pull him from one intersection to the next, thinking. Clenching and unclenching his fist, feeling strong. Dean the killer. A guy who you did not fuck with, who could end a life with a single blow. He was surprised how good he felt. Everything he'd heard before had led him to believe that killing another person would have severe emotional consequences. No one, not even Chip, who had killed three people, had told him how easy it would be. As with any other crime, it seemed, feelings of guilt came only when you got caught.

Am I a monster? he wondered. He had always thought that those guys who killed their relatives were nuts, but he didn't feel nuts at all. He felt clear and clean, as if he had shed a rotting old skin.

He wanted to tell someone. But of course that would undermine the feeling—others could look at him and have their own inconsequential thoughts, but only he would know what he had done. He turned onto I-80, drove east. Hours later, the sun fell behind him and the approaching headlights became balls of sparks. He felt totally alert, ready to drive all night long. As he approached Des Moines, a brown bat struck the windshield and stuck there for an instant—he could see its tiny, pointed teeth—before sliding up and over the Maverick. An omen, a sign that his life was about to get interesting. He turned north on I-35. For the first time since he'd been sentenced to the Nebraska State Penitentiary, he knew exactly where he was going.

———

The ringing telephone would not stop. Carmen opened her eyes. The room was dark except for two bright lines of daylight squeaking past the sides of the heavy curtain. She carefully elevated herself to a sitting position, feeling a little sick but overall not bad, considering that she didn't know where she was. She cleared her throat and stared down at the ringing telephone. The last thing she remembered was Axel meeting her at the airport. She was probably in a room at the Motel 6, or so she hoped. She picked up the handset between her thumb and forefinger, the way she might handle a dead bird.

"I'm sleeping," she reported.

"I can't get my lens in. Did I wake you up?"

It was Axel, of course, calling her from room 3. Axel had lived in room 3 ever since she had known him.

"Christ, Axel. What time is it?"

"Eight-thirty in the morning. You've been sleeping for twelve hours."

Carmen shook her head to clear it. "Oogh," she said, sinking slowly back onto the mattress. "Big mistake." The pain in her head, she recalled from her studies, was due to dehydration of the lining of the brain. She needed some water.

"What's that?"

"Talking to myself. I feel a little sick." Carmen groped for the light switch, squeezed her eyes closed, and flipped it up. She let her eyes open slowly, taking in the light a photon at a time. Axel was still yammering on about his contact lens.

"Okay. Okay. Give me a minute, okay?" One night, and already he needed a nurse. She looked down at her uniform and grimaced. The crisp whiteness had given way to the look of a well-used flour-sack dish towel. Carmen unzipped and unbuttoned, let the dress fall to the floor, then kicked it aside. Her mouth tasted awful. She could smell herself. She needed a hot shower, bad.

———

"It's open!" Axel shouted.

Carmen opened the door, stepped into room 3 and was instantly transported back in time. The smell of Mennen Skin Bracer. The bed made military style. The first time Carmen had visited Axel's room, he had tried to bounce a quarter off the taut bedspread to show her how tight it was. The quarter hadn't bounced very high. Actually, it hadn't bounced at all.

"How come you make your own bed?" she'd asked.

"I don't like the maids in here messing with my stuff," Axel had replied.

Axel's big thirty-one-inch TV dominated the wall opposite the bed. It was turned on to a fishing show, the sound off. The rest of his possessions—his "stuff"—were still neatly arranged in red plastic Coca-Cola crates stacked nine across and six high against the wall. Back in the sixties, he claimed, he had been able to make do with three crates: one for shirts and underwear, one for pants and shoes, and one for miscellaneous.

Miscellaneous, Carmen knew, included ten- and twenty-dollar bills, neatly rolled, held tight with wide rubber bands, nestled together in red Folgers coffee cans.

She made it a point to avert her eyes from the crates. It felt like bad luck. She remembered the last time she had been there. One year ago, on the third day of the fair, Axel's contacts had turned on him; he needed his eyeglasses and eyedrops, and he'd sent Carmen back to the motel with the key to room 3. It was during that visit that she had discovered the rolls of bills packed in a two-pound coffee can in one of the bottom crates. Shaking with excitement, she had pulled one bill from each of the eighteen fat, solid rolls that filled the can. It had been the single most exciting moment of her life. She wished she'd had the guts to take more. There had been at least seven other Folgers cans, which she had been too excited, too scared to open.

Just thinking about it now sent her pulse climbing. Her eyes shifted toward the Coca-Cola crates; she jerked them back.

Axel sat perched on a chair in front of the dressing mirror. His right eye was red and tearing. The end table at his elbow was covered with plastic squeeze bottles of lens cleaners, lubricants, and rinses. Several different brands were represented. Axel was looking at her in the mirror.

"You took your time."

"I took a shower. Give me a break. What's your problem?"

"I got one in, but this son-of-a-bitch won't sit right." He pointed at the contact lens, tinted blue, resting on a folded piece of toilet paper.

Carmen sat on the taut bedspread, forcing him to turn and look at her directly. She was wearing jeans and an oversize white V-neck T-shirt. No bra. She leaned forward. Axel stared into her shirt, letting his teary eyes rest on the cleavage, freckled and tanned. It was impossible to focus with only one eye working. Carmen shifted her shoulders, causing her breasts to swing to the left. Axel followed the path of her large nipples across the white cotton fabric. "I can't see for shit."

She leaned back and brought her legs up. Over a year he had been putting his contacts in all by himself; now suddenly he needs help. She wrapped her arms around her shins and rocked back and forth. If he wanted her to install his contact lenses, she wasn't going to make it easy for him. She did not want this to become a daily chore.

"How come you can't get it in yourself?"

"I don't know."

"How come you don't just wear your glasses?"

"I paid good money for these lenses. Besides, once I get them in I see better. Are you going to help me or not?"

Carmen sighed. She picked up the lens and squirted it with saline solution, then knelt on the carpet before him. "Lean forward."

She separated the upper and lower eyelids, letting her breasts brush against his forearm, and planted the lens over his bright-green iris.

"There. Now you got your eyes on." She sat back and crossed her arms. "There something you wanted to look at?"

———

Axel sat propped against the headboard, looking at his wall of Coca-Cola crates. Carmen had gone back to her room, insisting that she needed another hour of sleep. Axel couldn't remember the last time he had been able to sleep like that. He was lucky if he got four hours at a time. One of the things that happened when you got old. Tired all the time, but can't get a good night's sleep.

He wondered why he'd had so much trouble with his contacts. Had he been acting like a kid, looking for attention? Probably.

And that Carmen, thinking she was such hot stuff. Not that she wasn't a pretty girl, but that didn't make him so mush-brained that he hadn't noticed her looking at his coffee cans. Last year, she had grabbed just a few hundred dollars, thinking he wouldn't notice. He hadn't minded that so much and had never called her on it. But this year she might want more. Carmen liked money more than anything.

The last time he counted, the coffee cans contained two hundred sixty thousand dollars, cash money, most of it undeclared income. He'd thought about putting the whole pile in the bank, but he was scared the IRS would notice, and besides, Axel had never trusted bankers, doctors, politicians, or preachers. Still, he had to do something—it was far too easy to imagine Carmen stuffing her purse with roll after roll of his hard-earned green.

Axel wished, not for the first time, that he had a backyard. If he had a backyard he could bury it. Put it about four feet down, then plant a tree over it. That would make him feel good. Axel sighed. He had been through it in his head a hundred times before, but the money was still sitting in his room, where anybody with a spare key or a crowbar could bust in and walk off with it.

He would have to do something soon, make some decisions.

But not today.

Chapter

8

THIS TIME, Carmen was awake enough to notice his new truck.

"Cool!" she said, pressing the buttons on the radio. Her extra hour of sleep, plus a jumbo coffee from Denny's, had perked her up considerably. "Hey, you got them all set for WCCO."

"I *like* 'CCO," said Axel as he steered onto the freeway entrance ramp. He did not want to tell her that he had accidentally—no idea how he'd done it—set all the buttons on the same station. Besides, it was true. He *did* like WCCO, the Good Neighbor station. It was the only station where you could get the weather report anytime you wanted, and they didn't play any of that rock and roll.

Carmen did something to the radio and found a rock station. "Listen to this, Axel. Guns n' Roses. You got the same name as their lead singer. Except he spells it different. They're really cool. Listen." She twisted the volume knob.

The shrieking that poured out from his new speakers caused Axel to cross two lanes of freeway traffic before he found the volume knob, turned it down, and regained control of the vehicle. Angry motorists passed him on either side, glaring and honking. Carmen was doubled over, laughing.

"Goddamn it, Carmen, you want to get us both killed? The fair starts tomorrow!"

"Sorry," she gasped, wiping her eyes. "It was just too funny, you and Axl Rose singing. . . ."

"Well, don't do that anymore. You'll wreck the speakers." He guided the truck onto the Snelling Avenue exit ramp and turned toward the fairgrounds.

"How come we got to go out here, anyway?"

"I have to meet the Coke guy. Also, I want to check out the restaurant and make sure we're ready. Why? You have something else you wanted to do?"

"I thought Sophie was supposed to get everything ready."

"She did. I just want to take another look."

He pulled into the fairgrounds through the six-lane blue-and-green entrance gate. The quiet, peaceful fairgrounds he had visited the night before had transformed into a human anthill of activity, cars and trucks everywhere, the grounds crawling with exhibitors, concessionaires, deliverymen, and state fair employees. It was setup day, the last day before the first day of the fair. Axel nursed his truck along Dan Patch Avenue. Groundskeepers were mowing and trimming the grassy boulevards and lawns and sweeping the wide streets. As always, he was struck by the beauty of the freshly groomed fairgrounds. The grassy aprons were a deep rich green, perfectly manicured, looking almost artificial in the bright morning sunlight. Sculpted rock and flower gardens decorated the grassy medians, brilliantly colored, every plant at its florid peak. Even the streets and curbs were spotless. The benches sported fresh coats of green and blue paint, as did the trash receptacles and recycling bins and information kiosks and lampposts. Many of the concession stands were new or had been refurbished, each one striving to be unique and more visible than its neighbor.

"That's new," said Axel, pointing at a fresh-fried-potato-chip stand. "So's that." He nodded toward a small, brightly colored stand that advertised Tropical Shave Ice. "That'll give the sno-cone guys fits."

They turned on Underwood Avenue. Painters from Midway Sign

Company were adding a fresh coat of paint to the Beer Garden signs. "I'd love a piece of that action," said Axel. The Beer Garden was the ultimate fairgrounds concession. For twelve days, twelve hours a day, dozens of strong young bartenders poured 3.2 beer as fast as it would come out of the kegs. Ten thousand gallons a day, he'd heard. "I bet they clear a million bucks."

"You should sell beer," Carmen said.

Axel shook his head. "Wish I could, but the beer concessions are all tied up." He pulled the truck to the curb opposite a wide, sloping, tree-lined grassy mall. The mall ran the length of the block and was a good two hundred feet wide. The central area was dotted with small picnic tables, benches, and trash containers. To the left side, the squat, ugly shape of the Food Building ran the entire length of the mall, an assortment of concessions—Orange Treet, Pineapple-on-a-Stick, Black Walnut Taffy—lined up against its white cinder-block wall. On the other side of the grassy expanse, blazing red and white and green in the morning sunshine, sat Axel's Taco Shop. "Here we are."

Carmen said, "Hey . . . cool. You got new signs."

Axel climbed out of the truck and strode proudly toward his concession. It was beautiful. AXEL'S TACO SHOP, the overhead sign proclaimed in big red and green outlined letters. A red-and-black zigzag border made the letters pop out. That had been the sign painter's idea. To the left of the lettering a smiling Mexican wearing a sombrero was saying, *Muy bueno! It's good!* The Mexican's plywood sombrero extended out past the edge of the sign, giving him a larger-than-life look. That had been Axel's idea. The opposite end featured a picture of a taco overflowing with meat, cheese, and lettuce. The taco, too, extended out past the border, balancing nicely with the sombrero. It looked delicious.

The rest of the twenty-five-foot-long concession sported a new coat of bright white paint, with the corner posts painted red to match the new countertop. Axel unlocked the plywood front and swung it open. A small sign hanging from hooks above the serving window read: *Axel Speeter, Prop.* He turned to Carmen, but she had wandered off and was now standing forty feet away, smoking a cigarette, talking to a man wearing a white Stetson. The crown of the man's hat was level with the top of Carmen's head.

Tommy Fabian, the diminutive owner of Tiny Tot Donuts, looked up and waved. Axel waved back, then walked over to join them.

"Lookin' good, Ax," said Tommy. His small hand was swallowed in Axel's grip. Tommy was decked out in an embroidered western-style shirt with mother-of-pearl snap buttons, Wrangler jeans, and a pair of black lizard Tony Lamas with excessively high raked heels. His fingers glittered with an assortment of gold, including an oversize, diamond-encrusted horseshoe ring. He pointed at the taco shop. "Nice paint job."

"I thought I'd brighten it up a little this year."

"Got lots a flash. Makes me hungry just to look at it. That there taco is a beaut. And the guy in the sombrero—that you, Ax?"

"Sure it is," Axel said. "That was me in my heyday."

"Heyday? I guess I don't remember no heyday. I only known you— what—fifty years?"

"Ever since Sydney."

Tommy looked up at the Space Tower and squinted, searching in his mind for confirmation. "Forty-four," he said.

Carmen looked bored.

"Nineteen hundred and forty-four," said Tommy, with renewed certainty. "Met playin' cards on the *Henrietta.* I remember now. I won."

"We both won," said Axel.

"Yeah, but I won more."

"You always won more."

Tommy laughed and cuffed Axel on the shoulder.

Axel said, "Carmen? You want to get those boxes of napkins and cups out of the truck?"

"I s'pose," she said, walking toward the truck. She flipped her cigarette toward the sidewalk. It landed in the grass. Axel walked over to the cigarette, stepped on it, picked it up, and delivered it to a nearby trash can.

Tommy Fabian watched him, shaking his head. "I see little Carmen's still the same gal as before. I thought you sent her off to be a nurse or something."

"I flew her back for the fair."

"You're a glutton for punishment, Ax. Is the other one gonna be here again too? Her old lady?"

"Sophie. Yeah. I made Sophie my manager this year. She's pretty excited."

Tommy grinned and pulled out a short, slim cigar, licked it, held it up in the sunlight to inspect it, then set it ablaze with a battered stainless-steel Zippo.

"I oughta get the name a your sign guy," he said, sending up a cloud of blue smoke.

Axel looked down the mall at the faded Tiny Tot concession, one of three minidonut stands owned by Tommy Fabian. Tiny Tot was one of the big moneymakers at the fair. Tommy claimed he netted out at over a hundred thousand a fair. Every year, Axel watched the customers lining up for their little wax-paper bags of greasy sugared minidonuts. He figured Tommy was lowballing his net. Tommy had once boasted about the number of sacks of donut mix he'd used during the fair. Axel did some quick math and came up with numbers that made his nuts ache. One thing for sure, Tommy didn't waste any of his cash on paint—the red Tiny Tot lettering was faded, and the wooden sides of the forty-foot-long building showed through a ten-year-old layer of peeling yellow paint.

"Could use a little touch-up," Axel said.

Tommy puffed his cigar. "I'm thinking I'll throw some paint on next year. The space rental guy's been bugging me about it. Image of the fair and all that crap. What the hell—by this time tomorrow there'll be so many people here you won't even notice." He pointed with his cigar at the pristine mall. "All that grass? You remember what it looks like at the end of the fair? And last year, you remember the mud? What the hell."

Axel had to admit there was something to that. By the time one and a half million people had trampled over the three-hundred-plus-acre fairgrounds, there would be little evidence remaining of the groundskeepers' labors. This time tomorrow, the mall would be covered with fairgoers. After a few days the grass would be pounded flat and brown, and the streets would be dark and sticky with a pungent slick of spilled beer and sno-cones. The sea of munching, gawking people would obscure any view of the concession buildings, especially the ever popular Tiny Tot Donut stands. Axel looked back at his taco stand. He didn't care if his new paint and signage paid off; it was worth the money just to see it standing out clean and proud against the lush green grass.

"You know," said Tommy, "just so's you don't come back at me later and say I didn't warn you, you're outta your mind lettin' those two broads run your operation."

"They don't run it," Axel said. "They just work for me."

Tommy raised his short, comma-shaped eyebrows and sucked hard on his cigar.

"They do," said Axel.

The Coke guy showed up on schedule, for a change. As soon as he left, Axel discovered one of the syrup hoses leaking, a sticky mess sure to draw ants and yellow jackets. Over Carmen's complaints, they drove into downtown Saint Paul to pick up a hose fitting.

"How come you don't just have the Coke guy come back out and fix it?" Carmen wanted to know.

Axel said, "I just want to get it taken care of. I don't want to have to worry whether he's gonna show up."

Carmen sulkily maintained that riding around in his truck all day was not her job; she had thought they were just going to look at the stand and go straight back to the motel. At first, he ignored her demands because he thought he wanted her company, but by the time the guy at the parts store had located and sold them the fitting, her whining was wearing on him. He could've dropped her off at the motel, but he made her ride with him all the way back to the fairgrounds out of pure stubbornness, telling her he didn't have time to drive ten miles out of the way. That didn't stop her complaining, though. Axel set his jaw and kept on driving.

———

Carmen was pissed. Bad enough she'd have to sell tacos for the next couple weeks. At least she was getting paid for that. This riding around with Axel was boring. She'd rather watch TV.

They were almost back to the fairgrounds, coming up to Snelling and University, when a blue BMW passed them on the right, then cut in front of them and stopped at the light. Axel had to hit the brakes hard; Carmen, who was not wearing her seat belt, slid forward with a shout and cracked both knees on the glove compartment door. Axel slammed his palm down on the horn, giving the guy a ten-second blast. An arm appeared from the Beamer's window, a middle finger shot up.

For a brief moment, Axel held on to the wheel, his knuckles white and shiny. Then he jammed the gear selector into Park, unbuckled his seat belt, and opened the door.

"Hey," Carmen said, "I'm okay. Really."

Axel turned his head toward her for an instant. He didn't seem to see her. His face and the dome of his head had turned pink, with deeper red spots forming on his cheeks and forehead. His jaw was twitching, and the pupils of his eyes had contracted to poppy seeds. He jumped out of the truck. Carmen watched him run up to the BMW, jerk open the driver's door. She saw a hand, the same one that had flipped them the bird, reach for the door handle, trying to pull it closed. Axel grabbed the wrist and jerked the driver, a soft-looking young man wearing a gray suit with a yellow tie, out of the car. Carmen thought he was going to hit the guy. Instead, grabbing the yellow tie in one fist and the guy's belt in the other, Axel lifted him and sat him on top of the Beamer. He then ducked into the car and came out holding a key chain. He bared his teeth, shook the keys in the man's face, then threw them across the street into a row of bushes fronting the Midway State Bank.

Axel, his face afire, returned to the truck, backed up, and drove around the Beamer. Carmen looked back. The young man still sat on top of his Beamer, staring after them with his mouth open. She released a nervous burst of laughter.

"Shut up," Axel snapped, staring straight ahead. "It's not funny."

Carmen choked off her laughter and said, "Hey, I just—"

"Just shut the fuck up."

Carmen clamped her lips together. This side of Axel, rarely seen, scared the shit out of her. He drove with his hands stiff on the wheel and didn't say a word the rest of the way back to the fairgrounds. Carmen played with her hair, winding it around her left forefinger, trying to act bored. She wished she'd brought a Valium with her. Or two.

—

Axel was embarrassed. He parked the truck by the taco stand and went in with the new hose fitting. Carmen sat in the truck, listening to some god-awful shrieking rock music while he replaced the fitting.

He couldn't believe he'd lost it that way, right in the middle of Snelling Avenue. His back hurt from lifting the guy.

On the way back to the motel he pulled in to a Kmart. Leaving Carmen in the truck, he went in and bought a Sony Walkman with Mega Bass.

Carmen's mood leapt from sullenness to childish joy as she tore into the box. She gave Axel an enthusiastic hug and kiss. The Walkman had cost him $49.95 plus tax, plus another four bucks for the batteries. Expensive, but worth it if it made him feel less guilty for his outburst, not to mention the wear and tear it would save on his truck speakers. Carmen plugged in the headphones, installed the batteries, and cranked up the music. Axel could hear the tinny shrieking spill from the miniature headphones. Smiling, Carmen bounced up and down on the seat all the way back to the Motel 6.

Carmen gave him another hug when he parked the truck in the motel lot.

"You sure you don't want to drive over to Landfall with me later?" he asked.

"What?" She pulled the headphones away from her ears.

"You want to go see your mom? I'm going to pick her up in a couple hours and go back out to the fairgrounds. The employment office is sending me some kids to look at—supposed to meet them by the stand at three. We need to hire three more girls."

"Gimme a break, Axel. I'm going to be spending too much time already with Sophie. Besides, you had me out there all morning." She put the headphones back in her ears. "Thanks for the tunes," she said, waving the Walkman, her voice two notches louder than usual.

Axel locked the truck, watched her enter her room, then walked slowly over to his own room, keeping his back straight, hoping that a handful of Advils and a short nap would get him through the rest of the day.

———

He woke up with his heart pounding. That dream again. The one where the fair was starting, and he hadn't ordered any tortillas, and he hadn't hired any help, and he couldn't find his restaurant. Carmen was following him, laughing.

He eased himself off his bed. The back felt stiff but serviceable.

Must've been a muscle spasm, nothing to worry about. He looked at the clock. Two-thirty. Damn. Axel's naps usually lasted about twenty minutes, but this one had gone nearly two hours. He washed his face, rinsed his mouth, splashed on an extra dose of Skin Bracer, and combed back the white remnants of his hair. He thought about calling Sophie to tell her he was going to be a few minutes late. Either way, she'd be pissed. But then, that was nothing unusual.

Chapter

9

"OKAY, OKAY, OKAY," Axel said. "You can drive it. Just don't crash it, okay?"

"I'm not going to crash it," Sophie said, her voice tense.

Axel was puzzled. What was she so mad about? He'd agreed to buy all her sugar and salt and stuff at the regular wholesale price, the same price he always paid at Pillow Foods. He'd even rounded up the amount to an even twenty bucks. She'd snatched the money away from him, practically tore the twenty in half, mad as hell.

Sophie put the truck in gear and rolled out of the trailer court about twice as fast as Axel liked. "Jesus!" he said, grabbing at the armrest. "We being chased or something?"

Sophie, her jaw set tight, drove directly from the access road onto the entrance ramp, a slight tap on the brakes her only acknowledgment of the stop sign.

"I said you could drive it. I didn't know we were going to do the Indy 500." Axel did not like being a passenger in his own truck. Sophie was always talking him into doing things he didn't like. "The hell's the matter with you?"

"You know."

Axel considered. "You mad about the sugar and stuff?"

Sophie stared grimly ahead.

So that was it. "Jesus, Sophie, that stuff is cheap as hell. What am I supposed to do, pay you ten times what it usually costs me?"

"I been saving it up all year. And I saved all those coffee cans for you."

"So you made twenty bucks—what the heck's wrong with that? And I don't need any more coffee cans. Would you please slow down?"

"My purse is ruined."

"What?"

"Those sugar packs break open, you know. My purse is all sticky inside. My purse cost more than twenty dollars."

"I'll buy you a new purse," Axel said.

"I was going to buy a new awning. I need an awning."

Axel looked out the window and took a deep breath.

"You don't even appreciate it. I been saving sugar and salt for you for a year, and you just think how much cheaper you can get it from Pillow Foods." She pushed down on the accelerator pedal until the speedometer reached seventy.

Axel cleared his throat, reached into his pocket, extracted a small plastic box, and took a yellow pill.

"What's that?"

"Nothing."

"That was a heart pill, wasn't it?"

Axel shrugged. "I'll be okay."

"Then how come you had to take a pill?"

He did not reply. It had only been a vitamin tablet, but it was working beautifully. Sophie slowed the truck to fifty-five miles per hour, and they rode the rest of the way to the fairgrounds listening to the mellifluous voice of Cannon on 'CCO, Sophie giving Axel an occasional worried side glance.

———

Kirsten Lund wore lip gloss, a pink oxford shirt, stone-washed blue jeans, and her newest, whitest, white-on-white L.A. Gear cross-trainers for her job interview. Her mother had told her she should wear a dress, but her best friend, Sheila, who had worked last year at the Cheese-on-a-Stick stand, said to just wear blue jeans. Kirsten usually tried to please her mother, but this job was important to her. She was supposed to meet the guy at three o'clock but had been waiting since two forty-five, sitting at one of the picnic tables on the mall in front of the concession. It was almost quarter after. A couple of the other kids had gotten tired of waiting and left, but Kirsten needed this job really bad. All of her clothes from last year were totally embarrassing. She crossed her legs and looked up at the sign. AXEL'S TACO SHOP. There was this picture of a guy with a Mexican hat on. He was smiling, and he looked like a nice guy. She caught herself biting her fingernail, took a file from her purse, and repaired the rough edge she had left. The fair would last twelve days. Sheila had told her if she worked every day she could make six or seven hundred dollars. That would buy a lot of clothes. Kirsten unwrapped a stick of Freedent and folded it into her mouth.

At three-twenty, two more girls walked up to Axel's Taco Shop. They both had dark-brown hair and were wearing jeans and T-shirts. Kirsten thought they looked Mexican, which was not good. She figured that Axel, who might be the guy on the sign, would hire Mexican girls first. The two girls stood looking at the stand, pointing and talking, then sat down on the grass, in the shade provided by the stand, and lit cigarettes. A boy with long hair, wearing a Metallica T-shirt, wandered over and squatted in front of them. One of the girls gave him a cigarette and lit it. A few minutes later, two more girls, fortunately not Mexican, had arrived. Kirsten frowned at her competition. She had to get this job.

Five minutes later, a white pickup truck pulled up to the curb at the lower end of the mall. A tall, balding old man and a woman with bleached hair and sunglasses got out and approached the taco stand. The old man didn't look like the guy on the sign, but Kirsten was sure he was the one. He looked like an Axel. She closed her eyes and swallowed the wad of gum, took a deep breath, stood up, and walked to meet them.

"Hi," she said, intercepting them twenty feet away from the taco stand. She put out her right hand. "My name is Kirsten Lund, and I'm here to apply for a job."

———

Axel stopped, a little startled. He reached out and shook the girl's hand, then looked past her at the five kids who were sitting in the shade, watching sullenly. Kirsten Lund was tall and healthy-looking, and her shoes were white and clean. Her blond hair was teased up into a sort of halo around her forehead; the rest of it cascaded down her back in a torrent of heat-treated curls. She looked strong, her shoulders pulled back and her breasts thrust forward, and she was smiling so he could see her excellent teeth. She looked like a tennis player.

"You're hired," he said. He turned to Sophie. "Okay with you?"

Sophie frowned, crossed her arms, and examined Kirsten Lund. She wasn't sure she liked the way the girl had come right up to them and asked for the job. A girl like that would be asking for things all day long. She would be wanting to have her way.

"You have any fast-food experience?" she asked.

"Sure," said Kirsten. "I always work at the pancake breakfasts at my church."

Sophie looked at Axel. "She makes pancakes at church. You still want to hire her?"

"I'm real fast," Kirsten said.

"Can you work Friday and Saturday nights?" Axel asked.

Kirsten hesitated, then said, "Sure. I can work whenever you want. I'll take all the work you can give me."

"You're hired," said Axel. He regarded the other five applicants. "We need two more," he said to Sophie. "You go ahead and pick 'em. Ask 'em if they know the difference between a taco and a burrito." He turned back to Kirsten. "Are you a tennis player?"

———

Wow. Kirsten couldn't believe she had actually done it. Walked right up to him and got the job. And he said she could make $700 easy, maybe even more if she worked every day. In less than two weeks she would have all that money, more money than she had ever had at one time ever in her life. Plus, Axel was a really nice guy. He was going to give her six dollars an hour, which he said was a dollar an hour more than he was paying anybody else, because he said he knew right away she was a hard worker. He told her not to mention this to any of the other help.

Waiting for the bus that would take her back home, Kirsten began mentally to spend her earnings. By the time the bus arrived, she had gone through three hundred dollars, and she still saw herself in the sweater department at Dayton's.

Chapter

10

CARMEN HELD THE FRENCH FRY between her thumb and forefinger, smiling at it. Sophie looked up from her salad, irritated.

"Are you going to eat it?" she asked.

Slowly, Carmen inserted the fry in her mouth, bit the tip off, and chewed.

"I don't think she's hungry," Axel said.

"I'm hungry. I just like to eat slow." She took another small bite.

Sophie fished an olive from her salad bowl, watching Carmen.

"So," Axel said. "Tomorrow's the big day. The weather's supposed to be perfect. Should be a good crowd."

Both Carmen and Sophie ignored him. Sophie's narrowed eyes were locked on her daughter; Carmen gazed dreamily back at her.

"You're acting like a zombie," Sophie said. "Why don't you sit up straight?"

Carmen giggled and slumped farther down in the vinyl booth.

"We should've let her stay in Omaha," Sophie said. "Look at her."

"She looks all right to me," Axel said. "She's just tired."

"That's right, I'm just tired."

"You're both nuts." Sophie stabbed a chunk of lettuce.

Axel, who had finished his porterhouse a few minutes before, rattled the ice in his glass. Every year, he took Sophie and Carmen out to dinner at Flannery's Steakhouse the night before the fair. Neither of them ever ordered steak, and every year they found something to argue about. It wasn't worth it. Next year he'd just give them each some flowers and let them order takeout.

Carmen was slowly dissecting her deep-fried walleye, scraping off the breading, separating the fillet, picking out the tiny black veins, every now and then placing a small piece of white flesh in her mouth. Axel could see Sophie struggling to keep her mouth shut. It wouldn't last. She was right about her daughter, of course. Carmen was acting as if she was terminally bored. Maybe this was one of those things young people did to drive old folks crazy. He'd done his share, Axel recalled. He wasn't going to worry about it. Once the fair started, she wouldn't have time to be bored. Once those customers got a load of his new menu item, the Bueno Burrito, she'd be too busy to feel anything.

———

"Can I watch TV in your room?" Carmen asked as she stepped down from the truck. They were stopped in front of her room, number 19.

Axel put the transmission in Park and leaned past Sophie. "Why? Don't you have a TV?"

"It's a little one. You got that big screen."

"Well, you can't watch it. I don't like people in my room when I'm not there."

Carmen pushed out her lower lip. "I just want to watch for a little while."

"Not tonight. I have to take your mother home."

Carmen slammed the truck door. Axel waited until she had let herself into her room, then he rolled out of the parking lot.

"Why wouldn't you let her watch your TV?" Sophie asked.

Axel took a minute to reply. "I don't want to get home, have my room stinking of cigarettes."

Sophie nodded. "I'm glad she wanted to be dropped off first. She was getting on my nerves."

"She's always got on your nerves."

"Not always. Only since she turned twelve."

"That's a tough age."

"So's thirty-nine."

Axel laughed. Sophie had been thirty-nine for nearly a decade. Sophie said, "What's so funny?"

———

Carmen lay on her back on the bed, finding animal shapes in the ceiling tiles. So far she had found a wolf, a kangaroo, and two bunnies. The bunnies were screwing. She was glad she hadn't had to ride all the way over to Sophie's. Axel was probably pissed that she'd insisted on being dropped off first.

Actually, now that she thought about it, he had seemed sort of relieved.

She wished she had something to drink. The Valium was nice, it had kept her calm during dinner, but a drink would make it even better.

Someone knocked on the door. Carmen sat up, startled. Was Axel back already? She went to the window and peeked out around the edge of the curtain, but she couldn't see who was knocking. Axel's truck was gone. She opened the door.

"Hey, Carmen," said James Dean. He buried his index finger in her left breast. "How they hangin'?"

———

Axel did not think it was love. Not the kind of heart-floating, bowel-stopping love he had experienced in his younger years. He could not think of himself loving this woman, with her bleached hair and her aging body. He thought about her dark eyes, always squinting because she would never admit to needing glasses. It was not love.

Nor was it lust. There was not the hunger, the desire, or the breathlessness.

Beneath him, in the dark, Sophie was breathing through her nose. Sounds like short, sharp sighs. Axel moved his hips slowly and rhythmically, feeling himself sliding inside her, separated only by a generous layer of K-Y jelly.

There was affection, certainly. For all her pretentious snottiness and selfishness, he cared about her. There was a bond. He wanted her to be happy. But the sex had nothing to do with that.

Once every couple of months they fell into bed together. They did not talk, never discussed it before or later, never acknowledged their physical relationship in the light of day. It was something that just happened between them, almost accidentally, a kind of random bonding, like molecules colliding, briefly adhering, flying apart. No sense of dominance, or of tenderness, or of submission. They remained separate, inside themselves. She never flattered him, and she displayed no particular interest in pleasing him.

The patient rhythm of their movement flowed through the narrow bed to the shell of the mobile home; Axel could hear faint creaks as the trailer body flexed in sympathy.

If it was neither love nor lust that drew them down onto this foam mattress, then perhaps it was the need to know that it was still possible that affection could manifest itself physically. That the plumbing still worked.

Sophie's breathing was coming more rapidly now; he increased the tempo of his movement. It was good. In the dark, though he could not see it, he was sure that her face was changing. She would look more like her daughter now, younger and softer, without the hard shell of fear and mistrust. At these times he wished that he could have met Sophie in her younger years, before they had both grown their hard, dry shells. Sometimes he could even believe it was still possible, that they could both become young again.

He felt himself unlocking inside; the swirl of sensation low in his gut would soon become an orgasm. A thought from some other part of his mind appeared: In twelve hours, they would be at the fair. The smell of hot oil. Sophie's breath had become harsh and loud. He pictured her in the taco stand, rolling a burrito. Her mouth was wide open now, and he could hear air rushing through her throat, feel it hot in his ear.

His thoughts fragmenting, Axel came.

——

Bill Quist, night manager of the Motel 6, stood behind the glass door in the lobby and watched room number 19. What he should've done, he should have called her and told her she had a visitor. He shouldn't've just given the kid her room number, especially a kid as weird-looking as that one, especially with the kid not even knowing her last name or anything. But he'd been watching *Rescue 911,* and it had been easier to just tell the kid what he wanted to know.

He had turned away from the TV long enough to watch the kid drive his beat-up Maverick across the parking lot to her room. Carmen, old Axel's daughter or niece or whatever the hell she was, had let the kid into her room. After *Rescue 911* was over, he noticed the kid's car was gone. A little later, he saw the kid return with a shopping bag, and she let him in again. So he figured everything must be okay.

Tired of watching, Quist replaced his greasy eyeglasses in the front pocket of his flannel shirt and returned to the comfortable chair behind the counter. He leaned back and closed his eyes and thought about what he had seen. He wondered if old Axel knew what was going on. Probably not.

Quist smiled. Mostly his job was a snore, but now and then it got sort of interesting. Shit happened. Opportunities occurred. He sat up and put on his glasses and looked again at number 19. He was pretty sure they were in there screwing. He figured she would be on top, hanging those big tits in the kid's face, bouncing them off his cheeks. None of his business, of course, but it was interesting to think about.

Chapter

11

SOPHIE MADE HER FIRST SALE at eight fifty-five in the morning, a bean burrito and a cup of coffee to Willie the glassblower, who ran a concession at the top of the mall.

"You owe me five," Axel said to Tommy Fabian. The two men were standing on the shallow slope leading up to the Horticulture Building, a vantage point from which they could keep an eye on their respective businesses.

Tommy said, "That don't count. He's a carny. The bet was you wouldn't break ice before nine."

"So? I made a sale, didn't I?"

"Yeah, well, I don't call that breakin' ice. Carnies don't count."

Axel held out a hand, palm up.

Tommy muttered, "Fuckin' Willie." He pulled a thick roll of bills from his back pocket, peeled off a five. "Technically, I shouldn't be paying you. How 'bout we go double or naught on if it's gonna rain."

"Gonna rain when?"

Tommy looked up at the clear blue sky. "I'm saying it's gonna rain before Monday."

"Monday's four days away. I'd need some odds on that."

"It don't rain, I pay you twenty."

"Fifty. And it doesn't count if it rains between midnight and eight A.M."

"You're killing me, Ax."

"Then pay me the fin."

Tommy slapped the bill into Axel's hand. "You watch, though. See if it don't fucking pour."

"I hope to hell you're wrong. Wet people don't like to eat."

Tommy grunted, then pointed. "Look who's here," he said. "Sammy the motorhead. Come to the fair to look at the tractors, I bet."

Sam O'Gara, hands buried in the pockets of his coveralls, cigarette planted dead center in his mouth, sauntered across the mall toward them, wearing a spotless green John Deere mesh baseball cap.

"Hey, Ax," Sam said, "how do you know if a carny girl likes you?"

Tommy looked away.

"She shows you her tooth." Sam cackled.

"I don't get it," Axel said.

"That's because it's not funny," Tommy snapped. He didn't like carny jokes, unless he was the one telling them.

"Where'd you get that fancy chapeau?" Axel asked.

"I stole the motherfucker," Sam said. His cigarette bobbed up and down, losing an ash. "Where the hell you think I got it? What does it say on it? I got it from showing genuine interest in purchasing a new John Deere tractor."

"You never owned a new vehicle in your life," Tommy said.

Sam inhaled through his cigarette, then spat it onto the grass. "You should see these harvesters they got up there on Machinery Hill. Even got CD players in 'em. Like fuckin' Mercedes with six-foot tires. I shoulda been a farmer."

"You were a farmer, you'd have to work all day."

"That's true," Sam said. "So when we gonna play some cards?" He reached out and bipped the top of Tommy's Stetson. "Ax is gonna give us a shot at his coffee can—right, Ax?"

Tommy pushed his hat back up. "You still keeping your money in coffee cans, Ax?"

Axel crossed his arms. "What do you mean, 'still'?"

"I heard you owned the First National Bank of Folgers."

"Who told you that?"

"That little gal a yours, Carmen. She told me last year. I figured she was bullshitting me, y'know? I mean, what kind of idiot would keep his money in coffee cans?"

"I don't know," Axel muttered, looking over at his taco shop. A small line had formed. Sophie was serving, and he could see Carmen in the back of the stand, draining a rack of tortillas. It's beginning, he thought. The money is starting to flow.

———

Carmen poured herself another cup of coffee, her sixth that morning. It wasn't helping. The morning of the first day, and already she was beat.

"Three beef tacos, one bean tostada," Sophie shouted over her shoulder.

Carmen set her coffee on the shelf above the prep table, proceeded to build three tacos. "Where's our help? I thought they were supposed to be here."

"It's only nine-fifteen. I told them to come at nine-thirty. Don't forget the tostada."

"I got it, I got it." It was all that James Dean's fault, showing up that way. It had been a long night.

"What are you doing here?" she'd asked him.

"I missed you. What's the matter, you aren't glad to see me?"

"How'd you find me?"

"There's only a couple Motel 6's. It wasn't too hard."

He had been dressed the same way she remembered: jeans, leather jacket, no shirt, heavy military boots. Only now he seemed jazzed up, talking too fast, wired from driving straight through from Omaha.

"You drove all the way up here to see me?"

"I sure did. You got anything to drink? Beer or anything? I gotta jack down. I'm thirsty."

Seeing her chance to get rid of him for a few minutes, give her some time to think, she'd suggested that he run over to the liquor store for some of those canned martinis, maybe a twelve-pack of beer too. After he left she'd considered locking the door, not letting him back inside. A guy like Dean, he could really make her life complicated. On the other hand, no one had ever driven that far just to see her before. And he was sort of cute, if you didn't look too close. By the time he knocked on her door again, she was thinking that it might be sort of fun to have him around. They'd sat up drinking martinis and talking till after two.

Carmen wrapped the tacos and the tostada, delivered them to the front counter.

"I need two Bueno Burritos and a nachos," Sophie said. "We've got a line, girl."

"Okay, okay, okay," she muttered. "Keep your shirt on." Those fucking Bueno Burritos, another one of Axel's dumb ideas, took twice as long to make. They had so much stuff in them, the tortillas kept tearing.

Some of the things Dean had been saying had been interesting. He kept talking about Puerto Penasco, about how good you could live if you had money.

"So get some money and let's go," she had said.

"I'm working on it." Dean had grinned, his teeth bright. "Maybe we'll stumble across some coffee cans or something."

At that, Carmen had felt her belly go thumpity-thump, and a shiver had crawled up her back. "That's not funny."

"Hey, I was just kidding you." Then he'd started reading poetry from this book he had, and she'd tuned him out. Really boring. And *then,* all night long, he'd tossed and turned and muttered to himself. He'd still been twitching and rolling around on the bed when she'd left the room to ride over to the fairgrounds with Axel. Would he still be around when she got back? She sort of hoped he'd just go away. On the other hand, she wanted to hear more about Puerto Penasco. It gave her something to think about while she was rolling burros. Maybe it wasn't such a crazy idea after all. She wondered how many coffee cans full of cash it would take to buy a villa on the ocean.

Axel leaned through the door at the back of the stand, smiling. "Carmen, what's up?"

"Nothing!" she said, startled.

"Those Buenos selling?"

"Yeah. I'm busy as hell. You want to give us a hand?"

"Can't. I've got some business to take care of. Those girls haven't shown up yet?"

"You see them? I don't." Carmen loaded a pair of chimichanga-size tortillas with meat, beans, lettuce, and cheese. She added a few olive slices, a spoonful of sour cream, and a glob of guacamole, which was what put the *Bueno* in the Bueno Burrito. She popped a tray of nachos into the microwave, then proceeded to roll and wrap the burros.

"Carmen?" Axel said.

"*What?*"

"I need you to roll me six Buenos. And I need a bag to carry them in."

"What for?"

"Some friends of mine."

"I don't have time. Roll them yourself."

Axel continued to smile. He said, "Just roll me six, would you, sweetheart?"

———

Dean's naked body snapped up into sitting position, pouring sweat. He was in his cell—no! He was in his sister's apartment—no! Muscles rippled and twitched, vibrating his frame. Dream images of Mickey screaming at him gave way to the tangled mess of twisted sheets and bedspread, sunlight slanting past the heavy curtains, the collection of aluminum beer cans on the nightstand. He was alone. A headache gripped the back of his neck, and his jaw hurt from gritting his teeth. He breathed out, swung his legs over the edge of the mattress, and stood up; the room tilted, righted itself. "Where the hell is she?" he muttered, moving toward the bathroom.

Dean hadn't shaved his scalp in two or three days. His hair was about an eighth of an inch long already, and starting to curl. If he didn't take care of it soon, it would start looking like a mat of tiny ginger-colored springs. He found a disposable razor on the sink, soaped up his head, and went at it. He was a little shaky, cut himself three or four times. The bright-red spots on the white Motel 6 towel made him dizzy. He wondered whether Mickey's death would have bothered him more if there had been blood involved. Say, if she'd cut her head open. Maybe he'd have called 911. Or maybe he'd have had to leave the apartment right away. She would still be dead, but he wouldn't know it.

Now that he thought about it, it was *possible* that she *wasn't* dead. It was *possible* that she was in a coma. He'd heard that people in comas were cold and that their pulse was so weak you couldn't feel it. It could be.

He thought, Do I feel better now, knowing that she might be alive? He stared at his reflection in the mirror, circles beneath his eyes, soap bubbles on his head, a jailhouse tattoo of a burning cross on his right shoulder. He felt exactly the same. She could be dead or alive; it made no difference. Weird.

Twenty minutes later, he was dressed in his jeans and one of Carmen's T-shirts, the orange Bugs Bunny shirt he'd seen her wear back in Omaha. His stomach needed food. He thought he remembered a Denny's just up the street. The image of eggs and bacon and hash brown potatoes propelled him out the door. He was just getting into his car when he saw this old guy coming out of a room at the other end of the motel. Was that him? The Coffee Can Man? He was old enough. Dean crossed his arms on the roof of the Maverick, rested his chin on his wrists, and watched the old man walking toward him, a green plastic garbage bag swinging from one hand. For a few seconds, he thought the guy might be coming over to talk to him, but it turned out he was heading for the white pickup parked on the passenger side of the Maverick. The old man opened the door and threw the bag into the cab, then noticed Dean and jerked his chin up, startled.

Dean said, "Morning."

The old man nodded, his eyes quickly checking out the interior of the Maverick, then looking to each side. "Nice day," he said. He had a big voice, but he seemed on edge, like he'd gotten caught doing something.

Dean smiled. "Yeah, it sure is." He still wasn't sure if this was the Coffee Can Man. The guy was staring at the rings in his eyebrow. Dean could always tell.

"You staying here?" the old man asked.

"Maybe. Thinking about it."

"It's a nice place." They regarded each other uncomfortably, having talked a moment too long.

Dean said, "So I hear there's some kind of big fair going on here."

The guy brightened at that, seemed to relax a little. "There sure is," he said. "The state fair. You must be from out of town."

"Nebraska."

"Well, how about that." The old man gave him a sort of wave, climbed into his truck, closed the door.

Dean said, "Hey!"

The old man rolled down his window.

"You know how to get there?" Dean asked.

"Depends on where you're going, son."

"To the state fair."

The old man leaned out the window and pointed. "You just head on up Larpenteur there, turn south on Snelling. You can't miss it. Once you get there, stop by Axel's Taco Shop and grab yourself a free taco. Just tell 'em Axel said it was okay."

———

Kirsten Lund showed up for work wearing a Benetton top that matched her pink lips and nails perfectly. Her hair was bound back in a French braid, and the pimple that had erupted on her nose the day before was hardly noticeable beneath the layer of medicated makeup. She put her head into the back door of the stand and said, "Hello?"

Sophie, back at the worktable trying to build two tacos and a Bueno Burrito while a line of customers formed at the front of the stand, snapped at her. "Don't just stand there, girl. Get in here."

Kirsten stepped into the stand, looking around uncertainly. "What do you want me to do?"

Sophie rolled her eyes and shook grated cheese off her hands, scooped up the order she had assembled, and brought it to the front counter. Kirsten looked around the stand helplessly, spied an apron hanging on a hook near the door, and tied it on. Sophie took another order and rushed back to the prep table. "Watch me," she said, laying out a row of four flour tortillas like a dealer spreading a new deck of cards. Kirsten watched her fill the flour disks with blinding speed, roll them, wrap them, and deliver them to her waiting customers. Kirsten took Sophie's place at the table and, trying to remember, set out four tortillas. Sophie looked over her shoulder. "No, no, no. Now I need two tacos and a side of beans." Kirsten stepped back, helpless. Carmen stepped in through the back door.

"Where've you been?" Sophie snapped at Carmen.

Carmen ignored her. "Hi," she said to Kirsten, looking her up and down. "You got my apron on."

Kirsten said "Oh!" and reached back to untie it.

Carmen motioned for her to stop. She took a last long drag off her Marlboro and flicked it into the grass. "Relax, I don't need one." She was wearing a T-shirt that read *Axel's Taco Shop* in red and green letters. "You must be one of the new girls, huh?"

"I just started."

Sophie interrupted. "I need two tacos and a side of beans. I've been busy as hell."

Carmen shrugged and said to Kirsten, "She show you anything yet?"

"I just got here."

"My name's Carmen."

"Kirsten Lund."

Carmen looked down at Kirsten's hands. "That polish ain't gonna last long around here."

"I don't mind," said Kirsten.

"Okay, here's how you build a taco. By tomorrow you're gonna be so good at this you can do it dead drunk."

"Really?" Kirsten had never been drunk.

"Really. It'll be like you never did anything else. First off, you get your taco shell. Here."

Chapter

12

THE OLD MAN WAS RIGHT. You couldn't miss it. But getting in was another story. All the parking lots—the biggest parking lots he had ever seen—were full. Dean finally had to pay some lady in a pink sweatshirt five dollars to park his car on her front lawn. Then he had to walk a mile just to get to the fairground gates. Then stand in line behind the Fat family, Mom and Pop and three towheaded, pear-shaped kids, hulking through the revolving wooden turnstiles like hogs going to slaughter. He should've just eaten breakfast at Denny's.

Inside, the landscape teemed with pale, light-haired Minnesotans, all of them eating. The Fat family melted into the crowd, merging with their own kind. Everyone he looked at had a face full of something, even the skinny ones. And if they weren't eating, they were crowding in front of some rickety-looking shack or trailer or tent, buying something: corn dogs or minidonuts or zucchini-on-a-stick or sno-cones or foot-longs or whatever—some of the stuff they were eating didn't even look like food. People walking and eating at the same time. Dean tried to remember when he had last eaten. A bag of dill-pickle-flavored potato chips he'd bought in Iowa. Unless you counted all the beer he'd drunk last night.

He'd been on the fairgrounds only a few minutes when he lost his bearings completely. The number of people milling about was staggering—like a rock festival, only without the stage to provide direction and focus. He had never seen so many people, especially so many chunked-out people, all in motion at the same time. Where the hell was he? The crowd moved in and out of itself, groups of pedestrians twining together and separating like a confluence of molasses and oil; Dean was drawn along in the wake of passing bodies, unable to stop. Where were they all going?

They were going nowhere and everywhere. The sounds of people talking, chewing, shuffling and dragging their feet over the streets and sidewalks, some sort of aerial cable car clattering overhead, vendors shouting, an engine revving in the distance, music coming from every direction, all different tunes. It was insane. Dean had been to carnivals and fairs before, but nothing on this scale.

How was he going to find the taco place? A man carrying a five-foot-tall purple dinosaur nearly ran him down. Dean stepped aside, bumping into a pair of big-shouldered farm kids, both of them wearing caps that read *MoorMan Feeds*. One kid grinned at him and said, "Nice day, huh?"

Nice day? That was what the old man had said. He looked up at the clear blue sky, then back at the kid, whose red hat was the only part of him still visible as the crowd on the street closed. He had a bad thought then, out of nowhere. What if Carmen didn't really like him? How did he know Carmen hadn't been faking it, just using him to get her weed and her Valiums? The notion rolled uncomfortably in his gut. He forced his mind to engage the problem. Suppose she didn't like him? When he thought of her that way, she didn't seem so interesting. If she didn't like him, then she wasn't who he thought she was, and if that's what she was, then it didn't really bother him. The concepts clicked neatly into place. If she didn't really like him, that wouldn't change anything, as long as she continued to fake it. They could still go to Puerto Penasco.

Another bad thought hit him then. What if she'd lied about liking him and lied about the coffee cans full of money too? What if she'd made that up, just to get him to like her? He veered to the sidewalk, grabbed hold of a light post, and breathed slowly, filtering the greasy-smelling air through undersize nostrils. He really had to get something in his stomach.

He spotted a sign ahead, INFORMATION, and angled toward it. A smiling, cockeyed older man wearing a *Great Minnesota Get-Together* mesh cap stood in a small kiosk, scanning the crowd. Dean approached him, was about to ask him where he could find the taco place, when the man said, "Nice day, huh?"

Dean turned, thinking the man was talking to someone behind him, but no one seemed to be looking his way.

"Low eighties this afternoon," the man said. Apparently this was the type of information booth where you didn't have to ask questions. You simply passed within earshot, and information was delivered. The man continued: "They're saying we might get rained on some this weekend, but we sure did get a good one today!"

Dean regarded the man curiously, waiting for the next weather report.

"There something I can help you with, son?" the man asked.

"Yeah," Dean said. "I'm looking for this Mexican restaurant."

The man raised his gray eyebrows. "You mean like tacos and stuff?"

"That's it." What the hell did he think he meant?

"Well, there's lots of little taco stands around, only I don't know that you'd call 'em restaurants. There's one over on Judson Avenue, back the way you were coming from. And then there's a couple of them, I believe, up by the Food Building."

"I'm looking for one owned by a guy named Axel."

"Ah!" The man thrust a forefinger into the air. "Then you'd be looking for Axel's Taco Shop."

"Yeah, that's it."

"I can tell you just how to get there. But tell me something, son—how come you got those rings in your head?"

"How come you got one eye pointing the wrong way?"

"On account of I was in the war, son."

"You gonna tell me how to get where I'm going?"

"Seems to me a fellow can't help but get where he's going, but if you want to get to Axel's, you just go straight up the street here to the Food Building. Axel's is right across the mall from it."

"Thanks," Dean said.

"You betcha," the man called after him.

Dean imagined the Food Building as being this huge shrine surrounded by a sea of obesity. Maybe it was made out of food, like a gingerbread house. Or made out of corn dogs and bomb pops. He walked right past it and finally had to ask a guy who was selling plastic cowboy hats and Mylar balloons and yardstick canes where the hell was the Food Building. The guy pointed him back the way he'd come. When Dean started walking away, the guy said, "Hey, aren't you gonna buy something?" So Dean paid him three dollars for a heavy green yardstick cane with a leather loop on the end.

The Food Building turned out to be a squat, ugly, cinder-block structure, painted white, covering half a city block, surrounded by and filled with food vendors. Dean walked into the building, letting himself be pushed and jostled past the Navaho fry bread, caramel apple sundaes, giant Vietnamese egg rolls, strawberry cream puffs, deep-fried cheese curds . . . deep-fried what? He had to get out of there. The cacophony of smells was making his eyes water, exciting both his appetite and a desire to vomit. He pushed through the crowd, past the fried elephant ears and mini-Reubens and Soups-of-the-World, emerging at last onto a wide, grassy mall covered with picnic tables and surrounded by more food concessions. Frozfruit bars, Orange Treet, Black Walnut Taffy, Rainbow Cones, chocolate-chip cookies, fried chicken, sno-cones, Pronto Pups, French-Fried Ice Cream, Tiny Tot Donuts . . . Where was the Mexican restaurant? This had to be the place. When he finally spotted Axel's Taco Shop, the bright red-and-green sign jumping out at him, he felt as if his Mexican dinner had turned into a taco chip.

Dean stood staring at Axel's Taco Shop. This was no restaurant. This was a little wooden shack. A crummy little shack, no larger than most living rooms, about the size of three cells at Lincoln, if that, with the front wide open like a big window and a sign up above, a picture of a taco and a guy in a sombrero.

The lower part of the stand was also covered with signs. Dean squinted but couldn't read them. Probably menus. A blond woman stood at the counter. Behind her, he spotted Carmen. At least he was in the right place.

A man wearing overalls stopped and ordered something. The

blond woman took his money and handed him what looked like a burrito. The man walked away, pushing the paper-wrapped burrito into his mouth. Dean thought, Another—what—dollar fifty? Great. He tried to imagine that burrito multiplying into a coffee can fortune. He shook his head. This was bullshit. No way this guy was rich, selling burritos to farmers in overalls and baseball caps. He was going to have to have a talk with Carmen. All the way from Omaha for burrito money.

Chapter

13

SOPHIE WAS USED TO seeing a lot of strange people at the fair, so when the bald kid with the rings in his eyebrow approached, she thought nothing of it. In fact, she would likely have forgotten him within seconds if he had not drawn attention to himself by demanding a free taco.

"Excuse me?" she said.

The kid smiled. He had small, neat teeth, very white. He looked past her.

"Hey, Carmen!" he said in a loud voice.

Carmen approached the counter. "Dean?"

"I can't have you giving away food to your friends," Sophie said. "It'll come out of your pay." It was best to put a stop to it now, before it got out of hand.

"Do I look like I'm giving away food?" Carmen said.

Sophie set her jaw. "I'm just saying."

"I can't believe you actually came out here. I mean to the fair," Carmen said.

A couple wearing matching black cowboy hats and Garth Brooks T-shirts stopped a few feet away from the stand and read the menu signs.

Sophie said, "You want to step to the side, uh, Gene. I have some customers here."

"His name's *Dean*," Carmen said.

"Yeah, and I'm a customer too. I talked to your boss, Axel, and he told me to stop by for a free taco. So here I am."

"You talked to *Axel*?" Carmen said.

Sophie said, "Look, let's not tie up the counter here, okay?"

Carmen motioned with her head. "Come on around the back."

Dean circled the stand. Carmen handed him a taco through the back door. "You talked to *Axel*?" she repeated in a low voice.

Dean nodded, biting into the taco. He chewed as he spoke. "Saw him at the motel. In the parking lot."

Carmen stepped out the door. "What was he doing there?"

Dean shrugged. "He had a garbage bag full of something."

"You tell him you knew me?"

"Hey, do I look stupid?" he asked, his mouth full of taco. A glob of salsa dropped onto Carmen's orange Bugs Bunny T-shirt.

Carmen thought it best not to answer his question.

"You got my T-shirt on," she said.

Dean said, "How about you take a break, show me around a little?"

Sophie appeared in the doorway, grabbed Carmen's apron strap. "No way, José," she said, dragging her daughter back into the stand.

Dean finished his taco, watching the women work. A few seconds later, Carmen poked her head out. "Stick around," she whispered. "I'll be out of here in no time."

———

"So what do you think?"

"I don't think your mom likes me."

"I mean the cheese curds."

Dean chewed the deep-fried cheese curd, searching for flavor. He examined the remaining batter-fried nodules in the paper tray. He brought the tray up to his face and sniffed, then picked out another curd, bit into it, chewed for a few moments, and swallowed. He looked at Carmen, bewildered.

"So what do you think?" she asked.

"I don't get it."

"People love them. Axel told me they take in twenty thousand a day out of this one stand."

"Dollars? What is it? It's got no taste. Needs salsa or mustard or something."

"You know when they make cheese? What Axel says is, this is the stuff they used to just throw it away. You can deep-fry anything here and sell it. Deep-fried ice cream—they even got that."

They were walking up the hill past a concession stand made in the shape of a giant baked potato. Dean shook his head and tossed the remaining cheese curds toward an overflowing trash can, missing it by three feet. "Do you take in twenty grand a day at the taco shop?"

"You kidding? We're lucky to break five on a good day."

"That much?" It wasn't twenty grand a day, but he was impressed. Maybe there was something to those coffee cans after all. "I thought you told me this guy Axel had a restaurant."

"Axel calls it a restaurant. He says if a building stays up all year, it's a restaurant. If you knock it down and move it after every fair, it's a stick joint. If you can pull it behind a car, it's a trailer."

"I was expecting something bigger. You were telling me about all this money he makes, I thought there would at least be tables people could sit down at."

"Axel says you don't want them to sit down. You want them to keep moving."

"I gotta sit down. I had to park, I don't know where. I feel like I walked ten miles." Dean veered off the sidewalk and sat down on an empty bench. Carmen stood in front of him and lit a cigarette.

Dean said, "So he makes, like—what—fifty thousand in twelve days?"

"I guess."

"So he won't miss a few thousand, right?"

Carmen crossed her arms and looked away. "What do you mean?" she said.

"Well, it's just sitting there, isn't it? Sit down." He patted the bench.

Carmen sat down beside him, puffing on her cigarette. The conversation was making her uncomfortable. She liked the idea of getting her hands on some of Axel's money, but Dean was moving too fast for her. She said, "Maybe we ought to think about it."

"That's what I've been doing," Dean said. He laid his yardstick on her thigh, rolled it back and forth. "All that money. What's he gonna do with it, anyways? He lives in a Motel 6, f'Chrissakes."

Carmen stood up, knocking the yardstick aside. She needed time to think.

"Listen, you want to see a real money machine? Come here." She turned her back and started walking. Dean watched until she was nearly out of sight, then got up and followed her across the street and back toward the mall. He caught up with her in front of a large, rickety concession, a bank of glass-fronted mechanisms surrounded by a crowd of people five deep. There were fourteen machines, each operating with relentless precision. A batter-filled hopper plopped tiny rings of sweet, sticky dough into a moat of bubbling oil. The rings floated single file around the oil-filled trough, were flipped by a clever metal arm at the halfway point, and finally fell into a basket to drain, briefly, before being rolled in sugar and scooped into waxpaper bags.

"Little donuts," Dean said. "I've seen those before."

"Check out the guy with the hat."

Dean looked past the machines and saw a short, stocky man with a deeply tanned and wrinkled face sitting on an elevated stool. He wore an enormous black cowboy hat.

"That's Tommy. He owns Tiny Tot. He's a millionaire. Axel says he takes in more money in a day than we do the whole fair. Takes a bag of cash down to the bank two, three times a day. Axel says he's got the hottest concession at the fair, except for the Beer Garden. I bet Tommy's got ten times as much money as Axel, and he lives in a trailer!"

Dean squinted at the stocky little man. "He looks pissed."

"He always looks like that. Me and Tommy are buddies." She waved over the crowd, but Tommy didn't see her.

Dean shook his head slowly. "The guy is miniature. Like his donuts."

Carmen grabbed his arm. "Shit! There's Axel. He better not see us together."

Dean looked but could not pick Axel out of the crowd. "What's the problem?"

"You don't know Axel. He gets really weird around my boyfriends. I'll see you later, okay?"

Dean said, "Wait a minute . . ." But she was already out of sight. Boyfriend? Was that what he was? He watched the donut machines for a few minutes, trying to think of himself as Carmen's boyfriend but soon becoming fascinated by the little guy in the cowboy hat. He couldn't get over how small the guy was, almost like a midget. A midget millionaire. It was something to think about.

Chapter

14

KIRSTEN LUND STARED with open fascination at the daughter, Carmen, telling the mother, Sophie, to go fuck herself.

Carmen in her food-stained T-shirt, breasts moving up and down behind the Axel's Taco Shop logo, shaking as she thrust her middle finger at Sophie and stamped her feet on the painted plywood floor of the stand. Kirsten wondered what it would be like to have breasts like that, to have them hanging out there twenty-four hours a day.

The mother and daughter were different but the same. Sophie was taller, thinner, and paler than her daughter. She looked like a version of Carmen that had been leeched, milked, stretched, and bleached. Kirsten waited for Sophie to slap Carmen, or start crying, or throw something, but all she did was yell back, calling her daughter a spoiled little bitch. Kirsten, gripping her apron, pressed her back against the cooler, giving them plenty of room. Carmen was on a roll now. "I take a five-minute break, you'd think the fucking world ended," she shouted as she slapped a tortilla onto the prep table. "Look at me! I'm fucking working! I'm putting the fucking beans on." She slammed a scoop of crushed pink beans across the tortilla. "I'm putting the fucking cheese on." She slapped a handful of bright-orange cheese down on top of the beans. "The fucking lettuce. Fold the fucker up—here, stick it up your fucking ass you don't like it." She threw the taco on the floor and stomped out of the stand.

Kirsten tried to imagine talking to her mother that way. The thought made her heart accelerate. Screw you, Mom, she imagined herself saying. Put it in your butt.

Sophie, her face having gone from pink to red to white, let her breath out and turned back to the serving window. A plump, gray-haired woman with a determined smile was waiting there, holding her purse on the counter with two hands. Behind her, an old man in a misshapen felt hat, the man old enough to be her father or even her grandfather, was crouched over a cane.

The woman said, "Could we buy some beans from you? Just a cup of beans?"

"It'll be a dollar," Sophie said. "Thank you for waiting." Her hands were shaking.

"That's all right. I could see you were busy. I have a daughter too." The woman dug in her purse, found a wallet, and extracted a dollar bill. "We'll take one cup." The old man behind her was shaking visibly, holding himself up by gripping the handle of his cane with both hands. Sophie deposited the money in the steel cash box under the counter. Kirsten filled a small Styrofoam container with beans. She set a spoon and a napkin alongside it, aware of Sophie's eyes on her. The gray-haired woman led the old man to a nearby bench, sat him down, and presented him with the cup of beans.

"When you get old," Sophie said, twisting her hands together, "they make you eat beans all the time. My dad had to eat beans every day. He liked those green ones. Lima beans."

"I like lima beans," said Kirsten.

Axel stepped in through the back door. "What's going on? Where's Carmen?"

"She took a break," Sophie said. "It's about time you showed up. Where've you been?"

Axel shrugged.

Sophie said, "Can you give us a hand here? I need three Buenos."

Axel looked at Kirsten and raised his eyebrows.

"She doesn't know how to make them," Sophie explained. "Juanita won't be here for another hour, and I need three Buenos."

Axel smiled at Kirsten. "Never rolled a burro, eh?"

Kirsten shook her head. "But I made some tacos. Carmen showed me how to do the tacos and tostadas and nachos."

"Waiting for three Buenos," Sophie said.

"The secret of a Bueno," Axel said to Kirsten, "is getting the right proportion of ingredients on the tortilla. You always start with the beans. Not too much, though. Come over here where you can see. A little closer. Now watch how I do this."

———

James Dean found a bench where he could eat his bag of donuts while keeping an eye on the guy, Lord of the Donuts, perched on this stool that was high enough so he could sit down and still be taller than the kids working for him. Sit and yell at them. What was the guy's name? He couldn't remember what Carmen had told him, so he thought of him as Tiny Tot, Lord of the Donuts. Dean sat and waited until Tiny Tot got down off his stool and left the stand, passing so close Dean could have reached out his yardstick cane and tripped him. When he was almost lost from sight in the crowd, Dean abandoned the bench and followed him. As it turned out, he was visiting the rest rooms. Dean went in and stood down from him at the long steel trough, pretending to piss. Tiny Tot stood about five two in his pointy cowboy boots, a good five inches shorter than Dean. Tiny Tot pissed quickly, rattling the stainless with angry bursts of urine, then returned to the donut stand. Dean followed, swinging his cane.

The next time Tiny Tot climbed down off his stool, he took a plaid canvas shoulder bag and filled it with cash from the metal drawers under the donut machines. Dean followed him again, this time to a second donut stand, near the Beer Garden. While Dean bought a third bag of donuts, thinking of the dollar fifty as money in the bank, Tiny Tot collected the cash and left off several rolls of coins, then walked away in another direction. Dean, stuffing his cheeks full of greasy little donuts, stayed ten yards behind, enjoying the idea of so much money being carried by such a small man. He was not planning to actually do anything, of course. This was a simple reconnaissance. Later he could think about what to do with his knowledge. Right now it was just a game.

The third donut stand was tucked in under the grandstand. Tiny Tot collected the cash, then got into a discussion with two of his employees, which ended with him angrily hanging an out-of-order sign on one of the seven machines. Dean sat on a grassy spot across the street, tapping his stick on the curb and watching. When Tiny Tot finally left, red-faced, biting down hard on one of his little cigars, Dean closed the gap between them to less than twenty feet. The guy had no idea he was there. Totally oblivious. Dean might as well have been invisible.

Tiny Tot crossed Carnes Avenue, fat shoulder bag swinging, jamming his feet into the toes of his cowboy boots with each short, angry step. He cut across a large grassy area dotted with groups of fairgoers, past an exhibit promising a look at a Real, Live Albino Whale, $10,000 Reward If Not Alive, then turned up a wide alley behind a row of food concessions. Where was he going? Dean tucked his yardstick under his arm and stepped up his pace. Tiny Tot rounded a corner; Dean followed and almost collided with him. They stood frozen for a moment, their eyes locked.

"How are you doing?" Dean said, waggling his yardstick cane back and forth between them.

Tiny Tot grasped the cane with his right hand, smiled around his cigar, then slowly reached his left hand toward Dean's face. For a moment, Dean thought the little old man was going to caress him. Instead, Tiny Tot hooked his fingers through Dean's eyebrow rings. Dean lowered his head, following the sudden pain in his brow, to a place beneath the brim of the black cowboy hat, down to the level of Tiny Tot's bright blue eyes.

"I'm doing fine," Tiny Tot said. "How are you doing?"

Dean felt as if his brow was separating from his skull.

Tiny Tot growled, "You better let go that stick."

Dean released his grip on the cane, thinking he'd have his shot later, as soon as the son-of-a-bitch let go of his rings. "Okay," he said.

Tiny Tot blinked. The smoldering tip of his cigar was an inch from Dean's nose.

"I let go," Dean pointed out.

Tiny Tot grinned and exhaled a cloud of smoke. Dean felt him tense, then heard the whoosh of the cane, felt it whip up between his legs and crash into his testicles. He jerked back, felt a tearing sensation in his forehead, and dropped to the ground, globules of pain bubbling up through his abdomen, his eyes pulsing with black flashes.

———

"I can't hardly stand to work with her," Carmen said.

Axel pulled out of the lot onto Como Avenue. It was nearly midnight, and he was feeling old. The first day of the fair was always a killer. The body needed time to adapt.

"I mean, we're in there for a couple hours, and she's all over me. Like I can't do anything right. Like I don't know my job. The bitch." Carmen lit a cigarette.

"Crack the window, would you?"

Carmen rolled her window down.

"We have eleven days to go, Carmen."

"Christ, tell me something good."

"I need you two working together. Can't you humor her?"

"That's what I did all night. Me and Juanita just made food and let her and that Kirsten girl serve. Juanita's all right. Sophie doesn't bother her."

"How did Kirsten do?"

Carmen shrugged. "She was okay. She sure is clean. I don't know how she stays so clean. It's like food doesn't stick to her."

Axel smiled, thinking that Carmen was right. Kirsten Lund could walk through a shit storm and come out looking like she'd just had a bubble bath. "We did good today," he said.

"Oh, yeah?" Carmen looked at Axel. "How good?"

Axel patted the canvas bank bag on the seat beside him. "About thirty-five hundred and change. That's a good first day. Maybe once you get some sleep it'll be easier to work with her."

"I don't know about that." Carmen could now feel the two Valiums she had swallowed while they were cleaning up the stand. They helped. Eleven more days working with Sophie. She told herself it would be the last time, ever. Puerto Penasco was looking better than ever. Rich and free in Mexico. Flicking her cigarette out the window, she closed her eyes and imagined herself on the beach, dipping into a coffee can to pay for her rum punch. She let her mind drift.

"Here we are."

Carmen opened her eyes as they turned into the Motel 6 parking lot. "Want to drop me at the lobby? I need some cigarettes."

Axel swung the truck over to the brightly lit lobby and let Carmen out. "See you in the morning," he said. Carmen walked into the lobby, digging in her purse for change. Cigarettes were up to two fifty. She dropped ten quarters into the slot and pressed the Marlboro button.

"Back again, eh?"

Carmen turned away from the cigarette machine to look at the man sitting behind the counter. He was holding a copy of *Penthouse,* looking at her over the top of it.

"You talking to me?" she asked.

The man lowered his magazine. His eyes were small, gray, and moist.

"You stayed here last year," he said. "I remember you. You work with Mr. Speeter. Out at the fair, right?"

Carmen picked up the fresh pack of Marlboros. "That's right," she said. "Good night." She took a step toward the door.

"I hear you're gonna be a nurse now," the man said.

Carmen stopped. "Axel tells you stuff, huh?"

"Now and again. He's my best customer, you know. He's stayed in number three since before I even worked here. We're like neighbors; we talk." Quist looked back down at his magazine. "I see you got a roomie now." He turned a page.

Carmen lifted a cigarette out of the pack, placed it directly in the center of her mouth, then rested both elbows on the counter between the rack of postcards and the American Express applications. She waited. After fourteen hours at the fair, she was too beat to figure out what was going on. She waited for him to explain it to her.

"He's in there now," Bill said, keeping his eyes glued to the magazine. "Your skinhead boyfriend. I saw him go in your room a couple of hours ago."

"So? Hey, you got a light?"

Bill dug in his shirt pocket and extracted a book of matches. He looked at the matchbook cover. "'Call 1-900 QUICKIE,'" he read, then tossed them to her. Watching her light the cigarette, he continued: "You know, I'm supposed to get more for double occupancy.

Since the old man's footing the bill, you think I should maybe ask him for the money?"

Carmen shrugged, blew out a long stream of blue smoke, examined her fingernails. They were yellow and orange from handling processed cheese.

"Or maybe I shouldn't bother him. What do you think?"

"I wouldn't bother him with it. You know how it is."

"So how am I going to get paid?"

"I'll see what I can do. How much do you want?"

"Twenty cash ought to do it. Twenty a night."

"I'll have to get back to you on that. In the meantime, let's just keep it between you and me."

"Gotcha, babe. You and me."

Carmen crossed the parking lot, let herself into room 19, dropped her purse on the near bed. One day at the fair, and already she was exhausted. She took a canned martini from the cooler by the nightstand and popped it open. The Valiums were stroking the base of her neck. She sipped at the martini and felt the tension roll away, felt her shoulders dropping, felt her legs growing longer. The clock read 12:24. In eight hours she would be back at the fair, spreading beans over fried tortillas.

Dean lay on his side on the other bed. He was wearing his underwear and holding a wet towel against the left side of his head. His brown eyes followed her.

Carmen took another sip of martini. She said, "I got blackmailed about five minutes ago." Dean did not reply. "So what happened to you?" she asked.

After several seconds, Dean replied, "I don't want to talk about it."

Carmen shook a cigarette loose and lit it. She would be asleep soon; she could feel it gathering. But at the moment, she was staying up on a few untamed shreds of anxiety. She traced a design on Dean's muscular belly with her forefinger.

"You want to fuck around?" she asked.

This time, he took even longer to reply. In fact, he never did. Well, what the hell. She didn't care. It was just an idea to kill some time. She was all but asleep when he got up to go to the bathroom, walking funny, keeping his legs apart, almost like a chimpanzee. Carmen fell asleep thinking of him as James Dean, the naked ape.

Chapter

15

NEAR THE BACK of the south parking lot, deep in the RV ghetto, Tommy Fabian emerged from his sun-bleached Winnebago at six-thirty in the morning. It was a nice day, the second day of the fair, still cool from the night but with plenty of sunshine promising a warm afternoon. He crossed the parking lot, his short legs pumping, and paid his way into the fairgrounds. He bought a cup of coffee from a grab joint in the Coliseum, added plenty of sugar and coffee creamer, then walked up to Tiny Tot #1 and sat on a folding stool to watch the early-morning action. Fairgrounds employees and conces-sionaires were moving about, carrying things, opening stands, and unloading supply trucks. A street sweeper passed by, its enormous rotary brushes hissing over the asphalt. A man wearing a Minnesota State Fair windbreaker was handing out copies of the *State Fair Daily News* to anyone who looked as though he might be in charge of something. Tommy accepted a copy without looking at it. Years ago he had read things like that, but lately it seemed to be too much trouble.

At seven o'clock he visited the doniker behind the deep-fried-zucchini joint. They were actually clean, this time of day, and plenty of toilet paper available. A few more hours, you wouldn't want your bare ass anywhere near those toilet seats. Tommy snapped off a loaf, then walked back up to the Jaycees' and bought another cup of coffee. He returned to his seat outside his donut joint, sat, and sipped slowly.

A few farmers were straggling onto the fairgrounds now, wearing their clean overalls and go-to-town feed caps. The farmers were always the first suckers to arrive. Then the families. The couples and the teenagers wouldn't show up until much later, an hour or two before dark. Tommy lit one of his small cigars, his first of the day.

At seven-thirty, he saw Axel's manager, Sophie, pass by, carrying a grocery bag. Holding the paper bag in one arm, she tried to unlock the back door of Axel's Taco Shop. The bag started to slide from her grasp. She grabbed at it, and the bag tore open, spilling several plastic pouches of flour tortillas onto the ground. Tommy watched as she picked them up, let herself into the stand.

Duane, the kid who managed Tiny Tot #1 for him, showed up at seven-forty, five minutes early. Tommy unlocked the stand, fired up four of the machines, then picked his new yardstick cane from its hook on the wall and, swinging it jauntily, strolled off toward the grandstand to get his next joint up and running. By eight o'clock sharp, he expected to sell his first bag of donuts.

———

The second time, Carmen woke up to the sound of Axel's fist beating on the door. She sat up, looked at the clock.

"Shit!"

Dean, who was sitting up, reading, watched her scramble out of bed, naked except for the cellophane wrapper from a pack of cigarettes stuck to her ass.

"Shit, I'm late. How come you didn't get me up?" Vaguely, she remembered waking the first time, grabbing the ringing phone, talking to Axel, hanging up. She must've gone back to sleep.

Axel's muffled voice came through the door. "Carmen! Let's go!"

She looked helplessly around the room, still too sleepy to know what to do next.

Dean said, "Why don't you tell him you're not ready. I'll drive you over later."

Axel beat his fist on the door.

Carmen took a deep breath, opened the chained door a crack. "Axel? I fell back asleep. I'm sorry."

"How long will it take you to get your butt out here?"

"I gotta take a shower."

"Christ, Carmen. We're going to be late!"

"Why don't you go ahead. I'll catch a cab or something, okay?"

Axel threw up his arms and marched back to his idling truck.

Carmen closed the door. "He's pretty pissed," she reported.

Dean touched his brow lightly, looked at his finger.

"It's still sort of puffy," Carmen said.

Dean's jaw twitched. "Listen to this. . . ." He had his poetry book open.

"Isn't it sort of early for that?" She pulled the curtain aside, letting more light into the room.

"Listen: *This Soule, now free from prison, and passion, hath yet a little indignation.*"

"So?"

"So what do you think?"

"I think maybe some of your brains leaked out."

Dean closed the book and swung his legs over the edge of the bed. He said, "Life is too short to let an opportunity slide—you know what I mean?"

Carmen didn't. "All I know is Axel's gonna be really pissed if he gets stuck in the stand rolling burritos all day."

"So what? What I'm thinking is we just go to Puerto Penasco. What do you say?"

Carmen stared at the scab on his eyebrow. "What do you mean?"

"I mean, let's take a look in the old man's room. See what we find."

"We can't do that."

"Why not?"

"He'll know who did it."

"So?"

"So . . . I don't know." She felt her belly tingling, like she was coming on to some good acid, or like she was standing at the edge of a high cliff, looking down. The same reckless, scary feeling she got when she climbed into bed with a new guy, or lifted a twenty from the Taco Shop till, only more intense. "I don't have a key," she said.

Dean shrugged. "My guess, from what you told me about that guy in the office, that won't be a problem."

———

Tommy Fabian was taller than a lot of guys. His cowboy boots, which he wore because they were comfortable, brought him up to an even sixty-two inches. Lots of guys weren't that tall. The Stetson added a few more inches to his stature and, he felt, made it clear to all just who was in charge at Tiny Tot Donuts.

Tommy stood beside the rock garden on the mall, keeping an eye on Tiny Tot #1, his flagship location. The day had started off with a bang. He'd had twelve machines going before ten, and he'd made his daily nut by eleven. The rest of the day, the next twelve hours, that was gravy.

It was almost noon, and the lines were lengthening. Lines were good for business, if they weren't too long. One of the things he told his kids over and over was to work slow when there were only a few customers. Shut off a few of the machines if you have to, because you got to have a line to get a line. Then you got to kick ass when you get busy, keep them from getting too long. People would wait only a minute or so before they decided to go instead for some cotton candy, or a caramel apple, or a paper cup full of french fries. It was just like his days with the carnival. You wanted to make any money, you had to know how to work the tip. That was what made this fair great. Most of the joints were run by amateurs, didn't know what the hell they were doing. A guy like Tommy, who'd grown up in the carnival, could make a small fortune.

They were starting to get hungry now; the donut lines were growing. He could see people eyeing the crowd in front of his stand, looking to see what they were missing. Tommy willed Duane, his assistant, to open up the last two machines. As he watched, Duane did exactly that.

He was a good kid.

"Hey, Tommy." Axel Speeter came up the slope and stood beside him. Tiny Tot Donuts was two spaces down and across the mall from Axel's Taco Shop. This was their usual observation point, the only place on the mall where both stands could be comfortably observed. This was their place for exchanging gossip and speculating about the weather. They were the old pros.

Tommy nodded and waved his cigar. They stood for a few moments in silence, surveying the crowd.

"Look at that pair," Axel said.

The two girls were walking, laughing, eating Pronto Pups and drinking Orange Treets. Both were wearing jeans that had been carefully ripped, shredded, and safety-pinned to dramatic effect. They were wearing thin tank tops, one pink and the other yellow. The one in yellow was wearing a Minnesota Twins baseball cap with a fuzzy green plastic butterfly pinned to the front.

"Easter eggs," said Tommy.

"What?"

"Like four Easter eggs. That's why all the old cooch shows folded up. Who needs 'em, you got that young stuff struttin' around for free?"

Axel licked his upper lip and nodded. "I wonder how they get past their mothers that way. I wouldn't let my kid go out like that."

"You ain't got a kid."

Axel raised his eyebrows. "Now, how the hell do you know that? I might have one someplace."

Tommy shrugged. "You know what she's wearing today?"

Axel frowned. The thought was doubly disturbing: that he might have a daughter and that she might be half dressed in public. He shook it off. Sophie and Kirsten were starting to get busy. If Carmen didn't show up soon, he would have to get in there and help them.

"How's your help this year?" Tommy ashed his cigar.

"Not bad. Only one major battle so far."

"Yeah, I saw that one. Heard it from way over here." Tommy chewed his cigar, spat, then said, "You know the blonde is H.O.'ing on you."

Axel looked down at Tommy, his cheeks slack.

"I seen her show up this morning with a sack of grocery store tortillas," Tommy elaborated.

Axel said, "So? What makes you think she's holding out?"

Tommy rolled his cigar in his mouth. "I know when I'm getting ripped on account of I keep a count of the donut bags. I know how many bags I got at the start of the day and how many I got at the end, and I just match up the cash and the bags, and if it don't come out I know I'm getting ripped. Now, I'm guessin' you do something like that with tortillas, right?"

"It's only approximate."

"But it gives you an idea, right? You have 'em give you a tortilla count so you know about how much money you're supposed to have, right? So I'm wondering, this morning I see the old broad—"

"Her name's Sophie."

"Yeah, Sophie. I ask myself, why's she bringing in grocery store tortillas?"

Axel nodded sadly. He didn't want to know this stuff. He trusted Sophie. Carmen, he'd have believed anything. But not Sophie. Maybe she was H.O.'ing. Maybe not. Either way, he was inclined to ignore the situation, as long as she didn't take too much.

As if reading his thoughts, Tommy said, "Look, you want to let her cop a piece, that's your business. I'm just telling you."

"Okay, you told me."

"Also," Tommy continued, "long as I'm telling you stuff you don't want to know, that little Carmen has a boyfriend she probably don't want you to know about."

"What?" This was new. Carmen had a boyfriend? The thought made his stomach drop an inch.

"Yeah. A punk kid, followed me on my cash run yesterday like I'm some jerk don't know any better than to get rolled, like I ain't been doing this my whole goddamn life." Tommy sucked furiously at his cigar, his cheeks flaming with the memory. "I'm making my run, and I noticed this ball-headed kid following me—walking right behind me like I'm deaf, dumb, and blind. I'm taking my usual shortcut." He drew a line in the air with his cigar. "I got about six thousand bucks with me and this weird-lookin' kid on my ass. So I stop, and he waves one a them yardsticks in my face and says, 'How you doing?'" Tommy dropped his cigar and ground it into the grass with the tip of a cowboy boot. "So I grab the stick and I give the son-of-a-bitch a little nut massage."

"Just like that?" Axel was impressed.

"Went down like a sack a mix. I got his stick hanging over in my joint there. One a those canes they sell, you know, got markings on it like a yardstick."

"What did he do?"

"He just laid right down."

"I mean, what did he do that you hit him for?"

"He was up to no good. I could tell, the way he was watching me. Watching me pull the money out of the tills. And I seen him with Carmen, sitting with her."

"Jesus, you just hit him? Did you think about . . . what if he was just going to ask you where's the bathroom or something?"

Tommy grinned. "Probably that's exactly what he was going to do. He wasn't actually going to try to roll me, not in the middle of the day like that. But he was thinking about it, thinking how he could do it later on. I figured I could save us both some trouble. You shoulda seen him go down. Now there's one more son-of-a-bitch knows not to mess with Tommy Fabian."

Axel blew out his cheeks and pushed back a thin strand of hair. "You say he's bald?"

"Like he shaves his head. Creepy-looking."

"You saw him with Carmen?"

"Hand on her ass and everything. You watch yourself, Ax. Those two are cookin' up somethin', and it don't smell like frijoles."

"What does the kid look like?"

"Like a bald monkey. He's got this flat face. Used to have these rings in his eyebrow. I even got myself a little souvenir." He held up his right hand, showing off the two gold rings rattling loose on his middle finger.

Axel said, "Oh." He felt sick.

Chapter

16

CARMEN SET TWO twenty-dollar bills on the counter, hit the bell with her fist, then went to the coffeemaker and filled two paper cups with "complimentary coffee." Bill Quist, yawning, near the end of his shift, came out from the office, saw the money, then saw Carmen, then smiled broadly.

"Why, thank you, darling. I was starting to wonder about you."

Carmen added three packets of sugar to each of the coffees. "I told you I was gonna pay you," she said.

"That you did."

Carmen started toward the door, stopped, and turned back to Quist. "I almost forgot. Axel just called and asked me to bring him his eyedrops. He said you had a key to his room I could use."

Quist tipped his head to the side like a robin listening for a worm. "Say what?"

"I need a key to get in Axel's room."

"Mr. S. didn't say nothing to me about that."

Carmen set the coffees back on the counter, reached in her

pocket, and pulled out a handful of bills. She counted out three more twenties. "He also said I should pay you a few days in advance. Also, I'm gonna need another key for my room."

"I could get in big trouble."

Carmen sipped one of her coffees, waiting.

"You just gonna go in and get something for Mr. S.?"

Carmen nodded.

Quist swallowed, looking at the money. "I think I need a little more deposit." He cleared his throat. "I mean, if you don't want me to bother Mr. S. about it."

Carmen said, "I'll see what I can do. But I need the keys right now. Axel doesn't get his eyedrops, we're both gonna be in deep shit."

———

The Coca-Cola crates were stacked against the wall just like she had described. Dean lifted one down from the top row and looked inside. It was full of boxer shorts. He grinned and looked at Carmen, who was standing in the doorway watching the parking lot. She looked scared.

"What are you worried about?"

"You don't know Axel," she said. "You never seen him get pissed. He finds out we were in his stuff, he's gonna be pretty mad."

"Relax, Carmen. You never seen me get mad, either." Dean thought about Mickey, something he hadn't done for more than twenty-four hours. He couldn't remember what she had done to make him mad. The memory, three days old, had grown fuzzy. He brought another crate down and set it on the bed. It contained several pressed and folded white shirts. This guy is strange, he thought.

"Why don't you just look through the sides of them," Carmen said. "He keeps the ones with the coffee cans on the bottom row. You can look through the sides of the crates and see the coffee cans."

Dean got down on his hands and knees and examined the bottom row of crates. Two of them, the two on the end, contained red coffee cans. Dean could feel his heart start up. He stood and lifted another crate off the top.

"He's gonna know we were here. He'll know his crates are all mixed up."

Dean ignored her and continued to dismantle the wall of red plastic crates. When he reached the bottom layer, he lifted one of the red cans. There were ten of them. He dug his nails under the edge of the plastic lid and lifted it away.

The can was jammed full of black fabric. He grabbed a fold and pulled, extracting a pair of black nylon calf-length men's stockings. He shook the contents of the can out onto the bed. The can was full of identical pairs of stockings. Dean looked at Carmen, puzzled. Carmen gaped at the stockings with an expression of utter incomprehension. Dean grabbed another can and opened it. It too was filled with black nylon calf-length men's stockings. They were held together with the original plastic hanger and still had the size and fiber content stickers: 100% nylon, fits sizes 10–13.

"Those are the kind of socks he likes," she said. "He must've found a sale."

The other coffee cans were different. They contained, in order of discovery, nine three-packs of cheap ballpoint pens, several dozen Hav-a-Hank handkerchiefs, and six new decks of Bicycle brand poker-size playing cards. Three of the cans contained fourteen pairs of new white cotton boxer shorts. One held a dried-out and yellowed set of dentures, and strangest of all, the last can was half full of ground coffee.

By the time he discovered the coffee, Dean had grown a grim little smile. He walked around the bed, stood in front of Carmen, circled her neck with his hands, and gently massaged her throat with his thumbs. She didn't look so attractive to him now. She looked like any other stupid bitch. "Carmen," he said, "I am beyond shock."

"It was there," Carmen said, her face gone white.

"Sure it was."

She shook her head. "I have to get to work. We have to put everything back like we found it."

"Tell me something—do you like me?"

Carmen nodded, feeling his thumbs on either side of her Adam's apple.

Dean held her for another five seconds, then let go and began repacking and closing the coffee cans. "You think he put it in a bank?"

"Axel doesn't like banks. But I don't know. I never know what Axel will do." She took the prescription bottle from her purse, tapped out three blue Valiums, swallowed them dry, then watched Dean re-assemble the wall of Coke crates. "What are you gonna do?" she asked.

"I don't know yet."

"You just came here to get Axel's money, didn't you?"

Dean paused and stared back at her. He hadn't thought that was why he came, but now he wasn't sure. He said, "If I'd a known that you were lying to me about the money, I might not've liked you enough to drive all the way up here to see you."

Carmen thought about that. "I wasn't lying," she said.

Dean said, "Hey . . ." He pulled a grease-spotted, khaki-colored canvas bag out of one of the crates and tugged open the drawstring top. Reaching into the sack, he grinned and pulled out something wrapped in an oily rag, unwrapped it to reveal a .45-caliber pistol and a loaded clip. He popped the clip into the handle and pointed the old army weapon at Carmen's face.

"Bang," he said.

Carmen rolled her eyes and waited for the Valiums to kick in.

———

After helping the girls with the lunch rush, Axel poured himself a Coke and left the stand, telling them he'd be gone for a while. He wandered down Carnes Avenue, heading toward the midway. He needed the anonymity that came with the clatter and flash of the rides and games. He kept thinking about Tommy and the bald kid, imagining the scene again and again in his mind, remembering the kid he'd met at the Motel 6. It had to be the same one, the bald monkey with the rings in his head.

He would not be Carmen's first boyfriend, nor, probably, her last. He knew he would have to get used to it, and he knew he never would. Like it or not, he was beset by a father's protective fears and a lover's jealous rage. Carmen would have men, and they would have her. This one, though, this one was bad news. Even if he could not trust his own instincts in these matters, he could certainly trust Tommy's.

Axel sipped his Coke and stared up at the Ferris wheel—what Tommy would call a "chump heister"—rising above the entrance to the midway. The worm turns, he thought. Perhaps this bald monkey was a manifestation of his wicked thoughts. He imagined what Sam O'Gara would say to that, and he laughed.

Axel liked to walk the midway, a clattering, roaring, flashing, spinning quarter mile of rides, games, and sideshows that dominated the west end of the fairgrounds. He liked the noise and the action, and he liked to stand and watch the carnies work the tip, proving again and again that beneath the tight-lipped, practical exterior of the typical Minnesotan there lies yet another compulsive fool. This year, the suckers were being lured into tossing rings, basketballs, and coins by four-foot-tall Bart Simpson dolls, Inflatable Power Rangers, and Nirvana posters. Axel stopped to watch a clean, athletic-looking young man trying to win a Pink Panther doll for his girlfriend by throwing a highly inflated basketball through an undersize hoop that was farther away than it looked. He watched the kid spend twenty dollars before giving up, shaking his head, embarrassed more by his lack of skill than at his lack of good sense.

Axel walked to the end of the midway, where *Serpentina, the Snake Woman* was doing a teaser routine with a reticulated python on a small stage in front of the freak show. The freak show had evolved over the years—now it was called the Cavalcade of Human Oddities. *Three-Legged Lonna,* the *Siamese Twins from Darkest Africa,* and *Bigfoot, Monster or Mutant?* were no longer featured acts. The "freaks" were now performance artists. Serpentina could be any of three women, depending on what time of day it was. The one up there now was wearing thick eyeglasses, her thighs spilling past the edges of her faux-snakeskin leotard. Two of the women who played Serpentina also did duty as *Tortura, the Puncture-Proof Girl.* The third woman, a gaunt, hollow-eyed blonde, was occasionally featured as *Electra, Mistress of the Megawatt.* Axel preferred this modern approach. It seemed kinder than the ogling of physical deformities that had gone on a decade or two earlier. Down in the South—Mississippi, Alabama, Louisiana—the freak shows were still popular, but up here the fascination with birth defects had given way to other perversions. He had to admit, though, that watching a sword swallower, a contortionist, or a woman who could stand on an electrified plate that made her hair stand on end was not as powerfully evocative as staring at the man with feet swollen to the size of watermelons, or the young girl with an extra leg jutting from her inner thigh.

He paused at the Dump Bozo joint, watched a trio of small-town football heroes spend ten dollars for the privilege of trying to dump the obnoxious "Bozo" into a tank of water. The carny playing Bozo hurled taunts and insults at the players, driving them into a frenzy. When one of the players hit the target and dropped Bozo into the tank, Bozo would be back on his seat in seconds, spitting water and imprecations back at the ball throwers. It looked like a tough job, making people hate you so much they'd pay to get you wet. Tommy would have been good at it.

Axel was feeling fine. The buzz and clatter of the midway made him feel sane and normal. And he felt good about what he'd done with his money. He felt he could relax a little now, not be worrying about it all the time. Carmen always had been a little too interested in his money. Dipping into his coffee cans last year, thinking he wouldn't notice. He'd meant to talk to her about that but had kept putting it off, thinking about things he had done when he was her age, half a century ago, thinking she would change as she got older.

Change into what?

Yesterday, when he'd learned that she'd been blabbing it around, mentioning it to Tommy and who knew who else, he'd finally moved it all to a new, safer location. Now the entire $260,000 rested three feet underground, wrapped in two layers of Hefty bags, beneath his old pickup truck in Sam O'Gara's backyard. Axel smiled, remembering the way Sam's supposedly vicious guard hounds, Chester and Festus, had quickly lowered their hackles when presented with a half-dozen Bueno Burritos. The Bueno was a great product—even the dogs knew it. They'd wolfed the burros, then lain in the shade and watched contentedly as Axel dug the hole, dropped in the money, covered it up, and returned the old pickup to its original position. Except for the fact that the dogs were a little fatter, there was no evidence that he'd ever been there. Only he and the hounds would know. The money was safe, for now.

Axel stared sightlessly across the sea of bobbing faces moving in and out of the midway, drifting comfortably on the familiar current.

———

A few minutes after 4:00 P.M., Carmen stepped into the back of the taco stand. She put her purse under the counter but did not remove the mirrored sunglasses she was wearing. Sophie stood at the front counter, waiting for a customer. If she noticed Carmen's arrival, she gave no sign.

"You guys been busy?" Carmen asked.

Sophie jerked her head to the side, like she was shaking a fly off her nose.

"Sorry I'm late," Carmen offered after a moment. "Axel didn't wake me up. I overslept."

"Eight hours," Sophie said.

"Where's Axel?"

"He didn't say," Sophie said.

"Axel's weird," said Carmen. "Probably went to sit in his truck and space out."

Sophie arched an eyebrow and regarded her daughter. "He's not so weird."

"Yes he is. He's one of the weirdest guys I ever knew."

"You think he's as weird as your friend that was here yesterday?"

"Who, Dean? Dean's weird too. How come it's so dark out? It's not that late, is it?"

Kirsten and Sophie looked at Carmen, seeing themselves reflected in mirrored lenses.

"Take off your sunglasses," Sophie said.

Carmen said, "Oh!" She reached up and touched the glasses, pushing them up on her nose, but didn't remove them. Sophie shook her head, muttering, and turned back to the counter to wait for customers. She had not noticed the purple bruise that showed just past the edge of the right lens, but Kirsten did. "Did somebody punch you?" she asked in a whisper.

Carmen shook her head. It had not been a punch, exactly. More like a slap. "I ran into something I didn't know was there," she said.

After putting Axel's room back in order that morning, Carmen and Dean had walked down the street to Denny's to get something to eat. Dean had Axel's .45 stuck in his belt, under his motorcycle jacket. He asked the waitress to bring him steak and eggs, Canadian bacon, sausage links, and two glasses of apple juice. Carmen ordered pigs-in-a-blanket, her favorite breakfast when she'd been a little girl. While they waited for their food to arrive, she had asked him what he planned to do next.

"Next?"

"Yeah. You going back to Omaha?"

Dean shook his head. "Can't do that."

"How come?"

Dean stroked her kneecap with the barrel of the .45. That was when he'd told her about Mickey. Carmen was glad she'd had the foresight to eat the three Valiums.

"It's all your fault, you know," Dean said. "If you hadn't wanted those Valiums, it never would've happened."

"Wait a second," Carmen said. "I didn't do anything."

"And if you hadn't wanted to go to Puerto Penasco, I wouldn't even be here. Now it turns out you were lying to me about the coffee can thing."

"The money used to be there," Carmen said. "He must've done something with it." She didn't like how calm he was acting.

"What? What did he do with it, Carmy?"

Carmen shrugged. She didn't like being called "Carmy," either. Their breakfasts arrived. She watched Dean eat his meat. He held on to the plate, lowered his face, and forked the food in quickly. He ate the steak, then the bacon, then the sausage, then the eggs. Carmen unrolled her pancake-wrapped sausages and ate a few pieces of pancake, wondering in a distant sort of way what was going to happen next. Even filtered through the Valium, Dean was making her nervous as a mouse in a cage with a sleeping cat.

She pushed her plate aside. "What are you gonna do now?" she asked.

Dean drank his second glass of apple juice. "What would you do?"

"I don't know."

"Maybe I'll rob a bank. What do you think?" He lifted the .45 and set it on the table beside the remnants of his breakfast.

"You better put that away before somebody sees it."

"Don't tell me what to do, Carmy." He stared at her, unblinking. After a few seconds, he picked up the gun and put it in his belt. "I just can't believe you got me all the way up here for nothing."

"I didn't ask you to come," she heard herself say, knowing before the sentence was finished that she'd made a mistake. She saw his left hand close, then drift toward her across the table. The fist looked large, soft, and inflated. It floated toward her, growing larger until she could see nothing else. Her head snapped back and hit the plastic booth divider. She gasped and slid down in the vinyl seat. Dean stood and walked calmly out of the restaurant. Carmen felt no pain. She touched her eyebrow, saw blood on her hand. She dipped her napkin in her ice water, dabbed at her brow. None of the other customers seemed to have noticed anything. The waitress stepped up to the table and delivered the check, raising an eyebrow but making no comment about the blood-spotted napkin Carmen held against her brow.

Carmen paid the check and walked back to the motel. Dean's car was gone. His bag was gone too, but he'd left his poetry book behind. She lay back on the unmade bed and stared up at the thousands of tiny black holes in the ceiling tiles.

A few hours later, she had awakened, put on her sunglasses, picked up a bus on Larpenteur, and gone to work. It was better than waiting, not knowing whether or when he would come back.

Now, standing in front of the prep table, her hands greasy from the ground beef and spattering oil, reliving the morning in her mind, she was surprised to discover that it was making her slightly aroused. She could still feel the warm gun barrel touching her knee. The sensation ran up the inside of her thigh into her belly. He could have shot her. He had considered it—she had seen it in his eyes—but he had chosen not to. His fist had cut her, given her a black eye, but it had felt solid and real, and compared to what he might have done, what might have happened to her, the blow had felt like a caress.

Dean might be dangerous, but he wasn't boring. He really did like her. He'd killed his own sister, but the way he told it, it wasn't exactly his fault. A part of Carmen hoped he would disappear from her life, but another part wanted to see him again. And somehow she knew she would.

Chapter

17

AFTER DEAN PAID HIS FIVE BUCKS and pushed through the turnstile, he bought a Harley-Davidson painter cap and a pair of cheap, dark sunglasses from one of the souvenir kiosks. It was late, ten o'clock at night, and everybody else was moving the other way, out the exits and into the parking lots to search for their cars. Dean moved against the flow of bodies, toward the center of the fairgrounds. His new sunglasses blurred the details of the late-night fairground action. A bank of low clouds had moved in over the city; the air was warm and moist. At the corner of Carnes and Nelson, he bought a foot-long hot dog, piled high with onions, and ate it while he watched the flickering, wheeling lights from the midway reflect off the clouds. When he had finished, he strolled up Carnes to the mall, where he bought a blue-raspberry sno-cone and found a comfortable bench where he could suck on the flavored ice and watch the donut guy.

Tiny Tot Donuts was surrounded by people picking up their final snack of the night. Through occasional breaks in the crowd, Dean could see the black cowboy hat bobbing up and down. It didn't look like the stand would be closing anytime soon. Dean finished sucking the blue juice out of his sno-cone and dropped its flavorless remains on the trampled grass. The trash bins were overflowing anyway, nearly invisible beneath mounds of greasy paper. Two hundred thousand people had come to eat and spread their refuse over the three hundred acres. Dean strolled farther up the mall toward Axel's Taco Shop. He watched Carmen serving a small group of hungry customers. He waited a few minutes for a break in the action, then walked right up to Carmen with his new cap and shades and ordered a bean tostada.

Carmen took his order without recognizing him.

"Hey," he said. "How late you think that donut place'll stay open?"

"What?" she asked. She looked tired. A long strand of hair was pasted down one cheek. The blond girl brought his tostada and set it on the counter.

Carmen's mom had her head in the sink, cleaning it or something. Dean leaned in over the counter and said in Carmen's ear, "Wake up, Carmy. It's me."

Carmen jumped back, bumping into the blond girl.

"Hey!"

Dean laughed.

Carmen said, "Dean?" She looked quickly back over her shoulder at her mother.

"I just need to know how late the donut guy stays open."

"Probably eleven-thirty or so. Why?"

"What time is it?"

"Quarter to. Why? What are you gonna do?"

"See you later." He turned and walked away.

Kirsten Lund, still holding her arm where Carmen's elbow had hit her, yelled, "Hey! Don't you want your tostada?"

Dean kept walking. Sophie turned away from the sink and asked, "What happened?"

Carmen picked up the tostada and put it back on the prep table. "Some guy didn't want his food."

Sophie looked at the rejected tostada. "Something wrong with it?"

"No. He was just some weirdo. He decided to have some donuts instead."

"Did he pay for it?"

Carmen shook her head.

Sophie frowned. "Anybody hungry?" she asked. Carmen and Kirsten shook their heads and watched Sophie regretfully push the tostada over the edge of the table into the trash can. "Another one wasted," she sighed. She looked tired, and sad.

———

One of the things Axel always said was, "You got to leave a little for the next guy."

Not too many years ago, he had stayed open until the last customer had left the fairgrounds, sometimes until after midnight, unable to bear the thought of a missed sale. To let even one customer walk away hungry was an opportunity forever gone, or so he had believed. In those days he had been younger, able to function on three or four hours of sleep. And he had been hungrier, more desperate for the green.

Age had mellowed him in many ways. He could now close his restaurant before eleven, sometimes before ten-thirty. When the weather was bad he could close it earlier yet. The toll demanded by the late, long hours he had once worked was not commensurate with the few paltry dollars they had generated. He could leave that business for the other, younger concessionaires. Or for the next day, or the next year.

He could see, as he approached the restaurant, that his girls were beat, moving slow, their faces lacking animation. He stepped in through the back door. Sophie gave him a look but didn't say anything. She hated it when he disappeared. She sent Kirsten home, then the three of them proceeded with their evening wrap-up, packing the perishables into the cooler, sweeping, making everything ready for the next day. Carmen wore sunglasses. Axel wondered why, but chose not to ask. He went outside and hooked up his hose and started spraying down the grass and cement around the taco shop, sending bits of tortilla, lettuce, and miscellaneous jetsam flowing into the gutter. Axel enjoyed this part of the cleanup ritual, seeking out invading bits of cheese curd, cigarette butts, and candy wrappers, sending them on their journey into the sewer system. A pair of large, round young men stopped and tried to order a couple of burritos. Axel smiled and held out his hands helplessly.

"Sorry," he said. "We're closed."

———

Dean watched from a bench at the other side of the mall. The blond girl left the stand and walked toward the east exit, giving Dean a cautious look as she passed him. Stuck-up suburban bitch. He could tell she didn't like him. He returned his gaze to Axel and his women, watched them closing up. The old guy had a thing going with his hose, like he was taking the world's longest piss. The longer Dean watched him, the more he became convinced that Carmen's story about the coffee cans had been a fabrication.

Funny how that had changed the way he felt about Carmen. He still liked her, but now it was more like John Donne had said, like she was an extension of his self.

It took Axel, Sophie, and Carmen twenty minutes to close up. None of them noticed Dean. He watched them walk away, then turned all his attention toward Tiny Tot. The black cowboy hat was moving around the machines, bobbing up and down. Now and then he could hear Tiny Tot shouting at his employees. Dean reclined on his bench, crossed his arms, and watched through dark lenses, waiting patiently as the donut machines shut down one by one.

Chapter

18

TOMMY FABIAN CLAIMED to be the hardest-working guy in the concession business, and he never got any argument. He opened his three
Tiny Tot stands every morning at a quarter to eight, worked them all
day long, and stayed until closing every night. During the Minnesota
State Fair, he figured he got maybe four or five hours of sleep a
night. He would hit the sack sometime south of midnight, then be
up with the poultry for his first cup of sugar-saturated coffee.

The first two days were always tough. By the third day, Saturday, he
would find his groove. Pacing was the secret. Plenty of coffee in the morning, sip a little JD starting around ten, and make sure to keep sipping
all day long—but keep it low key. Two or three half pints was about
right. A sip here and a sip there, just enough to keep the earth level, the
gears meshed, and the engine humming. He never got stumbling
drunk, although by the end of the day his motions became noticeably
deliberate, and while he always remembered having locked his stands,
he rarely recalled the long nightly walk back to his Winnebago.

Back in the old days, he'd actually slept in his donut stand. That was how it had been when he was growing up, working the county fairs with his old man, running alibi joints. Six Cats, Cover the Spot, String Game—they'd run them all. Whatever the game, they'd always slept with it. It was the carny way. But the last few years, as his limbs stiffened and his digestive system began to assert itself, Tommy had compromised by spending nights in his Winnie, which had all the comforts of home—a soft bed, a shower, and, most important, a toilet. Much as he hated to leave his stands, it was worth it.

The thirty-foot RV was parked way out at the end of the southern lot, back in the middle of the horse trailer ghetto. This year he was sandwiched between a Peterbilt semitractor and an old silver Airstream occupied by the Mexican candlemaker and his harelipped daughter. The Peterbilt had a high red wind deflector that was easy to spot from a distance, even late at night. After closing up, he could point himself at the Peterbilt, and the next thing he knew, he would be asleep in the Winnebago. His legs carried him home like a good horse.

On this night, only the second day of the fair, Tommy felt that something was not right. After locking up, swinging shut the plywood front, and fastening it with a Yale padlock the size of a hockey puck, he stood beneath the wooden eaves and watched the late-night action.

Most of the people still on the grounds were late-closing concessionaires and the state fair cleanup crews. With all the grab joints closed, there was no food available, and the few fairgoers still wandering around the grounds were finding little to entertain them. The late-summer air cooled quickly, the greasy, beery fairground odor purged by breezes sweeping across the grounds from the north. The garbage trucks were out in full force now; every few seconds he could hear the groan of a dumpster being upended, the wet crunching of paper and uneaten food being crushed by powerful hydraulics. The gutters ran with greasy water: someone up the hill was hosing down the picnic tables. He watched a waxed cardboard carton float by, carrying fragments of cheese curds.

Everything looked perfectly normal.

Tommy reached into his hip pocket and extracted the last half pint of the day. He unscrewed the plastic cap and took his usual moderate sip, then said the hell with it and had a good belt. He still felt funny. The carpetbag slung over his shoulder held nearly three thousand dollars in bills and change. Most of the day's receipts were already in the bank; the cash in his bag was from the last few hours of operation. It was too late to make another deposit. A couple of swallows remained in his bottle. He finished it on his way to the gate, tossed the bottle into a trash can, and pushed out through the wooden turnstile. The Peterbilt was easy to spot, even from two hundred yards away. Tommy sighted on it and launched himself out across the desolate parking lot, trying to ignore the bad feeling, hoping for another forgettable walk home.

———

Dean could not believe how long it was taking the little son-of-a-bitch. First he stands around like a stunned gopher, doing nothing, then he decides to have a couple. When he finally gets moving, he's walking like the earth is made of Jell-O, holding his arms away from his body like an ape on a tightrope. Dean stayed well behind him, invisible in his black hat and sunglasses. This time, he would make sure he was not spotted.

He followed Tiny Tot out through the turnstile and across Como Avenue. There were only a few cars dotting the main parking lot. He could see the trucks and trailers parked at the back of the lot, four football fields away. Tiny Tot seemed drawn toward a big red-and-chrome semi. Dean stayed fifty yards back and to the side. Tommy disappeared behind the semi and did not emerge from the other side. Backtracking, Dean circled the semi until he could see what had not been visible to him before—an old Winnebago motor home tucked in between the semi and a big silver trailer. As he watched, a light came on in the Winnebago. A shadow began moving about inside.

After a few minutes, the light went out. Dean turned away and began the long walk to his car. He'd hoped for a chance at the little bastard tonight, but it hadn't worked out. He let his mind explore the details of his future, feeling himself take things one step at a time, being smart. He watched the fairground lights grow crisp and brilliant in the cooling night air.

———

Axel stopped the truck outside the door to number 19, put his hand on Carmen's shoulder, and gave it a gentle shake. Her head came up slowly and turned toward him; she blinked and licked her lips. "We here?" she asked.

"We're here." He watched Carmen fumble for the door latch, then step out onto the Motel 6 parking lot. She moved sleepily, like a little kid awakened from a nap. She wouldn't remember this in the morning. He waited until she let herself into her room, watching to make sure she got home okay. When she was safely inside, he drove around the building to his own room.

He kept thinking about her boyfriend. He didn't see the green Maverick in the lot. That was good. But he couldn't escape the feeling that he was losing her. Anger and sorrow flickered in random bursts—he was too tired to edit his emotions.

Axel unlocked his door and flipped on the light, wanting nothing more at that moment than to turn on his television and let the networks do his thinking until he could fall into sleep. He dropped the canvas moneybag on the bed, sat down on the wooden side chair, bent forward, and untied his shoes. Lately, it seemed, his feet were farther away than he remembered. He pulled off each shoe after untying it, set it beside the bed, toes pointing out, then sat back and shrugged out of his suspenders.

That always felt good.

Digging in his pockets, he came out with a handful of loose change and reached over to drop it into the ashtray on his bedside table, but he did not complete the motion.

The ashtray was empty. That was wrong. He was sure he had left a small collection of coins there. Not much, a few dollars' worth, maybe, but it had definitely been there the last time he'd left his room.

He stood up, feeling naked, a trickle of cold inching down his neck. Someone had been in his room. His eyes went to his crates. They looked different, not in the right order. Someone had been messing with his stuff. He checked the bathroom. Whoever it had been was gone. Feeling none of his earlier weariness, Axel dropped to his hands and knees and reached under the bed, feeling for the slit in the muslin bottom of the box spring. There. He reached through the opening, pulled out a waxed-tissue-wrapped bundle that had been wedged in a spring. He unwrapped it, sat and stared at yesterday's receipts, about thirty-five hundred, most of it in twenties and tens. The chill of fear warmed, coagulating into anger. Axel forced it back, forced himself to stand up, breathing deeply. This wasn't an emergency. Nothing bad had happened. His money was safe in Sam's backyard.

They hadn't gotten anything. He needed to take time, to think.

The alarm clock beside the bed read 12:17. He thought, I can deal with this tomorrow. Images of the bald monkey rooting through his crates. With Carmen? He couldn't be sure. Had he had anything in those crates that they'd take?

Crate by crate, he went through a mental inventory of his possessions.

A few minutes later, he started dismantling his wall of Coke crates. He found what he was looking for on the third row from the bottom: a khaki-colored canvas sack. He lifted it out of the crate. The weight was gone. Loosening the drawstring top, he looked inside, to discover three pairs of his black nylon socks.

———

Bill Quist thought that Chuck Woolery, the leering host of *Love Connection,* had one of the best jobs on TV. He'd read someplace that all the women who appeared on the show had to give Chuck a private audition. Or maybe he'd made that up in his head. Quist was very good at making things up. He thought he should have been a writer. Write those miniseries, get to meet the actresses. One of the women on *Love Connection* looked like a red-haired Heather Locklear. Now, there was an actress he would like to meet.

The redheaded Heather recrossed her legs. Quist thought he could hear the sound of nyloned thighs rubbing together. Or maybe that was the hydraulic closer on the lobby door, hissing air.

The chrome bell on the counter dinged.

"Okay, okay," Quist said, spinning his chair around. It was Axel Speeter. "Mr. S., how you doing?"

"Can't complain, Bill. How about you?"

"Just fine, just fine. What can I do you for?"

Axel rested his forearms on the counter and leaned into it. "I was wondering," he said, "if you know anything about this kid, this bald kid I've seen hanging around. Kid about yea high, with no hair and a little tiny nose?" He pointed a thick finger at his eyebrow. "Used to have these rings in his head."

Quist contorted his brow to show he was thinking, looking away from Axel's asymmetric green eyes. Inside, he was panicking. Never should've given the bitch the key. Damn, damn, damn! He didn't know what to say now. Didn't know if he should lie or just half lie.

"Wears army boots?" Axel prompted.

Quist nodded slowly. If he told Mr. S. that he'd never seen the kid, it would look like he hadn't been doing his job. It couldn't hurt to just have seen him. What did that have to do with anything? Nothing. It was safe. True, but safe. "Uh-huh," he said, nodding faster. "Uh-huh, I think so. A couple times, I'm pretty sure. Last couple of days. What about him?"

"He staying here?"

"Well . . . he's not a registered guest, if that's what you mean. What I saw was, I saw him a couple times. I figured he was just passing by, you know?"

"You sure he isn't staying here?"

"Like I say, Mr. S., he's not a registered guest. But he might be staying with somebody else. I mean, I'd have no way of knowing." Quist waited, his eyes on Axel's chest, hoping that the interview was over. Laughter from the TV made him turn his head, but as soon as he had the screen in view, Axel asked him something about a key.

"What? What's that?"

"I asked you, 'Who else has a key to my room?'"

Quist shook his head rapidly. "No one! Nobody goes in your room, Mr. S. Not even the maid, just the way you want it."

Axel raised his eyebrows, as if he was waiting for more. Quist didn't know what else to say.

Axel said, "Okay then, Bill, if you say so. But I'm having the lock changed tomorrow."

Quist said, "I don't know about that, Mr. S. I'd have to talk to the office on that."

"That's fine, Bill. You talk to them. Tell them how somebody's been going in and out of my room. Somebody with a key. In the meantime, I'm getting myself a lock." He turned and left.

Quist watched Axel's broad back receding. That was easy, he thought, returning his attention to Chuck Woolery. The redheaded Heather Locklear had been replaced by a guy with a ponytail. Quist changed the channel, hoping to stumble across a late-night rerun of *Baywatch,* something good like that.

—

James Dean pulled into the Motel 6 parking lot and backed the Maverick into the parking space opposite room 3. He was about to shut down the engine, when he saw Axel coming out of the motel office, walking funny, his chest pushed out like a marching soldier's. Dean stayed in his car, waiting for him to pass, but the old man looked up, saw the green Maverick, and stopped, not twenty feet away from the front bumper, looking right at him.

Dean thought, I could just step on the gas.

Axel stood with his feet apart, staring at him through the windshield. Dean remained expressionless and motionless, trying to think what to do. If he ran over him, someone would see. The guy in the office, or somebody passing by.

After a few seconds, Axel started walking toward him.

Dean thought, Shit, he knows we were in his room. He dropped the car in gear and hit the gas pedal. The old man didn't move. Dean cranked the wheel, missing him by a few feet, and sped out of the parking lot. Once on the street, he let the air rush out of his lungs. He felt weak and shaky, as though he had just survived an accident. Something about the old man scared him. He was two blocks away when he remembered that he had the .45 under his front seat, remembered that he had nothing to fear.

———

The Tonight Show was just ending. One thing that Axel missed these days was Johnny Carson. Axel didn't care for the new guy, but things changed and there wasn't a damn thing you could do about it. He sat on the edge of his carefully made bed and clicked through the cable channels. He watched a few minutes of a war movie, identified it as *Pork Chop Hill*, which he had seen already. That was okay; he didn't like the war movies anymore. What had once looked like heroic men fighting and dying now looked to him like children fighting and dying. He switched to channel 2, where he found a show about Australia. Herds of kangaroos bounding across the outback. Axel untied his shoes and placed them at the foot of the bed. He propped the pillows up against the headboard and settled back to watch the kangaroos. Axel liked animal shows, especially the ones about Australia. Maybe this would calm him down.

That little prick. He was the one who'd been in his room, all right.

The way he'd driven off proved it. He might've slipped the lock somehow, but more likely that sleazy clerk had something to do with it. Should bounce his face on the counter a few times, make him own up. Feeling his rage mount, Axel forced himself to jack down and watch the show. He didn't like himself when he got mad.

He liked kangaroos. Most people didn't realize how tough they were, how hard it was to be a kangaroo. Two males—boomers, the narrator called them—were clinched like boxers, kicking at each other with their big hind feet. Then the boomers broke apart and started making these flying kicks at one another, ripping at each other's abdomens with kangaroo claws. The big red boomer with the torn ear, according to the narrator, was the alpha male, the aging ruler and protector of a group of fliers, or female kangaroos, and their joeys. The fliers could be seen watching the battle from a shady eucalyptus grove a few yards away, waiting to see who would lead them. The challenger, a smaller but much quicker boomer, mounted a relentless attack, leaping again and again without pause, pounding the alpha male backward, shaking off return blows without apparent effect. Axel, no longer smiling, rooted silently for the alpha male, willing him to repel the smaller boomer's assault. The narrator noted that for the aging alpha male this was a fight to the death, that if he lost he would be forced out of the group, weakened and bleeding, forced out to die alone in the desert.

As Axel watched, the alpha male, looking as if he had just remembered another appointment, turned away from his challenger and loped weakly out of the grove onto the arid Australian plain, pursued for a few hundred yards by the kicking, biting challenger: the new alpha male.

He could have won, Axel thought, upset. The big 'roo could have stuck it out, used his greater size and experience to defeat the invader.

You could learn a lot from watching animals.

The scene shifted to a group of wallabies. The wallabies were smaller than the kangaroos, and they were grazing peacefully. Axel shut off the television, undressed, and got under the covers. He turned off the light. It seemed like a long time before sleep came for him. He couldn't stop thinking about the goddamn kangaroos.

Chapter

19

DEAN PUMPED ANOTHER QUARTER into the DeathMek machine in Tony's East Side Lounge. The machine was against the wall at the back of the bar, directly between the doors marked GALS and GENTS. Dean played the game automatically, his mind wandering as he destroyed one attacker after another, keeping his cyborg alive.

He was thinking about what to do next. Except for Carmen, he didn't know anybody in this town. All he had was about twenty dollars—the last of the money he'd got from Mickey. It wasn't enough to rent a room, and he wouldn't be able to get his donut money until the next night. What lousy luck, the taco guy seeing him. He'd been looking forward to telling Carmen about his plans for the donut guy. He should've just run the taco guy over.

He supposed he could use the gun to get some money, knock off a gas station or something, but he'd never done anything like that before. Walking into a lighted business and robbing it, that was not his style. Basically, he was a nonviolent person. Besides, robbing a gas station for fifty or a hundred bucks contradicted his new philosophy:

the fewer transactions, the better one's chances of getting away with it. Only the big scores were worth the risk. What he'd do, he'd play it smart, sleep in his car tonight. One more quarter in the machine, then he'd head out to the Maverick and crash. He wished he had some speed. He should've picked some up before he left Omaha. A few leapers, and he wouldn't need to sleep at all.

Dean had just disintegrated another mechanical dinosaur, when he felt someone breathing on his neck, watching him play the machine. He put up with it for about five seconds, then faked like he was giving the machine a little body English and brought his heel down hard on somebody's toe.

"Ow. Motherfucking ow!" The voice was whiny and nasal.

Dean looked over his shoulder. A narrow head, as hairless as his own.

"You stepped on my fucking foot," the skinhead said. He was young, no more than seventeen, and blade thin. Pimply hatchet face, pale-blue eyes, a faded and shredded T-shirt over a sunken chest. Beltless gray jeans, slung low on his narrow hips, puddled over a pair of disintegrating snakeskin cowboy boots. One of the boots was held together with a wrapping of silver duct tape.

Dean let himself relax. This skinhead cowboy was no threat. Just another punk kid. Reminded him of himself a few years earlier. He was about to come back at the punk with some really nasty crack, when he noticed another nearly hairless head coming toward them from the bar, carrying two bottles of beer.

The second skinhead was older and larger by about two hundred pounds. His eyes were set a few inches back inside his skull, little pig eyes, and he was wearing a black leather jacket that must have used up three cows and still looked a little tight around the shoulders. Dean, wishing he hadn't left the .45 in the car, grinned and held out his hands. "Sorry about your foot, man," he said. "You want I should buy you a beer or something?"

The kid stared at Dean, taking his time, letting the giant arrive with his beer.

"Where you from, man?" he finally asked.

"Chicago," said Dean. It was better to be from Chicago than from Omaha. People knew where it was. "Name's Dean," he added.

The kid said, "They call me Tigger, man." He reached out and gave Dean a complicated handshake, a sort of wrist-grabbing routine that reminded him of a biker handshake. Dean faked it. Tigger seemed satisfied.

"This here's Sweety." Tigger jerked his head toward the giant. "We're from here in Frogtown, man. Whole bunch of us."

Frogtown? He thought he was in Saint Paul. Dean looked around the bar. There were some factory-worker types, all white with small eyes, and a few horsey-looking women to match, but not other skins. Tigger sucked at his beer like he hadn't had a drink in days. Sweety stared down at Dean, looking at him as if he were a bug.

Dean said, "How's it going, Sweety?"

Sweety shrugged and looked away. The bottle of beer almost disappeared in his massive fist.

"So what the fuck you doing in Saint Paul?" Tigger asked.

"I thought I was in Frogtown," Dean said.

"Frogtown's in Saint Paul," Tigger said.

Dean scratched his chin. Three guys in a bar, drawn together by their mutual hairlessness. But these two were not your typical skinheads—not the Aryan Circle type, banded together to protect themselves from the other minorities, nor your garden-variety neo-Nazi skins with an unemployed-working-class hard-on—and that was fine with him. Dean had never cared for political agendas, with or without hair. Guys like these, they wouldn't even be looking for jobs. They had to have something going. They'd paid for two beers, and the money had come from somewhere. Maybe they knew where he could find some uppers. If nothing else, he might get a free place to crash.

Tigger waited for him to say something. Dean still wasn't entirely sure whether he'd found a friend or a fight. He pointed at Tigger's empty bottle. "How about I buy you another one?" he said.

A dull blue light flickered in Tigger's eyes. "I could see that," he said.

Dean said, "How about you, big guy?"

Sweety was out there someplace, not listening, glaring at the wall. Dean had seen guys like Sweety in Lincoln. You either got real close to them or stayed the hell away.

Tigger said, "You better get him one."

Dean bought the next round too. One more, and he'd be out of money. They were sitting in one of the booths near the back. Sweety, on the opposite side of the booth, was digging into the tabletop with a short, spade-shaped blade that he'd pulled out of his belt buckle, concentrating hard, his forehead red with effort, carving letters into the Formica surface. Tigger was bragging about some friend who had a Harley.

"So what's this guy do?" Dean asked. He couldn't figure out why Tigger was talking about him.

"Do? He don't do nothing. He deals."

"Deals what?"

"Whatever the fuck you want. Pork's connected, man."

Sweety said, "Fuckin' Pork." Dean tried to read what Sweety was carving.

"You want to score, I can get it for you. Pork and me, we're like this." Tigger crossed his fingers.

Dean shrugged. He didn't have any money left. "Maybe tomorrow," he said. "Can this guy get any speed?"

"You kidding me? Pork's got this crank, man, you wouldn't believe. Crystal meth, man. He knows a guy fuckin' makes the shit in his bathtub. Like I was telling you, he's connected."

Dean had never tried crystal meth before. In Omaha, it was not common on the street. Omaha was a weed and acid town, although lately it was becoming a crack town too. "Is it any good?" he asked, thinking if the price was right, he could maybe buy some weight, haul it over to Sioux Falls, and sell it to a guy he knew there. Double his money; maybe even triple it. The real question was, were these guys for real? The kid with the taped-up cowboy boot was a punk, showing off and trying to act tough. And the big one, the cyborg, looked like he had the walnut-size brain of a tyrannosaurus.

"It's fucking dynamite," Tigger was saying. "Right, Sweety?"

"Huh?"

"Pork's crank."

"Fuckin' Pork," said Sweety.

Chapter

20

AXEL SEEMED DIFFERENT the next morning. Even through her morning fog, Carmen could sense the difference. He was acting sort of crisp and nasty, and he took off the second she got in the pickup.

"Whoa," she said, slamming the truck door closed.

Axel pulled out of the parking lot onto Larpenteur Avenue without stopping, prompting a horn blast from a passing Honda.

"What's going on?" Carmen asked, wide awake now.

"You have a good night's sleep?" Axel asked. He hunched forward over the steering wheel, like a little kid trying to make his car go faster.

"I slept okay," said Carmen cautiously.

"Have a little trouble waking up?"

Carmen considered her answer. "No." It was safest, when the correct answer did not suggest itself, to lie.

"I was sitting out there almost five minutes."

Was he mad because she'd made him wait? Carmen was confused.

She had made him wait plenty of times before. Suddenly she was afraid. Maybe he'd noticed someone had been in his room.

"Are you sure you're okay?" she asked.

Axel pushed back from the wheel. "I'm fine," he said, not looking at her. "I just wish you'd be a little more responsible."

Carmen settled into her seat. If he didn't want to talk about it, that was fine with her. The first Saturday of the fair was going to be a long, hard day. The sky was bright blue, and the air was warming quickly. In most ways she dreaded the long hours ahead, but a part of her was looking forward to the energy and focus the day would bring. Responsible? The word had a strange flavor. Did he think he was her dad, or what?

———

The *Daily News,* official newsletter of the Minnesota State Fair, predicted a new attendance record that Saturday. As many as a quarter of a million people were expected. The weather looked like a perfect eighty-degree high, the sky appeared cloudless for two hundred miles in every direction, and Garth Brooks was scheduled to play the grandstand.

As usual, Sophie already had the front of the Taco Shop open and the deep-fryers heating by the time Axel and Carmen arrived. Ever since Axel had given her the title "manager" and promised her a bonus, Sophie had been putting in heroic hours. It was hard for him to believe that she was stealing from him. Nevertheless, as soon as she left the stand to visit the rest rooms, Axel took a careful look at the tortillas in the cooler. The flour tortillas came from Garcia's in plastic bags of one hundred, and the smaller corn tortillas in pouches of six dozen. He moved some of the bags aside and found eight ten-count pouches of Zapata tortillas, a grocery store brand, tucked in behind the regular stock.

So Tommy was right. Sophie was H.O.'ing. It was the only possible explanation. Eighty extra tortillas, assuming they were made into Bueno Burritos, would translate into over two hundred dollars. Over the course of the fair, that would add up to $2,400. Axel replaced the tortillas. So much for the five-hundred-dollar bonus he'd planned to give her. He would have to do something about it. But not today, not with a record crowd pouring through the gates. When Sophie got back from the john, it would be business as usual.

They had a line by ten that morning, and in the rush and bustle of business, Axel quickly purged his mind of Sophie's tortillas, the bald kid in the Maverick, and his missing .45. The day flew by without the usual midafternoon slump. Sophie, Carmen, Juanita, Kirsten, and Janice, the weekend girl, hardly stopped moving all day. By early evening they'd run out of cups, and Axel had to go begging from other concessionaires, none of whom were eager to dip into their supplies to help a competitor. He finally coaxed half a case out of the Orange Treet guy by promising to give him free tacos for the rest of the fair. At seven o'clock, Sophie told Carmen to start skimping on the cheese. At seven-thirty, they ran out of corn tortillas; and shortly after nine o'clock, they ran out of flour.

Twenty years in the business, and Axel had never run out of tortillas. Elated by record sales but distraught over the business he was losing, Axel ran to each of the three other Mexican food concessions on the fairgrounds and tried unsuccessfully to buy more tortillas. He thought about making the run to Cub Foods, but by the time he got back with them it would be too late to do any good. Garcia's truck would show up the next morning with Sunday's supply of fresh tortillas, and they could start all over again. He returned to the stand empty-handed but feeling better knowing that he had at least tried.

An exhausted Sophie stood proudly at the serving window, offering refried beans to each new customer. Axel stopped and watched as she actually sold some. A bubble of pride expanded in his chest; the woman really and honestly cared about his business. He had planned to talk to Sophie about the grocery-store tortillas that night, but he didn't have the heart to hit her with it after such a killer day. He told her to go home, told her he and Carmen would close up the stand. Wearily, Sophie agreed. Axel watched her walk off toward the parking lot, thinking she was worth every penny he paid her. Maybe even worth every penny she stole.

———

Carmen and Kirsten, with little to do in the way of food preparation, sat on folding chairs by the side of the stand, smoking cigarettes. Kirsten was just getting started with her first pack of Virginia

Slims. She watched Carmen carefully, trying to emulate her stylish smoking technique. Carmen had a way of taking the smoke into her mouth, then letting it stream out over her upper lip into her nose. She called it a French inhale. When Kirsten tried to do it, she sneezed and started coughing.

"First you got to learn to inhale regular," Carmen said. "You got to start a little at a time."

Kirsten nodded, her eyes watering, and took a tiny puff from her Virginia Slim.

Juanita was perched on a cheese carton, chewing on a fingernail. Carmen offered her a cigarette.

"No, thank you," Juanita said.

Carmen said to Kirsten, "Juanita is very polite."

That cracked them up, all three of them. It had been a long day.

———

James Dean stood between the railroad tracks at the back of the forty-acre parking lot, tossing stones up in the air and trying to hit them with an old broom handle. He was a lefty. Because it was dark, he could only connect with about one out of every four or five swings, and most of those he drove straight into the ground. Now and then, though, he got a good piece of one, and the rock would go sailing out into the parking lot. He caught this one rock perfect, listened, heard the sharp crack of stone on safety glass.

Last night, he'd closed up the bar with Tigger and Sweety. They'd been on the sidewalk, just leaving, when Tigger had suggested that Dean stay with them at "Headquarters."

That had sounded good to Dean. Tigger had an aging, oil-burning Cadillac Fleetwood, about a '76, rust-spotted black, with tinted windows and a peeling black vinyl roof. Dean got in his Maverick and followed the smoke through a tangled neighborhood, parked on the street, then accompanied his new friends down an alley, over a fence, and through the broken basement window of a dark, boarded-up house. The air smelled of spray paint, mildew, piss, and cigarette butts.

Tigger lit a candle, then said he had to go grab the juice. At first, Dean thought he was going for a bottle, but Tigger crawled back out through the window trailing a long orange extension cord. A minute later, the work lamp at the end of the extension cord blinked on.

"Headquarters" contained two mattresses on the floor, a torn vinyl beanbag chair, a few hundred beer bottles, an old TV. Empty spray cans were scattered among the beer bottles. Spray-painted slogans and drawings covered the walls. *Heil Hitler. White Power. Fuck Off and Die.* A few scattered swastikas, crosses, and skulls. One wall bore an enormous stylized vagina, fluorescent pink labia stretching from floor to ceiling. A pile of well-thumbed magazines—*Soldier of Fortune, High Times,* assorted skin mags—sat atop an upended cardboard box.

"This is, like, our meeting place," Tigger explained as he climbed back in through the window. "A bunch of us hang here."

"What's the deal with the light?" Dean asked.

"The guy next door has an outside outlet. We just plug ourselves in. He don't miss it."

Dean nodded. A real four-star operation, this. He'd have been better off sleeping in his car. "There a bathroom here?"

"Yeah. What they used to call the furnace room. The toilet paper's on top of the water heater."

Despite all that, he'd slept pretty good. The mattress wasn't bad, and nothing ran over him or bit him during the night, although he had heard some scurrying.

Tonight things would be different. Tonight he'd get himself a real room, and tomorrow, if Tigger could be believed, he'd be scoring himself a chunk of very pure, very cheap, very marketable methedrine.

Dean tossed a rock into the air, swung the broom handle as hard as he could. He hit the rock low. It went up in the air, came down a few feet away.

Enough. He decided to quit before he dropped a rock on his head, or before some guy with a busted windshield came looking for him.

———

Axel bought Carmen a bomb pop on the way to the truck. Carmen liked bomb pops. She liked to bite away the ridges, feeling the red, white, and blue ice cold on her front teeth. Twelve hours of action had left her numb; she sucked the bomb pop and listened to Axel chatter about what a great day they'd had. The day's receipts were inside his burlap shoulder bag. Axel patted the side of the bag affectionately.

"A great day," he said. "You did a great job, Carmen. You're a great kid."

"Uh-huh."

"If the rest of the fair is good—hell, even if it's not good—I'm going to be giving you a nice bonus. Buy yourself some new clothes."

Carmen bit the tip off her bomb pop and looked at the money bag.

"That would be great."

"You worked hard. You deserve it."

"I sure do."

Axel gave her a sharp look. He unlocked the passenger door and opened it, then circled the truck and let himself in the other door.

"You stick with me, Carmen, and you'll do all right."

"Uh-huh."

"I'm not kidding you. Hang in there with me, Carmen. I'll take care of you. I really will. We're a team."

Carmen pulled the bomb pop out of her mouth and looked at Axel. He was staring at her, looking right into her eyes. He looked like he was going to cry.

"Okay," she said, looking away. She hated it when Axel got maudlin. She thought about the six-pack of canned martinis waiting in her room, wondering whether they would still be cool from the night before. Not that it mattered. They went down just as fast warm.

———

Two hundred yards away, James Dean sat against the back of Tommy Fabian's Winnebago, playing with Axel's .45, feeling the checkered wooden handle, smelling the tangy odor of gun oil. He had never fired a pistol. Cocking the hammer, he sighted along the top of the barrel. The gun was heavy. He uncocked it carefully, set it in his lap. The long wait had diminished much of his excitement. He was getting hungry. To pass the time, he played the scene out again in his mind, seeing Tiny Tot's face when he showed him the gun. He wasn't sure what he would do after that, but whatever it was, Tiny Tot wouldn't like it.

He gripped the gun and listened. He could hear footsteps.

The footsteps passed. It was still too early.

He let his head fall back on the rear bumper of the RV and watched the moon, not quite full. A faint ringing sound wound its way through the RV camp—someone's mobile phone, perhaps. Dean thought, It tolls for thee, Tiny Tot.

What he would have to do, he had decided, was show him the gun about two seconds after he got to the door. Take charge of the situation before Tiny Tot could figure out which key to use. Come around the side of the Winnebago fast.

Nearby, someone in one of the RVs turned on a radio. Some old disco music from the seventies, before his time. Dean closed his eyes and listened, breathing deeply.

Something jarred him awake, a movement of the Winnebago's bumper against his head. He jumped up, heard the gun flip off his lap, hit the ground. Shit! He looked around the corner of the motor home.

Shit! The donut guy was there, already standing on the fucking step, turning the key. Where had the gun fallen?

No time. Tiny Tot had the door open. He was stepping inside. His plan forgotten, Dean ran straight at him, caught the door just before it closed, tore it open. He saw Tiny Tot turn toward him, mouth open, then twist away, reaching for something. Dean grabbed him by the ankles, jerked. Tiny Tot went down hard, the RV shaking, then twisted around with something in his hand, bringing it down on Dean's shoulder. Galvanized by a shock of pain, Dean threw himself backward out the door, dragging Tiny Tot with him, hurling the little man hard against the wheel of the Peterbilt. A baseball bat flew from Tiny Tot's hands, thudded to the gravel a few yards away. His cowboy hat fell forward onto his lap. He sagged against the big tire of the semi, his eyes bugging out, gasping for breath. Dean ran for the bat, scooped it up as Tiny Tot drew a loud breath, started to rise, saw Dean coming at him with the bat, and raised his arms.

Dean swung the bat, a downward chopping motion, hitting the donut man's forearm. Tiny Tot howled and fell back against the tire. Dean struck again, the bat glancing off Tiny Tot's skull. The little man's face went slack, his eyes pointing in two different directions, blood curtaining over his right ear. The sight of blood made the earth tilt; Dean dropped to his knees and closed his eyes. His ears filled with a rushing sound. He swallowed. The sound in his ears abruptly ceased. Voices. He heard someone shouting something. He pushed aside the dizziness, dropped the bat, and jumped up into the Winnebago, searching frantically for Tiny Tot's money bag. Everything was so bright, so in focus, it was hard to see, like a television with the contrast set too high. There, on the floor. He scooped up the bag in one hand, jumped out. The donut guy was moving, crawling away. Dean kicked him twice in the ribs till he curled up, his hands over his bloody head, fingers glittering. A flashing horseshoe snapped into hard focus. Dean kicked again, and again, until Tiny Tot's arms flopped away from his head. He ripped the horseshoe ring from Tiny Tot's slack fingers.

Someone yelled, "Hey! What's going on back there?"

There was a watch too, glittering in the faint light. Dean tore it from Tiny Tot's wrist. The band broke. He threw the watch away and started to run, then remembered his gun. He found it immediately, right where he'd dropped it at the back of the RV. His senses were totally keyed; he was seeing like a fucking owl.

"Hey!" A figure appeared from the other side of the Peterbilt. "What the hell's going on here?"

Dean pointed the .45 at the figure, a tall, burly man with a dark beard. He could see every detail of the man's face, every wrinkle, every pore. He was too out of breath to reply, so he just waited for the man to get close enough to see the gun.

Chapter

21

THE CUTE ONE that worked in the donut place, the one that reminded Kirsten of Luke Perry, showed up at the taco stand before they even had the fryer up to temperature. Kirsten leaned over the counter.

"Morning," she said.

He smiled at her.

"How's it going?" Kirsten asked. "You hungry already?" God, did that ever sound lame. She wished she knew his name, but since they had been trading tacos and donuts back and forth for three days now, it seemed like it would be rude to ask him. He didn't know her name, either, but he called her Blondie, which she liked. So she just thought of him as Luke. She loved that name: Luke.

"Mr. Speeter around?" he asked.

Kirsten shook her head. "Huh-uh."

The kid, Luke, frowned and looked up and down the mall. "You seen Mr. Fabian?" he asked.

"Who?"

"My boss?"

"Huh-uh." Thinking, God, do I sound like a dork, or what?

He looked past Kirsten into the stand, where Sophie was shredding lettuce.

"We're supposed to be open now, only he never showed up this morning."

Sophie came up to the counter, wiping her hands on her apron. "Tommy hasn't shown up?"

"He's like two hours late already. What do you think we should do?" He pointed at the locked-up donut stand, where eight girls in Tiny Tot T-shirts were standing under the eaves, watching him. "They're talking about going home."

Now that Luke was talking to Sophie, Kirsten could look at him real close. She liked the way his upper lip sort of folded back when he smiled, and she was hoping he would smile now while she could get a good look. He had a few pimples, but she let her eyes slide away from them, and anyway, they weren't permanent. His eyes, though, his eyes were the best thing of all. When I have my kids, Kirsten thought, I want all nine of them to have eyes that same bright sparkly blue.

Sophie pointed up the mall, her arm blocking Kirsten's view. "Here comes Axel now."

The kid intercepted Axel several yards away, talking and pointing at the Tiny Tot stand. Sophie went back to shredding lettuce. Kirsten watched Axel hand Luke a ring of keys, clap him on the shoulder, and point at the donut stand. Luke, a determined look on his TV-star face, nodded several times, then trotted toward the bored octet of Tiny Tot girls, holding the keys in the air and waving them.

"Where's Carmen?" Sophie asked as Axel stuck his head through the back door.

"She'll be taking the bus in this morning. I had to leave early. Tom Fabian called me from the hospital at six o'clock this morning."

Sophie scraped shredded lettuce into a stainless-steel bin and pressed it down with the lid. "He have a heart attack?" she asked, tearing open a five-pound plastic bag filled with grated cheese.

"He got jumped. Somebody beat him up. He looks pretty ugly. He can hardly talk."

Kirsten said, "Wow!"

"I had to pick up the keys from him. It was either that or he was going to crawl out of the hospital on his hands and knees and open the stands himself. The doctor made him call me."

He looked across the mall at the Tiny Tot concession, where the nine teenagers in their Tiny Tot T-shirts were moving around with an excess of confused energy.

"Look at that," Sophie said. "They don't know what they're doing. Tommy should have a manager. I mean a real manager, not some high school kid."

"I don't know," Axel said. "Looks to me like they're doing okay. In any case, Sam's going to come out later. Tommy asked him to run things while he was laid up."

"Sam *O'Gara*?" Sophie let her mouth drop open.

Axel smiled, almost laughing. "Hey, he'll do fine. All he's got to do is sit on the stool and eat donuts. Those kids know what they're doing. Look at them. They already got the front of the stand open. Another ten minutes they'll be frying and bagging. Look, I've got to go get his other two stands up and running."

Sophie pushed out her chin. "What about *our* stand?"

"What about it? You can't run things without me?"

Sophie crushed her lips together.

"I'll be right back," Axel said. "Listen, if Sam shows up, take him over and introduce him to Duane, would you?"

"Who's Duane?" Sophie asked.

Axel pointed toward the Tiny Tot stand, at the Luke Perry clone. A look that fell somewhere between horror and nausea crossed Kirsten Lund's face. *"Duane?"* she said.

———

Carmen drifted into work around ten, still wearing her sunglasses even though the day was overcast, getting darker, thunder rumbling in the distance. She'd tried covering up her black eye with makeup, but it hadn't worked.

She had dreamed that night about James Dean, the original one. Dreamed she was on this beach . . . Puerto Penasco? Maybe. A nice beach, and James Dean comes up on a motorcycle and gives her a breakfast sausage, then roars off. She was getting all her Deans mixed up. Anyway, she was glad he was gone. It had been a bad zigzag in her life, but now it was over. He'd probably driven back to Omaha. Left

his stupid poetry book and booked. And that was okay with her, because she could damn well take care of herself. Maybe she'd go to
Puerto Penasco herself. Maybe she could get Axel to send her. Maybe
they had a nursing school down there. Maybe she could just take the
money, few hundred dollars a day, just slip it in her pocket.

She was thinking about that as she stepped into the Taco Shop,
trying to figure out how much she could take before he noticed. Axel
grabbed her wrist. "Come here, Carmen." He pulled her out of the
stand, jerking her arm.

Carmen flashed that she was being arrested, as if he'd been reading her thoughts. He led her out onto the mall, to an empty picnic
table, sat her down, sat beside her. He leaned forward and turned his
head so that his face was only a few inches from hers. He said, "Talk
to me, Carmen. Tell me about your friend."

Carmen leaned back. "Friend?" She pulled her purse onto her lap
and dug for her cigarettes.

Axel dropped his hand to her wrist. "Don't bullshit me, Carmen.
You know who I'm talking about. Your friend beat up Tommy last
night. Hurt him real bad. Robbed him. I want to know who he is and
where I can find him."

"Oh!" So he'd gone and done it. A nervous laugh bubbled out of
her.

"You think that's funny? He coulda been killed. If Mack hadn't
shown up, he probably would've been."

"Mack?"

"Big Mack, the guy runs the high-striker. He says the kid had a
gun. Pointed it right at him. Could've got himself shot."

Carmen shook her head. She could almost see it, like in a movie.
Big Mack, who could ring the high-striker with a one-handed sledge-
hammer blow, against Dean. Dean with Axel's gun. Like a showdown.

Axel's hand closed on her wrist. "Talk to me, Carmen. You know
who I'm talking about."

Carmen said, "That hurts."

Axel let go.

"I don't really know him," she said. "He's just this guy."

"What's his name?"

"Dean. James Dean."

Axel snorted.

"That's what he says it is. Look, I just met him, you know? I met him in Omaha, and then he followed me up here. I had no idea he was coming."

"You let him stay with you."

Carmen shrugged, put a cigarette in her mouth. "Yeah, well, he's gone now." She spoke around the unlit cigarette as she searched for her lighter. Axel reached up and plucked her sunglasses from her face.

"He hit you, didn't he?"

Carmen shrugged.

"You're lucky he didn't shoot you."

"Why would he do that?"

"Maybe just to try out my gun. He's got my gun, doesn't he?"

Carmen's eyes slid away. "I told him not to take it. It wasn't like I had any choice, you know."

"You always have a choice."

"Yeah, right." Carmen found her lighter, lit her cigarette, blew smoke. "I could live or I could get myself killed. Some choice." She fixed her eyes on Axel's shoes. They were planted solidly on the tarmac, pointing right at her. His hand appeared in front of her face, cupped her chin, and gently lifted her head.

"You should get that eye looked at."

"Axel, you're talking to a nurse, almost. I'm gonna be okay. I just don't want people staring at it is all." She twisted her head away, snatched her sunglasses from his other hand, and backed away from him.

Axel did not move. He stood with his hand still out where her chin had been, his face stiff and hard like one of those old-fashioned photographs where the men all have beards. A drop of rain hit her face. A curtain of gray moved across the fairgrounds from the east. Another large drop hit her knee. Suddenly it was raining hard, sending people running toward the buildings.

Axel said, "Where is he, Carmen?"

She turned her hand, shielding her cigarette from the rain. "I swear to God, Axel, I haven't got a clue." Then, unable to stop herself, she asked, "How much money did he get?"

———

Axel sat on a stool at the Beef Hut, watching a Styrofoam cup of coffee cool. The creamer he had added produced an oil slick, which shimmered prismatically under the fluorescent lights. All those colors in his cup, yet when he looked up he saw only gray sheets of cold rain. He felt ill.

Not sick in his body or in his head. He felt sick in his life. His carefully nurtured and controlled life was coming apart like an overfilled burrito. His friend had been put in the hospital by some skinhead freak. That same bald monkey—Axel couldn't bear to think of him as "James Dean"—had beat up his . . . Carmen. The rain was killing his business on what should have been a big day. And Sophie—what was going on with Sophie? Bringing in her own tortillas—he knew that for sure—but the money, the money was good. If anything, it was too good. The last two nights, he'd matched up his cash receipts with the tortilla count, and both times he'd come out two to three hundred dollars rich, almost as if she was doing some sort of reverse rip-off. At first, he'd thought that the Bueno Burrito was throwing off his estimates, but even taking the new product into account, the money was coming out too damn good. Axel didn't like it. It would bug the shit out of him until he figured out what was going on.

He looked out at the flooded street, its slick black surface churning with raindrops. Maybe he *was* sick in his head. Maybe the tortilla thing could be explained. Maybe he had simply misplaced his .45. Maybe Carmen had run into a door. Maybe Tommy had gotten too drunk and fallen down twenty or thirty times. Maybe it wasn't raining.

Chapter

22

OF ALL THE THINGS Axel Speeter did not like, hospitals rated number one. Axel did not like the way they looked or the way they smelled, and he especially did not like the doctors who worked there. He hated their phony smiles, their dry hands, and the way they used all the buttons on their prissy white coats. Most of them wouldn't have made it through one busy Saturday at the Taco Shop.

He did, however, enjoy watching the nurses.

Tommy Fabian had a room on the fourth floor of Midway Hospital. Axel set the brown paper bag on the bedside table and sat down on the molded plastic chair. Tommy had his head turned away, staring out the window at the gray sky. A plastic bag filled with clear fluid drained into his left arm.

"I told you it was gonna rain," Tommy said, his voice a hoarse whisper. "Cost us both."

Axel shrugged. "Yesterday was good."

"Yeah. First part anyways." Tommy pressed a button, and the bed slowly contorted, bringing him to a sitting position. The left side of his face was undamaged. Tommy turned toward Axel. The other side was mottled maroon, with deep-purple patches. His right ear was completely covered with gauze, and portions of his scalp had been shaved, stitched, and taped over. The pale-blue iris of his right eye floated on a sea of cherry red.

"You're looking good," Axel said.

"Fuck you," whispered Tommy.

"Okay," Axel said. "You look like dog shit."

"Thank you. How my joints doing? Sam burned any of 'em down yet?"

"Sam's doing okay," Axel said. He thought for a moment, wondering whether he should say more.

Tommy asked, "Okay, what happened? He bust one a my machines?"

"No. Everything's fine. He did try to fire one of your help."

"Which one? There's a couple of 'em maybe need firing."

"It was Duane. The kid told him he couldn't smoke in the stand."

Tommy sat halfway up. "Goddamn right he can't! The health heat'll shut the joint down, they see him smoking in there." An agonized look flooded his face, and he fell back against the pillow.

Axel said, "Relax, Tom, it's all straightened out."

"I sure as fuck hope so. Fucking Sam. I told him to just sit there and fucking watch. I shoulda known better."

"Well, that's what he's doing. I told him he should go outside, he wants a smoke."

"I suppose he's sitting in there chewing that fucking snoose."

"Yeah, well, I told Duane to make sure he wasn't spitting it in the batter." Axel held up a paper bag. "I brought you some donuts."

Tommy tried to lift his left arm toward the bag, winced, let it fall back. His forearm was bound in a plastic splint.

"Here," Axel said, opening the bag and extracting a sugar-coated minidonut. "You want me to stick it in your mouth?"

"Screw you," he said. "You know I don't eat the fucking things anyways."

"Oh. Screw me." Axel ate the donut, watching Tommy's red eye watching him back. He finished chewing, swallowed, then looked in the bag. His eyes widened, and he said, "Now what's this, do you suppose?" He pulled out a half pint of Jack Daniel's, the black label

speckled with sugar from the donuts. Tommy reached across his abdomen with his right arm. Axel brushed the sugar off the bottle,
opened it, and placed it in Tommy's hand.

"Thank you," Tommy said.

"You're welcome." Axel watched Tommy empty a quarter of the
bottle. "So, you tell the cops who hit you?"

Tommy said, "I don't tell the heat nothing, Ax. You know that. I
take care of myself."

"Looks like you take care of yourself real good."

"That fucking Bald Monkey blindsided me. Got six grand off me."

"This is the guy you said was never gonna mess with Tommy
Fabian again? Doesn't sound to me like he stayed scared for long."

"He'll be plenty scared, I ever see him again."

"They found a baseball bat by your Winnie."

"My own fucking bat."

"Doctor says you're gonna be here at least a week. You got blood
clots." He pointed at the fluid dripping into Tommy's arm. "They
have to get you thinned out."

"I ain't being here no week." He took another pull at the Jack
Daniel's. "It'll thin out faster with Jack."

"You know what his name is?" Axel asked.

"Who?"

"Bald Monkey. He says his name is James Dean."

Tommy blinked. "What, you mean like the sausage guy?"

———

When Axel got back to the fair, the three girls—Carmen, Kirsten,
and Juanita—were huddled in the stand, looking out at the nearly
deserted mall. It was raining, getting dark, and the only people outside were crouching under umbrellas or running from one building
to another, shielding their heads with plastic bags or newspapers.

He'd be lucky to clear a thousand bucks. The day was a bust. None
of the concessionaires would do well, not even the joints inside the
buildings, where the crowds clustered in stagnant, sodden masses. A
rainy day was bad for everybody. Even Tiny Tot Donuts, possibly the
most weatherproof concession at the fair, looked dead. They had
only two machines going. Sam O'Gara's green feed cap showed
above the top of the machines, moving from one end of the stand to

the other, then back. He still had eight kids working; all of them standing at one end of the stand, talking.

Axel changed course, veering away from the Taco Shop, heading for Tiny Tot.

"Hey, Sam."

Sam looked up, met Axel at the side door. "What the hell do you call this?" He made a gesture that included the entire universe outside the stand.

"I call it rain, Sam."

"So what are they sayin', Ax? They saying the fucker's gonna let up?"

"Won't make any difference at this point, Sam. It's after eight. Won't be anybody more coming to the fair this day. Maybe you ought to send some of your help home. What do you think?"

Sam regarded the group of teenagers at the other end of the stand. "I don't know," he said. "What if it gets busy?"

"It's not going to get busy."

"I mean, what the fuck do I know about donuts? I never sold a fucking one of 'em before this morning, Ax. Swear to Christ, that fucking Tommy—even when he gets the crap beat out of him he's making trouble for me. You remember that time in Deadwood?"

Axel nodded.

"Fucking Tommy-the-Mouth fucking Fabian. Probably how he got his ass kicked last night, mouthin' off."

"You know, you don't have to do this, Sam. I can keep an eye on things, you got something else you got to be doing."

Sam rolled his shoulders. "Fuck it. He wants me to run his business, I got no problem with that. How is the little shit anyway?"

"He's hurting. But he's got all the nurses pissed at him, so I'd say the prognosis is good. They'll have him out of there as soon as they can."

"I sure as fuck hope so. I got this Camaro I'm working on. Got a guy wants to buy it if I can get the fucker running." He tugged his cap down low over his eyes. "So you think I got too much help?"

"Send half of them home. The other two stands too. Waste of money. Besides, they'll just be thinking too much, getting into trouble."

Sam nodded uncertainly, wiping his mouth with the back of a

hand. Axel enjoyed seeing him out of his element. He was such a cocky son-of-a-bitch, it was good to see him floundering for once.

———

Sophie had gone home at seven, according to Carmen.

"She said she wasn't feeling good. I dunno."

"She was sick?" Axel asked.

"I don't think so. More like she was pissed off about the weather. You couldn't hardly talk to her. Bite your head off. Maybe she was having her hot flashes again. She said she'd be opening in the morning."

That Sunday night, the grandstand featured something called a Christian Rock Festival. The rumor was that advance ticket sales had come in at a record low, and the rain had reduced attendance even further. Axel closed the Taco Shop at nine-thirty and sent the help home. He didn't even have the heart to wait for the small rush of business that would come after the show. He just couldn't see a bunch of wet Jesus rockers getting excited about his Bueno Burrito. He lowered the front of the stand and performed the end-of-day cleaning and counting rituals.

Once again, the numbers didn't make any sense. He'd started the day with 1,500 flour tortillas and 764 corn tortillas, more than enough for a busy Sunday. But the day had been a bust. He'd taken in $1,407, roughly a break-even day. But based on his tortilla count, he had sold only 260 burritos and 126 tacos and tostadas. Again, he was three hundred dollars long. In other words, he thought, about what he'd expect if someone was adding a hundred tortillas to his stock.

Somewhere in all this, there had to be a scam. But for the life of him, Axel couldn't figure it. It just didn't make any sense.

———

Something Axel had told her that she couldn't get out of her head: "A bad day is a bad day. You can't unlive it. You try to get it back, you go nuts."

Sophie thought she knew what he meant, but it didn't help. She took the rain personally. She felt herself responsible. Saturday had been such a great day. Record sales. Axel had been elated. Then they get rained out the very next day. It killed her to have to pay those girls to stand there watching it rain. She wished now she'd sent one of them home. But she'd been thinking all day that it might clear up, the people might come.

Pouring herself a second glass of white zinfandel, Sophie listened to the sound of steady rain filtered through the mosquito screen. Landfall could be a noisy community—some summer nights, the parties and fights went on till dawn—but on this wet Sunday the only sounds were those of rain on aluminum and the hissing of traffic from Interstate 94.

She wished Axel were with her.

As soon as the desire reached her conscious mind, Sophie recoiled from it. He was busy. Too busy. And anyway, why should she care? All the things she did for him, did he ever say thank you? Actually, he did. But there were a lot of things she did that he didn't know about. Like coming in early. Like taking responsibility for the shrinkage—how many managers would do that? Sophie set her jaw, the quickly dissipating but heady joy of martyrdom flowing through her. One way or another, she would make this the Taco Shop's best year ever. She would show him what a good manager could accomplish. They still had a shot at setting a record gross, if next weekend was good. And even if the gross was off, she'd show Axel a net like he'd never seen before—she would cut back the help, eliminate shrinkage, and push every sale like a pro. Sell those nachos, those extra-large Cokes. She'd show him. When he saw what she could do, he'd come up with one beluga of a bonus. How could he not?

Chapter

23

THE WEEK STARTED OUT COOL, in the sixties but mostly clear, with just a few cirrus clouds off to the south. The *State Fair Daily News* predicted attendance at 110,000—a solid weekday showing that would provide steady, profitable business for most of the concessionaires. By eleven o'clock, sales at Axel's Taco Shop had already matched Sunday's totals. Axel could count the number of times that had happened on one hand and have five fingers left over. The first Monday was usually for shit.

Sam O'Gara, heading into his second day at the donut stand, was feeling his oats.

"Maybe I'll get into it," he said. "Get myself a joint like this, sell deep-fried lutefisk on a stick or some goddamn thing. Get myself rich like you and Tommy."

"I'm not rich," Axel said, a bit nettled. "And besides, it's not that easy." He had worked hard to build his business. His first years at the fair had been tough, and not very profitable. Axel hated it when people looked at his operation as if it were a cash cow gifted to him by the state. It was a business, like any other, only maybe tougher. And the money wasn't nearly what people thought. The taco shop might net thirty in a good year, and if he was lucky he could make another twenty doing special events and county fairs, but it wasn't as if he was rolling in it. There were guys spinning nuts in factories making better money.

Tommy, on the other hand, *was* rolling in it—a fact that had not escaped Sam.

"What do you figure they cost, a little bag of donuts?" Sam asked.

Axel shrugged. They were standing in the same spot on the mall where Axel usually stood with Tommy. Every now and then, Axel would realize with a jolt that the man standing beside him was not Tommy.

"I figure about a dime," Sam said. "So he makes a dollar forty a bag. You know how many of them bags we sold today? Man, I could get into that. Now, I'm just talkin' out loud here, but it seems to me it'd be one hell of a lot easier'n fixing cars, that's for sure. Seems to me a guy could just kick back and let the green roll in, just like findin' buried treasure."

"You think it's so goddamn easy, I hope you take a run at it, Sam. I like the idea of lutefisk on a stick. I think you should go for it."

"You bein' a little sarky on me, Ax?"

Axel said, "Ninety percent of new concessions, they're history in six months. Of course, those guys went broke, they didn't have the lutefisk-on-a-stick idea."

Sam scratched his neck. "Better odds'n a inside straight, and I won plenty of times with those. Besides, how hard could it be, a peasant like you doin' so good, a guy what keeps his money in freakin' coffee cans."

"I don't keep my money in coffee cans," Axel said.

"Oh, yeah? What'd you do with it, then? Put it in T-bills?"

"It's none of your goddamn business what I do with my money, Sam."

Sam bobbled his eyebrows. "That a fact?"

"That's right. I can take care of myself. I don't need your financial advice."

"Well, la-di-fucking-da," Sam said, fitting a Pall Mall between his lips. "You wanna be a peasant, that's your own damn problem. Jus' don't come cryin' to me if that bald-headed kid decides to hit you next."

"Since when did I ever come crying to you?"

"Sheeit, I pulled you outta so many scrapes I lost count."

"Well, you can just relax, on account of I don't need you looking after me. You understand?"

Sam said, "Hey, Ax?" He thrust up his middle finger. "Fuck you."

"I'll see you later," Axel said. He'd had his morning dose of Sam O'Gara.

———

"I don't like leaving her in charge," Sophie said. "She's like a zombie lately. I caught her giving out two burritos and only charging for one. And forgetting the cheese, twice! Better we should have left that Kirsten in charge. Or even Juanita."

"Carmen will be okay," Axel said. "She was having a problem with her boyfriend, but they broke up."

They were walking down Carnes Avenue, going to the Waffle Shop for breakfast.

"Sometimes I think she's on dope, the way she acts. I don't know how she does so well at school. Or anyway she says she does. What boyfriend?"

"A punk with no hair on his head."

Sophie said, "Oh, yeah, I met him. He was hanging around the stand the other day."

"He's the one beat up Tommy, you know."

"Oh?"

"Yeah. And Carmen too. You see what he did to her eye?"

"That how come she's wearing those glasses? She was probably asking for it. Are we going to eat breakfast or just stand around?"

Axel unclenched his fists and let his shoulders sag. "What the hell," he said. "He's probably a hundred miles away by now. Let's go get some waffles."

———

Sophie sipped her black coffee and watched Axel arrange five pats of butter on his waffle. He moved the pats around with his fork, getting a measure of molten butter into each waffle pit. When the butter was distributed to his satisfaction, he picked up the strawberry syrup, guiding the thin stream up and down the rows of square waffle pits.

The Waffle Shop was one of the older concessions at the fair. You could still get a full breakfast there, but most of their business these days was in oversize, hand-formed waffle cones with your choice of ice cream flavors.

Sophie felt jittery. Axel had never before asked her to have breakfast with him. Something was going on. "You shouldn't eat that," she said.

Axel cut into the waffle with the side of his fork, speared a large wedge, and pushed it into his mouth. When he had swallowed it, he said, "I've been wondering about something."

"You should wonder about what you eat." She didn't know why she ragged on him that way. She watched herself do it again and again, always with the invisible, internal wince, expecting to be hit. With her husband—ex-husband—that was how it had worked. Made remarks, poked at him until he hit her. Poked at him some more. He'd been so dense, if she said something subtle he never got it. Just asked her what the hell she was talking about. She could see his stupid face, hear herself berating him.

"I think about it all the time."

"You didn't eat that stuff, you'd still have all your teeth." Difference was, Axel got it all, but he never hit her. That made her mad too. If she couldn't get under his skin, how much could he like her?

"Sophie, my teeth are gone whether I eat this or not. I'm not worrying about my teeth today. What I'm worrying about is, how come I've got so many tortillas at the end of the day?"

"It's not just your teeth," she said. Then she replayed, in her mind, what Axel had just said, and this time she heard it. She felt the heat building in her cheeks, feeling his green eyes. Axel had told her he used to be a professional poker player. She had always thought that was just a story, but seeing him now, seeing his intense, utterly unreadable expression, she believed it. "It's your heart," she said weakly.

"See, what I don't understand is, if you're going to all that trouble to set me up with the tortillas, how come you don't take the money?"

Back in the 1960s, when she was in her twenties, before she met her jerk-off ex-husband and got pregnant and had Carmen, Sophie had spent a few months living with a bunch of pseudointellectual dropouts down on the West Bank. They'd taken over a trio of roomy apartments above the Triangle Bar and formed a commune loosely bonded by a lack of money, a taste for cheap wine, and a tolerance for the seismic event that occurred each night from nine till one in the morning, when the blues bands cranked up their Peaveys and started the walls shaking. She'd been with this guy back then, a proto-hippie they called Mr. Natural, Natch for short, an occasional bass player with Skogie and the Flaming Pachucos, who had thumbed his way out to San Francisco and returned in a VW bug with a cigar box full of discolored sugar cubes. Sophie had stirred one into her jasmine tea one morning and, shortly thereafter, noticed that the walls were breathing and that a microscopic receiver in her left ear was playing the theme to *I Dream of Jeannie* over and over again.

Which was much the same way she felt right now, only it was the table breathing and the theme to *Jeopardy*.

Axel said, "Are you okay?"

Sophie shook her head, meaning yes. She'd had moments like this before. Like when she got pulled over for speeding, or the time Carmen, at age eight, had come home from school unexpectedly and found Sophie on the bed astride a neighbor's undressed body. Her embarrassing moments always brought with them this sense of unreality.

"Did you hear what I asked you?"

Sophie cleared her throat but was unable to reply. The thing was, what did she have to be embarrassed about? Axel was the one who benefited. What right did he have to accuse her of anything?

Axel said, "Aren't you going to eat your muffin?"

Sophie regarded the untouched bran muffin on her plate. Of course, if you looked at it another way, he wasn't really accusing her of anything. "I'll eat it later," she said.

Axel nodded and ate a large bite of waffle, watching Sophie. She noticed that one of his eyes was tending to drift these days. It would wander off on its own, then snap back a second later.

Axel set his fork on his tray and said, "Look, I'm not accusing you of anything, Sophie—I swear I'm not. I mean, even if you were holding out a few bucks, which I'm not saying you are, I wouldn't mind it.

I mean, you work harder than anybody. But it's driving me nuts, try-ing to figure out why you've been sneaking in those extra tortillas."

Sophie crossed her arms. "Those Bueno Burritos, the girls ruin a lot of tortillas when they make them. Too much filling."

"So?"

"You told me part of my job was to reduce the shrinkage. You told me if I got the net up, you'd pay me a bonus." She pushed her chin forward and stared back at him, watched his face changing, saw his lips part, then curve into a loose smile, saw his left eye drift up and away. For a long time, he said nothing at all.

———

The kid, Duane, intercepted them as they were walking back to the donut stand. Axel let his arm fall from Sophie's shoulder, feeling sheepish, as if he'd been caught kissing on school grounds.

"Mr. Speeter? Can I talk to you a minute?" The kid seemed upset.

"Sure." Axel let his hand brush Sophie's arm. "I'll catch up with you," he said.

The kid was shifting nervously from one foot to the other, like he had to pee.

"What's the problem?" Axel asked.

"You know Mr. Sam?"

Axel nodded.

"I mean, he's a nice guy and everything, but I don't think Mr. Fabian would like it, you know?"

Axel said, "No. I don't. What are you trying to tell me, son?"

"Well, it's, like, he's changing the mix."

Axel wasn't sure he'd heard that right. He cocked his head and waited for more.

"I mean, he thinks the donuts need more salt, you know? So he's changing the mix."

"He's changing the *donut* mix?"

"They're tasting sort of weird now, you know?"

Axel had to say it again. "He's changing the *donut* mix?"

"I mean, they're not bad, but I don't think Mr. Fabian would like it. Can you talk to him, you think?"

Chapter

24

"I COULD GET ARRESTED for this," Axel said.

"You could get arrested for blocking traffic, f'Chrissakes. This is a freeway, not a cow path. You're driving like an old man." Tommy Fabian had one of his little cigars going, his first in three days. "Damn, this tastes good!"

"It smells like your bandages caught fire." Axel edged the truck up to fifty-five miles per hour and moved into the left lane. "Just don't let it kill you while you're in my truck. I don't want to go to jail. I don't know how the hell I let you talk me into this. I shouldn't have said anything."

"I got a reputation," Tommy said. "My donuts, they gotta be right every fucking time. Fucking Sam. Salt, f'Chrissakes!"

"I made him go back to the standard mix, Tom. We had a little talk. He's pretty pissed at me, but everything's okay now. You got some damn good kids running it for you. That kid Duane is humpin' like a camel. I think he runs it better than you do. Three days without you, and it's running smoother than ever, despite the fact you got Sam in there."

"Don't tell me that shit. All the more reason I gotta get back. These kids figure out they can make it without you, and the next thing you know, you tell 'em to do something and you might as well be pissin' at the moon."

"Maybe you oughta relax, quit yelling at them. I've been thinking lately that we try to do too much ourselves. Besides, you got bunged up pretty bad there. I don't like doctors either, but when they say you gotta stay in the hospital you ought to at least think about taking it easy. Let Sam and the kids run the stand a couple more days. I mean, you can't do it all yourself, right?"

"Speak for yourself. Anyway, those doctors haven't got no sense of priorities. All they worry about is if somebody's gonna sue them. Once I get back in the saddle, I'll heal up faster anyway. By the way, you seen our bald friend hanging around anyplace?"

Axel hesitated. "He's gone," he said.

"What?"

"He was staying with Carmen, like you said. But he's gone now. Got in his car and took off. We probably won't see him again."

"Shit. I was looking forward to jumping up and down on his face. You think he's really gone?"

Axel guided the truck up the Snelling Avenue exit ramp. "Yeah," he said, "I do." It felt like a lie.

"Son-of-a-bitch."

Axel drove down Snelling at twenty-five miles per hour. He turned west at Como Avenue. While they were sitting in line, waiting to get into the parking lot, Axel said, "Hey, Tommy, you know kangaroos?"

"Kangaroos?" Tommy blinked and looked at Axel, who was staring vacantly out the windshield. "What about 'em?"

"You ever see how they fight? They tear each other up. They got these big kangaroo feet and claws, and they just take turns jumping on each other and tearing each other's bellies open until one of them goes off in the desert and dies."

"Yeah? What are they fighting about?"

"Lady roos, what else?"

"Lots of stuff. They could be fighting about who gets the kids, or about politics, or about money." Tommy flicked away his cigar.

Axel looked at his bruised and bandaged friend. "Don't be stupid," he said. "Roos don't care about that kind of stuff."

———

"I gotta sit down." Tommy Fabian veered to the right and collapsed on a bench.

"You okay?" Axel sat down beside him. They were on the fairgrounds just north of the Coliseum, halfway between Tommy's Winnebago, where he had changed his clothes, and the main Tiny Tot stand on the mall. "You don't look so good. Maybe you ought to go back, take a little nap."

"I just gotta rest a minute. I get to the stand, I can sit down, relax."

"Let's go back to your Winnie. You can take a nap."

Tommy shook his head. The two men sat in silence and watched the flow of people passing before them. It was a beautiful day, warm but not too warm, the sky a clear, distant blue. A mild, changing breeze kept the fairground odors moving and shifting, and even here, at the periphery of the grounds, Axel could pick out the hot, greasy smell of frying corn dogs, the tangy raw-onion scent from the foot-long stand half a block away, and the sour reek of spilled beer. Underlying the food odors were earthy animal aromas from the hogs, horses, cattle, sheep, goats, chickens, geese, turkeys, rabbits, and other blue-ribbon contenders contained in the barns and exhibition halls that dominated the southern quarter of the fairgrounds. Thinking about it that way made the odors overwhelming; Axel shifted to breathing through his mouth.

"I got a feeling he's still around someplace," Tommy said.

"Who?"

"Bald Monkey."

"He's not staying with Carmen anymore, I can tell you that."

"You wondering how come he went after me instead of you?"

"I think he was thinking about both of us. He got in my room and went through my stuff," Axel said. He was about to mention the missing .45 auto but decided it could keep until later. He didn't want to get Tommy thinking about guns. Until a few years back, Tommy had carried a little nickel-plated .32 in his belt. Then he'd gotten into an argument with the fried-zucchini guy, pulled out his piece, and started waving it under the other vendor's nose. The zucchini guy made a big stink and got the cops and the fair administration involved, and there had been a bunch of meetings that added up to

Tommy retiring his pistol and—worst of all, according to Tommy—having to apologize to the fried-zucchini guy. "After all, it wasn't like I shot the son-of-a-bitch," Tommy had complained. Axel thought it just as well, the way Tommy could blow his cork over nothing, that he didn't carry his gun around anymore. "He didn't get anything," Axel continued. "And my guess is he's left town. Carmen says he's from Omaha. Maybe he went back."

"Didn't get into your coffee cans, huh?"

"I got rid of the cans."

"You put it in a bank like a normal person?"

"Something like that."

Tommy took a breath, then pushed himself up off the bench. As Axel watched Tommy walking away, he thought, Maybe I drive like an old man, but *he's* the one that's *walking* like an old man. Is that how I'll be walking soon? Like the world is made of Jell-O? Axel remembered something then.

He remembered being in a duck blind with old Andy, his dad, on a rainy but unseasonably warm November day in 1940, waiting for the ducks to come, his last hunt before signing up for the Merchant Marine, the father and son wearing nothing but cotton dungarees, hip boots, flannel shirts, and light raincoats; standing in the wet cattails with seventeen cork decoys floating on Long Lake, searching the horizon for the black specks that would become mallards, bluebills, canvasbacks, teal. The sky was close and gray and wet. Old Andy's faded canvas hat rested on top of his ears, flaring them at the tips. Axel remembered standing on the trampled cattails that made up the floor of the blind, watching his dad, wondering how the old man could see with his eyes squinted down into little wrinkled slits. Andy had pointed across the lake and said, "Lookie dere, Ax."

Axel looked, expecting to see an approaching flock, but what he saw was a disturbance of the lake's surface. The water on the far side of the lake was leaping and chattering, yet the water directly in front of the blind was perfectly calm. As they watched, the disturbance raced toward them, and then the wind hit the cattails and bent them back, and Andy's hat went up into the air and disappeared. The temperature dropped twenty degrees. Axel looked at Andy then and saw the fear in his father's face as the weather struck.

The temperature continued to fall as the wind whipped their

faces with stinging sheets of ice and snow. It was over a mile to where they had parked the '36 Ford. They trudged along the dirt road, heads down, slogging through the freezing mud and gathering snow-drifts, moving their hands from their armpits to their ears. Axel remembered looking at Andy, thinking: He's an old man. He's not gonna make it.

But they had survived. Andy had lived another twenty-two years. Now, watching Tommy Fabian's painful gait, he counted back and realized with some sadness that on that day in 1940 old Andy had been only sixty-two years old, younger by eleven years than Axel was today.

Axel caught up with Tommy. "You ever feel old?" he asked.

Tommy shook his head. "Just a little sore sometimes."

"You ever think about taking a partner on? Somebody to help you when you get old? I mean, older?"

Tommy said, "No way."

"I've been thinking about my future," Axel said. "I get sick or something, I don't want to have to close up shop, you know?"

Tommy Fabian wasn't listening. They had reached the mall, and he was staring at Tiny Tot #1. The lines were good, and most of the machines were cooking. Tommy watched the stand as though he could not quite believe it could run without him. His employees, most of whom had cooked their first donut only a week before, were cranking the little rings out like they owned the place. Sam sat atop Tommy's stool, an unlit cigarette in his mouth.

Tommy turned to Axel, shaking his head in wonder. "Just stay with it and don't get old. The best thing you can do about it is don't get old."

Axel said, "I don't know, Tom. I can't say I much like the other choice."

——

Kirsten sat on the folding chair behind the stand, smoking a cigarette, blowing smoke out through her nose like Madonna. She was halfway through her second pack ever of Virginia Slims. It was her first break practically all day, and now it was starting to rain again. And wouldn't you know, Sophie shows up with her evil eye and says, "Can't you find anything to do?" She never showed up when Carmen was taking a nap behind the stand, no way. Kirsten wanted to stomp her feet and say, "You can have your stupid job, you smelly old . . . witch!"

Instead, she dropped her Virginia Slim and followed Sophie into the stand.

Carmen, moving as if the air were syrup, was making a Bueno Burrito for a rosy-cheeked, alert young man wearing a mesh Wayne Feeds cap.

Sophie glared. "For Christ's sake, Carmen. What did you do, take a slow pill today?"

Carmen said, "Hi, Sophie." She folded the burrito, giving it a final delicate pat, and presented it to her customer. "Thank you," she said, turning away, ignoring the five-dollar bill in his hand.

"Don't you want my money?" he asked Carmen, who seemed not to hear him.

Sophie stepped forward, snatched the bill out of his hand, and gave him his change. She grabbed Carmen by the arm and spun her around. "What is *wrong* with you?"

"Oh, I don't know. Why do you ask?"

For a second, Kirsten thought Sophie might rip the sunglasses off and claw Carmen's eyes out. A group of kids approached the stand. Sophie took Carmen by her shoulders and shook her; Carmen's head flopped back and forth. The group of kids stopped and watched for a moment, then left. Seeing this, Sophie let go and told Carmen to go sit behind the stand.

Carmen said, as though nothing had happened, "We need change."

Sophie checked the cash box. They were out of ones and quarters.

"Well, then, go tell Axel. He's over at Tiny Tot, talking with Tommy."

Carmen nodded, hung her purse over her shoulder, and drifted across the mall toward Tiny Tot Donuts.

———

Axel and Tommy, sitting on a pair of canvas chairs behind Tiny Tot, watched the light rain darken the street. People were moving into the buildings, some of them holding plastic bags over their heads.

Axel said, "You were a little hard on Sam there, Tom. I mean, he deserved it and all, but it's not like he was one of your employees."

"Son-of-a-bitch smoking in my stand."

"He was just trying to help you out while you were laid up."

"I ain't laid up anymore. Changing my mix, f'Chrissakes."

"Sometimes you got to let people help you the way they know how."

Tommy shrugged and lit a fresh cigar, his hand shaking.

"You feeling okay?" Axel asked.

"I feel great. How the fuck are you feeling?"

Axel took the question seriously. "I'm feeling alone," he said. "That's why I decided about Sophie, you know?"

"I still think you're nuts," Tommy said. "The broad's rippin' you off every day, and you want her for a partner? That's nuts."

"I told you, she's not ripping me off. She was just trying to make herself look good."

"You believe that, you oughta be down on the midway, trying to win yourself some plush."

"I'm tired of doing it all myself."

"What the hell? It looks to me like you got a bunch a broads in there doing it for you."

"You know what I mean. You ought to, anyways—I mean, look at you. You got a head all covered up with bandages, and every time you stand up you get dizzy—"

"That was earlier. I feel fine now."

"Whatever. The point is, if you had a partner you wouldn't even have to be here."

"A few hours ago you were telling me I didn't have to be here anyway."

"You wouldn't even want to be here. Besides, we're talking about me, and I'm tired of running the show all by myself. Sophie works her ass off. Sometimes I think she cares more about that stand than I do."

"She's so great, how come you don't marry her?"

"Too old."

"Seventy-three's not so old."

"I mean her."

Tommy, who had been drawing on his cigar, broke into a coughing fit. He leaned forward in his chair, and Axel thumped him on the back. When he got his breath back, he said, "Chrissakes, Ax, she's young enough to be your daughter."

"She's almost *fifty*," Axel said.

Tommy's eyes were still watering. "Pretty goddamn selective for an old cocker, you ask me."

"I'm gonna take her over to this lawyer tomorrow," Axel said. "Get it all set up. Why wait?"

"Christ, Ax, why don't you wait till the fair's over, at least. Give yourself a chance to think on it."

"I think on it, I might not do it, and I want to do it, Tom. If I wait till the fair's over, I'll forget what it's like to be alone in this business."

Tommy said, "You're always alone in this business. Well, look what we got here—speak of the devil's daughter. How you doing, Carmen?"

"Hi, Tommy," said Carmen. "I'm doing okay."

"How's the eye?" Tommy asked her. "I hear you got a heck of a shiner under those shades."

Carmen shrugged and turned toward Axel. "Sophie says for me to go get some change," she said.

Axel dug in his pocket and pulled out a set of keys. He handed them to Carmen. "You know where the truck is? Along the far row, way over on the other side of the lot. About ten cars in from the back. The change is in the back; you have to use the round key."

"Thanks." Carmen floated off.

"You're lucky he didn't use a baseball bat," Tommy called after her. Carmen gave no sign she had heard. "She looks sort of out of it," he said to Axel. "If she worked for the railroad they'd have her pissin' in a cup."

"She's just sleepy," Axel said.

"Yeah, right. Prob'ly been up all night banging Bald Monkey."

"He's gone, I told you. He's been gone almost three days."

"You mean you ain't seen him in three days. Guys like that don't go away until you make 'em. It's like trying to get rid of a hungry dog. They just lie in the weeds and wait." He looked up and pointed at the thirty-story-tall, blue-and-white Space Tower, with its rotating elevator. "He's probably sitting up there looking down at us right now."

Chapter

25

CARMEN ARRIVED AT THE TRUCK, it seemed to her, only moments after she left Axel and Tommy at the Tiny Tot stand. Her hair was wet. She didn't remember the walk at all. She let herself into the cab and, resting her hands on the wheel, let her mind wander, hoping to remember what she was doing there. It started raining harder; she watched through the windshield as the world went out of focus. Dean had been gone going on three days now. She might never see him again. She knew she should be glad he was gone. It was no fun getting punched in the eye; it was hard to see in the rain, looking through mirrored sunglasses. Now, though, she found herself bored into a near-catatonic state. The days and nights of her future appeared endless and gray and smelled of frying tortillas. She almost wished some guy would come along and blacken her other eye.

After a time, more than a minute but less than half an hour, she remembered why she was there. She was supposed to get change. Sophie was out of change.

The back of the truck was as precisely organized as Axel's room at the Motel 6. Cartons of cups and napkins and plastic forks were laid out along the left wall; condiments, chips, and other nonperishables were arranged on the opposite side. Carmen stood at the back of the truck, looking in through the open tailgate, feeling the rain on her bare arms. Where would he keep the change? She was supposed to know this. The bed of the truck was covered with a green packing pad. Carmen climbed inside. At the far end, against the cab, the packing pad stepped up and over a boxlike shape. Carmen pulled the pad back and discovered an oblong wooden box with an open top. The box contained a row of coffee cans. She felt excitement struggling to penetrate the Valium haze as she pried the top off one of the coffee cans.

It was filled with packets of sugar.

The second can was full of salt packets. She opened the rest of the cans. Taco sauce. Horseradish. Horseradish? More sugar. Equal. She replaced the covers and drew the pad back up over the box, wondering in a mild Valium sort of way why Axel was saving coffee cans full of condiments. Where was the change? She had done this before, last year, and she was supposed to remember. Axel kept the change in a special place, but where? She took inventory of the items surrounding her. Cups, napkins, paper servers, forks, canned chilies, chips, taco sauce . . . Wait. Back up. Cups. She opened the top of the carton and reached inside. There it was, the canvas bank bag. She opened it, emptied the contents out onto the packing pad, took five rolls of quarters, a roll of dimes, and three fifty-dollar bundles of one-dollar bills, and stuffed it all in her purse. That left three rolls of pennies, a roll of dimes, two fifty-dollar bundles, and two rolls of fives, tens, and twenties, held together with thick blue rubber bands. Carmen took a twenty from each roll, folded the two into a small square, and slid it into her back pocket.

Wandering back toward the Taco Shop, she wondered what Axel had done with his coffee can money. One thing she was pretty sure about—it had to be somewhere. Cheap as Axel was, there was no way he could have spent it. It occurred to her that he might have put it in a bank, which was what any normal person would have done a long time ago. But Axel hated banks. He said you could not trust them. He even hated going into a bank to buy change, always counting it twice, right there in front of the teller. It was embarrassing. Carmen experienced a moment of disorientation. She stopped and let her brain spin free for a moment, enjoying the floating sensation.

Her mind returned to the physical task at hand. Her hair was heavy with water. The rain was lighter now, but steady, and the parking lot had become a maze of puddles, the larger of which Carmen walked around. She paid no attention to the smaller puddles; there were just too goddamn many of them.

———

James Dean sat in the torn and stained beanbag chair and watched Tigger tattooing Sweety's forehead.

"Sweety's even got muscles on his forehead," Tigger said, pausing to wipe away the blood and excess ink. Sweety turned toward Dean and contorted his brow, which writhed impressively. The words FUCK ME were carefully outlined in black. Sweety himself had conceived the message. Dean had helped draw the letters with a felt-tip pen, and Tigger was working now on filling them in, using a pushpin to open the skin and a red Sanford marker for color.

"You know, it's not going to last," Dean said. "You want it to last, you should use ashes from Styrofoam. That's how we did it in Lincoln."

Tigger said, "Yeah, well, we ain't in Lincoln, and we don't have any Styrofoam."

"When's the guy going to be here?" Dean asked.

"He'll be here. Pork always does what he says he's gonna."

"That's what you said yesterday."

"Yesterday he was in Wisconsin. He didn't get my message."

"Fuckin' Pork," Sweety said, gritting his teeth as Tigger performed a series of pricks on the letter *C*.

"Hold still," Tigger said. "You want this to look good, don't you?"

He worked in silence for a few minutes.

Dean was bored. He figured he'd give Pork another hour, then take his money and leave. The more time he spent with Tigger and Sweety, the less he was inclined to trust their choice of drug dealers.

For the past two nights he'd had a room at the Golden Steer out on I-94, watching MTV, counting and recounting his money, and waiting for Tigger to arrange an introduction with "Pork," the supposed connection, the guy with the meth. His idea was to parlay most of the six thousand seven hundred dollars into a half kilo of crystal methedrine—an incredible price, if it was any good—then double his money by selling it to a guy he'd met in Lincoln named Stinger, who, if all went as planned, had got out of prison on schedule, had returned to Sioux Falls, had got back into the drug business, and had as much cash as he'd claimed to have. And even if Stinger didn't work out—a distinct possibility—there were always people looking to get high.

He hadn't minded waiting at first. The Golden Steer wasn't a bad place, but late last night he'd heard a crash outside his room and looked out to see that some drunk in a Cadillac had crushed his Maverick, driven right up onto the trunk. The guy was staggering around, muttering to himself, every few seconds giving the Cadillac a kick in the side.

Dean's first reaction was to go out and beat the hell out of the guy, but then he started thinking about how the cops would be showing up pretty soon. At first, they'd be interested in the Cadillac guy, but sooner or later they'd be looking at those Nebraska license plates on the Maverick, and if they ran the plates, well, that couldn't be good. He threw his stuff into his bag, walked down the hill to Concord Avenue, and called a cab. Since then, he'd been staying with Tigger and Sweety.

A scraping sound came from the window.

"There he is." Tigger set the pushpin on the table. "That you, Pork?" he called.

A pair of black lace-up motorcycle boots entered through the basement window, followed by a blocky man with a stubble of dark hair covering his scalp and jaw. His eyes were black and alert.

"This here's Pork," Tigger said.

Pork was wearing a camouflage-pattern sweatshirt and a pair of baggy olive-drab pants with cargo pockets. Though he was about Dean's height, he carried another forty pounds. His fingers were thick and short, and he held his arms a few inches out from his body, letting everybody know that he'd put in his hours on the bench. The guys Dean knew with bodies like that, they'd spent at least five calendars in Lincoln.

Pork grinned, his mouth forming a wide, pointed vee. "This place reeks," he said. He looked at Sweety. "What did you do to your head, Sweety?"

"I'm giving him a tattoo," Tigger said. "It was his idea."

Pork took a closer look. "Hope you don't land in jail with that on your head, my man."

"They can fucking try," Sweety growled.

Pork shrugged. "Believe me, they do." He looked at Dean. "You the guy?"

Dean, half buried in the beanbag chair, gave a slight nod.

"How good you know this guy, Tig?"

"He's cool," Tigger said.

Pork put his hands in his back pockets, raised his eyebrows, and looked at the ceiling, still smiling, shaking his head like he couldn't believe it. Dean didn't blame him. Tigger was not the kind of guy you would believe anything he said. But Pork looked like a guy you could do business with. A guy who'd paid some dues, learned how it's done.

"Look," Dean said, "you don't know me; I don't know you. That's cool. You don't want to talk, I can take my business someplace else."

"Relax," said Pork. He was looking at Dean, his alert eyes probing. Noticing the antitheft strip on Dean's jacket sleeve, he said, "How come you don't cut that thing off there?"

Dean looked at the plastic strip anchored to his jacket sleeve. "I kind of like it," he said.

"So you walk down the street and everybody knows you're a bad guy?"

Dean shrugged. "They can think what they want."

Pork shook his head, but the stolen jacket seemed to make him more comfortable. What kind of cop would go around wearing something like that?

"What you looking for?"

Dean said, "What do you got?"

"Tigger said you were asking about some crank."

Dean shrugged.

"I can get it."

"Good."

"How much you looking for?"

"I was thinking a half key, if the price is what Tigger said."

"The price is good. I suppose you'll want to sample the merch."

"You got it with you?"

Pork laughed. "You got your money with *you*?"

Dean, who did in fact have the money stuffed in his jacket pockets, shook his head.

Pork said, "Let's take this one step at a time, then. How about we get together tomorrow night for a little taste. You got someplace we can meet? I mean someplace besides this pisshole?"

Chapter

26

AT TEN-THIRTY THURSDAY MORNING, Frank Knox greeted Axel and Sophie at the front door of his aging two-story South Minneapolis Tudor. The house smelled like Lysol and something that Sophie could not identify. The attorney nodded to Axel, then smiled at Sophie and said, "You must be Sophia Roman." He did not offer his hand but rather backed away from her, then he turned and led them through a cluttered hallway and up the wooden stairs, which were half covered with stuffed manila folders, notebooks, and loose stacks of paper. Knox moved through his possessions with a kind of sinuous grace, like a cat, keeping his hands close to his sides and touching nothing.

His office may have once been the master bedroom. Sophie halted at the door, fearful of entering. The far wall was braced by a collection of four-, five-, and six-drawer file cabinets, all different heights, widths, makes, and colors, all featuring no fewer than two open drawers, and all capped by piles of folders and papers that could only be the result of years of careful stacking. The floor of the office also supported a mass of paperwork, mostly piled along the walls and, except for one teetering stack, limited to a height of four feet. Everything seemed to lean in toward the center of the room, drawn in by the mountainous jumble of books and files that dominated the space and served to mark the location of Knox's desk. Sophie was afraid it was all going to come crashing in on her.

Axel put his hand on Sophie's back and coaxed her into the room. Knox moved two piles of documents from a pair of wooden side chairs, then wiped his hands on the shiny lapels of his black twill suit. Axel directed Sophie to one of the chairs and sat beside her.

Knox sat behind his desk and smiled at them, his chin barely clearing the stacked documents. Frank Knox was an ashen, wispy-haired man. The hands he folded in front of his chin had a gray, powdery aspect, the nails stark yellow in contrast to the surrounding flesh. Large-lensed, black-rimmed bifocals made his face seem insubstantial, as though he were made of dust and the shiny suit was all that contained him. Sophie thought he looked like a ghost.

"I guess I should congratulate you," he said to Sophie, sliding his glasses up his long nose with a gray forefinger.

Sophie folded her arms over her breasts and nodded, her expression serious. The air in the room was suffused with a familiar chemical smell. What was it?

Knox looked at Axel and raised his eyebrows.

Axel said, "Frank has put together a contract for us, Sophie. Frank? You want to explain to her how we're going to do this?"

Knox nodded, causing his glasses to slide down his nose. He cleared his throat and began to talk.

By the time he had finished his explanation, Sophie's lips had become a thin line, her face was pink, and her breasts hurt from the pressure of her tightly crossed arms.

"You said you were going to make me your partner," she said, not looking at Axel.

Axel, as relaxed as Sophie was tense, smiled broadly and said, "That's what we're trying to do. But we have to do these things right."

"What's he talking about, ten percent?"

"Excuse me," Knox said. "I'll be right back." He left the room.

"He's going to wash his hands," Axel whispered. "Kill the germs."

"What's that smell?"

"Rubbing alcohol. That's what he washes his hands with."

"What's this about ten percent? You said we were going to be full partners."

"It's ten percent a year," Axel said. "Every year you get another ten percent, and in five years you own half of Axel's Taco Shop. Fifty percent. We have to do it that way because of taxes."

Sophie shook her head.

"I can't just give you half the business all at once," Axel said. "It doesn't work that way. We're valuing the business at one hundred thousand dollars, even though it's worth twice that, and you'd never be able to pay the taxes on fifty grand. If I just up and gave it to you, you'd be stuck with a twenty-thousand-dollar tax bill."

Sophie said, "Five years? What if . . ."

Axel waited a moment, but she did not finish her sentence. "You want to know what if I die," he said for her.

Sophie nodded.

"Then you'll have to negotiate with your new partner. My share of the business will go to my heir."

"Your heir?"

"Yeah. Alice."

She looked at Axel. "Alice from California? You're leaving it to Alice?"

"Yup." Axel grinned. Alice Zimmerman was his sister, a bad-tempered, disapproving, formidable matron who, contrary to the usual aging sequence, had grown taller, louder, and stronger in her advancing years. Axel had seen her only once in the last decade—two years ago she had flown out from San Diego for an unannounced seven-day visit, a week that left Axel with a bad stomach and a lifetime's worth of unsolicited advice. Alice had never approved of Axel or his friends, particularly his women friends.

"You don't even like her. You told me you never wanted to see her again as long as you lived."

"That's right, I don't. And I won't have to."

"Alice hates me."

Axel shook his head sympathetically. "Yeah, that could be a problem. But you don't have to worry about it now. I've decided I'm not gonna die till later."

———

On the ride back to the fairgrounds, Axel kept the conversation going by telling Sophie how great it would be to be partners. Sophie watched the traffic, gripping the armrest and pushing her right foot against the floor, trying to make the truck go faster. She didn't like being a passenger.

"I'll stop by Midway Sign and get a guy out to paint your name on the stand. *Axel and Sophie Speeter, Proprietors.*"

Sophie gave Axel a sharp look. "Sophie *Roman,*" she said.

Axel turned red.

"You're blushing!" Sophie said, her face breaking up into laughter.

"Anyway, I'll get the guy out to paint it."

They rode along in silence. Axel rested his hand on her back. It felt good. She had never seen Axel blush before.

"It's going to be great," he said again. "We'll make one hell of a team."

Sophie was starting to believe it. She reached up and put her hand over his, held it there against the back of her neck.

———

Axel's Taco Shop was still standing when they returned. Carmen and Kirsten had handled a few minor emergencies, and failed to deal with a few others, but people were still lining up and pushing their money across the counter. That was what counted. Sophie tied on an apron and dove into the fray. Axel went for a walk, heading down Carnes Avenue with no destination in mind.

The idea of making Sophie his partner had grown quickly, like the idea of buying a new truck, or the decision to pay for Carmen's schooling. He was glad he'd acted while the idea was still fresh and clean and free from doubts and overanalytical thinking. This streak of impulsiveness had been with him all his life. It didn't hit him as often now, but when it did, he embraced it as a sign that the young man still resided within him.

He no longer had to wonder whether he wanted Sophie in his life. It was done. They were partners now, for better or worse. He'd felt this way after committing himself to a big poker hand, after buying the Taco Shop, after burying his money in Sam's backyard.

A sudden movement from above caught his eye. He looked up, to see a round metal cage fly straight up into the air, reach a height of about one hundred feet, then tumble earthward. Two screaming figures were locked into the cage. The Ejection Seat, one of the fair's newest attractions, was a cross between a giant slingshot and a bungee cord. Sixty bucks a ride, and they had a constant line of thrill-seekers waiting to get strapped in and shot skyward. Axel grinned and watched the cage bounce up and down between the sixty-foot-high towers. He understood how they felt, and why they paid the money. The thrill was in the decision to go for it, the idea of being strapped in, the moment before the slingshot was triggered.

Chapter

27

AXEL SNAPPED THE PADLOCK closed and took one last walk around the outside of the restaurant. Everything seemed to be in order. Most of the concessions on the mall were closed, or closing. Sophie had gone home. Carmen slumped on a bench, smoking a cigarette. Axel wished, as he often did, that he still smoked. The end of the day was a good time for a cigarette. He missed the break, and the morsel of warmth that came with a good cigarette.

Tiny Tot Donuts remained open, feeding the last of the grand-stand crowd. Tommy Fabian sat on his stool, looking as though he might fall off at any moment.

It took fifteen minutes for Axel to talk Tommy into closing. By the time the kids had shut down the machines and finished cleaning, it was nearly midnight. Axel helped Tommy lock down the stand.

Carmen had fallen asleep on her bench. Axel gave her a gentle shake.

"Let's hit the road, kiddo."

They walked to the truck in silence. Both Carmen and Tommy

looked like they were going to pass out. Tommy walked with one hand inside his shirt, like his gut hurt. They were almost to the Winnebago when it occurred to Axel that Tommy might be holding on to something besides himself.

Axel gave Tommy's elbow a nudge. "What you got there, Tom?"

Tommy glared up at him. "I don't want to hear it, Ax."

"Administration sees you packing a gun again, you could lose your spots."

"I run into that Bald Monkey again, it'll be worth it."

———

In the truck, as they pulled into the motel parking lot, Carmen roused herself to ask, "What's Sophie so hyper about, anyway?"

Axel said, "Sophie? What do you mean, hyper?"

"All day she was all over my case. All of a sudden she's worried about I might put too much meat in somebody's taco. You'd think I was giving away money, the way she's been acting."

Axel forced his face to assume a serious expression. "Really?"

"Yeah. She's turned into a real bitch all of a sudden. I don't get it."

Axel could hardly contain himself. This partnership was going to work out great. Grinning, he asked, "So how much meat are we talking about here?"

Carmen opened the passenger door and said, "You're just as weird as she is."

"Get some sleep," Axel said. "You'll feel better tomorrow. Try to get in before the lunch rush, okay?"

Carmen closed the truck door and waved him away. Her head hurt. She was tired and she was bored.

She could hear Dean's voice before she opened the door.

He was sitting on the writing table, his booted feet resting on the chair, reading from his poetry book. He looked up briefly as Carmen entered, then continued reading. On the bed directly in front of him sat a young giant with arms the circumference of her waist. He wore an olive-drab tank top, khaki-colored cotton duck pants, and a pair of boots like Dean's, only bigger. His head was shaved, and most of his forehead was covered by a swollen, scabby bruise. He didn't look up at Carmen but kept his eyes fixed on Dean, his arms rigid and flexed, his jaw pulsing every few seconds.

"No man hath affliction enough, that is not matured and ripened by it, and made fit for God by that affliction . . . ," Dean read.

Behind the giant, who took up most of the bed, a boy of perhaps seventeen, also bald, lay gazing up at the ceiling tiles, hands laced behind his head. He wore shredded black denim jeans and a pair of snakeskin cowboy boots held together with silver duct tape. Carmen closed the door and leaned against it.

"How'd you get in?" she asked Dean.

The boy with the cowboy boots turned his head. "Pork just fuckin' picked it," he said, showing her his collection of mottled gray teeth.

"Pork?"

Dean read, *"This Soule, now free from prison, and passion, hath yet a little indignation."*

This, Carmen thought, is too weird. She walked quickly between Dean and the giant, heading for the bathroom, hoping to give herself a minute to think. She found another intruder, bent over the back of the toilet tank, using a razor blade to chop chunks of dry white matter into powder.

"What you got there?" Carmen asked, forgetting her confusion. "Coke?"

The man turned his head and leered at her while he continued chopping the lumps into powder with short, rapid strokes. He was the most feral-looking of the group, possibly due to the furry patch that served to connect his eyebrows with his long, meaty nose. Also, he had neglected to shave for some time, and his head and face were covered with short, dense dark hairs.

"We don't do yuppie dope," he said.

Carmen looked curiously at the lines he was now making on the white porcelain. "What is it?" she asked.

"Crank. You're Carmen, I bet. I'm Pork."

"Pork? Crank?" Carmen was looking at the lines. "Is it any good?" she asked.

Pork grinned. "Pure crystal meth. You could drive all the way to L.A. on a quarter gram." He rolled a five-dollar bill into a tube the diameter of a pencil and handed it to her. "Want a little wake-up?"

A few minutes later, Pork followed Carmen out of the bathroom, carrying the top to the toilet tank. Carmen's nose throbbed agonizingly, but it was getting better. She could feel the amphetamine flooding her system.

Dean was explaining something to the kid in the shredded denim, who was now sitting up on the bed, next to the giant. They were both leaning forward intently, listening. The words spilled from Dean's mouth, tumbling over one another. "It's not you, Tigger. That's the whole point. It's everybody. So it's like you are part of the nigger, and part of the yuppie, and part of the whore, and like they are part of you."

"Bullshit," said Tigger.

"Look," said Dean. "What do you do when you got a big zit, big old whitehead, hanging off the end of your nose. You squeeze it off, right? And you got a right and an obligation to do that, right? On account of you don't want people to get sick from looking at you, right? And what do you do when your little sister, who is a part of you—"

"I ain't got a sister."

"Well, suppose you did, and she's like a part of you, which she would be, and she starts hooking, doing coke and smack, and hanging out with the niggers. What's the righteous thing to do?"

"Me an' Sweety fuckin' kick ass on her and the niggers both."

"Exactly. What I'm saying is, it's on account of *you got to* because they are a part of you. Which is what my man Donne is on about. When the fucking bell fucking tolls, you better fucking listen, on account of it means somebody needs to get their fuckin' head kicked."

The giant, who had been nodding energetically, curled a meaty arm around Tigger's head and started rapping his knuckles against his skull. "Lemme soften his head up. He don't listen."

Tigger twisted loose. "Fuck you, Sweety."

"'Fuck you, Sweety,'" Sweety parroted, pitching his voice as high as he could get it.

"Hey," said Pork, still holding the ceramic toilet tank top. "I gotta set this down someplace."

Dean slid off the writing desk. "Right here," he said. He looked at the lines, six neat parallel slashes of white on white.

"Me and Carmen here, we already got our consciousnesses raised. This is for you guys. You ready for seconds, Deano?"

"You better go first," Sweety said to Tigger. "Your conscious got more climbing to do."

Tigger said, "Fuck you," but he took the rolled-up bill from Pork and did his two lines quickly, one up each nostril, and threw himself back on the bed, holding his hands over his nose.

Pork laughed. "Stings, don't it? That's how you know it's good."

Pork and Carmen watched Sweety and Dean do their lines, then Carmen opened the cooler and distributed warm canned martinis.

"Awright," said Sweety. "We gonna have a party."

"Where'd you guys come from?" Carmen asked.

"Headquarters," Tigger said.

"Drove over here in Tigger's Caddy," Dean said. "Man, that is one big ugly car you got there, Tigger."

Tigger grinned. "The Black Beauty."

"It's a fuckin' tank."

"Got a big old five-hundred-cubie V-8."

"So we drove on over here, sitting around reading John Donne, working on Sweety's head, man. These guys never heard of Donne before. Sitting around waiting all day for the Porker to show—"

"I got hung up," said Pork.

"It was worth it," said Dean, pinching his nose. "This is great shit. I want it. I want it all. So anyway, we sit around here waiting, but at least Tigger got done with Sweety's tattoo, man. What do you think?"

Carmen, enjoying the buzz but with no idea what was going on, asked, "Are you guys from Omaha?" She pulled a cigarette out of her pack.

"Gimme one of them," Sweety said. "Gimme two." Carmen handed him two cigarettes.

"We're from Frogtown, man," Tigger said.

"I found 'em," Dean said.

"Bullshit," Sweety said. "We found you. You didn't know where the fuck you were." He had both cigarettes in his mouth. Carmen lit them.

Dean said to Carmen, "Went into this bar, place full of factory creeps, and Tigger comes up."

"Stepped on my fucking toe," Tigger said.

"So we start bullshittin'."

"Skins hang together," Sweety said, sucking hard on his cigarettes.

"So I asked these guys if they knew where I could get some speed."

Carmen's head was waggling back and forth as she tried to follow the conversation, retaining almost none of it. Her eyes settled on Sweety's forehead. "What happened to your head?"

Sweety grinned, contorting his brow.

"It's a tattoo," Dean said.

Carmen looked at it for several seconds before distinguishing the words FUCK ME.

"Fuck you?"

"You got it, bitch. Fuck me fuck me fuck me." He stood up and moved toward Carmen, his arms held out before him.

Dean pulled Axel's .45 out of his jacket, pointed it at Sweety, and said, "Bang."

Sweety clapped his hands over his chest and fell back on the bed. "Arrrgh. You got me. I'm fucking dead."

Tigger was giggling.

Dean blew imaginary smoke from the muzzle and slid the pistol back into his jacket pocket. "You got to watch these guys every minute," he said to Carmen. "They're a buncha fuckin' animals."

An hour or so later, even as he was talking—telling Carmen and the skins about how he'd avenged himself on Tiny Tot, telling them how much cash he'd scored, telling them about how easy it was—a little man behind his left eyeball was telling Dean to shut up, to be discreet, to not trust this bunch with every thought that ran through his head. But that small portion of his consciousness could not withstand the tongue-loosening power of the methedrine. He was gabbing away like a speed freak!

Dean barked out a laugh, interrupting himself.

"What's so funny?" Tigger asked.

"I'm talking like a fucking speed freak!"

That turned out to be the funniest thing anybody'd heard all night. Dean basked in their admiration, feeling his chest expand. He decided to read them some more passages from John Donne, but when Pork saw him reaching for the book, he turned to Carmen.

"I hear the guy you work for is really rich," he said.

"He keeps his money in coffee cans," she said.

"Bull*shit*!" Dean said. "We checked his damn coffee cans and didn't find shit."

"Well, it was there. I saw it. It's not my fault he moved it."

"Yeah, well, anyways, the donut guy is the one with all the money."

"He's back at work, you know," Carmen said.

Dean said, "No shit?" He was surprised. He thought he'd killed him.

"Maybe you ought to score off him again," Pork suggested.

Dean laughed. "Not a bad idea."

"I don't know," Carmen said, getting into the spirit of it. "Him and Axel, they walk back to his place together now."

"So hit 'em both," said Pork.

Tigger jumped in. "Fuck, why don't we hit the fuckin' gate? Man, would that be cool, or what? Get, like, a million bucks or something!"

Pork said, "Tigger, I ever tell you what a fucking idiot you are?"

Sweety made a rumbling sound in his chest.

"I ain't talking about you, Sweety," Pork said. "You're one of the smartest Aryan motherfuckers I know. And big too." He pulled a folded paper from his pocket. "What do you say we do a little booster?"

Sweety grinned, using his entire face. Dean could hear his scabbed brow crackle.

———

Sweety's stomach started growling a few minutes into the 6:00 A.M. edition of *Sesame Street*.

"He's hungry," Tigger explained. "We got to go get something to eat."

"I'm hungry too," said Dean. "Hey, Pork. You hungry?"

Pork nodded. Dean looked at Carmen, who was curled up on the floor. "You hungry, Carmen?"

Carmen did not answer. Two hours earlier, she had swallowed a few Valiums, and she was now on the floor, wrapped in the bedspread, snoring.

They took Tigger's car to a Perkins. Sweety ordered a breakfast steak and six eggs, scrambled. Tigger explained to the nervous waitress how to prepare them.

"He likes 'em just barely cooked. You go tell them to just stir the eggs up and dump 'em in a pan and then dump 'em right out again on a plate. Hardly cook 'em at all. He likes 'em real soupy like. And get him some extra toast too, so's he can sop it up. Okay?"

The waitress said, "Steak and eggs with a side order of six eggs, scrambled, very loose."

"Yeah, only you know how loose you think he wants 'em?"

The waitress nodded.

"He likes 'em even looser than that."

Pork was talking to Dean. "I can get it for you. But not till tonight."

"That's cool."

"I'd have brought it last night, but I didn't know for sure you wanted it. Besides, I don't like carrying weight."

"No problem. I can have the money for you whenever." Dean could feel the money pressing against his ribs, two thick bundles stuffed in the inside pockets of his jacket.

"So what do you guys want to do today?" Tigger asked. "You guys want to do something?"

Pork scratched his chin with a fork. "I was thinking I'd go some-place and crash."

"Fuck that," rumbled Sweety.

"Yeah," said Tigger. "Fuck that. Let's go do something. What do you guys want to do?"

Dean said, "You guys ever go to the state fair?"

They all looked at him.

"I mean, I was thinking we could go over there and get some donuts or something. Go look at the freaks."

Chapter

28

SHORTLY BEFORE FRIDAY NOON, Midges Flores, the maid, knocked lightly on the door to room 19, hoping that no one was there. She put her ear to the door and listened, then knocked again, louder this time. Midges did not like the girl who was staying there, and she liked the bald man even less. But he hadn't been around since last weekend, when he had sat and watched her make the bed, cleaning his teeth with a fingernail and not saying a word. And the girl, she was a slob. Midges knocked again. No response. She relaxed, inserted her passkey into the doorknob, and opened the door.

What a mess; this was the worst yet. The bed all undone, and it stank of cigarettes, sweat, and alcohol. Midges had pushed her cleaning cart all the way into the room before she noticed the girl lying on the floor.

"Oh! Excuse me!" Midges said.

The girl on the floor didn't move. Midges started to back her cart out of the room, then stopped. The girl was very still.

"Hey, are you okay?" Midges licked her lips and felt her heart accelerating. Was she dead? In the past, Midges had found money, drugs, children, clothing, interesting Polaroid photographs, and even someone's eight-foot-long pet boa constrictor . . . but never a corpse. She approached the girl, who was lying flat on her back, fully dressed but with only one button holding the front of her shirt together, and bent over her. She sure did look dead. Midges froze. What if she had been murdered? What if the murderer was still in the room? He could be in the bathroom. He could be under the bed. The bald man. Midges' hand was only inches from the girl's neck. She would just check, very quietly, for a pulse. Keeping her eyes on the bathroom door, she pressed her fingers against the girl's throat. The girl's eyes popped open. Midges jerked her hand away, took two steps backward, and screamed as she collided with her cleaning cart.

Carmen sat up, blinking. "What's going on?" she asked. "Where did everybody go?"

———

Sophie hated to admit it, even to herself, but Kirsten and Juanita were a hell of a lot faster, pleasanter, and more reliable than her daughter the sleepwalker. They both did their jobs, complained only a little, and never ever told her to shove a burrito up her ass. Sophie liked that. Also, she liked the idea of having a real Mexican girl like Juanita rolling burros and frying ground beef and every now and then waiting on customers. Business was brisk going into the last weekend of the fair. The rainy midweek had kept many of the fairgoers at home; now they were out in force for this final weekend of cheese curds and corn dogs, skyrides and giant slides, Machinery Hill and the twelve-hundred-pound prize hog, and, of course, Axel's Taco Shop. It was eleven-forty in the morning, and they'd had a steady stream of customers since ten.

The system that seemed to be working best was to keep Kirsten up front serving customers, Juanita building tacos, burros, and tostadas in back, and Sophie running the orders back and forth and doing the soft drinks and making sure Juanita was stocked and running the fryer and taking care of whatever else came up. Juanita wanted to take her break now, and she mentioned it every time she pushed an order across the stainless-steel table.

She said, "I gotta go to the ladies'."

"Wait till Carmen gets here," Sophie said, grabbing a pair of Buenos. "Anytime now."

When Sophie came back for an order of beans, Juanita said, "I got my period. I gotta go to the ladies'."

"You had your period last weekend," Sophie said. "Are you a rabbit, or what?"

"That Carmen, you know, she might never come, and I gotta go to the ladies'."

"Just wait." Sophie grabbed the beans and delivered them to the front counter. When she turned back, Juanita was gone. "Damn." She stepped around the food table and spread out three tortillas and spooned a layer of beans across each of them.

"Hey," Kirsten said, looking back. "How come she gets to take a break? I need two more tacos and a side of beans."

Sophie folded the burritos, snatched a pair of taco shells from the arms of the deep fryer, loaded them, wrapped them, and motioned Kirsten to come get them. "She'll be right back," she said.

"I was here first thing this morning. It's not fair. I came in early, and she gets to take a break."

Juanita was gone for over twenty minutes. "You got to wait in line," she said in response to the look Sophie gave her. Sophie scowled, knowing that it was probably true—the lines were longer at the women's rest rooms than they were at the cheese curd concession. A line had formed in front of the taco stand now, six hungry people staring in at the painted menu board. Sophie moved into high gear, loving the sense of crisis, seeing each customer now as another buck in her pocket.

Carmen showed up at twenty after twelve.

"Well, look who's here," Sophie said. "We thought you'd got lost."

"Can I go on break now?" Kirsten asked, untying her apron. Sophie nodded and took her place at the front counter.

Carmen looked at the people lined up waiting to be served, then at Juanita, who was trying to do about six things at once. "What do you want me to do?" Carmen asked her.

"Need more taco shells, cheese, beans, and roll two deluxe for the guy with the red hat."

Carmen thought about leaving, about just walking out and losing herself in the crowd. Walk right off the fairgrounds and onto the street and stick her thumb out and get picked up by some guy in a Mercedes, go have a few drinks.

"You want to get your lazy butt moving?" Sophie said.

Carmen tore into a bag of corn tortillas and loaded the fryer. She'd stay for a while, maybe leave later. If she felt like it. She still had some crystal folded into a square of paper tucked down deep in the front pocket of her jeans. Last night, Pork had looked through a magazine to find a good picture and finally found one of Nancy Reagan, tore it out, spooned some crystal meth over Nancy's nose, folded her up into a neat square with the corners tucked in, and handed it to Carmen. "This is for letting us use your room. What do you say?" he asked her.

She had said, "Thank you." Pork had laughed and told her she was supposed to "Just say no." Carmen didn't get it.

She laid out a row of six flour tortillas and started rolling burros, and by the time the sixth burrito was rolled and wrapped, she was caught up in the rhythm of the Taco Shop and almost enjoying herself. Carmen was capable of moving quickly and precisely, especially when she began the day with a nose full of methamphetamine.

———

The nearest rest rooms, located in the shadow of the Giant Slide, had grown a thirty-foot-long tail of females—about a ten-minute wait, by Kirsten's estimate. She took her place in line and watched enviously as men walked easily in and out of their side of the building. She had to pee too bad to let herself get mad, but it bugged her how slow most women were. Some of her friends complained that rest rooms were designed by men, that women *needed* more time, so they should have more toilets available. Kirsten did not agree. She could take care of business as fast as any guy, maybe faster. Unless she had her period, of course, but even then she wouldn't just sit there staring down between her legs like some of these women.

God, did she have to *go*!

The trick was to let your butt touch the toilet seat lightly, or not at all—at these rest rooms, she went for not at all—and just pee, wipe, and get out. Make room for the next person, who maybe had to go *really* bad.

Kirsten shifted her weight from one flexed leg to the other. She fantasized squatting down right where she was and letting loose. No, thinking about it that way didn't help at all. Maybe she was keeping her muscles *too* tense. She tried relaxing her belly. She imagined a hollow space inside her abdomen. All the room in the world. An empty lakebed. As her eyes danced over the heads of the people passing by, she wished she were one of them: people who did not have to pee. A dome of flesh caught her attention. One, two, three. Four. Four of them, standing over by the Pronto Pup stand. One of them, the one in the orange T-shirt, looked familiar.

———

Sweety was able to fit the entire Pronto Pup into his mouth without swallowing. He held it there, cheeks distended, and stared at the girl who had sold it to him. She wouldn't meet his eyes. He grinned, his lips parting to show her the floury, meaty, mustard-yellowed mass that strained at his teeth.

Tigger said, "C'mon, let's go do some rides, man."

Sweety forced his lips over the corn dog and began to work his jaw back and forth as he fell in behind Tigger. Pork gave Dean a look, shrugged, and followed.

Dean thought, This is like being the bionic man, the terminator. He was sweating like a pig, but that was okay. He'd left his jacket back in Tigger's car, and that helped. With just the T-shirt on, he could stay cool. He liked the way the .45 felt in his waistband, and the bulge it made in the T-shirt. He would be cool and bionic, cruising the fair with his bionic pards. He could feel his joints as he walked: snick, snick, snick. He could hear his engine humming.

———

Carmen admired the face she had created. The pinto beans formed a smooth layer over the tortilla disk. Two black olives made eyes. A green olive nose. A white sour-cream smile. Shredded lettuce hair. Who did it look like? She pulled off the lettuce. James Dean! No. It wasn't quite right. She moved the olives farther apart.

"I'm out of lettuce," Juanita said.

"Need three deluxe and two bean," Sophie called back. "Carmen! Let's get a move on. What are you doing back there?"

"She's making faces again," Juanita said.

Sophie shouted, "Carmen!"

Carmen's feet flexed, popping her a couple of inches into the air.

"I told you not to do that. Quit acting silly and do your job, girl!"

Regretfully, Carmen folded the tortilla face into a burrito, wrapped it, began again.

———

Axel was strolling up the mall toward the Taco Shop when Kirsten ran up to him, breathless.

"Mr. Speeter! I saw that guy."

Axel cupped her shoulders in his hands. "What guy?"

"That guy they say beat up Mr. Fabian. That skinhead guy."

"Where?"

Kirsten pointed down Carnes Avenue. "Down by the Giant Slide. He was with some other guys, some other skinhead guys."

Axel dropped his hands and started back down the mall, his jaw clamped so tight he could feel his bridge flexing.

Chapter

29

"THAT FUCKIN' TIGGER," Pork said. "He does this shit all the time." He reached in his pocket and came out with his fist wrapped in brass. "You can't take the little shit anywhere without him pissin' somebody off."

A pair of cowboy-hatted young studs had Tigger up against the side of the Headless Woman trailer, one of them holding Tigger's arms, the other slapping him in the face. After each blow he shouted at Tigger, "What did you say?"

Tigger kept replying, "Fuck you." They all seemed to be having a good time.

Sweety charged with his fist held straight out and hit the first cowboy on the side of his neck. The cowboy bounced off the aluminum side of the trailer and slid to the ground. Dean, not sure what was going on, followed Pork, who jumped on the other cowboy's back and pounded him several times on the temple with his metal-sheathed fist. The cowboy was spinning around, trying to throw him, when Sweety came in with his big fists locked together and brought them both up under the cowboy's jaw. The sound of that made Dean's stomach roll.

The cowboy went down hard. Tigger, bleeding from his nose, was kicking the other one, who was too dazed to resist. Pork grabbed Tigger and pulled him away. Several people had stopped to watch.

"Let's get the fuck out of here," Pork said. They moved out through the crowd, Pork looking pissed off, brushing dirt from his shoulders, Sweety with his arm locked around Tigger's neck, giving him knuckle raps on his hairless skull, Tigger going, "Ow, ow, ow . . ."

"What was that all about?" Dean asked.

"Our Tigger has trouble relating to people," Pork said over his shoulder. "Can't say three words in a row without somebody wanting to jump up and down on his ugly little face."

Dean's breathing slowed. Sweety had released Tigger and caught up with Dean and Pork. Tigger's face was flushed, and he was wearing a big gray grin.

Dean said, "Wipe your nose, would you?"

Tigger laughed and wiped the blood on his sleeve. "Man, those fuckers never fuckin' knew what hit 'em!" he said, kicking the air. "Fuckin' Sweety, man, pow! Like a fuckin' tank, man. Damn!"

"You're gonna get us killed one of these days," Pork said. "Go mouthing off to some guy, and it turns out he's got six friends."

"That would be okay," said Sweety.

Pork made a sour face. "I don't know about you guys, but I could use a blast."

With over a hundred thousand people milling about the fairgrounds, it was tough finding a private place where four guys could sit down and do a little crank. Tigger thought he knew a spot over near the grandstand where they could squeeze in between an egg roll joint and the back wall of a mechanical horse race game, but when they got there it was full of high school kids passing a joint. Tigger wanted to kick them out, but Pork said what do you want to do, fight or get high? "I mean, let's get our priorities straight here. We already had one fight, right?"

Sweety finally said, after they had wandered around for twenty minutes or so, "We just sit down someplace and fuckin' do it."

"Too many cops around," Pork said.

"I don't see no cops."

"Yeah," said Tigger. "Let's just do it. What do you say, Dean?"

Dean shrugged, going with the flow.

"You guys ain't on probation," Pork complained. "You guys get cracked, it's no big deal. I fucking go back to Stillwater for another three years."

Dean agreed with that.

"You guys don't got to do it with us," Tigger said.

"It's my shit!"

Tigger said, "You guys can each go in the can. Me and Sweety, we'll just do it here. Fuck 'em." He pointed at a patch of flattened brown grass between the curb and the sidewalk.

Pork didn't like it, but he didn't have an argument ready, so he handed the paper to Tigger. Dean and Pork crossed the street and watched Sweety and Tigger sit right there in front of a hundred thousand people and snort crystal, scooping it from the paper with a Popsicle stick, staring down anyone who gave them a double look. Pork frowned as he watched Sweety treat himself to an extra blast before refolding the paper. Sweety grinned and waved.

———

Dean couldn't get the hang of the dodgem cars. Sweety and Tigger had him pinned down; every time he got moving, one or the other of them would slam into him from the side. He was glad when it was over. Pork, who had been watching, laughed and punched him on the shoulder. "Now you know why I don't do dodgem cars," he said.

Dean rubbed his shoulder. "Let's go see if Carmen showed up yet. I'm getting hungry."

"Go ahead," Sweety said. "We'll be around someplace. I want to go see the freaks."

"Maybe we could get some free burritos or something. I bet she'd feed us." Dean didn't want to be alone. He had a good buzz going with the meth, and he was getting off on the skinhead energy. "Come on, we can stop at the Beer Garden. I'll buy you guys a beer."

"C'mon, Sweety," said Pork. "Let's go see Dean's bitch. We can do the freaks later."

Sweety was clicking his teeth together, swinging his head back and forth, looking like a big lizard on the prowl. Dean started to say something, then noticed Pork shaking his head. Pork gestured in the direction of the Beer Garden, and he and Dean started walking. "He gets real pumped sometimes, and you got to be careful," said Pork.

Dean looked back over his shoulder. Sweety was following them, trailed by Tigger. "He'll follow us, but you can't argue with him when he gets this way. I seen him once throw this guy. Just picked him right up and threw him about ten feet like he was a shot put."

"What did the guy do?"

"You mean to get tossed? He was wearing a baseball cap. Sweety don't like baseball caps. That might've been it. With Sweety you never know. This was downtown, right in the middle of the day on Hennepin Avenue. The guy landed and just up and started running, so no harm done, but this other time he went after this cop, and the next thing you know there was three cops beating on him with their sticks, and Sweety, he don't even care, he's just beating on them right back. They were hitting him on the head with their sticks and every-thing, and it took the three of them it seemed like hours to knock him down. Cops all had nosebleeds and shit. Sweety, blood all over his head, was just having a good old time. Point is, he's got no judg-ment and he's about as strong as the Incredible Hulk. We used to call him that, but he likes Sweety better."

"So what are you telling me?"

"Just that when he's like this he doesn't care what happens. You just got to be real easy around him, he gets this way. Couple beers might calm him down some. He likes beer. It makes him happy, usually."

Dean bought a round of watery Leinenkugels at the Beer Garden, then he bought another round. Sweety was making him nervous, staring at people and sticking his tongue out about a yard, with that FUCK ME scrawled across his forehead. Dean didn't like the way he was making his jaw muscle twitch. He said, "You guys want a hot dog or something?" Nobody did, so they had another beer. Except for wor-rying about Sweety, Dean still felt great, had a nice buzz running up and down the back of his neck, eyes getting sharper all the time. Crys-tal clear. Hanging with these guys, looking dangerous, cruising on the meth, the good stuff, made in America, makes you faster and stronger and smarter and improves the eyesight too. That was some-thing he really liked, how good it made him see. Not like coke, which was for niggers and yuppies, or like weed, which was for punks and hippies. Yeah, it was a good feeling. Not like Carmen and her Vali-ums, falling asleep all the time. Dean liked the wound-up, tight-jawed power he got from the meth, and he liked the smooth-rolling easy confidence that came from being with his new friends. He liked the feeling of the .45 stuck in the waistband of his jeans, the barrel just touching the tip of his dick, the grip barely concealed by Carmen's Bugs Bunny T-shirt. If you knew what to look for, you could see the shape pushing through the thin orange cotton. He liked the way it felt when he walked. He wasn't so sure, though, about Sweety, who was now sitting in this big room full of guys, half of them wearing baseball caps, Sweety all wound up, his eyes fixed forward, his head swinging back and forth, jaw working, neck muscles bulging, blinking now and again. He made Dean think of a double-barreled sawed-off he'd seen back in Omaha. Some guy had cut it off right across the chamber, letting most of the shell stick out past the end of the barrel; it was about as close as you could get to a hand grenade—pull the trigger and who knows? Nobody'd ever had the nerve to shoot the thing. Sweety looked like that, like his eyes were those two red plastic twelve-gauge shells full of shot sticking out an inch and a half, hanging out there looking for some excuse to explode.

Sweety finished his third jumbo beer, and Pork, who kept giving Dean this raised-eyebrow look, filled Sweety's plastic cup from his own. Tigger was cutting into the tabletop with the key to his Caddy, writing the word FUCK, checking Sweety's forehead to make sure he was spelling it right. Pork spoke in a low voice to Sweety, who seemed not to hear him. A group of college-student types, all wearing baseball caps with college logos, sat down at the next table with their tall plastic cups full of beer. Sweety rotated his head and fixed his eyes on them. Dean thought, Here it comes.

Pork was on his feet now, tugging at Sweety's arm, then dropping it and walking toward the exit. Dean stood and followed, not looking back.

"He might just follow us out," Pork said. "He's mean as hell, but he's just a big old dog. He don't like to be alone."

They were out on the street, blinking in the afternoon sunlight, when Sweety and Tigger caught up with them. Pork said to Dean, "See?"

"Where we goin'?" Tigger asked.

Pork shrugged and looked up at Sweety. "How you doing?"

Sweety said, "Those fuckers."

"Who?" Tigger asked.

"Fuck you," Sweety said. "This place sucks. What the fuck are we doing here?"

"You want to go home?" Pork asked. "You want to go someplace else?"

"You want a taco?" Dean asked.

Sweety swung his head toward Dean. "Yeah," he said. "That's it. A fuckin' taco."

"Then let's go get us some tacos."

Dean got his good feeling back then; they were all back on track, back on the taco track. They were moving together, moving through the crowd with Dean on point. Behind him, sticking up a head above the rest, came Sweety, then Pork and Tigger hanging back, the four of them giving off that dangerous vibe that made people slide their eyes off and away.

Dean said, "All these guys are rich out here, every one."

Pork had his own buzz going, bopping his head back and forth to some tune buried deep in his head. Dean didn't think anybody was listening, but he kept talking anyway.

"All that cash money, man. We oughta just set up a business, score off a new one every day. That's what John Donne would do. All these guys with their money, man. Make 'em share the wealth." Dean searched his mind to see how it would be. The master plan would appear before him at any moment now, logical and complete. He would lay it out for Pork, Tigger, and Sweety. Show them how smart he was. He imagined the respectful look he would get from Pork, like he really knew his shit. Read them some more John Donne. He imagined himself talking to the old man, Axel, asking him questions. He reached a hand under his T-shirt and felt the warm wooden grip of the .45, imagined working the steel barrel between the old man's teeth. That would definitely be part of the plan, get the taco man sucking his own gun.

Except for one thing. It was probably all a figment of Carmen's stoned-out imagination. He had no reason to think the old man had that kind of money. It sure as hell wasn't sitting in his motel room. Reluctantly, Dean let the fantasy slide away. He would have to settle for some free tacos and just do the drug deal with his Tiny Tot money. That would be cool. He could turn the six K into twelve K when he got to Sioux Falls, and from there who knew? Set himself up as a distributor. The world was looking sharp, clear, and full of opportunities. They rounded the corner of the Food Building, slicing through a crowd of people in front of a busy french fry stand, and moved up the mall toward Axel's Taco Shop.

Pork said, "You say this guy has a million bucks in cash?"

"That's what Carmen says," Dean said. "Only she's probably full of shit."

They were passing Tiny Tot Donuts. Dean looked inside and stopped. Sweety ran into him and asked him what the fuck he was doing. Dean pointed into the donut stand. "See that guy with the bandage on his head? The little guy with the hat? I don't believe it. The guy, the guy is up and walking? I must be losing my touch."

As Dean spoke, the guy, Tiny Tot, looked up from his work and saw him and dropped the bag of sugar he was holding and disappeared out the back of the stand. Dean laughed. "Guy's scared shitless. You see him take off?" He turned back to Pork and Tigger.

Pork was grinning. Then his face closed and he said, "He don't look scared to me." He started walking backward. Dean turned and saw Tiny Tot, limping, coming around the side of the donut stand, red-faced, coming right at him with something in his hand.

Dean said, "Shit." He backed away, bumped into Sweety, moved sideways away from the donut guy. The kids in the donut stand were leaning out over the counter, watching, and the crowd of customers was now turning to see what was happening. Dean turned and ran twenty yards up the mall, then stopped and looked back. He didn't see the guy at first, then he did. What was he holding in his hand? Tiny Tot was limping, not moving fast but moving steady. Dean relaxed, knowing now that he could outrun the little man. He waited for him to get closer. When he was less than twenty feet away, Dean recognized the object in his hand. It was a bright, shiny revolver. Dean backed away, holding one hand out palm forward like a shield and reaching with the other hand for the .45 in his belt. He lost sight of Tiny Tot behind a cluster of people, then saw him again, still coming. Dean had the gun out now, trying to keep it pointed at Tiny Tot as the guy raised his own gun, holding it with both hands, pointing it at Dean's chest. Dean pulled on the trigger, but the .45 did not fire. Shit, what was wrong? Was the safety on? He looked down at the gun and tripped, falling backward, seeing as he went down Sweety's broad leather-clad back eclipse the image of the donut guy, and he heard a loud snap, then another, not so loud, then screams.

Chapter

30

SOPHIE WAS ON HER KNEES, trying to change a tank of Coca-Cola pre-mix, when she heard Kirsten say, "What's going on? Oh my God!" The urgency in Kirsten's voice brought Sophie quickly to her feet, and she cracked her head on the edge of the counter. Holding a hand to her head, she looked out across the mall. At first, she couldn't tell what she was seeing. Then she saw Carmen's bald friend, James Dean, stumbling backward through the crowd, crashing into people, spilling a little boy's sno-cone, the kid's mother shouting through a mouthful of cheese curd. The expression on James Dean's face was so wide-eyed and openmouthed that Sophie started to laugh. What was he doing? Then Kirsten screamed "Oh my God!" again, only louder and right in her ear.

Carmen pushed between them. "What?"

Sophie saw Tommy Fabian limping toward Dean, pointing with one hand, bringing up his other hand, holding something shiny. A huge bald man in a black leather jacket appeared, seeming to sprout up between the two, and dove at Tommy—Sophie was seeing it in slow motion now—and as the pistol flashed and bucked in Tommy's hands, Sophie saw it for what it was, heard the sharp explosion echo off the white brick sides of the Food Building as Tommy disappeared beneath the big man, then she heard another muted pop. The two men rolled, spilling a blue recycling can, white plastic cups exploding across the trampled grass mall. Those within a few yards of the tumbling pair fled, others rushed forward for a better view. The big man regained his feet and came up with one of Tommy's hands and a foot locked in his grip. Sophie heard a high-pitched keening. Tommy was screaming, and so were several people in the crowd. The big man swung his shoulders and his arms, and Tommy came up off the ground. Spinning like a shot-putter, the big man swung Tommy around in an airplane ride, a couple of complete orbits, then let go and sent the little man cartwheeling through the air. Tommy hit the lamppost hard, with an audible crack.

A man in a white shirt and black suspenders appeared from the crowd. Sophie recognized Axel the way she might suddenly recognize an actor in an unfamiliar role. Where had he come from? Sophie leaned out past the edge of the counter and shouted a warning, but her voice was devoured by the buzzing crowd.

———

Axel had been feeling a little silly. He had walked up and down Carnes Avenue twice, from the Giant Slide to the midway, doing a double take at every bald head in the crowd. No Bald Monkey.

What did he think he was going to do if he found the kid? Lecture him? Beat him up? Make a citizen's arrest? He shook his head, smiling at himself. Just another old fool rushing off half-cocked, too mad to think straight. Besides, the girl was probably mistaken. These teenage girls, always looking for drama.

He was only a few yards from the Taco Shop when he heard Kirsten scream "Oh my God!" His first thought was that Carmen had put her hand in the deep fryer. He ran to the back of the stand, saw that they were all, Sophie and Kirsten and Carmen, staring at something outside, on the mall. Someone is having a heart attack, was his next thought, then he heard the unmistakable sound of a gun firing once—loud and sharp—then again, muffled. He was afraid he knew whose gun. He rushed around to the front of the stand in time to see Tommy

Fabian's cartwheeling flight, arms and legs spread out like a sky diver's. Axel's senses grew suddenly, painfully acute. Everything stopped for an instant, formed a tableau: the big black-jacketed man, frozen in mid-stagger, Tommy striking the lamppost, and, a few feet away, sitting on his butt on the grass, Bald Monkey, holding his arm out toward the place where Tommy had been, one hand gripping a .45, the other hand fumbling with the trigger guard. Axel broke loose and ran, forcing his body through air gone thick as sand. He heard a strange howl, felt his throat shuddering, and realized that he was screaming. Bald Monkey's head swiveled, his eyes widened, he rose to his feet, and his arm came around with the gun. Axel saw the kid's thumb find the hammer, draw it back, saw the end of the barrel fix on his chest. He stopped, an arm's length away, eyes on the hole in the end of the barrel. The kid's hands were shaking. A glitter caught Axel's eye, and he saw a familiar horseshoe-shaped diamond ring on the kid's finger.

The sight of Tommy's ring shattered Axel's instinct for self-preservation. He threw himself forward, slapped his right hand down hard on the .45, a sharp pain lancing his finger. His palm wrapped warm steel. He hit the ground with his shoulder, rolled, came up with the .45 in his hand, swung it, giving it everything he had, slapping the steel slide hard against the kid's bald skull. He felt the shock travel up his arm, causing intense explosions of pain in his elbow and shoulder. He expected Bald Monkey to go down and stay down, but instead the kid jumped to his feet and took off like a startled rabbit, legs churning, his shiny head quickly melting into the crowd.

Axel pulled the hammer back, released his trapped and torn finger, and locked the safety. His right hand had gone numb.

The big skinhead had fallen to his hands and knees. Axel circled him and ran to Tommy, whose head had flopped sideways at an impossible angle. He tried to push Tommy's head back where it belonged, thinking that if he straightened it out quickly enough he might be able to undo what had happened. There was no response, no complaint, no sign of life. He looked up in time to see the big man crawling toward him.

"What did you do?" Axel shouted, the words rolling out deep and slow, as if shouted through molasses.

"I don't feel good," the big man said. A peculiar-looking bruise covered most of his forehead, blood pulsed from his chest. "I gotta lie down." He listed to his left, then relaxed and let himself fall onto his side on the grass.

Axel struggled to put it together, to make sense of things. The crowd had drawn back, forming a circle about thirty feet across, with Axel in the center. He looked down at the bleeding man, then back at Tommy. He didn't understand. The crowd was moving in on him, needing to be nearer the blood. He heard a siren. Axel stood. He could see two cops pushing through the crowd. He eased back through the crowd toward the taco stand, slipping the .45 into his pants pocket. There was nothing more he could do.

———

The fence at the north end of the fairgrounds finally stopped him. James Dean fell against the galvanized steel, pressed his face against the mesh, gasping for breath. He remembered his flight as a series of frozen, garish images. The back of his head radiated bright tendrils of pain. Had he been shot? He could not bring himself to touch it, afraid he might find a soft, pulpy mass of erupted brain tissue. Unlacing his fingers from the steel mesh, he turned his back to the fence, let himself slide down onto the grass, drew his knees up to his chest, wrapped his arms around his shins. His heart was beating too fast. How old did you have to be to have a heart attack?

The donut guy coming at him with a gun. Unbelievable. He could have been killed! And he'd lost his gun. How could he lose the gun? One moment he'd had it, then a glimpse of the old man, then Wham, something had hit him in the head, and suddenly he was running faster than he'd ever run before.

Curiosity overcame fear. Dean reached back and delicately probed his skull. It was swollen and tender, but not bleeding. The knowledge that his brain was still inside his skull helped him regain his feet. He had to get out of there. He had to get to Tigger's car. That was the most important thing.

It took him twenty minutes to cross the fairgrounds. He pushed through the turnstile in time to see Tigger's rusted Cadillac pulling out of the parking lot onto Como Avenue. Dean ran into the street, shouting at them to wait. He could see Pork's face through the tinted glass, looking right at him. The car turned away and accelerated, leaving behind an oily blue cloud. A blast from the horn of a Ford station wagon sent Dean hopping back to the curb. He couldn't believe it. Pork had been looking right at him. They left him there on purpose. A wave of dizziness, then of nausea, forced him to sit down on the curb. He closed his eyes, squeezed them until he saw flashes of light, remembering with a thud that he'd left his leather jacket in Tigger's back seat, its pockets solid with cash.

———

If someone had asked Axel how he was feeling, he would have said that he was feeling very, very old. And very sore. He would have said that his mind was hurting from too many fresh memories, and that his right arm was throbbing painfully, and that his finger was bleeding where he had caught it under the hammer. He would have said that it is the things you have to remember that kill you. Like it was the things that Tommy remembered that killed him. Memories and his friend Axel Speeter, who had busted him out of the hospital so he could keep his appointment with death.

If someone had asked Axel how he was feeling, he might have said something like that. Or he might have simply said that he felt lousy.

But nobody was asking.

He could hear the honking and short siren blasts of an ambulance working its way through the crowd. It pulled up onto the pounded grass mall, and two paramedics rushed toward Tommy and the bald giant. After a brief examination the paramedics relaxed, their movements becoming slower and more deliberate.

None of the police officers—there were five of them now—asked him how he was feeling. One of them, yellow-haired, still with a trace of his grandfather's Swedish in his voice, asked Axel if he had seen what happened. "Not a thing," Axel said. "When I got here, it was all over." The officer took his name and address anyway, then turned to Sophie.

Axel wrapped a few scoops of ice in a towel and held it against his elbow.

Sophie said she had been under the counter, changing the Coke canister. She hadn't seen a thing, either. Carmen, sitting on the grass behind the stand, hugging her knees to her chest, claimed she had been busy making a Bueno Burrito. The police officer wrote their full names and addresses on his clipboard. He had better luck with Kirsten Lund, who was anxious to share her experience. She related the events in detail, pointing to places on the mall, acting out the way Tommy had waved his gun, describing with her hands the way he had sailed through the air; her face was flushed and bright. Axel had never seen her so animated, her Nordic reserve forgotten in the thrill of violent events.

Making careful notes, the yellow-haired cop asked her to go over several points again. Axel listened carefully as Kirsten related the events of twenty minutes earlier.

So Tommy had been the shooter, just like he had thought, and it was the big man who had broken Tommy's neck. And Bald Monkey was mixed up in it somehow. Tommy chasing the monkey with his six-gun, that made sense. Tommy would do something like that, probably thinking he was going to make a citizen's arrest. Or maybe he was just going to shoot the kid. Either way, it hadn't worked.

The ambulance backed off the mall out onto Carnes Avenue and moved slowly through the crowd. The cop was asking Kirsten to tell him again, was the man from the Tiny Tot stand firing the gun before the big man tried to stop him? Or was he just waving it about in a threatening manner? What the hell difference does it make, Axel wondered, with both of them dead? Kirsten went over her story again, adding some detail about the wild look on Mr. Fabian's face. She described how Axel had run to help Mr. Fabian and how the big man had fallen almost on top of them. The cop frowned at Axel, who smiled grimly and nodded, relieved that Kirsten had not noticed or had at the least failed to mention that there were two guns and that one of them was at this moment distending the lining of Axel's right-hand pants pocket.

Axel put his hand on the gun, discovering a prideful place inside himself. He'd disarmed the little shit, just like that. And given him one hell of a headache to boot. Bald Monkey must have a thick skull to take a hit like that and then go running off. He'd think twice before messing with Axel Speeter again. Axel inhaled deeply, taking in the smells of the restaurant—the hot oil, the tangy aroma of fresh salsa, the heady mix of scents from Sophie, Kirsten, and Carmen. He could even smell himself, the old boomer, reeking a little after defending his fliers. Axel shifted the ice pack to a new spot on his elbow and smiled, seeing himself as this grizzled old kangaroo. Then it hit him again, low and hard. Tommy Fabian was dead. He closed his eyes, shutting out the color and heat of the fair, letting the cold truth settle deep in his gut.

Chapter

31

JAMES DEAN SAT ON THE CURB outside the fairground fence, waiting for the numbness to pass. He needed an idea, an impulse, a reason to move. It could have been anything at all. A pang of hunger, an itch that needed scratching, a question demanding an answer. He kept seeing Pork's face in the car window. The donut guy pointing the silver gun. Sweety's broad, black-jacketed back. Tigger nailing him with the dodgem car, pinning him against the rail, not letting him move, laughing. He could not move now. How could he stand up? He had nothing left, no place to go.

A horse stopped in front of him, nearly crushing his foot. He looked up and saw a helmeted cop sitting on the beast, leaning over, asking him if he was okay.

Dean said he was fine. He said he was waiting for somebody to pick him up.

The cop gave him the look, waited for him to stand up, then clopped off down the fenceline, his horse leaving behind a pile of steaming manure. Dean tried to remember a line from Donne, something he had read weeks before. Something like if you cut off part of your body, you save what is left, but it's better to cut off part of a dead man. Something like that. He wished he had the book, but he had left it back in Carmen's room. He started walking along the curb, placing one foot after the other.

Everything seemed complicated and uninteresting; he needed one clear idea, something to get him going. Or maybe what he needed was some more crank. He thought about some other things he wanted, listed them in his mind.

His book. At the motel.

Carmen? Did he want Carmen? He wasn't exactly aching for her, but it was nice to have company.

His money. Shit. What was he thinking of, leaving his jacket in Tigger's car? Stupid, stupid. He had forgotten to be smart. He didn't even know their real names—he sure as hell wasn't going to find a Tigger or a Pork in the phone book.

He stopped walking. Would Tigger and Pork be dumb enough to return to that basement after ripping him off? It didn't seem possible. On the other hand, he had nothing to lose by going there and waiting for them. He dug in his pockets, coming out with two twenties, a five, and a few ones. Whatever else, he would need some money, and soon.

A block ahead of him, an ambulance pulled out of the fairgrounds, lights dead, and drove up Como Avenue. First thing he had to do, he had to get out of there. Maybe just get on one of the buses and figure out where he was going later. He had just turned back toward the bus stand when he saw the old man, Axel, not fifty feet in front of him, crossing the street toward the parking lot, moving slow, looking like he was about two hundred years old. Dean froze. The old man didn't see him. Dean felt his face grow warm with anger and dread. He watched until Axel faded into the parking lot. As soon as the old man was out of sight, the heat in Dean's face flowed right down into his balls.

It felt good. Suddenly he felt his perspective shift, as if he had stepped around a dark corner and found himself in full sunlight. He had been thinking that everything was fucked up, but what if it wasn't? If you looked at it another way, he was the luckiest guy in the world to come through all that with just a bump on the head. He *could* have been shot, like Sweety, or had his neck broke like Tiny Tot. As it was, he still had his moves to make, and nobody to stop him. The old man had given him his best shot. Next time, next time he'd be ready, he'd be the man in charge.

It was all about attitude. You had to be smart, and you had to have the right attitude. You couldn't afford to feel sorry for yourself. It was the same thing as doing time. You had to be cool and smart, and you couldn't afford to get all emotional.

He recalled another line from the book. Mostly, reading John Donne had been a show-off thing, a way to prove to Mickey that he wasn't the illiterate she took him for, a way to fuck with Carmen's head, a way to impress Tigger and Sweety and Pork. But there were a few times when he'd sat by himself and tried to make sense of the words. It was nothing like reading a newspaper or magazine. Everything was spelled weird. He could pick his way through a few pages, but the type would quickly fuzz into a gray, meaningless mass.

But then some stuff would jump out at him. This one thing was coming back to him. Shit, he wished he hadn't left the book in Carmen's room. But he remembered the one line, word for word: *This Soule, now free from prison, and passion, hath yet a little indignation. . . .*

———

Carmen remembered a thing she used to do. When she was a little girl and she and Sophie were living in the projects up north of University, she had learned to turn the world into a cartoon. Sometimes she could force it, other times it would just happen on its own. Colors would brighten and flatten, and people would form black outlines and move in little jerks, like Yogi Bear. In the cartoon world, she would get her own black outline, and she could make her arms and legs stretch or shrink or get heavy or change color or disappear. Usually she would do this at night in her bed, closing her eyes and watching it happen, but sometimes she could make it happen outside in the daylight. Carmen had not turned the world into a cartoon or even thought about it for many years until now, watching Sweety get shot and Tommy Fabian flying through the air and Axel bending over him and Dean standing there and then running and the cops asking her questions, and all of a sudden the outlines came back and the colors were cranked way up. Carmen looked at her hand and made her fingers stretch.

"What are you doing?" Sophie asked.

The cartoon version of Sophie was pretty, Carmen thought. Prettier than the regular Sophie. She looked a lot like Wilma Flintstone. No wrinkles. "I'm looking at my hand," she said.

"I can see that. We've got a business to run, don't forget. People don't stop eating just because somebody gets killed."

Carmen looked toward the front of the stand. "We don't have any customers," she said. "What do you want me to do?"

"I don't know. Clean something. Never mind. Take your break. Be back here in a half hour, okay? Kirsten and I will handle things. You get out of here—you're dangerous. You and your friend."

Carmen said, "Friend?"

"Your friend with the gun. Just because I didn't tell the police, don't think I didn't see him."

"You mean Dean? It was Tommy shot the gun."

"Your friend had a gun too. I saw it in his hand. Now get out of here, take a break."

Carmen shrugged and left the stand. Who knew *what* Dean was doing? Him and his cranked-up hairless friends. She was glad she and Dean hadn't found the money in Axel's room. That was crazy, the idea of going to Mexico with Dean. A sense of release rolled up her body; she did a little dance step, causing a few people to veer aside, giving her room. An image appeared in her mind of a Mexican village on the sea, a thick packet of U.S. dollars in her purse, an icy pitcher of margaritas, and a man. Not James Dean, but a new man, with hair. Curly hair on his head and on his chest, and buried in it a nice gold necklace. Tropical sun beating down on them, a nice breeze coming in over the surf . . .

Without warning, the image faded and she became suddenly aware of herself as alone, without substantial funds, standing in the midst of a hundred thousand corn-dog-eating yokels. She was nobody, nothing, going nowhere. The realization nearly caused her knees to buckle. She felt it in her stomach, and in a band of pressure against the nape of her neck. She stumbled toward an empty bench a few yards away. Carmen knew what was happening. She was crashing, coming down off the meth. She'd come down off Dexedrine before, and coke, but never crank. This was different, more intense. She sat on the bench and squeezed her eyes shut and forced her thoughts away from herself, back to the image of a wad of money. Thinking about money was good. That was the trick to crashing— you had to keep grabbing onto the good thoughts. If you let the bad thoughts in, it would get bad. She summoned up the image of Axel's coffee cans.

Cans and cans and cans. She felt her chest swell, her breasts rise. The thought of the money stroked her body like a plunge into warm water. She could see herself walking along the ocean toward her Mexican beach house. She could see a shelf in her bedroom lined with a row of Folgers cans, cans full of green corn cash tamales.

Axel's nylon socks. Like a slow-motion punch to the stomach, the thought brought her crashing down again. How could she think about the money when she didn't know where the money had gone? She tried to think of places he might have hidden it, but she couldn't think while she was crashing. She squeezed her teeth together until the pain in her jaw shattered her thoughts, focusing her senses on the outside world. A few yards away, a cartoon Indian was selling cartoon fry bread to cartoon fairgoers. The outlines were there, but the colors seemed muted. She watched him until his movements began to recycle.

Carmen lit a cigarette and sat back and closed her eyes. She was getting a new buzz now, not unpleasant, a sort of smooth, rolling vibration. She imagined herself floating over the fairgrounds. She thought about the places the money might be. In Axel's room. In Axel's truck. Her imagination stopped there. In his room or in his truck. What did he do with the money every night? He put it in his burlap shoulder bag. They walked to his truck. He dropped her off at her room. In the morning they drove back to the fair. Was the bag empty in the morning? She thought that it was. Her mind drifted back to an imagined Mexico.

When she opened her eyes, the cartoon show had ended. Objects had become dull and three-dimensional. How long had she been sitting there? Had she been sleeping? Carmen wasn't sure. When she stood up, she knew from the way her legs felt that she'd been there for quite a while.

Everything felt and looked different. The day crowd had begun to thin out. There was a general movement toward the fairground exits, eaters of cheese curds and Pronto Pups and Tiny Tot donuts and sno-cones moving slowly and uncomfortably toward the turnstiles, parents herding flocks of exhausted kids, ignoring their automatic whining about having to leave so soon.

It was still daylight, but the crowd was changing. The after-work crowd had begun to arrive: the teenagers and the beer drinkers, adults in groups of two and four, people coming to see the show at the grandstand or to ride the Ferris wheel in the dark or to stroll up and down the clattering, blinking chaos of the midway, trying to win a four-foot-tall Barney. There were fewer farmers, fewer children, and fewer old folks. The people looked fresher, not yet bagged out from massive infusions of sugar and lard.

Before returning to the taco stand, Carmen went to one of the rest rooms and unfolded the square of paper Pork had given her. She licked the last traces of crystal from Nancy Reagan's smiling face, then flushed her image down the toilet.

Sophie was loading the fryer with tortillas when Carmen entered the stand.

"Sorry I took so long," Carmen said.

Sophie said, "You're fired."

———

Axel fiddled with the truck radio until he stumbled across a classical music station. He was thinking that it would make him feel better to listen to a wordless yet coherent progression of sounds. It wasn't working; the sounds were too complex and insistent. He turned off the radio and sat in silence, giving in to the flickering memories of Tommy alive, Tommy dead. Trying not to think about the Bald Monkey, struggling to find a tolerable balance between anger and grief. He would feel the tears mounting his lower eyelids, will them to come to wash it all away, then his jaw would clench and anger would squeeze his eyes dry. It was too soon to grieve. He sat and let his mind turn this way and that, like a driver lost in a strange city.

Carmen rapped on the window, startling him. He touched a dry eye with the back of his hand and rolled down the window. "What's the problem?" he asked, his voice ragged. He cleared his throat.

Carmen was smoking a cigarette, kicking the packed dirt with her pink-and-white Reeboks.

"What's the problem?" he asked again, forcing concern into his voice.

She flicked her cigarette straight down and ground it out with her toe, crossed her arms, and looked up at Axel. "Can Sophie fire me?"

"Why would she want to do that?"

"You got me. She says I'm fired."

"What did you do?"

"Nothing. I took a break, and when I got back she says, 'You're fired.'"

Axel waited.

"Maybe I was a few minutes late getting back. I don't know. Can she fire me? I mean, am I working for Sophie or am I working for you?" She had her arms crossed, squeezing her breasts in her Axel's Taco Shop T-shirt. Her eyes half scared and half angry, she waited for Axel to pronounce his judgment.

Axel said, "Carmen, what do you want me to do? Sophie's running the stand; I can't just tell her to hire you back."

"So fire *her*!"

Axel said, "Why?"

"I can run the stand better than Sophie any day. She's so cheap she's got us counting olives. I put four olive slices on a tostada, and she's all over me. People like lots of olives."

"I can't do that, Carmen. Your mother's my partner now, you know."

"She's what?"

"I took her on as a partner, and part of the deal is she runs the stand the way she wants. Maybe if you go back and talk to her . . ." He shrugged. Carmen was lighting another cigarette.

"No way. You don't know my mom."

She's right, Axel thought. Both of them are right. Sophie was probably right to fire Carmen, and Carmen was right—no way would Sophie change her mind so easily. She would stay mad for at least a day, maybe longer. If he told her to hire Carmen back, she would fight him on it through the last day of the fair. He sighed and wondered how he was going to keep his family together.

Carmen paced a circle on the packed dirt. The sun was near the horizon. She moved in and out of the shadow of the truck, smoking her cigarette with rapid, jerking motions. My family, Axel thought.

He had never before thought of it that way. Or maybe he had, but without using the word out loud in his mind. What did that make Carmen—his daughter? Something like that, he decided. Or something else. In any case, he knew what he should do. He should let the women deal with each other, keep his nose out of it.

But he knew he wouldn't.

"Tell you what," he said. "Let me talk to Sophie. You stay out of her way tonight, and we'll see about tomorrow."

"What am I supposed to do till then? Can I take the truck back to the motel? I'll come back tonight and pick you up."

Axel hesitated, imagining himself standing in the empty parking lot at one o'clock in the morning, his shoulder bag full of money, waiting for Carmen to show up, thinking about her flat on her back at the Motel 6, snoring at the television.

"I have a better idea," he said. "How about if you take the bus?"

———

The sky glittered with the nightly fireworks show as Axel returned to the Taco Shop. Sophie was frying a final batch of taco shells, getting ready for the small rush of business that would come after the grandstand show let out. She looked at Axel, her jaw set, saying nothing. Kirsten was gone, her shift over at nine o'clock. Sonya, one of the part-time girls, leaned out over the counter, chewing on a plastic straw and watching the groups of people drift slowly toward the exits. Axel decided to let Sophie break the news to him right away.

"Where's Carmen?" he asked.

"I fired her," Sophie said.

"Oh. Well, she probably deserved it." He decided to leave it at that for now. "How did we do today?"

Sophie hesitated. "She took a three-hour break. I don't have to put up with that from any of my girls."

"It's your show, Sophie. So how did we do today?" He pointed at the cash box under the counter.

"I'd guess close to six thousand. Maybe more. And no help from Carmen."

"You must've been busy. Who do you have for tomorrow?"

"Juanita starts at eight, Kirsten comes in at twelve. Sonya won't be here."

Axel nodded. "It's gonna be busy. Supposed to be a nice day, and they got Kenny Rogers in the grandstand. You want me to find you another girl?"

"We only have three days to go. I don't want to be training somebody new right now."

"I don't blame you."

Sonya said, "I need two tacos and a Bueno and one nachos." Axel watched Sophie prepare the order. He could see she was tired; her movements had the needful precision of one whose energy reserves are dangerously low.

"You know," Axel said as he watched her loading the pair of tacos, "it might be smart to keep Carmen on tap, just in case you need her. Get her in here for the lunch rush, so you can take a break."

Sophie, focused on making the tacos, did not reply. Axel waited, letting her process his words.

"What makes you think she'd even show up?" Sophie said after handing the order to Sonya.

"Maybe she won't, but we'd be no worse off than before, would we?"

"I fired her."

"That's right, you did. I was just thinking that we might want to keep our options open."

"You can keep your options open. I have a stand to manage. I can't afford to count on her."

"You're right," Axel said. "You can't count on her."

"She's completely unreliable."

"I suppose if she did show up, though, and we were really busy, you might find some use for her."

Sophie considered. "We don't need her."

"I know that. But maybe we can use her."

Sophie shrugged. "She's fired as far as I'm concerned. She shows up here, she's working for you. It comes out of your share."

"I'll talk to her," Axel said.

———

Timothy Alan Skeller, aka Tigger, lowered himself feet first through the basement window, the pointed toes of his duct-taped boots scrabbling against the cinder-block wall. He dropped the last ten inches to the concrete floor, then felt around in the dark for the end of the extension cord, muttering to himself. "Where's the, shit, fuckin' thing—" A beer can crackled under his boot. "Fuckin' fuck shit, fuckin' shit." He dug in his pockets. "Goddamn, goddamn son-of-a-bitch." Two coins fell from his pocket and clacked on the concrete. "Fuck! Shit!" He found the matchbook in his hip pocket, fumbled loose a match, made three attempts to light it before it flared up, casting a weak orange glow.

The extension cord was not where he had dropped it. Tigger had perhaps a half second to wonder where it had gone, then had his question answered when a length of thick orange electrical cord dropped past his face and tightened over his Adam's apple.

Chapter

32

AXEL UNTIED HIS SHOES, placed them at the foot of his bed, set the .45 on the nightstand, then carefully arranged himself on top of the spread and stared up at the ceiling, arms crossed over his chest. He knew he wouldn't be able to sleep. Too much bouncing around inside his head. Closing his eyes, he tried to find a comforting thought. After a few minutes, he reached down and unsnapped the front clips of his suspenders. The bands of pressure on his shoulders disappeared, but his arm still throbbed, his finger burned, and the money hidden in his bed—over twenty thousand dollars now—produced a dull ache in the center of his back. He wasn't sure he could actually *feel* the money. It was tucked down in the box spring. In theory, it should have been undetectable to anyone lying on the mattress. But it didn't matter whether the sensation was a physical thing, since it was undeniably there, pressing up at him.

They'd been in his room once. He couldn't count on a simple dead bolt to keep them from coming back, and maybe next time they'd look a little harder. Carmen had to figure that he was stashing the money in his room. Was she still hooked up with that kid, that Bald Monkey? Axel took a deep breath. Carmen was driven by forces he could not understand. Why had she gotten involved with a punk like that in the first place? He could see it if the kid was good-looking or had something going for him. Maybe she was just going through a delayed adolescent thing, trying to drive her parents crazy— Shit! He was doing it again, thinking of her like she was his daughter. He shifted the position of his legs. The fight with the kid had really taken it out of him—he must have used every muscle in his body. He could already feel his limbs stiffening. His right elbow felt like a throbbing ball of concrete. It would be a rough morning.

He wondered how Bald Monkey was feeling. Did he have a little headache? Axel hoped so. He hoped he had a huge one. He hoped his head hurt so bad he'd go back to wherever the hell he came from. That was what he hoped, but what he feared was that the kid wasn't finished. He had a feeling about Bald Monkey, the same way he'd had a feeling about those guys in Deadwood, three decades ago.

One thing he had to do for sure, he had to do something about this cash. He couldn't just leave it in his room. He had to move it, put it with the rest of his money. Unfortunately, when he had entombed the bulk of his fortune, he hadn't thought about how difficult it would be to make deposits.

The thought of digging made his elbow throb even harder.

———

What Sam O'Gara hated most about middle-of-the-night phone calls was that when the fucker went off, goddamn Chester started howling. And when Chester howled, then Festus, he'd jump up on the bed and start licking for all he was worth. It was like a goddamn air raid siren going off in his bedroom, then getting drowned in dog spit.

He sat up, throwing Festus and his blankets off the bed in one motion. "All right, goddamn your tongue— Chester! You shut up 'fore I have your balls lopped!" He swung his legs off the bed and staggered toward the kitchen, where his vintage Princess dial phone was giving forth another insistent ring, followed immediately by another howl from Chester. "Goddamn it, I'm coming!" He snatched the phone off its base and shouted into the receiver, "If this is a wrong number,

I'm gonna find you and shove this fucker right up your misdialing ass, you sorry son-of-a-bitch!"

"Hi, Sam, it's me."

"Jesus fucking Christ, Ax. You know what happens in this house when the phone goes off?"

"Let me guess. You use a lot of bad words, then you answer it."

"You don't know the fucking half of it." Chester and Festus sat in front of him, panting happily now that they'd done their job.

"Sam, I've got to tell you something."

Sam shook his head, suddenly wishing he hadn't picked up the phone. Festus whined nervously. Chester slumped to the floor and rested his chin on his paws.

"Sam, I can't believe I didn't call you before. I must've been all messed up in my head. I just thought to call you now."

"Jesus Christ, Ax." Sam's voice came out soft and ragged. "You're gonna tell me somebody's dead, ain't you?"

"Tommy."

"Aw, f'Chrissakes."

That was the other thing he hated about middle-of-the-night phone calls. It was always some goddamn awful thing he didn't want to know about.

—

Tigger drove with one hand on the wheel, touching his neck gently with the other. "I swear to God, man, it wasn't my idea to leave you there, man." His voice sounded hoarse. "It was that fuckin' Pork, man." He swallowed, winced.

"You were driving the car," Dean said.

"He told me if I stopped he'd fucking kill me."

"And he took my jacket."

"What was I supposed to do? You seen the guy. I mean, Sweety was big, but Pork, man, the dude's kinda scary, y'know?"

"Scarier than me?" Dean asked.

Tigger shifted his eyes to Dean, then looked back at the road. "Not right now he ain't," he said.

"Where is this place?"

"We're almost there, man."

"You think he's still gonna be there?"

"He'll close the fucker up."

"Good."

"Here it is." Tigger turned into a small parking lot crowded with pickup trucks, Chevy Camaros, and Harley-Davidsons. A flickering red neon sign read: THE RECOVERY ROOM.

Dean said, "How come you aren't still in there drinking?"

Tigger pulled his car into one of the few open spaces. "I got eighty-sixed, those fuckers."

"Show me which one's his bike."

Tigger pointed at a black-and-silver Harley. "The one with the rebel flag on the tank, okay? Can I go home now?"

"No." Dean pulled the keys from the ignition. "We're partners now, asshole. Partners stick together."

Tigger drew his head back, squinting at Dean. The speed and the lack of sleep made Tigger look much older, like maybe twenty-three. "Whaddya mean?"

"You want to make some money, don't you?"

"Well . . . sure."

"Good. Then we're partners."

"You mean, like, half and half?"

"We'll work something out," Dean said as he opened the door. "I need something out of your trunk."

"What? There ain't nothing in there."

"Nothing? You got a spare tire, right?"

"Sure. Only it's flat."

"That all? You don't have anything to go with it?"

Tigger struggled to understand. "What, you mean like a jack?"

"I was thinking more like a tire iron. You got one of those, don't you, partner?"

Tigger shook his head. "Nope." He brightened. "But I do got a crowbar."

———

Pork was feeling hard and tight and fast. His new jacket squeezed his shoulders, constricting his movements. It made him move different, made him swing his upper body with each step, giving him a don't-fuck-with-me walk like a weight lifter's, only much more dangerous-looking. He liked the way that felt. He especially liked the feel of all that money hanging against his sides. Who would've thought it would be so easy? That punk Dean, thinking he was some kind of gangster. What an idiot! He couldn't believe it when he'd stuck his hands in the jacket pocket and come out with a fistful of twenties.

With that kind of money, Pork could have made a lot of friends at The Recovery Room, but that wasn't his style. Anybody could make friends. What Pork wanted was respect. He went for the lone biker image, parked himself at a table in the back of the bar, flashed some cash, got himself a whole bottle of Jack Daniel's, then lay back and watched the scene, seeing himself as a modern-day Mafia boss. Guys that knew him would swing by, nod, then fade. That was cool. One of the bitches sat down with him for a while, grabbed his hand, and put it on her tit. He gave her a vicious squeeze, which got rid of her in a damn hurry. He didn't need any of her biker cooties, nor anybody else's. The kind of money he had now, he could afford the good stuff. Right now he just wanted to relax and moderate his amphetamine buzz with a few shots of Jack.

By the time the bar closed, Pork was ready to hop on his Harley and take a ride out in the country, letting the night air scour him clean. He sat and watched everybody else file out of the club. It was best to be the last to leave. That was the cool way to do it. Let everybody know he was in no hurry. He let the bartender give him a few looks, then got to his feet and did the don't-fuck-with-me walk over to the bar, slapped down a pair of twenties, headed for the door.

The first thing he saw—unbelievable!—some asshole sitting on his bike. More curious than angry, he walked across the dirt parking lot toward his Harley. The light from the flickering neon sign made it hard to see. He was only a few feet away when he recognized the figure on his bike as Tigger.

Pork said, "Man, what the fuck are you doing back here?" He saw Tigger's eyes shift, look past him. Pork had seen that look before. It was the look you saw in the prison yard when somebody was about to get a shank between the ribs. Instinctively, he ducked and twisted, bringing up an arm to protect his face. Something hit him hard on the elbow. He caught a snapshot of Dean's face, expressionless, then a blur of movement and an explosion of intense pain as the backswing caught him on the side of his neck. He fell, crashing into the

Harley, hearing Tigger shout something, hearing the bike crash to the asphalt, feeling the footrest jab into his kidney. The three ravaged points—elbow, neck, kidney—joined in a triangle of agony, and for a moment, as his vision filled with black bubbles, he thought he was passing out. He squeezed his eyes and rolled to the side, felt the gritty surface of the parking lot beneath his palms. He took a breath, heard the sound of air rushing into his body, tasted dust, opened his eyes. There was the packed dirt, the earth, right there in front of him, real and solid.

The worst of it is over, he thought. He knows he hurt me, knows he can have what he wants. Now we talk.

He turned his head, slowly. This was no time to play the tough guy. Again, Dean's face appeared in his eyes, looking as slack and dead as any mug shot. It was not a talking face, or even a fighting face. It was a killing face. Pork saw the hooked end of the crowbar silhouetted against the red neon. He tried to roll away, got one hand in front of his face just as the steel bar came chopping down. The force of the blow audibly snapped his fingers, slammed his hand into his cheekbone, his head into the packed dirt. He felt a scream in his throat, smelled the earth rising up to swallow him, heard the dull slapping sound of steel striking leather and flesh. He heard it again, then heard nothing at all.

Chapter

33

THE MORNING STARTED OUT cool and moist, with a dew point in the middle sixties. During the night, the picnic tables and benches on the mall had gathered an oily slick of moisture that remained until after eight o'clock, when the sun rose high and hot enough to steam it away.

Axel sat on his folding metal chair behind the Taco Shop, holding an ice-filled towel against his elbow, listening to Sophie and Juanita setting up for the day. Sophie gave her orders in a quiet voice, not her usual snapping tones. Fairgoers filtered slowly onto the grounds. All three Tiny Tot Donut stands were closed. A TV news team rolled in and shot some film of the dead stand on the mall, probably planning a follow-up report on violence at the state fair. People who had been coming to the fair for thirty years for their bag of minidonuts would walk right up to the plywood window covers and try to see in, unable to believe that they were to be denied their ritual. Often they would then come up to Axel's Taco Shop, not to buy tacos but to ask about Tiny Tot Donuts.

If they asked Sophie where they could get some donuts, she would direct them to the Tom Thumb Donut stand down on the midway, or to the Mini-Loops stand on Judson Avenue. If they asked Axel, he would simply respond by saying that the owner had passed away and deny all other knowledge. He could not bring himself to send customers to one of Tommy Fabian's competitors. Even if Tommy no longer cared, Axel did. He was in no mood to be reminded every five minutes that his oldest and best friend was gone. It was just as well. It would have killed Tommy to see all those customers walk away without their donuts.

Every now and then, one of Tommy's carny friends would walk up from the midway to pay his respects by standing silently in front of the Tiny Tot stand, smoking a cigarette. A few of them drifted farther up the mall to exchange a few words with Axel. They all seemed to take Tommy's death philosophically. One, Froggy Sims, the aging, chain-smoking mike man for Wee Wanda, the World's Smallest Woman, didn't want to leave.

"Tommy, he was a good un. Real old-time carny, him." Froggy put his cigarette in his crumpled mouth, made a pair of fists, clacked his rings together. The first time Axel had seen him do that, he'd wondered whether it was some obscure carny thing. He'd asked Tommy about it, and Tommy had said it was just Froggy's way of making sure you noticed his jewelry. Tommy hadn't cared much for old Froggy, but he'd always given him free donuts.

Axel shifted the ice pack to a new spot on his elbow. He resented this guy hanging around, making out like he'd been Tommy's best friend. He figured Froggy was mostly sad about losing his donut connection. The guy had about five thousand bucks in gold on him, not counting what was on his teeth, but he'd walk a half mile across the fairgrounds for free food.

"Use to run an alibi joint, me and him. Those were the days, I got to tell you."

"I bet they were," Axel said. "Listen, Froggy, you want a taco or something?" Maybe that would get rid of him.

Froggy made a face like he was surprised. "Jeez, Ax, that's white a you."

Axel smiled with his mouth and told Juanita to get Froggy a taco and a Coke.

Froggy said, "You don't got no Pepsi?"

By nine-thirty the outside temperature had risen to eighty-four degrees. It was going to be a hot one, a late-summer Minnesota sauna. Every third person in the state would say, at some point, "It's not the heat; it's the humidity."

The ice helped. Axel flexed his arm. The swelling had gone. It felt almost normal. He stared across the mall at the dead hulk of the Tiny Tot stand. Tommy's ghost was hovering over the mall, staring down at the boarded-up remnant of his life. Axel didn't want to know what that felt like, ever.

A familiar figure stopped in front of the Tiny Tot concession, then walked slowly up to Axel.

"Hey, Ax," said Sam.

Axel looked up. "What are you doing here?"

Sam lit a cigarette. "I'm not sure," he said. "I couldn't get no work done, thinking about Tom."

Axel nodded. He understood. Another of Tommy's friends, paying his respects.

"I didn't think he'd be the first one of us, Ax."

"Yeah? Who'd you think it would be?"

Sam spat out a fragment of tobacco, looked critically at his cigarette, then grinned at Axel. "Fact is, I thought it'd be you."

"Thanks a lot." Axel was not amused.

———

Carmen, still wearing yesterday's clothes, woke up with a headache. It wasn't a bad headache. In fact, it was the mildest one so far that week.

Someone was pounding on the door. She had the sense that it had been going on for some time.

"Just a minute!" She looked at the clock: ten-fourteen. "Who is it?"

"Management!"

Carmen opened the door. Bill Quist stood in the doorway and looked past her, smiling.

"Where's your friend?"

"What do you want?"

"I haven't heard from you lately. Is your friend still staying here?"

"No. He's gone."

"Oh. Mr. Speeter called. He says you're supposed to go in to work."

"I was fired."

Quist shrugged. "I don't know about that. I just know he called and asked me to wake you up and tell you."

"He could've just called my room."

"He's been trying all morning." He pointed. "Your phone's off the hook."

Carmen remembered dreaming about this incessant ringing noise, then making it stop.

"Did that key I loaned you work out?" Quist asked.

"What key?"

Quist laughed. "That's what I say: 'What key?' You were going to give me some money, remember?"

"No. Did Axel say anything else?"

"Just that you're supposed to go to work. How about you give me twenty bucks now and the rest later?"

Carmen slammed the door.

Quist blinked at the closed door, still smiling, then shrugged and walked back across the parking lot to his office. It was always worth asking. You never knew.

———

"You're leaving?"

"I called Carmen. She'll be here anytime now." Axel found a paper bag and started filling it with burritos.

"But—" Sophie looked at the line forming in front of the restaurant, shook her head like she couldn't believe it. "You're leaving *now*? Just me and Juanita?"

"Kirsten and Carmen should be here soon."

Juanita shouted over her shoulder. "I maybe need some help right now, you know."

"I'll be right there," Sophie said. She gave Axel a dark look. "Kirsten's an hour late, and you know Carmen."

Axel said, "I'll be back in an hour. Look, I've asked Sam to help out. He needs to be doing something. He'll be right back—he just went to the john."

"Sam O'Gara? I don't want him anywhere near here. I heard what he did to Tommy's donut mix."

"It's up to you. I gotta go, Sophie. Back in a couple hours, okay?" He added the paper sack of Bueno Burritos to his burlap bag, slung it over his shoulder, and walked across the mall. He heard her shout that it was goddamn well not okay, but he kept moving.

———

"Now where's he going?"

"How the fuck do I know?"

"He's got that bag with him."

"The money's in the bag?"

"Some of it is, I bet. C'mon, podna, let's get a move on." Dean stood up, his straw cowboy hat riding low on his forehead. He felt ridiculous. He wore a light-blue western-style shirt and a red paisley bandanna around his neck. The shirt was made of polyester or something, hot as hell, sticking to him like a sheet of glue. All three items had been purchased at a western-wear stand in the Coliseum. The only good thing was, next to Tigger he looked great.

Tigger had selected a colorful shirt with *Let's Rodeo* embroidered in rope letters, front and back. His hat was white felt with an outrageously high crown. It had cost fifty-nine bucks, but Dean figured it was worth it if it made the kid happy. He needed him, for now. But he'd drawn the line at new boots. They didn't have time. He planned to keep an eye on the old man every minute. This was serious business, and there would be no mistakes.

Somehow, Pork had managed to spend or lose over four thousand dollars during the few hours he'd had Dean's jacket. When Dean had discovered how little money was remaining, he'd told Tigger to drive back to The Recovery Room's parking lot and drive over him a couple times, just in case the beating hadn't killed him. Tigger had not responded well to that suggestion, so he'd let it go. He realized now that it wouldn't have been the smart thing to do. From now on, he was going to do only smart things. The plastic bag Pork had left in the chest pocket of Dean's jacket helped. It contained several grams of powdered methamphetamine. A few fat lines, and he'd got so smart it was like he could predict the future.

"Don't get too close," Dean said. One bad thing about wearing disguises on a day like this: He was sweating buckets. The speed made his sweat smell like chicken soup. Chicken soup running down his cheeks and trickling along his ribs. He smelled like a high school cafeteria.

"He ain't looking," Tigger said. "He's heading out through the gate."

"Going out to his truck."

"What're we gonna do?"

"Just stay cool, podna. We get in your car and follow him, see where he goes."

———

Kirsten Lund was late, and it wasn't her fault. It was her mom's fault. Kirsten had made a big mistake, a huge mistake, a mondo mistake, when she'd told her mom about the fight at the fair.

"Young lady, if you think I am going to let you go back to that horrible taco shack, you have got another think coming."

Wow. Kirsten never thought her mom would get so twisted about it. It wasn't like people got shot at the fair every day. In fact, it was probably the only time ever in history. Not go back to work? Not possible, she explained, but her mom was being a real load.

"You don't need the money that bad, dear. Most of your school clothes from last year still fit you fine."

Kirsten was horrified. "Jesus, Mom, what are you trying to do to me?"

That was another mistake.

"I won't have language like that in my house! You are not going back to that awful place, and that, young lady, is final!"

Big, huge, mondo mistake. She'd had to wait for her mom to leave for work, then rush to the bus stop. Her mom would kill her if she found out, but that was better than going back to school wearing last year's clothes. And Sophie was going to be mad too. Everybody was going to be mad at her. She might even get fired, like Carmen.

———

"What's he doing? Can you see?"

"He's got a little, like, stepladder. He's setting it up next to the fence."

"Has he got his bag with him?"

"Yeah. Now he's got a shovel. He's throwing it over the fence. He's up on the ladder now. He's taking something out of the bag."

"Can he see us?"

"He's not looking this way."

"I hear dogs barking."

"Now he's throwing some stuff over. It looks like food."

"Food?"

"Yeah. It looks like tacos or something. . . . He's climbing over now. He's climbed over. I can't see him anymore."

"Shit. Okay, let's go see what he's doing." Dean jumped out of the car and trotted down the sidewalk, Tigger close behind. The fence, in violation of city ordinance, was seven feet high. "Okay. Boost me up so I can see," Dean said in a low voice.

Tigger crouched beside the privacy fence and let Dean straddle his shoulders. He tried to rise, groaned.

"Come on!" Dean said, grabbing the top of the wooden fence.

Tigger straightened his legs, gasped, and fell over, sending both of them sprawling onto the sidewalk. "I can't," he gasped.

Dean climbed to his feet, rubbing his elbow. "What a fucking wuss. C'mere, I'll lift you up. Tell me what the fuck he's doing in there." They exchanged positions, Tigger on Dean's shoulders.

"Can you see?"

"Yeah."

"Well?"

"It's some kind of junkyard. A bunch of cars. Shit. There's a couple big motherfucking dogs in there, man. Looks like they're having lunch."

"What about the guy?"

"I can't see him. Wait a minute. He's in one of them. He's in this old pickup truck, trying to get it started. He's backing it up now. Okay. He's getting out. There's—he's—he's standing there looking at this hole, man. Like a big hole somebody dug up, you know? He's just looking at it. . . . He don't look happy, man. He looks pissed. His fuckin' face, man, he looks like he's gonna blow. Shit! Shit, lemme down, man! Lemme down!" Tigger pushed away from the fence, sending Dean staggering backward just as something heavy hit the fence from the other side and dual howls shattered the quiet neighborhood.

—

The dogs.

The goddamn dogs. Now they were barking, howling at something on the other side of the fence. First they ruin his life, then they bark about it.

Axel stared down into the shallow pit at the fluttering remnants of a dark-green Hefty bag. He thought, If I ever have a heart attack, please, God, let it be now. He looked up at Sam's dogs jumping against the wooden fence and amended his wish. First, God, give me time to kill the dogs. He reached into his bag, pulled out the .45, cocked it, and pointed it toward the bellowing mutts.

He held it on them for several seconds, knowing there was no way he could do it. It wasn't the dogs' fault. A week back, he'd invaded their territory carrying two bags, one filled with Bueno Burritos, the other filled with cash money. He'd given one to the dogs, then buried the other right before their hungry canine eyes. Axel uncocked the pistol and put it back in his bag.

The dogs had started digging at the back bumper. He could almost see it, the two dogs working together, or maybe in shifts, sending a steady spray of loose dirt flying out from under the truck. Yeah, he knew a dog-dug hole when he saw one.

But where was the money? He stepped into the pit, lifted the torn Hefty bag. Nothing. He kicked aside some dirt, thinking for a moment that perhaps this was some other doubled-up garbage bag and that the one with the money still lay beneath his feet. A corner of gray-green caught his eye. He bent down and tugged a twenty-dollar bill from the earth. Falling to his hands and knees, Axel shoveled aside handfuls of dirt, throwing some at the dogs, who had sauntered over to watch him.

The twenty was all he found. He stood up, distastefully regarding his dirt-caked fingernails. He hated that. Dirt under his nails.

One loose twenty. Where had it all gone? Had high wind passed through the neighborhood and blown it all away? Not likely. He threaded his way among the derelict vehicles, trying to follow the perimeter of the fence, keeping his eyes on the ground. After five minutes of searching, he found another twenty, stuck in the grille of the Dodge Charger. At the base of the fence, between the two VW

Beetles, he discovered an entire roll, still held together with its rubber band, the bills slightly chewed but still spendable. The dogs? The dogs wouldn't be able to eat an entire quarter-million dollars, even if it did smell like Mexican food.

No, he knew who had his money. He just wasn't sure what he should do about it.

Chapter

34

THE WALK FROM THE BUS stop to the mall would normally take about three minutes. Carmen stretched it out to forty. She did not want to go to work. The tactile memory of the texture of a flour tortilla gave her the shudders.

Also, it had kind of bothered her, being fired by Sophie. Fired by her own mom.

It was getting so she couldn't count on anybody.

She stopped to watch a yellow Skyride capsule pass overhead. All day long, the Skyride ferried people, two to a capsule, from the Horticulture Building, at the head of the mall, to Heritage Square, at the far corner of the fairgrounds. Carmen had worked under the cable for five seasons and had yet to ride it herself. She didn't like the idea of being locked in a bobbing capsule, riding along an unchangeable route.

She couldn't count on any of them. Not Sophie, not Axel, and certainly not James Dean. Now that *he* was gone—gone for sure this time, she thought—she really needed to firm up her position with

Axel. If he wanted her to work with Sophie, then that's what she'd have to do. At least for now. She opened her purse and took two more Valiums from the prescription bottle, swallowed them, and lit a cigarette. The two she had taken back at the motel didn't seem to be working. She decided to wait for these to kick in before giving herself up to the Taco Shop.

Carmen noticed that the Tiny Tot stand was boarded up, then remembered that Tommy Fabian had been killed. She'd forgotten all about it. She couldn't count on him, either. Next thing she knew, Axel would go and die on her too.

———

"How's this?" Sam O'Gara held up his latest effort at rolling a Bueno Burrito.

Sophie groaned. "Would you eat that?" she asked.

Sam frowned at the lumpy, leaking wad in his hand, shrugged, and tossed it into the trash. "I never claimed to be a goddamn cook," he said. "Besides, those tortillas are like wet toilet paper. Don't take nothing to rip 'em."

"Try again, only take your time with it. And be gentle. You're not changing a tire; you're making someone's dinner."

"If you wasn't so goddamn picky, I'd be doing fine." Sam was in an ugly mood. This was turning into one of the worst weeks of the first half, or two thirds, or fifteen sixteenths, or whatever the hell fraction of his life it was that he'd lived so far. First thing, Axel waking him up, then finding out that Tommy had finally got hisself killed, then the damned dogs dig up the yard and make the worst goddamn mess he'd ever seen. It had taken him near an hour to clean it up. And then his Chevy wouldn't start. Nor his truck. All those vehicles, and every last one of them a junker. What a guy ought to do, a guy ought to go buy himself a horse. He'd had to take the bus to get to the fairgrounds. Axel was going to owe him big for this one. Make no mistake, Axel would pay big time for this.

"I'm not picky," Sophie said. "It's just that we have certain quality standards here. Kirsten doesn't seem to have any problems with it. At least not when she decides to show up for work."

Kirsten wrinkled her brow. "I said I was sorry."

"Sorry doesn't make up for lost business."

"Now ladies," Sam said. "Bitchin' ain't gonna get the people fed."

Sophie threw up her hands. "Fine. Fine. Kirsten, will you please give Mr. O'Gara a lesson?"

Kirsten smiled at Sam. "It just takes practice is all." She rapidly put together four Buenos, had them folded and wrapped within seconds. "I can do them as fast as Carmen now."

"Faster," Sophie amended.

Sam snorted, a flapping sound that made both women jump. He had to get out of there, and the only way he was going to do it would be to find himself a replacement. He pointed across the mall.

"What about the little princess? You gonna leave her stand there all day?"

Carmen, wearing her sunglasses, stood a hundred feet away, leaning against the white cinder-block wall of the Food Building, facing them, smoking a cigarette. "She's been holding up that wall half an hour now. And what about that little Mex gal was here? Where'd she take off to?"

Sophie said, "If you mean Juanita, she was only scheduled for the morning shift. As for my daughter—if she wants to work, all she has to do is ask."

"Yeah? Well, maybe she's just sitting over there waiting for *you* to ask *her*."

"Well, I do not intend to do any such thing."

"You want me to go get her?" Anything to escape.

Sophie considered. "I suppose. Even Carmen is an improvement on you, Sam."

"Thanks a hell of a lot." Sam untied his apron, let it fall to the floor, and stalked out of the stand.

———

Carmen watched Sam O'Gara walking toward her. His gait was smooth and rolling, almost as though he were on a ship. Other people on the mall, she noticed, were also walking that way.

She figured she was coming on to the Valiums.

Suddenly he was there, in his bib overalls and V-neck T-shirt and green cap. "Hot one, isn't it?"

"Hi, Sam. Is it hot? I guess I didn't notice."

"Well, actually it ain't the heat so much. It's the humidity. You want to work? Your mama could use you."

Carmen looked past him at the taco stand, nine or ten people in line, Sophie and Kirsten moving around inside at dangerous velocities.

"You sure she wants me?"

"Sure she does. She told me to come and get you. She said you're the best burrito roller she's ever seen."

"Really?" Carmen agreed with that, but she didn't think Sophie had ever noticed.

"Yeah. You help your mama out now, okay?"

Carmen nodded. Sam gave her a grin, buried his hands in his overalls, and turned away.

Carmen said, "Hey! Aren't you gonna be there?"

Sam looked over his shoulder. "Who, me? I'm gonna go eyeball the animules, honey. I hear they got a hog runs twelve hunnert pounds this year."

Carmen said, "Yuck."

Sam muttered, "Besides, another minute in that stand with your mom, I'm a goddamn basket case."

Carmen laughed. "You just got to ignore her," she said.

Five minutes later, she was finding Sophie impossible to ignore. She'd seen her mom in foul moods before, but never like this.

"Dammit, Carmen, did you forget everything you ever knew, girl? First I lose that fumble-fingered Sam O'Gara, then I get you. What do you call this?"

"That," Carmen said, "is a beef tostada."

"I asked for a beef *taco!*"

"Sorry! Jesus!" Carmen couldn't seem to do anything right. She tried not to let it bother her, relying on the Valium to buffer Sophie's flak. That worked for a while, until Kirsten had to make an emergency run to the rest room. As soon as she was out of the stand, Sophie turned up the volume on her complaints.

"Kirsten would never do that," Sophie said. "When I ask for 'two bean,' I mean tacos, not burritos."

"How am I s'posed to know that? Do I look like a mind reader?" Carmen said.

"We've been doing it that way for five years now. What's wrong with you, girl?"

"Jesus, Sophie, would you just jack down?"

"Jack down? I have a business to run here. I need two bean tacos, pronto. Try to get it right this time, would you please?"

Carmen got it right that time, almost. Sophie yelled at her again for being too generous with the cheese. Carmen didn't understand why she was being so hyper. What Sophie needed, she thought, was a Valium. This idea took root in her mind and grew on its own for several minutes. The more she thought about it, the more Carmen liked the idea of a calm, benevolent Sophie Roman. She considered simply offering her a Valium—or maybe two—but rejected the idea. Sophie would never agree to take a pill from a prescription bottle without her name on it.

There was another possibility, however. Sophie kept a six-pack of Canada Dry seltzer under the front counter. She always had an open can going, from which she would sip at frequent intervals. All Carmen had to do to mellow her out was to drop a few Valiums in Sophie's seltzer. It made all kinds of sense. Everyone would benefit, even Sophie.

Carmen couldn't believe she'd never thought of this before. She only needed an opportunity, a few seconds when Sophie wasn't paying attention.

———

Axel remembered driving his old pickup back over the hole, shutting it down, and climbing the fence again. He remembered being in his new truck. He did not remember driving back across town, but he must have done so, because here he was, clutching his burlap shoulder bag, following a line of people through the gates into the fairgrounds.

Must have gone on autopilot, Axel thought. His mind on his missing money, trying to imagine what Sam would do if he came home to find his backyard full of cash. Would he guess where it had come from? Would he want to know? Or would he just squirrel it away. Just stash it and wait to see if anybody came looking.

Axel's biggest question was, why hadn't Sam mentioned it to him? They'd been friends going on forty years now. If a guy finds a quarter-million dollars cash in his backyard, wouldn't you think he'd want to tell his friends about it? A guy might, but what about Sam O'Gara?

Either someone else had found the money—could be anybody who'd had the good fortune to peek over the fence at the right moment—or Sam didn't want Axel to know he'd found it. Yet if Sam had wanted to conceal the fact that he'd found the money, you'd think he would have filled in the hole, made it look like nothing had happened.

Axel didn't know *what* Sam would do. He had always been like that, especially at the card table. Sam was harder to predict than Minnesota weather. He was a human randomizer, which was what had made him a great cardplayer. As far as Axel knew, Sam could have spent the money, burned it, given it to charity, or tossed it in a closet. Any, all, or none of the above seemed equally possible.

But the money was Axel's. Sam had to know that. It was under Axel's truck.

Thinking back over his friendship with Sam O'Gara, examining it in a way he never had before, Axel searched for chinks, flaws, misunderstandings, hidden resentments. They argued all the time, sure, but wasn't there an underlying trust between them? When it came right down to the nuts, couldn't he count on Sam? Of course he could.

On the other hand—how many hands was he up to now?—Sam had been pretty pissed at him the other day. What had that been about? Money. Sam had been telling him what to do with his money, and Axel had told Sam where to put his advice. He remembered telling Sam that he didn't need his interference, that he could take care of himself.

Well, shit, that had just been talk. They'd been arguing like that for forty years. They were still friends.

Axel caressed the rough exterior of his shoulder bag, felt the rolls of money pressing against the burlap. At least he still had this year's money. He reached into the bag and let his hand rest on the .45. He was passing a Pronto Pup joint. The concessionaire caught his eye, recognized him, gave a nod. Axel's grip tightened on the gun as he nodded back.

He tried to think of what to say when he saw Sam. He tried to simplify it, to reduce the problem to manageable proportions. He might say, "Suppose you lost, say, twenty bucks. Suppose you lost it in your friend's house and your friend finds it. Later you tell him you lost a twenty. He would say, 'I found your twenty. Here it is!'"

Even though you couldn't prove the twenty was yours, he would give it back to you because, for one thing, twenty bucks isn't worth losing a friend over. And he wouldn't have to ask, because you would just give it to him.

Now, make that twenty dollars a larger amount—say a quarter million. Axel put himself in Sam's place. What would he do if he found that much cash buried on his property and, the next day, Sam O'Gara showed up and claimed it was his? How good a friend would he have to be to believe him?

——

"You wanna know what really pisses me off?"

"No."

"What pisses me off is they made us pay to get back in. Don't that piss you off?"

"No, it doesn't," Dean said.

"I mean, we already paid to get in once. You'd think that'd be enough."

Dean lifted his cowboy hat and scratched the top of his head. His scalp felt odd, as if it were shrinking. Shrinking and itching. Before following Axel back into the fairgrounds, he and Tigger had done another line of Pork's crystal. It had seemed like a good idea at the time, but now he was wondering whether they'd done one line too many. Every time he blinked, the world shifted about a quarter inch up and to the left.

Tigger said, "We shoulda just sneaked in. Just climbed over the fence is what we shoulda done."

"You know what you should do?" Dean said. "You should shut the fuck up."

"I'm just sayin'," Tigger said.

"Well, don't. Just keep an eye on the guy, okay? That four bucks you paid won't add up to nothing. Think of it like an investment. That's what you gotta do."

"It just pisses me off is all."

"Okay, it pisses you off. Hey. Where'd he go?"

"He's still there. He's talking to Carmen."

—

When Axel stepped into the Taco Shop, Sophie grabbed him by the arm and pulled him back outside.

"She's acting awfully weird, Axel. I think you should take her back to the motel."

"What? Who?" He didn't need this right now. He had more important stuff on his mind. "Where's Sam?" he demanded.

Sophie, not about to be derailed, squeezed his arm and shook it, as if trying to wake him up. "Not Sam! Carmen! She told me I was a cartoon."

"Really?" Axel looked through the door at Carmen. She was making burritos. "She looks okay to me." He pulled his arm away from Sophie. "Where's Sam? Wasn't he helping you out here?"

"If you can call it help. Listen to me, I'm trying to tell you something. There's something wrong with her. I think she's on drugs or something. Just watch her for a few minutes, okay? You'll see what I mean."

"I have to find Sam," Axel said.

"Just wait a goddamn minute. And watch her." Sophie stepped back into the stand and took an order from a customer.

Axel washed his hands and put on an apron. "Was Sam here helping out?" he asked Kirsten.

Kirsten nodded. "He left about twenty minutes ago."

"He said he was gonna take a walk," Carmen said.

"He's gone, thank God," Sophie said. "I need four tacos and one Bueno."

"I need shells," Kirsten said.

Axel loaded the deep fryer and rotated a batch of tortillas into the hot oil. He watched Carmen moving around the stand, building tacos and burritos. She was moving slow, but maybe she was just tired. Maybe Carmen was right, maybe Sophie was too hyper. Axel relaxed, forcing his mind off his missing money, and let himself swing into the rhythm of Axel's Taco Shop, keeping the tortillas cooking, the meat frying, and the burritos rolling. There were four of them in the stand—Axel, Sophie, Carmen, and Kirsten—all working as one. The customers were stacked up out front, food was flying out the window, and money was flowing into the cash box. Axel thought it a bit strange when Carmen called him "Fred," but he didn't worry about it. The restaurant was humming, and for the moment all was right with the world.

He had known it wouldn't last, but he was stunned by how quickly things fell apart. He was lifting the batch of tortillas out of the oil when there was a thump, a squeal, and Sophie shrieking. Axel dropped the rack back into the oil and whirled in time to see Sophie shaking Carmen, holding her by the neck, slamming her back against the cooler. Kirsten was pressed against the counter, her eyes open wide.

"Is it poison? What are you trying to do to me?" Sophie shouted.

Carmen's face was turning red. She was trying to say something. Axel stepped between them, grabbing Sophie's arms and pulling her hands away from Carmen's neck. A small, appreciative crowd had gathered in front of the stand. Axel pushed the two women out the back door.

"What's going on?" he demanded.

Carmen was rubbing her neck. "She choked me," she said.

"She tried to poison me. I caught her putting something in my water."

"Your water? What water?" Axel asked.

"My Canada Dry. She was putting pills in my Canada Dry."

"Is that true?"

Carmen shrugged. "Did you know you look like Fred Flintstone?"

"She's insane. She tried to poison me," Sophie said. "She thinks we're the Flintstones."

"Wait a minute. Back up," Axel said, as much to himself as to them. "Carmen, did you put something in Sophie's water?"

Carmen pushed out her lower lip. "I was just giving her a couple Valiums."

"Dope?" Sophie shrieked. "You were trying to give me *dope?*"

"Just to calm you down a little," said Carmen reasonably.

"You were slipping your mother a mickey?" Axel asked, struggling with the concept.

"Just a couple Valiums." Carmen held up the prescription bottle.

Sophie pointed. "Look. She has them in her hand."

"Let's see," Axel said, reaching for the bottle.

Carmen backed away. "I don't have to. You're a cartoon."

"My God, she's on dope. My daughter's a drug addict."

"Give them to me, Carmen."

Carmen was walking backward. She pushed the bottle into her pocket, turned, and ran away through the crowded mall. Axel and Sophie watched her until she rounded the corner of the Food Building.

"I told you," Sophie said. "We should've just left her fired."

Axel shrugged. "She'll be okay," he said doubtfully.

"Are you kidding? She's on dope. An addict. I'm lucky she hasn't murdered me in my bed and stolen my VCR."

"Don't be silly," Axel said. "Carmen wouldn't hurt a bug."

"Hey, you guys," Kirsten called from the stand. "Are you just going to leave me in here alone?"

Chapter

35

It was too bad she hadn't got her mom to take the Valium, and really too bad that Sophie and Axel had busted her. At least they hadn't gotten the pills. Carmen shook the plastic bottle, held it up to the light. Only a few left. Maybe that was okay, seeing as she would probably get fired for real this time. She wouldn't have to work with Sophie anymore, so maybe she wouldn't need the Valium. At the moment, it wasn't something she wanted to worry about. She'd figure something out. Why not relax and enjoy the cartoons? They were the best ever. It was almost like being on acid, only smoother and not so scary. Everything had an outline. Some people became familiar characters. Axel and Sophie as Fred and Wilma Flintstone had been hilarious. Carmen wondered whether she would run into Barney and Betty Rubble. She knew people weren't cartoons, not really, but at the same time, they really *were*. The illusion was at least as convincing as the images on a TV set, and as a bonus, she could make her arms and legs stretch like Plastic Man. She could even float, though not more than a few inches off the ground. It was like wearing antigravity skates. Carmen moved down Carnes Avenue, letting herself drift toward the midway on the crowded, littered street. She was thinking about how it might be fun to go on a few rides, when a figure appeared before her wearing a straw cowboy hat, mirrored sunglasses, and a red paisley bandanna. He put out a hand, palm forward, and she ran into it with her left tit.

The glasses slid down and caught on the tip of his nose, revealing a pair of big brown cartoon eyes.

"Hey there, Carmy," said a familiar voice.

She tried to make him into Elmer Fudd. It didn't work. It was James Dean.

Carmen said, "Guess what?"

"What?"

Nothing occurred to her. "Just a minute." She squeezed her eyes down to slits, blurring his image. She heard another voice.

"What's she doing?"

"She's fucked up on something. Hey, Carmen, snap out of it. I gotta talk to you."

Carmen said, "What do you want?" She had an idea. "You want to go on the Tilt-A-Whirl?" They were on both sides of her now, James Dean and his friend with the big white hat—what was his name? Trigger, like Roy Rogers's horse. Carmen asked him, "Is that a ten-gallon hat?"

"I don't know," he said.

"I gotta go to the bathroom." She started walking again. They fell in on either side of her. "Then I wanna go on the Tilt-A-Whirl."

Dean said, "I do not want to go on the fucking Tilt-A-Whirl."

She ducked her head below the brim of Trigger's white hat and said, "How about you? You want to go on the Tilt-A-Whirl?"

"Those things make me puke. Hey, Dean, what about the guy?"

Dean grabbed Carmen's wrist, jerking her to a halt.

"Hey! I gotta pee, y'know."

"You want I should go back and watch him?"

"Yeah, you do that, and I'll take her to the can."

"Then we go on the Tilt-A-Whirl, okay?"

He squeezed her wrist, really hard. "Fuck the Tilt-A-Whirl, Carmy. Let's go. Talk to me about the man. What happened back there?"

"Sophie got mad." She pulled away, but her wrist was stuck in his hand. They were walking again.

"That bag he's got. You know what's in it?"

"Who?"

"Your taco guy."

"Axel?"

"Yeah. What's he got in the bag?"

"You want me to look?"

He seemed surprised. "You think you could?"

"Sure I could. Only I really gotta go to the bathroom, okay?"

The restrooms by the Giant Slide were in a long wooden structure, with entrances at both ends of the building. A line of women waited at the south entrance.

"I'll be just a minute."

He released her, and she squeezed past the women in line and pushed her way into the building, oblivious to the stares and comments from women who had been waiting for twenty minutes. She walked past the row of toilets, past the sinks, and out the opposite end of the building, where she turned toward the midway. She wanted to immerse herself in the flashing and the shouting and the overamped rock and roll. She needed to get back to cartoon land as soon as possible. Those skinhead cowboys, they were no fun. If she wanted to answer a bunch of questions, she'd have stayed at the Taco Shop.

———

Dean lifted his hat by its crown and fanned himself with it. "This fucking sun," he remarked to no one. He moved toward the shade of the Giant Slide, found a light pole to lean against, and examined his surroundings. His senses had become so acute that each blade of trampled grass stood out against its neighbors. An old guy in bib overalls and a green baseball cap stood a few yards away, hands buried in his pockets, looking at him. The old man nodded when he caught Dean's eye.

"Hot one, ain't she?" he called out in a cracked voice.

Dean gave the guy a cold stare, then returned his attention to the restroom entrance. What the hell was Carmen doing in there? He amused himself by fixing his gaze on a teenage girl waiting in line outside the restroom. If he focused, he felt, he could make her turn toward him. Lock eyes with her. He felt a presence behind him, turned his head. The guy with the green hat, inches away, an unlit cigarette in his mouth.

"You got a light, Mac?" The hair on his jaw was about the same length as the hair on Dean's head. They both needed a shave.

Dean said, "Get lost."

"What, you don't got a light?"

Dean took a quick look at the restrooms. No Carmen.

The old man said, "You waitin' on your gal?"

Dean stabbed a forefinger at the old man's chest. "What did I just tell you?"

The old man laughed.

"You think that's funny?" Dean said. He squeezed his right hand into a fist, thinking about letting the guy have it—bam!—right in the nose.

The old man widened his eyes and puffed out his lower lip, causing the unlit cigarette to point straight up at his left eye. He scratched the underside of his chin. "Guess I did," he said. "Women is funny. Use to have one myself, y'know. Built like a fuckin' Cadillac, bazooms like watermelons. Had a tattoo of an M-1 rifle on her left ass-cheek and a birthmark the shape of Texas on t'other. Name was Tricksy. Gal was fast as lightning every way you can think of 'cept for one. Used to take her twenty minutes just to take a leak. Fuckin' women. You go figure."

Dean stared at the old man, his lower lip moving up and down as he absorbed what he was hearing. The guy had eyes about six different colors, and more wrinkles than a ton of raisins. As Dean watched, the cigarette migrated from one side of his mouth to the other, bobbing up and down like a snake charmer's flute.

———

Axel had once seen a TV show about people who exploded. It had been one of those shows where they tell about UFOs and werewolves and people who can bend nails with their minds. Stuff he didn't really believe. But the segment about people who exploded—not *exploded*, really, just sort of burst into flames—had sounded very scientific and convincing. They even had a scientific name for it, he re-membered: spontaneous human combustion.

At the time, Axel had wondered what those people who exploded felt like just before it happened. Now he thought he knew. They felt like this.

His nest egg, all the money he'd managed to accumulate over the past twenty-five years, had been dug up by a couple of dogs, and the only person who *might* be able to return it to him, Sam O'Gara, had also disappeared. And *Sophie*—he'd never seen her like this before. She was raging, muttering under her breath, slamming things around the restaurant. Kirsten was so shook up she was screwing up every order, making tacos into tostadas, nachos into burros, and giving people Sprite when they'd ordered iced tea. Carmen was wandering the fairgrounds with a pocketful of dope. He wanted to run after Carmen and lock her in her room, where she'd be safe. He wanted to find Sam, find him and grab him by the ankles and shake loose his money. He wanted to be a thousand miles away from Sophie and her anger. But he couldn't have any of that, because there was a line in front of the restaurant, people who wanted—who *needed*—Bueno Burritos. He was trapped inside a cage he had made for himself, and if something didn't give, he was afraid he would ignite, leaving behind nothing but a horrified crowd of fairgoers and a charred spot on the restaurant floor. They would write about it in the *Enquirer,* and only fools like him would believe it to be true. But it would be.

"You're crazy," Axel muttered as he started building a row of six Buenos.

Sophie said, "What?" Hands like claws, ready to pounce on him.

"I was talking to myself," he said. Jesus Christ, he'd better be careful. He wasn't the only one ready to blow. One wrong word, a single bad burrito, a fly landing on the wrong person's nose at the wrong time—it was the goddamn Middle East, all packed inside a hundred eighty square feet. He felt the weight of the .45 in his pocket, tugging down on his right suspender. Every time he moved, it rubbed the outside of his thigh. Looking up from his work, he rolled his neck and let his eyes play across the crowded mall. He picked his way from face to face. Even after twenty-five years, they still looked like individuals to him. Then he saw a green cap making its bobbing progress in the direction of the Taco Shop, and for a moment he felt it, an intense burning sensation, just above his belly, hot enough to ignite human flesh.

———

Sophie had always wanted one of those *Shit Happens* bumper stickers. She saw them all the time, but she didn't know where to buy one. It was so true, especially now. It came in waves, like the weather. When had it started? She tried to think back. Even as she smiled at her customers, took their money, pushed their food across the counter, and shouted instructions at Kirsten and Axel, a part of her mind was reviewing the last few days, trying to remember when this latest shit storm had rolled in. Was it when Carmen arrived from Omaha? When the fair started? Or was it when Axel made her a partner? She was having mixed feelings about that. Ten percent a year. What did that mean? And in the meantime, she was doing most of the work. In years past, Axel had spent most of every day in the Taco Shop, doing whatever needed doing. But this year . . . This year, every time she turned around he was going somewhere, or gone, or just standing out back, doing nothing at all. Like he thought now he had a partner he didn't have to hold up his end anymore. Well, if he didn't care enough about the business to do his share, then the hell with him. Telling her she was crazy, when he was the one acting like a jerk. There was this other bumper sticker she liked: *Don't like my driving? Call 1-800-EAT-SHIT.* As long as she was the one running this restaurant, he was going to have to help out, and not just for a few minutes here and there. Sophie turned around, thinking to share her thoughts with Axel whether he liked it or not. But Axel was gone, his apron hanging by the door, still moving.

Chapter

36

THERE WAS ONLY ONE THING Sam could have said that would have prevented Axel from asking about his missing money, and he said it.

"Hey, Ax, I think I just met up with that guy you was telling me about. Your Bald Monkey fella. Just talked to him. Doggin' that little gal a yours, all dressed up like Roy Rogers."

"You—you *what* him?" Axel shook his head, trying to make sense of what he was hearing. "You mean, he's here?"

"I'd a grabbed 'im, only I wasn't a hundred percent sure I was dealing with the right asshole."

"Got his head shaved, right?"

"Yeah, only he's wearing one a them cheap cowboy hats."

"Got a cut on his eyebrow?"

"Couldn't see. He's wearing his Foster Grants. Your little gal, she gave 'im the slip. C'mon." Sam turned and started walking away.

Axel blinked back his confusion and followed, his eyes on the sagging seat of Sam's overalls. The crotch hung low, about eight inches north of his knees. Sam walked with a hip-swinging gait, each movement of his legs forming a shallow arc, as if he was trying to avoid chafing. Or like a toddler carrying a load in his diaper.

Axel hurried forward and came up alongside Sam, who had settled into a brisk waddle.

"What do you mean, she gave him the slip? Was he chasing her?" Confusion was becoming anger; he put a hand in his pocket and gripped the .45 to keep it from abrading his thigh.

"Don't think so."

"Where are we going? You know where they went?"

"Once he realized she'd got away, he asked me where was the Tilt-A-Whirl, then headed off toward the midway."

"You're sure it was the same guy?"

Sam shrugged.

"So it might not be him."

"Might not be. Only how many bald-headed friends can Carmen have?"

Axel did not reply. He really didn't know. The Ferris wheel, at the entrance to the midway, loomed above them. Beyond lay a quarter-mile-long, U-shaped gauntlet of rides and games, and a milling crowd of cash-carrying suckers being willingly harvested by an organized gang of carnies.

"There must be ten thousand people here," Axel said.

"Just look for a straw cowboy hat," Sam said.

"Maybe we ought to split up."

Sam grabbed Axel by the elbow. "Hold on, Ax. Talk to me here. What are you plannin' on doin' once we find 'im?"

Axel caressed the slide of the .45, slick with sweat and gun oil.

"I just want to make sure Carmen's okay. Get her back to the stand."

"What about the guy?"

Axel said, "You go down the right side. I'll go this way." He entered the midway, moving quickly, not looking back at Sam. As soon as he had passed through the gate, the decibel level climbed. Every ride hammered the crowd with rock and roll—overamped tape loops of heavy-metal electric guitar clawed at his ears. Axel didn't know any of the songs. To his ears it was noise, the same jarring, discordant crap Carmen liked. He tried to ignore the music and concentrate on looking at every face under a cowboy hat. There were a lot of them. Cowboy hats were big this year. Every one he saw produced another surge of adrenaline. He concentrated on keeping his cool. Tommy was dead, and he couldn't change that. Tommy had already killed his killer. Axel's priority had to be Carmen. If she was on dope, she needed his help, whether she was with Bald Monkey or not.

Cowboy hat, dead ahead.

Axel picked up his pace, came up beside the cowboy-hatted figure, caught a look at his profile.

Another blank, blond and bearded. He relaxed his grip on the gun.

As he was walking past a wheel game, a horn-shaped speaker blasted in his ear. "Every playah a winnah!" Axel veered away from the game. "Only way to lose is to not play the game," the mike man called after him.

He decided to continue down the length of the midway and meet up with Sam. If they hadn't found Carmen by then, then he'd say the hell with it and get back to the stand. He was passing the Headless Woman joint when something caused him to stop and look behind him.

White cowboy hat, a few paces behind him. Axel took three quick steps and snatched the oversize hat. The kid let out a yell and jumped back. The front of his shirt read: *Let's Rodeo*. His head was shaved like a new recruit, but it was the wrong kid. This one had a pointy nose and tiny, startled eyes. Axel let his breath hiss out.

"Sorry," he mumbled.

The kid grabbed his hat. His small eyes narrowed. "Crazy old fucker," he said in a nasal whine. He smashed the hat back onto his head and backed up a few steps.

"I thought you were somebody else," Axel said.

"You been eatin' too many tacos, old man." The kid took a few steps to the side, then continued up the midway, looking back over his shoulder every few steps.

Axel felt ridiculous. He was suddenly sure that that was the bald kid Sam had spotted. How many cowboy-hatted skinheads could there be? He shook his head and forced himself to smile. Wild-goose chase. He pulled his gun hand from his pocket and rolled his shoulders, willing the tension from his body, watching the white hat bob and disappear up ahead. The clamoring rock and roll, the clanking of the rides, the hammering of the generators, the voices and shouts and happy screams, all blended together. Carmen, he decided, had probably gone back to the Motel 6. It was time for him to return to the stand, time to take care of business.

He was thinking about how many tortillas he would need to get through the last weekend, when an unwelcome thought wriggled into his conscious mind. Something that kid had said. Something about eating too many tacos.

———

Dean found Carmen standing in line, waiting to board the Tilt-A-Whirl. An old AC/DC tune blasted from the speakers mounted on both sides of the ride. He cut in, draping an arm over her shoulder. She rolled her sleepy eyes toward him and said, "Where'd you go?"

"Didn't go anywhere, Carmy. Where'd *you* go?" He flexed his arm, pulling her face into his chest, giving her head a gentle squeeze. She felt loose, like wet clay.

She said, "You want to go with me on the Tilt-A-Whirl?"

"Sure, why not?" Maybe it would wake her up a little.

———

The more Axel thought about it, the more it bothered him. Why would the kid say anything about tacos if he didn't know Axel was in the taco business? And how would he know that Axel was in the taco business? Axel picked up his pace, weaving through the crowd, trying to relocate the white hat. He was nearing the end of the midway, where he'd have to turn and go back up the other side.

There. He broke into a run. The .45 slapped against his thigh. He felt something rip, stopped, reached in his pocket. The thin fabric had given way; the barrel of the gun now poked through a hole at the bottom of the pocket, hanging down to his knee. Axel looked around, saw no one watching, and pulled out the gun, turning his pocket liner inside out. He wedged the gun into his waistband, tugged loose his shirttails to cover the protruding grip.

The cowboy hat was no longer visible. Axel decided to cut across the center island, between the Gravitron and the Tilt-A-Whirl, and head the kid off as he came up the other side. He ducked through a yellow bally-cloth divider. The area between the rides was a jungle of snakelike electrical cables. Above him to his right, the Gravitron, an enormous saucer-shaped device covered with flashing yellow, red, and green lights, was picking up speed. Axel wasn't sure what happened to the people who entered the ride, but they always looked a little sick when they exited. The Tilt-A-Whirl, to his left, seemed tame by comparison.

Axel picked his way over the cables, reached the other side, and climbed the low fence. Before him, the canvas front of the Cavalcade of Human Oddities stretched for fifty feet in either direction. Each performer was depicted in a series of crude but exciting painted banners. The Pretzel Girl, shown with her limbs tied in pretzel-like knots. Tortura, the Puncture-Proof Girl. The Human Blast Furnace. Serpentina, the Snake Woman. Axel had met Serpentina, an old friend of Tommy's. She was also playing Electra, Mistress of the Megawatt, this year. Behind him, the Tilt-A-Whirl clanked into life. The kid could be anywhere. He might've gone into the Hard Rock Funhouse or one of the other attractions, or ducked between the rides as Axel had, or simply taken off his hat and melted into the crowd. The rattling and clattering of the Tilt-A-Whirl became louder. Axel moved away from the noise, throwing a glance back at the undulating, whirling platform. Something caught his eye. A cowboy hat, in one of the Tilt-A-Whirl's spinning tubs. It was there, then it was gone. He squinted, trying to track the spinning cupola. The hat appeared again, and then he saw Carmen, screaming, her eyes wide. The tub whirled, and they were gone.

The effect, when the ride was operating, was both elegant and bewildering. The tub swept by again, but this time facing the other way. Axel couldn't see them. On the third sweep they appeared again. He stepped to the side, followed their tub with his eyes through its looping course up and around. Carmen was screaming. She looked terrified. What was the kid doing to her? He was grabbing her, holding on to her, shouting at her.

———

"Let go!" Dean pried Carmen's hands away from his body, held them. His ear was ringing from her screams. Crazy bitch.

"Eeee!" she shrieked, her mouth a distended grin.

Dean closed his eyes, willing the ride to end, hoping he wouldn't ralph all over himself. He had business to take care of, and here he was on the Tilt-A-Whirl, having his guts scrambled.

Carmen shrieked again, sending a needle of sound tunneling into his right ear. He turned his head away and opened his eyes to a blurry, striped world of garish, rushing color. He clamped his jaw tight and shut his eyes again. He couldn't decide which was worse. Just when he thought he wasn't going to make it, the spinning slowed and the Tilt-A-Whirl slowed. The blurred horizon took form. The tub rocked to a complete stop. He tried to get out, but the safety bar remained locked across the top of his thighs.

Carmen said, "You got to wait for the guy to come let us out."

Dean had about had it with her. He said, "I oughta fuckin' smack you for getting me on this thing."

"You better not."

"Oh?" Did she *want* to get hit?

Carmen pointed. He followed her finger, at first seeing nothing, then, standing at the exit gate, the old man, staring up at him, less than thirty feet away. He was holding the pistol in both hands, not even attempting to conceal it. Dean twisted, trying to get his legs out from under the lap restraint.

"Ow! What are you doing?" Carmen said.

"I got to get out of here."

He had one leg out from under the bar.

Carmen waved. "Hey, Axel!"

"Move the fuck over!" Dean shouted.

"He's not gonna shoot you," Carmen said. "At least I don't think he is."

———

Axel had time to think while he was keeping his sights on Bald Monkey, but he was trying not to. The hot, animal flush felt too good. He fantasized pulling the trigger again and again. For Tommy. For Carmen. For the hell of it. Could he make the shot? Forty years ago he could have, but now he would be as likely to hit Carmen—or somebody else—as he was to hit his target. He thought about this and other technical aspects of shooting. He didn't let himself think about the consequences of a successful shot other than to imagine the monkey falling through the air, crumpled like a well-shot canvas-back.

Carmen smiled and waved. The scene had become unreal to Axel; he felt as if he was watching himself go through motions. He had felt this way when Tommy got shot—like he wasn't really there. Like someone else was making his decisions.

The feeling of unreality intensified when the monkey got loose, dashed across the metal surface of the Tilt-A-Whirl, toward the edge. He had him now; nothing in his sights but bald monkey and blue sky. He was squeezing the trigger when something hit him hard under the elbow. The .45 boomed and kicked and sent a round up into the air. Someone behind him. Axel brought his elbow back, hit something, heard a grunt, then felt his leg give way. He was falling before the pain in his knee reached his brain. The instant his butt hit the asphalt, two hands scooped under his armpits, lifting him back onto his feet, pushing him forward.

"Let's go, Ax. You can walk, can'cha?"

"Sam?" Axel took a step, nearly fell again. "He was there, Sam, I saw him!" He pointed at the Tilt-A-Whirl, where Carmen, still locked into her seat, sat staring at them, her mouth hanging loose.

Sam wrapped Axel's right arm over his shoulder. "C'mon, buddy. Let's get moving." He started forward, half dragging Axel.

"What the hell happened?" Axel said. "I had him, I had the little bastard in my sights. Somebody ran into me. Wait." He stopped. "My gun. Somebody grabbed it."

"That was me, you dumb fuck." Sam slapped the front pocket of his overalls. "You can have it back later."

"I—you did that? Ow, not so fast. My knee!"

"You were gonna shoot him! Right there in front of everybody. Christ, Ax, my dogs've got more sense than that. You want to go to jail?"

Axel tested his leg, transferring weight to it, leaning forward, quickly bringing the other foot around. He could walk on it. Sort of. If he hung tight to Sam.

"What about Carmen?"

"Just keep moving. She'll be fine. We've got to get you out of here."

"I had him," Axel said.

"Yeah, well, you're damn lucky you didn't get him."

———

The ride boy was confused. "What was that all about?" he asked.

Carmen ignored him, stepped out of the cupola shakily, and walked down the ramp. Where had they gone? She had seen Axel, and then Sam had knocked him over, and Dean had jumped off the Tilt-A-Whirl, then she was all alone. It was too confusing to think about. She guessed that if not for the Valium, she would be pretty upset right about now. As it was, she was just miffed that they had both left without her.

The midway felt too hot and too close. The people were no longer cartoons; they were sweaty, ugly animals. She felt greasy and gritty, and her T-shirt was chafing under her arms. She continued up the midway past the Cavalcade of Human Oddities. The sword swallower was doing his teaser routine, giving the gawkers something to look at as the mike man described the collection of bizarre humanity waiting inside the tent, willing to reveal all for the price of a ticket. Carmen watched the sword swallower insert the blade deep into his body, then pull it out shiny with olive oil and saliva. Her T-shirt was really bothering her. She tried pulling her arms in. Struggling, she was able to get her right arm back through the sleeve hole, but then her arm was stuck inside the T-shirt, pressed against her body, and she could not figure out how to get it back out through the sleeve. She turned around in a circle, twice, but found the situation unchanged. One hand was sticking out the bottom of the shirt. It occurred to her then that she was going to a lot of trouble for nothing, so she pulled the bottom of the shirt up over her head.

That felt much better. Carmen draped the T-shirt over her shoulder. People were looking at her. Even the sword swallower, who had lost his audience, was staring. Carmen shrugged and walked away. People were weird. The air felt soft on her breasts, just like when she'd been a little kid, wading in Tanners Lake.

Chapter

37

FOR A SECOND THERE, Tigger thought the guy had fuckin' shot James Dean. He imagined himself telling it. The guy's pointin' this gun, and then this other old dude, like, hits him! Fuckin' gun goes off: *Ka-boom!* Deano goes flying right off the fuckin' Tilt-A-Whirl, man, and it's like he got shot, but then I see Dean running like a fuckin' deer, man. And these old guys, they're limpin' the fuck off, like maybe one of 'em got shot in the fuckin' foot.

It was a good story, only Tigger couldn't think who he'd tell it to, what with Sweety and Pork gone. And Dean—if he ever caught up to him—Dean probably wouldn't think it was funny. Oh, well. He knew some other guys he could tell it to. Only now he had to make a decision—should he keep following the taco guy, like Dean said, or should he go after Dean, get the hell out of there?

Since he'd lost sight of Dean, he decided to go with the taco guy.

———

The first thing Sophie thought—seeing them like that, Axel hanging on Sam, staggering up the mall—was that they'd gone off and gotten drunk. Middle of the day, busy as hell, and they'd gone off and split a bottle. Sophie could feel the red blooming on her cheeks. She knew what she looked like when she got mad, but it wasn't as if she could stop it, and anyways, she'd got to where she didn't even want to stop it. This entire fair had been a disaster from the get-go. People getting killed, her worthless daughter trying to poison her, Sam O'Gara mangling tortillas by the dozen, and—worst of all—Axel spending practically no time in the stand, helping out. If this was what it was like being a partner, she didn't want any part of it. Turning her back to the approaching pair, Sophie regarded the cramped food preparation area, where Kirsten was frantically assembling an order. She lowered her eyes to the floor. Small particles of food peppered the brick-patterned linoleum surface: bits of orange cheese, sliced green and black olive, shredded lettuce, congealing crumbs of fatty ground beef. About five tacos' worth of filling. Soon it would be up to their ankles.

I could quit, she thought. The concept shivered her spine with orgasmic intensity. She could just walk away. That was it. When Axel walked in through that door, she'd drape her apron over his drunken skull and walk away. Go find a real job, something in an air-conditioned office where men wore suits and paychecks arrived every Friday at 4:30 P.M. and the floor wasn't covered with organic matter.

Kirsten said, "You okay?"

Sophie jerked herself back to the present. "I'm fine," she snapped.

"What's wrong with Mr. Speeter?"

Sophie followed Kirsten's pointing finger. At first, she didn't see him. "Where'd he go?"

"On that bench," Kirsten said.

There he was, sitting with his leg stretched out along the length of the bench.

"Hey, Soph!" It was Sam, standing behind her, in the doorway. Without Axel draped over his shoulder, he didn't look so drunk anymore.

"Don't call me that," Sophie said.

Sam bumped up his eyebrows, drew a malformed Pall Mall from somewhere inside his overalls, and fitted it to his mouth. "What you want I should call you? Her Holiness Madame Priss-Butt?"

Sophie's teeth clacked together. That was it. She was out of there, right now. She reached back to untie her apron.

Sam said, "Listen, before you go all lady-of-the-fucking-manor on me, how about you make up an ice pack for your partner out there. He's got himself a knee that's gonna be the size of a cantaloupe, he don't get some chill on it."

Sophie felt her anger begin to crumble. "He . . . what happened?"

"We ran into Carmen and her little no-hair friend, and old Ax, he had hisself an accident."

Kirsten was already filling a towel with crushed ice. It was just like making burritos—you got better with practice.

———

The younger cop, the tall one, was enjoying himself, but the older cop looked angry, embarrassed, and unhappy.

"Put your shirt on," he said, keeping his eyes averted.

"Okay," Carmen said. "Keep *your* shirt on." She laughed.

The younger cop, staring at her tits, laughed too. His partner glared at him. Carmen shook out her T-shirt and looked at it. It was inside out.

"It's inside out," she said. They were standing near the head of the midway, surrounded by gaping fairgoers. Carmen grinned at her audience and waved the shirt back and forth over her head.

"Just put the shirt on, honey."

"Are you going to take me to jail?"

"We just want you to put your shirt on."

"You should take it easy," said Carmen, pulling the shirt over her head. "You want something to calm you down? You look really unhappy."

"Are you going to keep your shirt on?" the older cop asked.

Carmen shrugged. "Is he always so uptight?" she asked the younger cop.

The cop smiled and looked away. His partner scowled at him, then looked back at Carmen, who was scratching her left breast through the T-shirt. He turned to his partner. "What do you think?"

The small crowd was dispersing.

"We'd have to walk her all the way back up there." He pointed. "I say forget it. It's not worth it." He turned to Carmen, put his hands on her shoulders, and spoke directly into her smiling face. "How about it, lady—are you going to keep your shirt on?" he asked Carmen. "Will you promise us that?"

Carmen was trying to get something out of her jeans pocket.

"We asked you a question," said the older cop.

Carmen got the bottle from her pocket, opened it, and shook two Valiums onto her palm. She offered them to the older cop. "Here," she said, "eat these. You'll feel better. You really will."

———

One time Tigger had gone to work for a temp agency, and they had sent him to this factory where all day long he loaded little white cardboard boxes into big brown cardboard boxes. He earned thirty-eight dollars for eight hours, then spent it all that same night at The Recovery Room, trying to wipe out the memory. It hadn't worked. He still had nightmares about that day, the white-into-brown-cardboard-box day, the most boring day of his life.

Sitting watching the taco guy was almost as bad. All the guy did was sit in his chair, holding a towel on his leg. Tigger, sitting on the grass up near the top of the sloped mall, could see the guy's foot. He had been looking at that foot for almost an hour. It hadn't moved an inch. And the other old guy, he was in the taco stand, working. That was boring too. Tigger really wanted to leave, since it was obvious the guy wasn't going anywhere, but he kept thinking how pissed Dean would be if he left. He didn't think he'd ever forget the sound of the steel crowbar hitting Pork's skull. Tigger had been in lots of fights and stuff, but he'd never heard anything like that before and he hoped he never did again. He kept remembering it, the sound, and thinking it was like the sound when you hold on to an ice cream cone too tight. When it shatters and you get ice cream all over yourself. That wasn't exactly the sound, but it was as close as he could come.

No, he didn't want to get Dean pissed off at him.

But Dean had run. The guy had shot at him and he had run. Did that mean Tigger was supposed to run too? He didn't know. But he did know that watching a guy's foot was cardboard-box boring. After a time—Tigger didn't know how long it had been or what had finally inspired him to move—he stood up and headed for the gate. The farther he got from the taco guy, the better he felt. This whole deal was getting too weird, what with people getting shot and everything. Maybe it was time to move back in with his dad again, see if the old son-of-a-bitch had mellowed out in the past six months. By the time he got to his car, he'd almost decided to do it. Just show up at his dad's house on Selby, walk right in, see what happened.

As he was unlocking the car door he decided. That was what he would do. If Dean wanted to take off the taco guy, then he could do it without Timothy Alan Skeller. Tigger opened the car door and slid in behind the wheel. He was all the way in before he realized that he was not alone.

Dean, slumped in the back seat, said, "Where the fuck *you* been?"

Tigger jumped, whacking his thighs on the steering wheel. "How'd you get in here?" he asked. Then he noticed the glass on the passenger seat, and the missing window. "You broke my window, man."

"Don't worry about your window. Taco Man's gonna buy you a whole new car."

"I don't want a new car, man. Besides, the dude's got a fuckin' *gun,* man. And he ain't afraid to use it. He *shot* at you, man. I fuckin' saw it."

"Yeah, well, he missed me, didn't he."

"He missed you on account of the other old guy *made* him miss."

Dean sat up and leaned over the seat back. "Reason he missed me," he said, "is on account of I got the fuck out of the way." He took the cowboy hat from Tigger's head and sailed it out the window. "Now start the car."

"Why? Where we going?"

"Just start the fucking car. I'll tell you where to go."

Tigger said, "I don't think I wanna."

"Yes you do."

———

After seven-plus decades of living, Axel had thought that he had experienced all the emotions his body was capable of producing. He had plumbed the dark, bottomless depths of terror, sailed the heights of pleasure and joy, waded through swamps of anger and disgust, and baked in the desert of despair. But he'd never felt like this before, as if the reins had been severed, as if the brake lines had ruptured, as if he was watching himself flail at life without purpose or effect. When things were going badly, Axel's thoughts took a literary turn. If life was a metaphor, perhaps he had the power to change it.

What if he had shot the kid? What if he'd killed him? Cold radiated up his leg from the ice pack on his knee. He would have gone to jail. The thought shivered his spine. Other thoughts, perhaps even worse, threatened to surface.

Feeling eyes on him, he tipped his head back and found Sophie standing in the doorway to the Taco Shop.

"How are you feeling?" she asked.

"I'm fine," he said.

Sophie shook her head. "She's a big girl, Axel. There's only so much we can do."

Axel felt his eyes heat up; he turned his face away from Sophie and blinked rapidly. She thought he was worried about Carmen. Hell, he hadn't even been *thinking* about Carmen. He'd been thinking about himself. Poor Carmen, wandering around out there by herself or—even worse—not by herself. What an all-time shitty day. He felt Sophie step back into the restaurant, heard her say something to Sam.

Damn.

Sam.

The other thing he was trying not to think about. The hole in Sam's backyard. Axel drew a deep breath, waiting for the fear and anger to hit him but feeling nothing beyond a sort of dull, distant thudding, the sound of a flaccid heart herding blood through a network of aging vessels. Not long ago that heart had been hammering, powered by the need for vengeance, driving a rage that had nearly caused him to commit murder. Now such emotion seemed unreal and impossible. He felt nothing other than weariness and the unpleasant pulsing from his swollen knee. The fact that his entire fortune had disappeared seemed meaningless. He knew he had to ask Sam about it, but he was afraid of what he might hear. Better, for the moment, not to know. Either Sam had the money and he would give it back, or he had it and he wouldn't, or the dogs had eaten it, or someone else had taken it. It didn't matter. What mattered was the fact that he did not seem to care. He'd lost his edge.

———

"I think we should take him to see a doctor," Sophie whispered.

"He don't want no doctor," Sam said. "Leave him be."

"He's just sitting out there staring. Did he get hit on the head or something?"

"He'll be okay. He's just noodlin'." Sam finished folding a lumpy Bueno Burrito. A glob of guacamole oozed out from a tear in the tortilla. A few hours earlier, Sophie wouldn't have dreamed of serving such an abortion to one of her customers, but now she simply watched as Sam wrapped it and handed it to a waiting Kirsten.

"What about his leg? He can hardly walk."

Sam said, "It'll get better or it'll get worser. Leave him be."

"I think he's worried about Carmen."

"Maybe he is, maybe he ain't. Maybe he's just pooped."

Sophie thought, Axel's worrying about my daughter, and I'm worrying about Axel, and Sam doesn't seem worried about anything. Thank God Kirsten is just doing her job, or this business would fall apart. She returned her thoughts to the restaurant. There was a small line in front of the window. One at a time, she said to herself wearily. Just keep on serving, and in time everyone will get fed. It had gotten to where all the customers' faces had morphed into a single identity-free blob. A couple of hours ago, when she had almost decided to quit the Taco Shop, much of the state fair energy had leaked out of her. But Axel's getting hurt, that had changed everything. She couldn't leave him hurt, couldn't let the business collapse. She wished, though, she could get that energy back.

She wanted Axel on his feet again. Seeing him sit on his folding chair with his leg out, his face sagging, his eyes staring across the mall toward the boarded-up Tiny Tot Donuts stand—it was hard to take.

"Can I help you?" she asked the next face in line.

The customer did not reply. Sophie forced herself to focus, to see the person more clearly. A woman. As her features came into focus, Sophie had a startled moment when she thought it was her mother, who had died nearly ten years before. The face displayed the same pinched nose, cold blue eyes, and determined, jutting jaw. But this woman was taller and had a large supply of gray-blond hair piled atop her head. A red spot burned high on each pale cheek.

Sophie smiled at her and repeated, "Can I help you?"

The woman's eyes were fixed on something behind her. Sophie turned her head and saw Kirsten pressed back against the stainless-steel cooler, staring wide-eyed at the angry customer.

Kirsten licked her lips. "Hi, Mom," she said in a small voice.

Chapter

38

BY SEVEN-THIRTY, Bill Quist had checked in his last guest. He turned on the NO VACANCY sign, used the vending machine keys to score himself three cans of Coke and a handful of candy bars, and settled in to watch a rerun of the *X-Files* episode where the guy with the pointy nose discovers that webbing has appeared between his toes. Quist liked *The X-Files*. In particular, he liked the guy with the pointy nose's partner, what's-her-name, the one with the bazooms. He liked her lower lip, the way it hung there almost quivering. And he liked how big her head was, too. The guy with the pointy nose, he had this little head, but the partner, she had this huge head. Quist imagined her as eight feet tall, acting the part on her knees.

He really liked *The X-Files*.

So he was sort of pissed when the bell on the lobby door dinged—just when the pointy-nose guy was showing his webbing to his partner. Probably some guy with a stupid question, or needing change, or some jerk who didn't believe the NO VACANCY sign. He kept his eyes glued to the TV, refusing to look away for a simple door ding. Maybe it was just somebody come in to use the vending machines. Maybe they'd just go away.

Then he heard the most irritating sound in the entire universe. The goddamn bell on the counter. Usually he hid the damn thing during his shift, but he'd forgotten and now they were dinging it. Not just once, but over and over: *Ding. Ding. Ding. Ding. Ding.*

He said, still not turning around, "I hear you. Just hold on." Big-head was touching the toe webbing. Man, did that send a tingle up his thigh!

Ding. Ding. Ding.

Quist spun around in his chair and looked up over the counter. "I said hold on!"

Ding.

It took maybe half a second for his eyes to go from the bell to the hand to the face. Shit, it was that punk kid hung out with that Carmen, old Axel's girlfriend or daughter or whatever the hell she was.

Ding. Standing there with his shaved head and his shitty little smile, hand suspended over the chrome bell.

Ding.

There was another one too, a scrawny, pimply kid, sitting in one of the chairs, scratching his neck.

Ding.

Quist stood up and approached the counter, picked up the bell, and put it in a drawer.

"I need a key," the kid said.

Quist shook his head. "No can do," he said. "You're eighty-sixed. Mr. Speeter told me so." He was of two minds. One mind was telling him that was that, the kid stays out of the guests' rooms. The other mind was wondering how much cash the kid might be able to come up with if he really wanted access.

Turned out the kid was of a third mind. Quist tried to step back, but the end of a crowbar snagged his neck like a stage hook and jerked him toward the counter.

With Kirsten gone, the Taco Shop was in serious trouble. Sophie put it to Axel this way: "If you can stand, you can help. If you can't, we might as well just close up."

Axel said, "It's only eight o'clock. We never close at eight."

"We need your help."

Sam's voice came from inside the Taco Shop. "Hold your horses there, young fella. I only got so goddamn many hands, y'know. You sure you wouldn't rather have a taco?"

Axel sighed and tried to stand up. His knee had a solid, heavy feel to it, as if packed with cement. He eased some weight onto it. For a moment, it felt all right, then a sharp pain lanced from the joint right up his thigh. He grabbed the edge of the doorway.

"I need a cane or something," he said.

Sam appeared in the doorway. "Hey, you two. I got my hands full up to my elbows here."

"He needs a cane, he says," said Sophie.

Sam stepped out of the stand. "You hang on there, Ax. I'll be back in a jiff." He set off toward the Tiny Tot Donut stand. Sophie ducked back inside, leaving Axel clinging to the doorway.

Sam returned in less than a minute, swinging the green yardstick cane that Tommy had taken away from Bald Monkey. He handed it to Axel, then helped him into the restaurant, propped him up against the prep table.

"Waiting on one tostada, two bean, one Bueno," Sophie said.

Axel began to assemble the order, slowly at first, then picking up speed as his body rediscovered familiar rhythms.

"What you want me to do?" Sam asked him.

"I don't care."

Sam scratched his three-day-old beard. "Maybe I shoulda let you shoot the monkey," he said.

Axel stopped moving his arms and gave Sam a nothing look. "You could fry up some shells," he said. Within minutes, they had developed a sort of system, and the production line began to shuffle along.

———

Tigger wanted to say, Man, I don't hardly know you no more. Only thing was, he didn't really know the dude in the first place anyways, so why should it surprise him the guy turns out to be this psycho nut. Tearing the room apart, snarling and muttering about coffee cans full of money. Sure, there were plenty of coffee cans, but forget about money. All they found was socks and underwear and a bunch of other junk, which was now scattered all over the floor. He was starting to think the money was just a figment somehow got stuck in Dean's head. James Dean the psycho nut, now sitting on the bed with a crowbar on his lap, reading fucking poetry. Tigger shivered and tried to listen to what Dean was saying. Not that it made any sense.

Dean read, *"Unvirtuous weeds might long unvexed have stood . . ."* He paused. "What do you think, Tig?"

Tigger said, "What's unvexed?"

"Like the motel guy. He's unvexed at us."

"It means, like, pissed off?"

"Right. And I'm unvexed too. And I'm gonna stay unvexed until I get my hands on that taco man's money. Listen. *But he's short liv'd, that with his death can doe most good."*

Tigger did his damnedest to look as if he agreed, even though he was afraid that what Dean was saying was that somebody else was going to get killed pretty soon. He'd gotten to the point where the money seemed unreal. All he wanted now was to get out of this deal alive. The money didn't matter.

Dean asked, "So what are you going to do, Tig, you get a couple hundred thousand bucks in cash? You gonna buy yourself a new car?"

Tigger thought for a moment. He kind of liked the idea of one of those big black Dodge pickups with the big engine and the big wheels and the lights up top. Maybe the money mattered some after all.

"I was thinking maybe this truck I seen," he said.

—

Axel stood outside the restaurant and watched Sophie closing the food bins and fitting the perishables into the cooler. She looked exhausted. He wanted to say something to her, but he couldn't think what it was. Using his yardstick cane, he limped around to the front. His good leg, the one doing all the work, was giving him trouble now. His burlap bag, with the day's receipts added to it, hung like a one-sided yoke from his shoulder. Axel moved a few feet to a picnic bench and lowered himself onto it, keeping his bad knee straight. He lifted the bag onto the bench and watched Sam lower the plywood over the service window, snap a combination lock into the hasp.

He said, "So, Sam." He was hurting, but he felt better than he had. Work helped.

Sam lit a cigarette and sat down beside Axel.

"I got to tell you, Ax, you got yourself one tough way to make a living."

"Beats fixing cars."

Sam puffed vigorously on his Pall Mall. The air was warm, moist, and still; a ghostly column of smoke gathered above his head. They sat in silence for a few moments, listening to the murmur of closing concessions, the grinding and whining of the sanitation trucks. "No it don't," he said.

Axel could feel a question boiling in his throat, getting itself ready. He said, "So, Sam. Let me ask you something. Suppose a guy found something that, say, was the property of this other individual, this friend of his. What would you think he should do about that?"

Sam rolled his cigarette between his thumb and his forefinger, examining it closely. "You find something, Ax?"

Axel shook his head. "Not me. But if I did—like, say, if you were to drop your wallet in my restaurant and I was to, say, find it—what I'd do then is I'd give it back."

Sam said, "I keep my wallet on a chain."

"Yeah, but hypothetically. Hypothetically, I'd give it back."

Sam snorted and took a huge drag off his cigarette, flicked it out onto the grass. Axel watched it land, suppressed an urge to hobble over and pick it up. There were a thousand other butts on the mall. One more wouldn't make any difference.

"Hypothetically," Sam said, "if a guy's dogs dig something up in his own backyard, then a guy ought to be entitled to keep whatever it is they dig up."

"I don't think you understand," Axel said.

"I mean, the whole point a private property is finders keepers."

"That doesn't make sense to me."

Sam shrugged. "You want to talk about who's making sense, I ain't the one was shooting off a forty-five on the midway a few hours back."

"Speaking of which, you gonna give me back my gun?"

"What for? So you can go get yourself killed like Tommy?"

"No, so I can get some answers from you."

Sam cackled and fired up another cigarette. "I might maybe be a horseshit burrito-roller, Ax, but I ain't a fucking idiot."

Sam turned his head away and stared at the Tiny Tot Donuts stand. Axel suppressed an urge to whap him with his cane. He wasn't sure what kind of twisted passageways were contained in Sam O'Gara's compact skull, but he figured it wouldn't do any good at this point to piss him off. He decided to open up the other subject they'd been avoiding, just to see what popped out.

"It's like he's not really dead, isn't it?"

Sam's head bobbed slightly; a cloud of smoke materialized and slowly dissipated. "I got this feeling we're not too far behind him, Ax. Tommy, he's down there getting warmed up, dealing hands with that leather-ass Satan."

"Telling him how to play," Axel said.

"Losing every hand too, I bet. Satan, he don't bet without he's sitting on the mortal nuts." Sam expelled a burst of smoke through his nose, laughed, then started sneezing. "And I bet you he gets 'em every time, Ax. Every fucking time."

"We never got together for that game, the three of us."

"No," Sam said. "We never did."

"I think Sophie's ready to go." Axel got his good leg under him, braced himself with his cane, and rose painfully to his feet. He started toward Sophie, who was locking the back door to the restaurant.

"Look at you," she said.

"Look at me what?"

"You can hardly walk. You should see a doctor."

"No way. Look what happened to Tommy. He went in the hospital, now he's dead."

"That's ridiculous."

"Well, I'm not going to any hospital. We've got two more days till the end of the fair. I'm not spending them on my back."

"Fine. How are you going to drive yourself home?"

"I don't think I can," Axel admitted. "I don't think I can bend my leg."

"I suppose I'll have to take you," she said.

"I don't think I can get in that little car of yours."

"We'll take your truck."

Sam said, "Y'know, I could use a ride home too. I took the bus over here, y'know. Cost me a buck and a quarter."

Sophie sighed, shaking her head as if disgusted, but a part of her was clearly enjoying her role. "What would you two do without me?"

Chapter

39

"**YOU SURE YOU CAN MAKE** it?" Sam asked.

Axel stepped carefully down from the cab. "It's only a few steps to my damn door, Sam." He transferred some weight to his yardstick cane, took a quick step, testing his bad knee. It had stiffened some more, but at least it didn't hurt worse.

Sophie, sitting behind the steering wheel, said, "Don't just sit there. Give him a hand, Sam."

Sam made a move to climb down.

Axel lifted the cane and waved its tip in Sam's face. "I can do it myself, goddamn it."

"He says he don't want no help," Sam said.

Sophie said, "Yeah. Like he didn't need any help walking to the truck."

"That was a quarter mile," Axel said, taking another painful step. "This is ten feet."

"I never seen anything so pitiful," Sam said. "Soph is right. You oughta be in the hospital."

"It's just a sprain." Axel took two quick steps, reached the door. "You know, you don't have to sit there gawking at me. Go on. I'll see you in the morning, okay?"

"I'll be here," Sophie said.

Axel inserted his key in his door and stood there watching as Sophie and Sam drove off. He turned the key, twisted the knob, pushed the door open. His hand had just hit the light switch when something crashed into his mouth, knocking his dentures back into his throat. His knee collapsed, and he fell to the floor, choking.

—

"That was easy," said Dean, kicking the door closed. It was always easy. Pork had been easy. And with Mickey, he hadn't even been trying.

"He's, like, having a fit or something," Tigger said.

Axel lay on the floor, holding his neck with one hand, digging the fingers of his other hand into his mouth. Dean tossed the crowbar on the bed, bent over Axel, and quickly felt under his arms and around his waist, looking for the heavy, solid shape of the .45. Axel writhed under his hands, red-faced, eyes bugged out, making wheezing, gagging noises.

"He don't have it," Dean said. "Unless it's in here." He grabbed the shoulder bag, pulled it away. Axel's body convulsed, he gave a loud cough, and something jettisoned from his mouth and bounced across the carpet toward Tigger.

Tigger jumped back. "Fuck, it's his fucking teeth!"

Dean laughed, stepping back. Nothing fazed him now. He had finally hit a plateau with the crystal, a perfectly level place where all things came easily under his control. His body had adapted to the high levels of amphetamine; he had the buzz under control. He was a machine now, turbocharged and running at peak capacity. He could see with perfect clarity. He unzipped the bag and dumped its contents onto the bed. Things fell out in slow motion. A pair of dirty socks. A bottle of aspirin. A heavy bank bag, obviously full of coins. And five white paper bags held closed with rubber bands. Dean ripped open one of the bags and found a thick bundle of paper money. He thumbed the bills, then tossed the packet to Tigger. "What did I tell you?"

"He's been carrying it with him?"

Dean shook his head. "This is just a taste. Carmen says he has coffee cans full of the stuff." He watched the old man pull himself up onto one hip, a rope of pink drool reaching from his mouth to the carpet, breathing heavily, still trying to catch his wind. "We just got to get him to tell us where."

———

Axel heard the kid's voice. "That's right, ain't it? You got more?"

He wiped his mouth, looked at the blood on his hand. The kid took a step toward him. "You hear me, old man?"

"I shoulda shot you." The missing dentures distorted his voice. He coughed, leaned to the side, spat a glob of spit and blood on the carpet.

"So talk to me. Where've you got those coffee cans stashed? All you got to do is tell me, and we leave you alone. Nobody gets hurt."

Axel shook his head. "Too late," he said. "I'm already hurt." His mouth tasted of blood, and his knee was pulsing unpleasantly, but oddly enough, he felt stronger, felt a kernel of anger where moments before there had been only empty spaces.

"And you don't want to get hurt more, right?"

Axel said, "That depends." This anger, it was not like the fury that had driven him that afternoon. This was a cooler, harder-edged emotion. Before, it had been his imagination driving him, but this time he could see it, right in front of him. He set his jaw, trying not to let what he was feeling show in his face.

"Depends on what?" the kid asked with a smirk.

Axel did not reply, thinking that he wouldn't mind getting hurt some more if it would get him a shot at this punk kid, this kid who'd been in his stuff, messing up his room. That would be worth getting hurt for. He had a sudden memory of the kangaroos he'd seen on television. The old boomer had run away, had survived the battle only to die alone out in the Australian desert. That wasn't for him. One way or another, he had to play this hand to the end. The only problem he could see was that there were two of them, and he was lying on the floor with a bad leg and no teeth. He couldn't kick. He couldn't even bite the son-of-a-bitch.

He said, "You're James Dean."

Dean shrugged. He didn't seem to care that his name was known.

Axel said, "He was a punk too. You see *East of Eden?*"

James Dean rested his weight on one hip, cocked his head. "The one where he got to be this rich guy," he said.

"The one where he started out a punk and then turned into a creep."

"Least he got the money. Only he didn't keep it in coffee cans."

Axel said, "You know what Tommy called you?"

Dean said, "Who the fuck's Tommy?"

Axel ran his tongue over his upper gum. "He called you the Bald Little Monkey," he said, adding the "Little" just to give it more punch.

The skinny kid laughed abruptly, shut it down when Dean snapped a look at him.

"Well, maybe I'll pay this Tommy a visit too," Dean growled.

"Maybe sooner than you think," Axel said.

Realization touched Dean's features. "Oh!" He laughed, then explained to Tigger. "He's talking about the donut guy, Tig. He's, like, *threatening* us!"

The thing to do, Axel decided, was to think of it like a game. The one with the muscles, James Dean, he was the one to beat. The skinny, slack-mouthed kid, the one called "Tig," wouldn't be much of a problem. He said, directing his words at Tig, "When it happens, you'd best run." The kid's mouth fell open another half inch. Axel figured that might just do it. Plant the idea, let it grow. Everything about the kid, his body language, said he didn't want to play this hand.

Dean said, "He's a tough guy. Look how tough he is, Tig. No teeth."

"Where's Carmen?" Axel demanded, shifting gears again.

Dean appeared genuinely confused. "How the fuck should I know?"

"You tell me where she is, maybe I'll tell you about the coffee cans."

Dean lifted the crowbar. "Maybe you'll tell me about the coffee cans anyways."

Axel watched the crowbar turning in Dean's hands. He had to say something. "It's in the safe," he said. Get out of the room, he was thinking, get outside. "I put it all in the motel safe."

Dean raised his eyebrows, then looked over his shoulder toward the bathroom.

"Hey, Motel 6! How come you didn't tell me about this?" he shouted.

"It's a lie!" came Bill Quist's frightened voice.

Axel said, "Bill? That you in there?"

"He's lying," Quist shouted.

Axel shook his head. "You in with these guys, Bill?"

No reply.

Dean said, "He says you're lying."

"What's he doing in the bathroom?"

"Let's talk coffee cans," Dean said.

"It's like I told you. I put the money in the safe. I did it when the other guy was on duty. Bill doesn't even know about it. You don't believe me, we can go look."

——

Sophie drifted toward the curb, then pulled a quick U-turn on Larpenteur Avenue, throwing Sam against the door.

He said, "Whoa! Hey! Hold on there, what you doing?"

"I don't care what he says," Sophie muttered.

"What? Who?"

"You saw him. The man can hardly walk."

"He don't need to walk to sleep."

"I can't leave him like that, all by himself. Somebody has to take care of him."

"Well, he ain't going to like it."

"I don't care what he likes. He needs me."

——

The parade moved slowly across the parking lot, Axel supported by a frightened-looking Bill Quist, with Dean and Tigger walking a few steps behind them. Axel, a glazed look in his eyes, had departed the present. As his body limped across the dimly lit parking lot, one arm hanging on Bill Quist's shoulder, his mind traveled into the past.

He saw himself in Deadwood, about to get the shit beat out of him by a trio of drunken cowboys. His mistake back then had been to wait too long. He had let the cowboys confront him in their own time and place. Now, he was thinking, he'd made the same damn mistake all over again. He should have dealt with this James Dean a long time ago, the first time he'd met him. Instead, he had offered the kid a free taco.

Was it too late? Axel expelled a mental sigh and returned to the present.

"I'm sorry about this, Bill," he said.

Quist said, "This isn't fair. I just work here." His hands were tied together in front with a pair of Axel's knee-high black nylon socks. A large bruise had formed on the side of his neck.

"You seen Carmen today?" Axel asked.

"She called. She wants you to go get her."

"Get her where?"

"Ramsey County detox."

"Oh." Detox? At least she was safe. One less thing to think about. They were almost to the lobby. Well, he decided, as well this time as another, and he let his good knee collapse and fell to the tarmac. Quist tried to hold him up, but Axel slipped his arm loose, groaning piteously. Behind them, Dean and Tigger stopped.

"Get him up," Dean commanded Quist.

Quist tugged at Axel's arm, but the only effect was to make him moan.

"My knee," Axel said, coughing.

Dean said, "You better get up, or we'll just drag you."

"Why don't we just leave him?" Tigger asked. "We don't need him, right?"

"If the money's not there, we need him." Dean pointed the crowbar at Quist, who had dropped Axel's arm, edged a half step back, and was rocking slightly on his feet. "Don't you even think about it."

Quist's shoulders sagged. Dean returned his attention to Axel.

"Time to get up, old man." He gave him a vicious poke in the ribs with the crowbar.

The crowbar stuck. Dean tugged at the steel, thinking for a moment that he had actually shoved it into the old man's body and gotten it stuck between two ribs, but in the quarter second it took for him to realize that Axel had grabbed the bar, the old man twisted and yanked, tearing the bar from Dean's grasp, coming back at him with a one-handed swing. With a shout, Dean jumped back. The crowbar missed his knee, but he felt it flutter the denim of his jeans. The amphetamine plateau had shifted; things were coming at him too fast now. From the corner of his eye, he saw the motel clerk moving, stumbling back, turning, running. Tigger somewhere behind him, saying, "Hey . . . hey . . ." A car stopped on the roadway opposite the parking lot, headlights glaring. Confusing shadows. His heart made his ribs vibrate. The old man rising from the parking lot, using the crowbar like a cane. Too much, all at the same time. Dean backed away, trying to focus his thoughts. He heard himself shout something to Tigger, but Tigger wasn't there. He looked back, saw Tigger running. The old man was standing now, hopping toward him on one leg, holding the crowbar like a baseball bat, his shoe slapping loudly on the asphalt with each hop.

There was a moment when Dean almost ran, but then the scene snapped into focus again and he saw that he was still in control, still on that plateau. The guy was old, he was tired, and he was hopping along on one leg. Everything had slowed down again. The old man's hops were shorter. He was getting tired. Every time he made another little jump, Dean took a step back, keeping about eight feet between them. Let the guy wear himself out, then take him.

Hop.

Dean took another step back. He could deal with Tigger later.

The old man stopped, balancing on one leg. He lowered the bar. Dean smiled, took a step forward.

"You done now?"

The old man glared, breathing loudly.

"How about you give me the bar." Dean reached out a hand. He saw the end of the bar start to move, started to jerk his hand back. The old man fell toward him, bringing the bar up over his head, chopping down with it. Dean saw it all in slow motion, plenty of time to get out of the way, but his body refused to match the speed of his mind. The hook end of the bar crashed into his sternum, driving the air from his lungs, raked down his belly, and snagged in the waistband of his jeans. He went down, his chest in spasms, and the old man was on him.

———

Axel wanted to split James Dean's head wide open. He managed to bang it on the pavement a couple of times, but it was like trying to hold on to an oily bowling ball. No hair to grab. Then the kid caught his breath, howled, and snapped his body into a reverse arch, sending Axel up and off. Axel's bad knee hit the pavement. A bright flash of light hit his eyes, a moment of blindness. He heard a roar. The kid rose up before him, silhouetted against a pair of headlights coming right at him. Axel picked a direction and rolled.

———

"Go!" shouted Sam. "Go-go-go-go-go!" He reached over with one foot and tromped on the accelerator. The truck lurched forward, hopped the curb, and headed down the grassy embankment toward the Motel 6 parking lot, spitting sod from its rear wheels. Sophie screamed, her hands white on the steering wheel. The truck hit the parking lot, bounced, a shiny, bloody head appeared above the hood, they felt a thud, and Sophie hit the brake, still screaming, her eyes closed. The truck skidded toward the motel office, hit one of the two overhang supports, and crashed through the plate-glass doorway into the lobby.

———

Axel didn't see the truck strike James Dean, but he saw his body airborne, saw him rotate in the air and land flat, facedown on the parking lot, the sound of his impact covered by the louder sound of the truck crashing into the lobby.

For a moment, everything stopped. Axel gave himself three seconds, then climbed to his feet and hopped slowly toward the office. The overhang, deprived of one support, sagged dangerously. Axel squeezed between the remains of the doorway and the back end of his pickup truck. He heard a grinding, whining noise coming from beneath the hood, the sound of the starter trying to crank a frozen engine. He hopped up to the driver's door, opened it, and saw Sophie twisting the ignition key, probably so that she could back over the kid in the parking lot. Axel opened the door. Sophie stared at him fiercely, cranking the starter, pumping the gas pedal. Her eyes were squeezed down to slits, her face and shoulders covered with white powder. Axel frowned at the steering wheel, at the limp white bag dangling from its center.

He reached out and gently removed her hand from the starter. He held her face. "Are you okay?"

Sophie nodded shakily. "Something went bang," she said.

Axel looked at Sam, who sat blinking stupidly out through the shattered windshield, a rivulet of blood running from his nose down his chin.

"You—son—of—a—bitch." Axel felt a smile flutter onto his face.

Sam wiped his sleeve across his chin, smearing blood. "What?"

"You never unhooked the goddamn air bag."

Chapter

40

"I RAISE," SAID SOPHIE. She looked across the table at Axel. "Can I do that?"

Axel frowned at his cards. "You don't want to," he said. His new dentures clicked when he talked. They didn't fit right with the stitches the doctor had taken in his gum.

They were sitting, the three of them, in Sam O'Gara's kitchen. Axel took up two chairs, one for his body and the other for his leg, now confined to a plastic cast. The refrigerator, an ancient Philco, emitted a low rumble. Chester and Festus were sacked out under the table, Festus giving Sophie an occasional interesting moment by licking her ankle. The first time, she'd squealed and jumped out of her chair, but she was getting used to it.

Sam fished a can of Copenhagen from his pocket. "Don't listen to 'im, Soph. Anyways, I fold." He pushed his cards away and shifted his chair closer to Sophie. "What you got there, sweetheart?"

Sophie pulled her cards against her breasts.

Sam said, "Don't worry, I'm out of this hand. Just show me your cards, I'll tell you if you wanna be raisin' ol' Ax. He's a tricky sumbitch. C'mon, I'm on your side."

Sophie hesitated, then tipped her cards toward Sam. He leaned closer. "Not bad," he said.

Axel snorted. "She's showing you her cards, Sam, not her boobs."

"I's talking about both."

Sophie shot out an elbow, forcing Sam to jerk his head back out of range, but she couldn't completely conceal a smile. "What should I do?" she asked.

Sam thrust a thumb in the air. "Raise it up!" he said. "Make 'im pay to see those babies." He twisted the top off the Copenhagen can, pinched up an enormous wad of the black tobacco, and packed his lower lip.

Axel groaned and watched as Sophie pushed four quarters into the pot.

He said, "What can you have?"

Sophie advanced her chin and fixed her eyes on Axel's stack.

Axel looked again at his cards. It wasn't a bad hand for five-card draw. He had a flush, jack high. Almost certainly a winner—unless Sophie's cards were better. That was the thing about poker. Any hand was a winner until it got beat.

Which seemed to happen a lot.

He fiddled with his pile of coins, found four quarters and five dimes, tossed them on the pot. "Let's see 'em," he said.

Sophie looked at Sam. "Do I have to?"

"If you want to win you do, sweetheart."

"Can I raise again?"

"You're called," Axel snapped.

Sophie carefully set her cards on the table, faceup. A full house, queens over fives. Axel rolled his eyes and threw away his hand.

"You have to show too!" Sophie said.

Axel said, "Why? You won."

Sam grabbed Axel's discarded hand and flipped it up.

Sophie said, "What's that? You didn't even have a pair."

"That's a flusher," said Sam. "A flusher and a loser. My deal." He swept the cards together.

"I win?" Sophie asked guardedly.

Axel snapped, "Yes, goddamn it, you win."

Sophie's mouth softened and spread into a wide smile as she scooped up the pot. For a moment, Axel saw her as a happy little kid on Christmas morning. What a strange woman this is, he thought. I give her half of my business, my life, and she's all frowns and doubts and suspicions, almost as if I'd given her nothing but trouble. Last night, when they'd paid off the help and counted their remaining take from the fair, her ten percent had come to over four thousand dollars. You'd think that would've made her happy, but all she could talk about was how much more they'd have made if it hadn't been for losing Kirsten and having Carmen flake out on them and Axel's being in such rough shape that he'd had to spend the last two days of the fair propped up on a stool, making burritos at half speed. Axel was glad to have made it through the weekend, period. But not Sophie. Four thousand dollars in her pocket, and all she could think about was how it should have been five. Now, a few hours later, she wins one lousy three-dollar pot, and she's all smiles and joy.

He never knew what she was going to do. Three nights ago, in the emergency room at St. Joseph's, she had surprised him then too. Throughout the entire ordeal—the scene in the parking lot, the cops, the questions, the long wait in the emergency room at St. Joseph's—she'd kept it together. He'd expected her to be hysterical, but she'd been like a rock. And then, after the doctor had finished with him, when they'd pushed him out of the examination room in that wheelchair, feeling about as bad as he ever remembered feeling, she looked at him and her face collapsed. They'd wheeled him out into the waiting room, and she'd looked at him and just lost it, started crying like a baby. He'd never seen her do that before. And then when Carmen had shown up at the stand on the last day of the fair, not wanting to work, just wanting to get paid . . . Axel had expected Sophie to lose it then. But all that happened was that she had wearily counted out Carmen's money, too tired or numb to argue. "I don't get a bonus this year?" Carmen had whined. Even then, Sophie hadn't said a word.

The blond girl, Kirsten, stopped by at the same time, all apologies and embarrassment over being hauled off by her mother in the middle of the day, but mostly wanting to collect her pay. Axel paid her off. She didn't ask for a bonus. A few minutes later, he had seen Carmen and Kirsten sitting out on the mall, smoking cigarettes and laughing. All Sophie had said was, "They don't know what's important."

Axel remembered thinking that she looked . . . not old, but mature. He thought she looked good.

She looked good now. Winning that pot had put some color in her face.

"Where's Carmen gone off to today?" Axel asked.

"She went shopping with that Kirsten." Sophie finished stacking her coins. "They went to the Mall of America. Can you imagine? What on earth could those two have in common anyway?"

Sam laughed.

"What's so funny?"

Sam squared up the deck of cards and riffled them. "They both got trouble with their mamas," he said.

Sophie made a face. "Excuse me." She left the kitchen. Sam and Axel listened to her footsteps climbing the stairs, the sound of the bathroom door closing.

Sam said, "She's got the touch, Ax. Maybe me and you and her ought to hit the road. Odds are, we'd do better, the three of us, than we ever did with old Tommy."

Axel smiled and shook his head. "Maybe we wouldn't get in so damn many fights."

"You got that right. And if we did, she'd just run 'em over."

"You know what it's going to cost to get my new truck fixed? About four dimes."

"Well, your old one's out back, ready to roll. I even gave 'er a little tune-up."

"I'm going to need what was under it too."

Sam raised his eyebrows. "Now, Ax, you say that money ol' Festus and Chester dug up was yours. Now explain to me again how come I'm s'posed to think that." He leaned back in his chair, shifted the wad of tobacco with his tongue.

"It was under my truck. I put it there."

"I said you could park your truck here, I didn't think I was including mineral rights. Besides, I don't see how come a smart fella like you would go burying his money like a goddamn dog in somebody's backyard not even his own."

Axel took a deep breath. Sam had been hanging him out there for the past two days, not admitting that the money was Axel's but not coming right out and saying he wasn't going to give it back, either. Axel was about eighty percent sure that Sam was just playing with him. He trusted Sam. Maybe not a hundred percent, but a solid ninety.

Sam said, "Even if you did find your money someplace, I don't know what the hell good it'd do you. You don't spend it. You'd probably go bury it in the goddamn park, leave it for the squirrels."

Axel did not reply.

"Suppose you did get it back," Sam went on. "What would you do with it?"

Axel looked at his old friend hopefully but saw nothing in Sam's face to encourage him. "Is this a test, or are you just trying to make me miserable?"

Sam shrugged and riffled the deck of cards with his thumb. "Just wondering."

"Maybe I'd invest it in something," Axel said.

Sam cocked an eyebrow.

"Maybe I'd put it in a bank," Axel growled. "Hell, I don't know. Does it matter?"

Sophie's footsteps sounded on the stairs.

"Don't matter to me," Sam said.

Axel muttered, "I suppose I should be glad you're letting me have my truck back." A click from his dentures took the edge off the sarcasm.

"The truck is yours."

"So's the cash."

Sam picked up the deck and shuffled. "You're a goddamn peasant, Ax. I ever tell you that?"

"I tell him that all the time," Sophie said.

Axel said, "You ready to go?" He didn't want to talk about the money in front of Sophie. He didn't want her to know. It was embarrassing.

"Where are we going?" she asked.

"The hell away from here." Axel got his good leg braced, squeezed his lips tight together, and stood up. "C'mon. We've got to go over to the fairgrounds. I want to get the rest of the stuff out of the cooler, get the restaurant closed up for the year."

Gripping his yardstick cane, Axel stood up and hobbled out the back door. Goddamn Sam O'Gara. You think you know a guy. The first few steps were tough, but once he got into the rhythm, walking wasn't all that bad. He jerked open the passenger door and climbed clumsily into the cab of his old pickup. His foot caught on something, a plastic bag on the floor. He grabbed the bag, tried to move it out of the way, then stopped. He felt through the black plastic. Rolls, like tight little burritos. He could feel them. He wanted to rip the bag open, to plunge his arms into it, but Sophie opened the other door and hopped in.

"What's going on with you two?" she asked.

Axel sat up straight. "Nothing," he said.

Sophie dropped her eyes to the bag. "What's that?"

"Just some stuff Sam was keeping for me." He rolled down the window and looked back at the house. Sam stood in the doorway, smoking a cigarette. One of the hounds poked its head out between his bowed legs.

Axel shouted, "You son-of-a-bitch! You just left it here? Where anybody coulda come and grabbed it?"

Sam just grinned.

Sophie said, "I swear to God, Axel, I don't know who'd want to steal this old pickup."

The aging Ford started right up, to Axel's surprise. She didn't have to pump the gas and grind away with the starter like before—just turned the key and they were in business. He liked the way the engine sounded. Sam must've worked some kind of magic. And once they got out onto the road, it even seemed to roll better. The shimmy had disappeared. Or maybe it was the plastic bag between his feet, maybe that was what made the ride so smooth.

Axel said, "You know that bank on Snelling? You mind stopping off there for a few minutes? I want to make a deposit."

Sophie looked at him in surprise. "You? Since when do you use a bank?"

"Things change," he said. He wouldn't put it all in. Maybe just a few thousand dollars; give himself time to get used to the idea.

"You want to know something?" Sophie asked.

"What?"

"Carmen was right. You're weird."

"You're weird too," Axel said.

Sophie shrugged. "Carmen would agree with you."

They rode down University Avenue without speaking, turned north on Snelling, Axel enjoying the comfortable silence. She was driving real nice for once, smooth and slow. As they turned into the fairgrounds, Axel was thinking that he wouldn't even get that new truck fixed, because he'd heard that once a vehicle got in an accident, it would never ride quite right again, and anyways, he'd never really gotten friendly with it. Never trusted the damn thing. He was thinking he'd sell it, or maybe give it to Sam, since, after all, the old one seemed to be working just fine.

About the Author

Pete Hautman's two previous novels are titled *Drawing Dead* and *Short Money*. He lives in Minneapolis with writer/poet Mary Logue and some animals to which he is allergic. Pete is currently working on a new novel featuring characters from *all* of his first three books.